"BROWNE IS THE NEXT BIG THING IN
HEART-STOPPING FICTION."
—Kathy Mackel, author of *The Hidden*

Praise for
The Paradise Prophecy

"Browne has not only conjured up an epic story—*The Paradise Prophecy* is thoroughly entertaining and imaginative. Just don't distract him with too much praise once you read it; I really need him to finish its sequel."
—*New York Times* bestselling author
Raymond Khoury

"Milton's *Paradise Lost* provides the backdrop for Browne's riveting, cinematic novel, which charts an epic battle between good and evil . . . consistently smart prose and an ending that points to future thrillers set in this fascinating world."   —*Publishers Weekly* (starred review)

"Browne has written a compelling page-turner, which kept me reading into the wee hours of the night while glancing over my shoulder looking for evil lurking in the shadows. This is a raise-the-hair-on-the-back-of-your-neck, frighteningly good story."   —Bookreporter.com

continued . . .

"A suspenseful thriller, *The Paradise Prophecy* is a wonderful and creepy book. If you ever thought *Paradise Lost* was boring, this book will give you a whole different view of that particular story. Highly recommended for fans of suspense, mystery, dark fantasy, and action adventures of a religious nature."   —Monster Librarian

"*The Paradise Prophecy* is a superb rendition of good and evil as the agents of God and Satan battle for the souls of mankind. Action-packed from the onset . . . [an] excellent thriller."   —The Mystery Gazette

"Browne illustrates his fictional world so beautifully that you can completely immerse yourself in the story and later suspend belief without hesitation. He also, quite brilliantly, brings his characters to life, faults and all, so that you may feel some pity for even the most evil characters. These people are not caricatures of good and evil, but instead are multidimensional characters with goodness, faults, and even sadness on the side of evil, that bring the story completely to life."   —Writer's Diary

Further Praise for the Author and His Novels

"Part Thomas Harris, part Dante's *Inferno*."
                    —*The Tampa Tribune*

"Browne's thrillers are lean, mean, and thoroughly entertaining . . . an adrenaline rush that leaves you breathless."
                    —*New York Times* bestselling author
                    Allison Brennan

"A real nail-biter." —Scott Wilson, *The Fringe*

"Edgy suspense mixed with a touch of the supernatural keeps pushing the reader forward." —Bookfinds

"An outstanding pulp-prose stylist."
—*The Daily Telegraph* (UK)

"Nonstop pacing, breathless prose, and page-turning urgency." —Kathy Mackel

"Heart-pounding suspense . . . a first-rate novel that will glue you to your chair until you finish the last satisfying word." —Gayle Lynds, author of *The Last Spymaster*

"A taut, absorbing page-turner . . . a writer to watch!"
—Carla Neggers, author of *The Widow*

"A nerve-racking race against time." —*Kirkus Reviews*

"[An] adrenaline-pumping thriller."
—*Midwest Book Review*

"Provocative and gritty." —*Tucson Citizen*

ROBERT BROWNE

The
PARADISE
Prophecy

A SIGNET SELECT BOOK

SIGNET SELECT
Published by New American Library, a division of
Penguin Group (USA) Inc., 375 Hudson Street,
New York, New York 10014, USA
Penguin Group (Canada), 90 Eglinton Avenue East, Suite 700, Toronto,
Ontario M4P 2Y3, Canada (a division of Pearson Penguin Canada Inc.)
Penguin Books Ltd., 80 Strand, London WC2R 0RL, England
Penguin Ireland, 25 St. Stephen's Green, Dublin 2,
Ireland (a division of Penguin Books Ltd.)
Penguin Group (Australia), 250 Camberwell Road, Camberwell, Victoria 3124,
Australia (a division of Pearson Australia Group Pty. Ltd.)
Penguin Books India Pvt. Ltd., 11 Community Centre, Panchsheel Park,
New Delhi - 110 017, India
Penguin Group (NZ), 67 Apollo Drive, Rosedale, Auckland 0632,
New Zealand (a division of Pearson New Zealand Ltd.)
Penguin Books (South Africa) (Pty.) Ltd., 24 Sturdee Avenue,
Rosebank, Johannesburg 2196, South Africa

Penguin Books Ltd., Registered Offices:
80 Strand, London WC2R 0RL, England

Published by Signet, an imprint of New American Library, a division of Penguin
Group (USA) Inc. Previously published in a Dutton edition.

First Signet Select Printing, June 2012
10 9 8 7 6 5 4 3 2 1

Copyright © Penguin Group (USA) Inc., 2011
Gustave Doré illustrations copyright © Dover Publications

PUBLISHER'S NOTE
This is a work of fiction. Names, characters, places, and incidents either are the
product of the author's imagination or are used fictitiously, and any resemblance
to actual persons, living or dead, business establishments, events, or locales is
entirely coincidental.

The publisher does not have any control over and does not assume any
responsibility for author or third-party Web sites or their content.

For my father
and for Brett, Bill, Tasha and Andrew,
friends old and new

Death is the golden key
that opens the palace of eternity.

—*John Milton*

BOOK I

A Priori

Better to reign in Hell, than serve in Heav'n.

—*Paradise Lost*, 1667 ed., I:263

1

Before they met, he knew nothing of the book, or the story surrounding it.

He hadn't known about its size or the scope of its contents or the blackening skin of its pages or the ornate, nearly perfect penmanship that adorned them. He hadn't known that it was housed in Prague, in one of the collections of a Holy Roman Emperor, patron of the arts and practicing alchemist. He hadn't known that a hundred and sixty donkeys had been slaughtered to further its creation.

And he was completely unaware of the seven missing pages.

The pages that would lead to his undoing.

But much to his regret, the poet learned these things and more on a visit to Florence—there in a small villa in Arcetri, where he first met the astronomer, a pale, bearded old man condemned to spend the last years of his life as a prisoner in his own home.

This was long before the evil days, before the darkness amid the blaze of noon. Back when the poet's life had been truly blessed, when day-to-day living had not only been pleasurable, but was often exhilarating. When he was filled with the freshness of spirit that comes with youth and intellect and an unyielding belief in newly formed ideals.

He'd been quite surprised to receive the old man's invitation, and after months of arduous travel, taking him from London to Calais, then on to Paris and Nice and Genoa, his first instinct was to send his apologies and return home to England.

But the astronomer not only possessed one of the finest minds known to man, he was, in many ways, a kindred soul. A follower of God, yet free in spirit. A believer in individual choice who abhorred tyranny of any kind, even when it wore prelatical robes.

And when the poet read the message waiting for him at his lodgings in Livorno, he knew it would be foolish to pass up this opportunity to further his education.

So he accepted the invitation and went to Florence.

A choice that would haunt him until his dying day.

The villa was tumbledown and smelled faintly of mildew, two guards standing watch at the front gates.

He was greeted at the door by a timid young maid who looked as if she'd come straight from the convent, here to do penance for some ungodly transgression. She averted her gaze as she introduced herself, and he wondered what sad demon possessed her that would prevent her from looking him in the eye.

"Please be gentle with him," she said softly as she escorted him down a long hallway past a row of doors. "He hasn't been well these last few weeks and he tires easily. And be warned. He has his good days and bad, and we never quite know which to expect."

Her words surprised the poet. He had heard that, despite his age, the astronomer was still in complete control of his faculties. But perhaps the *good days* this young woman spoke of were filled with enough brilliance to outweigh the bad. The old man's writings certainly reflected this.

They came to a stop at the end of the hallway and she opened a door, gesturing him into the room beyond. The shades were drawn to block out the afternoon sun, because no sun was needed.

The old man was blind. An affliction, the poet knew, he had suffered only recently.

But his hearing was good, and the moment the door swung open, he turned in their direction and said, "I cannot teach you anything. I can only put you on a course to self-discovery. What you find, and what you do with it, is up to you."

He sat in a chair by a blazing fireplace, his blank eyes staring out at nothing. The poet stood there in the doorway, a bit confounded, feeling as if he'd walked into the middle of a conversation and not quite knowing how to respond.

Was the old man even speaking to him?

He decided his best course of action was simply to introduce himself, but as he began forming the words, the astronomer cut him off.

"I know who you are. I invited you here, remember?"

"Yes. Yes, of course," the poet stuttered, feeling as if he'd just been chastised by his own father. "But to be quite frank, I'm not absolutely certain why."

The old man softened then, waving a hand at him. "Come in, come in. Have a seat. You must be weary after such a long journey."

This was certainly true. Traveling by horseback was

never easy. The poet closed the door behind him, and with the aid of the light from the fire, he found a chair and pulled it close to the old man.

It was at that very moment that the regret began to overcome him. As he sat down, an inexplicable sense of darkness descended upon him, as if the Devil himself were hovering nearby, watching and waiting with great anticipation.

"I've read your work," the astronomer said. "You strike me as a man of sound intellect, with a strong belief in God."

"I could say the same of you."

The old man shrugged. "There are those who claim I've rejected Scripture in favor of science, but even after my arrest and the death of my daughter, my faith in God and nature has remained firm. Whatever the course of our lives, we should receive them as the highest gift from His hand. Don't you agree?"

The poet nodded. "Of course. But I also believe the greatest liberty God has given us is the freedom to think and speak in whatever manner our conscience may guide us."

"As do I, my son."

"Which is why I find your confinement here nothing short of reprehensible."

The old man waved a hand dismissively. "Those who keep me prisoner in this cage have small, fearful minds."

"It would appear so, yes."

"They huddle together protectively and use their faith as a shield, rejecting anyone who questions the sanctity of their petty narrow-mindedness." He heaved a sigh. "But enough of such talk. I didn't ask you here to discuss politics."

The poet hesitated. "Then why, exactly, am I here?"

"We'll get to that. But first, let me share with you the story of my most recent discovery. As a man of letters, I think you of all people will appreciate it."

The poet raised his eyebrows, thinking of night skies and star clusters and wondering how someone who no longer had eyes could find much of anything out there. "What sort of discovery?"

The astronomer smiled, but it seemed forced, as if he were trying to hide some private fear that lay just beneath its surface. That sense of darkness grew deeper, and for a moment the poet wondered if he should flee this place and never return.

"I've found the pages," the old man said, offering no further explanation.

The poet was confused, once again feeling as if he'd stepped into a conversation he hadn't previously been part of. "Pages?"

Despite his blindness, something flickered in the astronomer's eyes and they seemed to come alive. "The seven missing pages from the Devil's Bible," he said. "The seven missing pages that, if placed into the right hands, will change the universe forever."

The poet couldn't leave the villa fast enough.

What he had hoped would be the highlight of his travels—an afternoon of fine wine and poetry and conversation with one of the great men of his time—had turned out to be anything but.

Instead he had witnessed what he believed to be one of the astronomer's *bad days* and found himself listening to the tale of a thirteenth-century Benedictine monk who had broken his monastic vows and was sentenced to be walled up alive—an image that gave the poet considerable pause.

Hoping for mercy, the monk begged his brethren to allow him to create a formidable tome, one that would contain all human knowledge and bring glory to their monastery. But the monk was given only a single night to complete this task, and when he realized that such a feat was impossible, he made a pact with the Devil, who offered to help him in exchange for his soul.

The astronomer told this story with quiet rapture in his voice and seemed to take great delight in describing the fruits of the monk's labor, assuming that because the poet was a student of literature, he would somehow share in that delight.

Written in Latin and roughly the size of a small storage trunk, the book, the Codex Gigas—or Devil's Bible, as it came to be known—contained painstakingly rendered transcriptions of both the Old and New Testaments; the *Chronicle of Bohemia*; a necrology of the time; various historical treatises; holy incantations and conjurings; and a number of starkly wrought illustrations, including a multicolored drawing of the rebel angel Satan that brought involuntary shivers to anyone who gazed upon it.

The astronomer claimed to have seen this book long before his arrest and trial and confinement to the villa. But it wasn't the book itself—as magnificent and perplexing as it might be—that had excited him.

It was those missing pages. Pages that had disappeared without explanation, removed from the middle of the Codex Gigas by unknown hands and rumored to contain the secret to one of God's greatest creations.

"Seven simple pages," the old man said. "And finding them was an obsession I carried with me for much of my life."

As the poet listened, he realized with great sadness that the astronomer's mind had been twisted by age and he had created this absurd fiction out of whole cloth. It surprised him that a man of science, a man who had dedicated his life to supporting his beliefs with concrete evidence, would allow himself to be consumed by such a dark and rather fanciful tale.

Surely no such secret existed. And the story of the monk and his pact with the Devil was nothing more than superstitious drivel.

But even more absurd was the astronomer's claim that he had recently found these missing pages. After spending the last two decades poring over monastery records, monks' diaries, private correspondences and sending out inquiries from Prague to Jerusalem, he traced all seven of them to an antiquities dealer in Rome, stored in a sealed portfolio in one of the dealer's many archive rooms.

"So I bribed my captors," he told the poet, "and slipped away in the dark of night, taken by carriage to the capital city. Then I locked myself in that archive room and swallowed the contents of those pages like a drunken old fool."

Fool, indeed, the poet thought. But he humored his host. "And did you find everything you had hoped to?"

"Oh, yes. And so much more. The promise of a greater source of power than any one man should hold."

Enough of this nonsense. Time to call his bluff. "I'd love to see these pages, then."

"I thought you would. That's why I've invited you here."

"I assume you brought them back with you?"

Now the astronomer lowered his head, struggling for an answer, and the poet almost felt guilty for asking. "Sadly, no. But I'm hoping you'll help me retrieve them."

The poet was surprised. "You just said yourself you had them in your hands."

"Yes," the old man murmured. "But I nearly collapsed, right there in the room. Had to be carried away before I could arrange to take possession of them—before I could even finish *viewing* them, as glorious as they were."

"But why?" the poet asked.

The astronomer lifted his head again, staring directly at him, the brown of his irises barely visible behind milky white membranes. The look was so unsettling it sent a chill straight through the poet's body.

"You see these eyes? They'd grown dim and tired, no question about it, but they could still see when I walked into that archive room."

The poet frowned. "I don't understand."

The old man swallowed, as if what he was about to say might choke him, his unseeing gaze burrowing into the poet's very soul.

"It's quite simple, my son. The curse upon those pages drove me blind."

2

ISTANBUL, TURKEY
PRESENT DAY

There were four of them, huddled in a corner of the café, half hidden by shadow.

Three men and a woman.

Ajda hadn't heard them enter. The bell above the door had somehow failed her. But the moment she emerged from the kitchen and saw them sitting there, she knew that they were strangers to the city.

Tourists.

Not that this was anything unusual. The streets of Istanbul were always filled with such people. They flew in from all over the world, marching like lemmings into foul-smelling buses that carted them around to all the usual landmarks, the museums, the wonders of a strange land.

But there were no tour buses this late at night, and Ajda was surprised to see these four.

One of them called to her in Turkish, ordering black tea, but his facility with her native tongue did nothing to endear them to her.

Even from a distance, they made her feel ill at ease.

As she carried the tray to their table, setting a cup in front of each of them, she avoided looking directly into their eyes for fear their gazes would somehow burn straight through her.

It was an irrational fear, she knew, but the hour was late; the café otherwise deserted, and her gut told her that there was something very wrong here.

She hoped they would quickly drink up and leave.

They spoke Russian then, although none of them looked to be natives of the country. It was a language Ajda knew fairly well, after summer studies in Saint Petersburg and two years rooming with a family near Brighton Beach in America before returning here to the city. But the strangers couldn't know this, and they spoke freely in front of her.

Or perhaps they simply didn't care.

"All right, my dear," one of the men said, turning his gaze to the woman. "The floor is yours. What's so important you had to drag us here at this hour?"

He was statuesque, dressed in impeccably tailored clothes. He reminded Ajda of the many American business-men she'd seen on television.

"I've just returned from Manasseh," the woman told him. "I have some disturbing news."

Ajda tried not to listen. Their business was not hers. And as she tucked the tray under her arm and turned away from the table, she attempted to distract herself from their conversation with thoughts of Ferid and his promise to marry her.

But it didn't work. The strangers, like most tourists, were speaking much louder than good manners dictated, and Ajda's curiosity had been piqued. The place the woman had spoken of—Manasseh—was not familiar to her, although she had long been a student of geography.

Was it a city? A country?

Ajda had a vague memory of hearing the name before,

but associated it with a king of some kind. Something she had learned in school, no doubt.

"Don't keep us in suspense," another of the men said. "What is this news?"

He was the oldest of the group, but he dressed like a much younger man, in a leather jacket and jeans—an aging rock star, wearing sunglasses at night. He was sitting next to the woman, and he casually reached over, running a hand along the small of her back. An intimate gesture that made Ajda shiver with revulsion. The thought of being alone with this man repulsed her.

The woman, however, didn't seem to mind. Far from it.

"*Custodes Sacri* is alive and well," she said.

A long silence followed, and Ajda made herself busy wiping a nearby table, chancing another glance in their direction.

All eyes were on the woman.

And who could blame them? She was beautiful. Exotic. Ethereal. Not that Ajda made a habit of admiring other women. But there was something about this one that compelled it.

At the moment, however, these men weren't interested in her beauty. Only in the words she had spoken.

"Ridiculous," the third man said. He was German, with the somewhat stiff, controlled bearing of a military man. He struck Ajda as someone who would take great pleasure in inflicting torture. "Their lot ended generations ago. Who told you this?"

The woman hesitated again. "No one of consequence. A laggard. A drunk."

The businessman raised an eyebrow. "One of your playthings, no doubt. Is he . . . committed yet?"

The woman shook her head.

"Then why believe him?"

"It's complicated. But I have my reasons. You think I'd waste everyone's time if I didn't?"

"What I think is that you tend to be an alarmist, my dear, and I'm not interested in listening to your cries that the sky is falling. But even if it's true, *Custodes Sacri* is no real threat to us."

Sunglasses turned to him. "Don't be naive, Radek. I'd think you, especially, would understand the threat of unseen enemies." He looked at the German now. "And you, Vogler, you know better than anyone what lurks behind an innocent face and a charming smile. Our last few attempts have failed spectacularly, gentlemen, and I think it's time we let Bel—" He stopped himself, glancing at Ajda, who kept busy behind the counter. "It's time to let our sister here have her chance."

The woman looked at him appreciatively, even lasciviously. Ajda shuddered at the thought that these two might be related.

The businessman gestured dismissively. "Look around you. The world is in chaos and we're closer than ever to realizing our goal. The fourth moon approaches, and a handful of true believers can't do anything to stop us."

"The fourth moon is useless to us if we fail to find what we're looking for."

The businessman scowled. "That's your particular obsession, my friend. You put too much stock in ancient rumors. For all we know, they're nothing but lies designed to distract us from what truly needs to be done."

"We've had this argument before," Sunglasses said.

"But even the execution of their so-called savior didn't give us the power we need."

The German snorted. "Proof that he was as mortal as the rest of them."

"But if those ancient rumors are true, the Telum will change the game. And I thought we all agreed what our first priority is."

The businessman shook his head. "I made no such agreement. I see no reason to abandon the tried and true in hopes that a fairy tale might bear fruit."

The woman leaned toward him now.

"Tried and true?" she said incredulously. "Like the Crusades? The Black Death? World War Two? Your efforts have fallen short time and again, Radek, and the sooner you put that ego of yours in check, the better off we'll all be."

The businessman flicked his gaze toward her, his eyes cold with contempt. "I'd advise you to watch your tongue, my dear. If you think I'd hesitate to cut it off, you're sadly mistaken."

"You're certainly welcome to try."

Ajda watched in horror as the two stared at each other, neither willing to look away.

"Enough," Sunglasses said. "These petty disputes only serve to divide us, and we can't afford that now. If *Custodes Sacri* is indeed active again, then we can use them to our advantage. They do, after all, hold the key to what we seek. And that knowledge is as important as the Telum itself."

The German looked doubtful. "What makes you think they'll be any different than the others of their kind? We've tried working with them before."

"It only takes one."

"Assuming you can find any of them."

The woman smiled now. "This is why I summoned you all to Esau."

"Oh?"

She gestured toward the window. "The auction house across the street. My friend seems to believe the owner is one of them. A rancid little beast named Ozan."

"And he knows this how?"

"He's a student of our world. Seems to know more about it than I do myself. And despite his failings, his intellect is quite formidable. He could be useful to us."

The businessman glanced at the other two men, then smirked at her. "It's quite obvious you have a soft spot for this pathetic creature."

She studied him coldly. "Now whose tongue is in danger?"

"Let's get back to the problem at hand," Sunglasses said, then turned again to the woman, once more stroking the small of her back. "I assume you'd prefer to handle the matter?"

"I think it's only fitting, don't you?"

"How so?" the businessman asked.

"You've all had your chances to prove yourselves. Now it's mine. And even if this Ozan creature fails to give us what we need, he'll no longer be an obstacle." She smiled. "By the time I'm finished, none of them will."

Sunglasses looked at the others. "There you have it then. You two can continue doing what you so love and leave the rest to us. Are we all in agreement?"

The other men seemed to hesitate a moment, as if giving in were somehow equivalent to a battle lost. Then there were nods all around as each of the four raised a palm, saying in unison, "*A posse ad esse.*"

Ajda froze in place as a shiver ran through her bones. She had dropped all pretense now and was staring openly at them, certain that what she was witnessing was the planning of a crime of some kind. Possibly even murder.

What else could it be?

The woman glanced up sharply and Ajda quickly averted her gaze. She had to speak to Ferid. He knew people. Could summon the police. The auction house was closed at this hour, so maybe they could warn this man Ozan before these horrid people got to him.

But as she turned to flee to the kitchen, she stopped short, surprised to find the woman standing directly in front of her—an impossible feat that confused Ajda, rendering her momentarily immobile.

"You speak Russian," the woman said.

A statement, not a question.

Alarmed, Ajda swiveled her head to look at the others, for fear they might be coming for her. But to her further surprise, the table was empty except for four untouched cups of tea. There was no other indication that the men had ever been here at all.

"You're quite lovely," the woman continued, now speaking Turkish with the fluency of a native. And as Ajda tried to move past her, she quickly discovered that her immobility was not temporary at all.

The woman looked her straight in the eyes. And just as Ajda had feared, this was no ordinary gaze. It felt as if a foreign entity had invaded her body.

But not, she realized, an unpleasant one.

"I'm sure all the boys adore you," the woman said, then gave her a small, knowing smile. "And perhaps some of their sisters, too?"

Then, without even a hint of hesitation, she reached forward and gently cupped Ajda's left breast, brushing a neatly manicured thumb across the fabric covering her nipple.

To Ajda's astonishment, she was not offended nor embarrassed by this. It didn't bother her that a complete stranger was touching her in a place that no woman had ever touched. It didn't even concern her that the door to the café was unlocked and that someone might walk in at any moment.

It was as if she were dreaming. A dream she had no desire to awaken from. One with no restrictions, no taboos.

Her senses were whirling. This woman's touch had stirred something inside her. Something primal. And as her body reacted, she suddenly felt . . . free. Free to act on her impulses without judgment.

"So beautiful," the woman said, then ran her hands down the front of Ajda's blouse, unbuttoning it, dropping it to the floor. With a quick, practiced motion, she unhooked Ajda's bra, then leaned forward and kissed the spot where her thumb had just been.

Ajda didn't resist.

Had no desire to.

Whatever fear she had felt before had vanished along with her modesty, and she found the sensation of this stranger's tongue to be quite exhilarating.

Something loosened inside of her, something wet and

wonderful—a feeling that Ferid, with all of his fumbling, had never been able to awaken.

And as they sank together to the floor, hands roaming, fingers exploring, all Ajda could think about was the hunger she felt.

She wanted more.

Give me more.

BOOK II

The Fall and Rise
of Gabriela Zuada

I fled and cry'd out, Death!
Hell trembl'd at the hideous Name, and sigh'd
From all her Caves, and back resounded Death!

—*Paradise Lost*, 1667 ed., II:787–89

3

SÃO PAULO, BRAZIL

Her screams were what told them she was in trouble.

Before that, Alejandro and the others had assumed that she'd merely wanted time alone, as she often did. And despite the danger, despite her utter carelessness, the moment the show was over, she had managed to slip away from them and disappear.

Some might have considered it a prima donna move. But Gabriela Zuada was no prima donna.

Alejandro knew this better than anyone.

After nearly a year as her personal manager, and three before that running *Lar do Coração*—Gabriela's Home of the Heart charity—he had never seen her throw a temper tantrum, had never seen her raise her voice in anger, had never seen her make a single reckless move that would lower her to the level of any of the flavor-of-the-week pop stars who had come and gone over the years.

But the woman liked her privacy. Especially after a performance. And Alejandro knew that the hordes of ravenous fans, the paparazzi, and all the trappings of superstardom sometimes got to be too much for her. So he had assumed, along with everyone else in Gabriela's entourage, that this was why she had quietly disappeared.

He had turned away for only a moment, to make another phone call. One minute she was walking alongside him, the next she was gone. A trick she had perfected after several months of practice.

Alejandro couldn't count the number of times he had patiently explained to her that she was not only a public figure, but a controversial one as well, and that she must stay with her bodyguards at all times.

But Gabriela rarely listened. She may not have been a prima donna, but she definitely had a mind of her own.

This was the last night of her Glory Revealed World Tour, and Gabriela had always liked to end with a show here in São Paulo. Had once said to Alejandro, back in the days when she had shared his bed, that home was the only place she truly felt safe.

"This is where God chose to put me on this earth," she'd said as she snuggled up close, pressing a warm breast against his arm. "Where his angel watches over me."

Alejandro had loved the feel of her skin against his. The rise and fall of her chest as she breathed into his ear. Missed it even now, all these months later.

They had both known that their affair was a sin, but had succumbed to temptation more than once—seventeen glorious times, to be precise—until the guilt had finally driven Gabriela to break it off.

"How can I preach chastity to young girls when I'm not chaste myself?"

It was a fair question. One that Alejandro couldn't argue with.

But when he had broached the subject of marriage, Gabriela had scoffed. She had no time for such things. Not with the ministry finally taking off, not with all the work that had to be done.

She would only allow herself to be committed to the

Lord and no one else. And she must serve as an example of purity in a world polluted by mankind's weaknesses— especially now, when that world was quickly headed toward the oblivion of hell, when economies were failing and the streets were filled with so much anger and hate.

She had never seen such unrest, she'd told Alejandro. Several months ago, at a concert in Greece, a near riot had broken out for no other reason than someone mistakenly sat in the wrong seat. It had taken a plea from Gabriela herself to calm the crowd.

Shortly after that night, she had broken it off with Alejandro. She had somehow gotten it into her head that her growing lack of attention to her own faith had rubbed off on others, and the only way she could fight against the chaos was to renew her vow to the Father.

It was bad enough, she said, that she was forced to get up on that stage and shake her hips. Some in the Church were appalled by her overtly sexual performances, but they couldn't complain about the results. Gabriela had brought young people from all over the globe into the fold, and she considered a few pelvic thrusts a small compromise, as long as they never overshadowed the larger message in her music:

God is good.

God is great.

God is the light in a world of darkness.

Besides, who ever said children of the Lord couldn't be sexual? Hadn't He given them these urges for a reason? And maybe, just maybe, He approved.

But Gabriela had eventually drawn the line at continuing to sleep with Alejandro. As much as she'd loved their nights together—or so she had claimed—she could no longer allow herself to sin.

"So this is it," she had said as she climbed atop him and guided him inside her for the very last time. "Tomorrow is a new beginning. Tomorrow I give myself to God and no one else."

God is a lucky man, Alejandro had thought.

Then he'd closed his eyes and reveled in the feel of that thrusting pelvis against his, in the knowledge that he had tasted the sweetness that was Gabriela Zuada, a sweetness that had brought him such unbridled pleasure that he would remember it with exquisite clarity for the rest of his life.

And now, as he strode with a platoon of bodyguards, searching the maze of corridors backstage for the woman he loved—a maze that hadn't seemed quite so confusing before this moment—Alejandro once again remembered that last sinful night, relishing his good fortune.

And despite being cut off from those amazing bodily treasures . . . the perfect breasts, the skilled hands, the rolling tongue, that dark, delicious hair . . . Despite the fact that Gabriela was nowhere to be found in this impossibly confusing place, a sense of calm washed over Alejandro and he felt at peace with the world.

Until the acrid smell of gasoline filled his nostrils, and Gabriela began to scream.

4

Ten minutes before those screams, Gabriela Zuada stood onstage with her bandmates, their hands locked together as they took their final bow.

The crowd was cheering, many of them on their feet, some even chanting, "Santa Gabriela, Santa Gabriela, Santa Gabriela . . ." as they showered the stage with flowers and candies.

Scooping up one of the flowers—a bloodred rose— Gabriela threw it into the air, then lifted her chin toward the rafters and shouted, "*Glória a Deus, nosso Pai!*"

The crowd went wild, hands thrusting heavenward as they repeated her words in unison, over and over, tears streaming down their faces, tears full of joy and hope and the promise of salvation.

And in that moment, Gabriela—bone weary, drenched in sweat—thought:

They would do anything for you.

Anything at all.

Then the thought was gone, skittering away like a roach exposed to a kitchen light, and Gabriela felt a chill run through her.

Where had that come from?

How could she think such a horrible thing?

It was true that she wasn't feeling well tonight, had

been concerned that she was coming down with a cold and fever and might not make it through the entire show, but was that enough to put such thoughts into her head?

Before she could take any time to analyze the moment, Francisco, Rafael and the others waved to the crowd and headed offstage. Gabriela fell in behind them, blowing one last kiss to her fans as she disappeared behind a wall of amplifiers.

By the time she reached the ramp at the back of the stage, the thought was forgotten, overtaken by the sudden realization that her feet were killing her. All she wanted was to get out of these shoes, into a limousine, take the short ride home to her penthouse in the heart of São Paulo, then swallow a handful of aspirin and go to bed.

That wasn't too much to ask, was it?

As she reached the bottom of the ramp and handed her headgear to the sound technician, Alejandro and her bodyguards surrounded her, escorting her toward a dimly lit hallway behind the stage.

Alejandro handed her a towel, a bottle of lemon-lime Gatorade and her cell phone. Their usual ritual.

The phone was Alejandro's idea. He thought it absolutely essential that she have one with her at all times. A security precaution.

It was true that Gabriela had ruffled some feathers by speaking out against the drug lords here in São Paulo, but she sometimes felt that Alejandro was too paranoid for his own good.

"Outstanding show, *querida*. We've finished the tour on a high note."

Gabriela tucked the phone into her back pocket, wiped her face and neck, then returned the towel to him and took a swig of Gatorade. "I was off-key half the night. I think my ears are going."

"Nonsense." He reached out and squeezed her hand. "They loved you. We all love you."

She gave him a small squeeze back, feeling a tiny twinge of guilt. Their history together would always be a source of discomfort for her, and she quickly withdrew her hand as they moved into the hallway.

Alejandro didn't seem to notice. He had his own phone pressed to his ear now and was calling for the limousine to be brought around back. He was in fine spirits tonight, but Gabriela often worried about him, feared that she had broken his heart.

It was easy to admit that she loved him, but there were things about her that Alejandro could never know. A secret she couldn't reveal. And the closer she had gotten to him, the more she had wanted to share that secret.

So she had stepped away. Just as she had stepped away from the streets. And the parties. And her addiction to *Poeira do diabo*.

Devil dust.

They veered left, taking an adjoining hallway, and Gabriela was surprised by this. She had played this venue many times before, yet the layout seemed different somehow. Backward. She could've sworn that the last time she was here, it had veered to the right, following a straight line to a set of double doors that led to the loading dock.

But not this time. And it occurred to her that either she was crazy or she was simply confused by the many weeks of touring and the hundred other backstage passageways she had traveled.

Up ahead, the fluorescent lights were flickering, and Gabriela was suddenly struck by the memory of a much darker time in her life. A time when she and her best friend, Sofie, would get high in a gas station bathroom, the light above the cracked, graffiti-laden mirror flickering endlessly as they shared a pipe.

It was Sofie's death that had brought Gabriela to God. And every night, when she spoke to Him, she made sure to include a prayer for her lost friend.

She was remembering one of their better times together (riding their bicycles on the streets of the *favela*) as she and the others passed under that harsh, flickering light.

Then something odd happened.

Gabriela felt a short, abrupt tug, as if she'd been hooked to a wire and yanked forward. For a moment she thought she was still wearing the harness she donned at the top of every show—the one that allowed her to make her entrance by swooping over the audience like a winged angel as she sang the opening bars of "Paradise City."

But that made no sense. She had discarded the harness by her second number and had gone through six costume changes since.

Yet she felt the pull of that wire as plainly as she had felt the squeeze of Alejandro's hand. And without warning, she stumbled forward into sudden darkness—seemed to be drowning in it—only to emerge on the other side to find herself alone. Standing in yet another dim corridor.

Gabriela stopped, whirled. "Alejandro?"

But Alejandro wasn't there. Neither were any of her

bodyguards. One minute she had been surrounded by them, listening to their voices reverberate against the walls—

—and now, nothing.

The corridor was empty. Silent.

What was going on here?

They would do anything for you.

Anything at all.

The thought again. Slipping without warning into her brain. But like the corridor around her, it was different this time. She couldn't be entirely sure that the thought was her own.

She felt her forehead. Warm.

A fever. She was definitely coming down with a fever. She needed that bed more than ever now.

"Alejandro?" she called again, wondering for a moment if he and the others were hiding somewhere and this was some kind of prank. Retaliation for all the times she'd slipped away on her own.

But, no, Alejandro would never do such a thing. Could never be so cruel. Even after she rejected him, he had continued to stay loyal to her. Always kind. Always loving. Always supportive.

Alejandro was her rock.

He would do anything for you.

Anything at all.

Gabriela stiffened, her gut tightening. She was no stranger to voices inside her head, but they always came to her in moments of prayer—not like this. This one wasn't friendly. A voice she thought she recognized.

What have you done for him, *Gabriela?*

And what did you ever do for me?

Sofie. It was *Sofie.*

Not the young, vibrant Sofie that Gabriela had met in middle school, but the raspy-throated powder monkey who had huddled with her in that dirty, foul-smelling gas station bathroom, sucking in endless hits of Devil Dust.

You left me to die.

Why did you leave me to die?

Sofie was right. Gabriela *had* left her. Had found her on the floor of that very same bathroom and watched her choke on her own vomit. But instead of helping her, instead of calling an ambulance, Gabriela had followed the rules of the jungle and fled. Had abandoned her best friend, leaving her to die in a puddle of urine.

It had taken Gabriela many months to come to terms with this. To find herself again and beg for the Lord's forgiveness. For Sofie's forgiveness. When her career had taken off and money was easy to come by, she had formed a charity in Sofie's honor. Several charities.

And when God's heavenly messenger spoke to her and asked her to be one of His soldiers, she had readily agreed. Had sacrificed her future with Alejandro for the honor.

Yet none of this absolved her.

She knew that.

She would live with the guilt of Sofie's death for the rest of her life. A constant reminder of what she had come from and who she had once been.

Someone laughed, and Gabriela whirled again, her heart lifting slightly as she looked toward the end of the hall.

"Alejandro?"

There was an open door there. One she hadn't noticed before. More flickering light inside.

Convinced now that she was in the midst of some kind of fever dream, that she had passed out from exhaustion and was probably, at this very moment, in Alejandro's arms, Gabriela moved cautiously toward the doorway and stepped inside, surprised by what she saw.

The gas station bathroom.

Just as she remembered it.

The dingy walls, the toilet splattered with feces, the smell of urine and dried blood, the filthy sink, the splintered mirror with the words *VA SE FODER* spray-painted across it in big red letters. *Go fuck yourself.*

And sitting on the edge of the sink, beneath that flickering light, was a familiar-looking glass pipe, once translucent, now scarred and blackened by years of abuse.

Sofie's pipe.

And lying next to it was a small, battered lighter. A faded sticker on its side read GOT JESUS?

Gabriela froze at the sight of them. Was barely able to suppress the feeling welling up inside her. A feeling of contempt, mixed with—dared she say it?

Desire.

She had long ago beat her addiction, had spent many torturous months in rehab to do so, but the dust was a powerful demon and it did not relinquish that power easily.

What are you waiting for, my angel?

A voice again. Not Sofie this time, but another woman. Soft. Soothing. Carrying a dark undercurrent that made Gabriela shiver.

Frightened now, she turned to the door, but it swung shut with a resounding boom. Then the latch clicked, locking her inside.

"Alejandro!" she shouted, pounding her fists against

the wood, suddenly afraid that this wasn't a nightmare after all. "Alejandro, help me!"

He won't help you, my darling. He doesn't love you as I do.

Gabriela spun, searching the small room, looking for the source of the voice. "What do you know about him? Who are you? What do want from me?"

Only that you return my love.

Gabriela shifted her gaze to the pipe again. Was it the dust speaking? How could that be possible?

No, no, she thought. Like before, the voice was inside her head. Brought on by the fever. What else could it be?

Tell me you love me, Gabriela.

Gabriela turned, searching the room again. "I love only the Father."

Oh? Do you see Him anywhere? He cares for you even less than sweet, attentive Alejandro.

"You're wrong," Gabriela cried. "He believes in me. He trusts me."

And how do you know this?

"Why else would he send His angel to . . ."

She stopped herself. All at once, she knew what this was about. And it had nothing to do with fevers or dreams at all.

To what, my darling?

Lowering her voice, she said, "Go away. You're wasting your time. I'll never give you what you want."

And what would that be?

"To betray my oath."

The voice laughed. *You make it sound so serious. But people break promises every day. What about all those promises you made to Sofie?*

"Leave me alone!"

Not until you tell me what I need to know. Don't worry about the Father. He abandoned us all a long, long time ago. There's no place in his kingdom for you. You're one of the forgotten.

"You're wrong," Gabriela cried. "He believes in me. Trusts me. And I won't betray that trust."

And what about all the scribbling in that precious book of yours? If that isn't a betrayal, what is?

Gabriela felt fingers skitter along her spine. "How do you know about that?"

I know everything about you, my darling. I'm part of you. I always have been. I'm the desire you feel when you look at Alejandro. When you stare longingly at Sofie's pipe.

Gabriela shifted her gaze to the sink again and looked at the pipe and lighter sitting there, perched on the edge, calling to her. But she knew she had to resist. "No. I'll never give in to you. Never."

Never is such a strong word, isn't it? Your pathetic old friend said much the same to me, but in the end he was willing to compromise. Everyone is.

"My friend?"

The collector. One of your brethren.

Mention of the collector startled Gabriela. If this woman knew about him and was now coming to *her*, then they were *all* at risk. And so was the secret they held. Despite the fear rocketing through her bloodstream, Gabriela could not let herself give in to her weaknesses. There was too much at stake.

"No—you can't seduce me. I'll tell you nothing."

What harm would it do, my angel? Who would know?

"*I* would know," Gabriela shouted. "*I* would know."

Then she turned again, pounding her fists against the door. "Alejandro! Where are you? Help me!"

But no one answered.

Suddenly remembering the phone in her back pocket, and silently thanking Alejandro for his paranoia, she pulled it free and fumbled it in her hands, nearly dropping it. Clutching it tightly, she pressed speed dial, then put it to her ear, waiting for it to ring.

But it didn't. Went straight to voice mail.

Damn him. Why was he always on the phone?

Then, without warning, Gabriela was confronted by a blur of motion. Something swung out at her, knocking the cell phone from her hand. It flew to the floor, bounced once, and settled faceup under the feces-stained toilet.

Startled, she snapped her head up and discovered that she was no longer alone in the room.

Sofie was there, standing before her, the pipe and lighter in her hands. Her skin was bone white, festering sores on her cheeks and forehead. A dribble of vomit on her chin.

It was far and away the most horrifying sight Gabriela had ever seen. She brought her hands to her mouth, stifling a scream, and backed away.

Then Sofie spoke.

"Look at you, so sweet and noble now. All those fools calling your name. What do you think they'd say if they knew you left me here to die?"

Gabriela shook her head violently. "It was the dust that made me do it. You know that as well as I do."

"The dust? The dust was our friend, Gabriela. Remember how happy it made us feel? Remember how we laughed?" Sofie lifted the hand holding the pipe. "If you won't tell us your secret, then why not take an offer of compromise? The same compromise the collector made. All we ask for is the name of one of your brethren. Nothing more."

"Stay away from me."

Sofie shoved the pipe toward her. "Give us a name, and this is yours. Just like old times. You can be with the ones who love you. Who love the *real* you, not this angelic monstrosity you pretend to be."

"No," Gabriela shouted, and swung an arm out, knocking the pipe and lighter to the floor.

Sofie watched them roll and land near the phone, then slowly lowered her head. She said nothing for a long moment. And when she spoke, there was sadness in her voice. "I was hoping it wouldn't come to this."

Suddenly the smell of gasoline filled the air, and Gabriela spun, saw liquid sluicing down the walls, coming down in sheets, pooling on the floor. Fumes rolled toward her and she began to choke and cough, feeling them burn her lungs.

"Give us a name, Gabriela. Now!"

"No." She gagged. ". . . Leave me alone . . . leave me—"

Sofie's face churned up in fury as she grabbed Gabriela by the shoulders and threw her against the nearest wall. Gabriela hit it hard and pain tore through her, gasoline pouring onto her head, soaking her hair and clothes, plastering them to her skin.

"Give us the name!" Sofia shouted, then grabbed her again, throwing her against the sink.

Gabriela slammed headfirst into the mirror, splintering the glass. A shard pierced her forehead and blood poured from the wound, mixing with the gasoline as it rolled down her face and into her mouth.

She hobbled forward, gagging and spitting. "Please . . . ," she begged, weeping now, adding tears to the mix.

But Sofie grabbed her a third time and flung her toward the toilet. Gabriela stumbled into it, landing in a heap on the floor, still coughing, barely able to breathe. She rolled onto her back, and her gaze once again went to the pipe and lighter, which lay only inches from her now, miraculously dry, untouched by the gasoline.

Tell me you love me, my angel.

And despite herself, she felt that familiar urge well up inside her again, stronger than ever.

"Give us a name," Sofie said. "That's all we ask. One simple name and you'll be free."

Gabriela tried to resist. Tried with all her might. Sent a desperate prayer up to God, but got only silence in return.

"Please," she sobbed, "please . . . help me . . ."

But no one heard. No one was listening.

Maybe the voice had been right. God *didn't* love her. And maybe He had been wrong to trust her. To think she was any different now than she was back then, all those nights so long ago.

What Sofie had said was true. The dust *had* made them happy. So very happy.

And what would be the harm in one small hit?

The moment Gabriela thought this, the gasoline stopped flowing, leaving behind soaked walls, puddles on the floor, and a room full of fumes.

Gabriela's gut was churning. The dust still calling out to her.

Tell me you love me, my darling.

Giving in, she reached out, grabbed for the pipe. But just as her fingers were about to close around it, Sofie's rotting bare foot pressed against her hand, stopping her.

"A name," she said. "That's all we require."

Defeated, drained, no longer feeling as if she had a will of her own, Gabriela sputtered and coughed again, then finally relented, giving them what they wanted, letting the name flutter through her mind like a passing bird. And the moment it did, Sofie was gone, leaving Gabriela alone with the pipe, the lighter, and her discarded phone.

Pulling herself up on her elbows, still crying, still coughing, but ever cognizant of the need burning inside her, Gabriela picked up the pipe and lighter with wet, trembling hands.

She thought of Alejandro, how devastated he'd be. She thought about how weak she truly was, and how easily she'd given in to them. Her only saving grace was that she hadn't given them everything. Hadn't revealed the secret she was sworn to protect.

That was something, wasn't it?

But she knew that she could no longer be trusted with that secret. That the dust had too strong of a hold on her. And with this knowledge, she leaned forward slightly, whispering softly into her cell phone, hoping someone out there would hear her and understand.

It was time to let the Father take her now. If she couldn't be useful to Him in this world, maybe she'd do better in His.

Anticipating sweet relief, she put the pipe to her lips, tightened her grip on the lighter and sent up one last prayer for forgiveness as she rolled her thumb against the flint wheel.

The explosion barely registered as Gabriela inhaled deeply, taking into herself that thing which had been missing from her life all these years.

It felt transcendent.

A split second later, however, when she realized that the smoke she was inhaling was no longer the narcotic she craved but the stinking, sweet essence of her own burning flesh, her final conscious thought arrived along with a searing, unbelievable pain.

That was when Gabriela Zuada started screaming.

BOOK III

The Boy Who Couldn't Forget
The Girl Who Couldn't Sleep

Embryos and idiots, eremites and friars,
White, black, and gray, with all their trumpery.

—*Paradise Lost*, 1667 ed., III:474–75

5

HARRISON, LOUISIANA

"Every story has a hero," he said. "Someone we invest ourselves in. But not all of those heroes are necessarily pretty. Or perfect. And I think any discussion of Milton's masterpiece has to consider this."

Sebastian LaLaurie squinted out at a lecture hall full of Louisiana's so-called best and brightest, almost daring one of them to contradict him.

Nobody did.

"Look at the stories we've talked about these past few weeks: Moses, Miriam, David, Gideon, Elijah, Noah, Ruth . . . The Old Testament is chock-full of heroic men and women."

A murmur of voices. Nods of agreement.

"Throw in part two of our biblical canon and you've got the greatest hero of them all. A simple carpenter's son who sacrificed his life to save every last one of us."

A chorus of amens filled the room, but Batty held up a hand, cutting them off. The last thing he wanted was to turn this lecture into some kind of revival meeting. He was here to educate, not run a cheerleading session.

He stumbled slightly and grabbed hold of the lectern to steady himself, getting a tentative ripple of laughter for his trouble.

He ignored it and pushed on. "But what if we adjust

the lens a little, just like Milton did, and look at things from a slightly different angle? What if the *true* hero of Paradise is someone else entirely? Someone we traditionally think of as the villain."

Another ripple, but it wasn't laughter this time, and there wasn't an amen within earshot. Instead, Batty saw enough startled frowns to know he'd hit a nerve. This wasn't surprising, considering that Trinity Baptist College had been built on strict, orthodox beliefs, and few of the students here were brave enough to take the contrarian point of view.

But Batty had always liked to shake things up a bit. These kids had no earthly idea what was going on out there.

He, on the other hand, did—which was why he was currently about two drinks shy of a midafternoon bender.

"Milton based much of his epic poem on the book of Genesis," he continued. "And in that book, God creates a perfect paradise, populates it with a nice young couple and puts them to work in His garden. They spend their days slaving away, doing whatever God commands—only there's this Tree of Knowledge nearby, bearing some nice juicy fruit, and it looks pretty damn tempting."

The fact that Batty could drink so much and still teach Religious Literature and Rhetoric without slurring his speech or falling flat on his face was something of a miracle. But he tried not to give it too much thought. If he did, he'd probably decide he wasn't quite drunk *enough*.

Images from his nightmare still lingered—

—*a screaming young girl consumed by a wall of fire*.

He had awakened to those screams in the middle of the night last night, disoriented and concerned, wondering if what he'd seen was real, and suddenly reminded of his own private horror.

A horror he preferred not to relive.

He said to the class, "But temptation or no temptation, God tells this nice young couple, 'No, no, no, you keep your hands off that tree. That knowledge stuff, that's a bad thing. You just listen to me, let me do the thinking, and I'll take good care of you.'"

Batty tried a smile, but figured it probably came off more like a grimace.

"Then along comes our new hero in the form of a serpent. He sees what's what and doesn't like it one bit. So he tells Eve, 'You know what? You go on, take a bite of that fruit if you want to. You deserve to live a little.'"

"Is this supposed to be funny?"

The question came from several rows up, somewhere near the middle of the lecture hall, and Batty swiveled his head, wobbling slightly, trying to focus in on its source.

One of his graduate students. An angry little beignet with startling brown eyes.

Rebecca's eyes, he thought, then immediately pushed the thought away as if it were tainted by something toxic.

He needed another drink. "I guess it *is* pretty funny. Because if it weren't for our new hero, Eve never would've exercised the free will God granted her. And without free will, there's no real purpose to life."

Murmurs all around. None of them friendly.

"Without free will, we just follow rules. And what fun is that? No adventure, no quests, no glory, no passion, no redemption. All those things that make us human." He paused. "Fortunately, somebody recognized that God's Paradise was a flawed creation, and that Man was living under a kind of blissful tyranny. So he decided to do something about it." Batty let his gaze sweep across the room. "And that, my friends, is the very definition of heroism."

"Oh, really?" The beignet was on her feet now, a fierce little thing filled with the indignation of a True Believer. "And what did this so-called hero give us? The Holocaust? Disease? Gang violence?"

Batty shrugged. "Why stop there? What about poverty? Starving children? Endless war? The oil spill? *Katrina?*"

That last one, Batty knew, was a trigger point. Hurricane Katrina was Louisiana's sorest of sore spots, had caused more pain and devastation than anyone here could remember, and the wounds were still festering, all these years later.

"Some might argue that the havoc Katrina brought us had more to do with God's abandonment of Man than Man's abandonment of Eden, and it doesn't really negate my point. None of those things do." He looked at the rest of the class. "Not everything in the Bible is black and white, ladies and gentlemen, which is why we've spent the last several centuries arguing about it. And I think John Milton himself understood this. He was a pious Puritan, but that didn't keep him from authoring an epic about an anguished rebel rising up against an all-powerful tyrant. There's no doubt his work was born out of a reaction to his times and his strong endorsement of regicide, but it makes you wonder if he knew something the rest of us don't." Batty paused. "Maybe he knew a true hero when he saw one."

And that was when the dam broke.

Something nasty stirred in the air and several of the students joined the True Believer, shooting to their feet in protest, while others headed straight for the doors. Some began shouting at Batty, calling him a fool and a charlatan and a few choice names that would have made their grandmothers blush.

This wasn't the first time he'd pissed them off, but it was the strongest reaction he'd ever managed to get from them. They were obviously fed up with his apparent lack of respect for their faith—an accusation he'd take issue with—and he didn't suppose the distinct smell of Tullamore Dew oozing from his pores helped matters much.

He was about to tell them that he was simply trying to stimulate their stagnating intellects; that they should sit back down and *think* for once in their short, useless lives, when a familiar voice called out to him—

"Professor LaLaurie. May I see you in my office, please?"

And standing in the doorway, a scowl on her face, was the associate dean of Trinity Baptist College, one Edith Rose Stillwater, widow of the late Reverend Arthur Stillwater, Batty's best friend and mentor.

Batty turned, gave her a tight smile and tried not to stagger.

This was not going to be pleasant.

"**P**oor Milton must be turning in his grave," Edith said.

She sat behind the big oak desk she had inherited from her husband a little over a year ago, looking as if she had just bitten into a peach and discovered it was rancid.

Batty sank into a chair across from her. "Milton was a

free thinker, Edith. He would have agreed with every word I said today. Arthur would have, too."

"Oh, please. Arthur was a good Christian who believed in the word of God. Not the nonsense you were spewing."

"He also had a world-class intellect. One he liked to use. Not everything he believed in was limited to the constipated mutterings of the gospel according to John Smyth."

Edith stared at him. "Are you purposely trying to get yourself fired?"

Batty had spent so much time in self-destruct mode lately, he wasn't sure he knew the answer to that. But he didn't let it hold him back. "The only thing I do with any real sense of purpose these days is seek out liquid sustenance."

"That's fairly obvious. You smell like a distillery."

Batty shrugged. "What can I say? Aftershave just doesn't have the same kick."

Edith sighed in exasperation. It was obvious she'd had more than enough of him and Batty couldn't really blame her. Insolence and sarcasm were his first line of defense these days and he doled them out with the abandon of a street-corner lunatic.

"For God's sake, Sebastian. Why do you insist on being so contrary? Arthur loved you like a brother but I sometimes have to wonder why."

"Not enough to fire me, apparently."

"Believe me, I only hired you here out of loyalty to him. And call me a fool, but I still hold hope that time in a nurturing environment like this might help turn you around. Unfortunately, you seem to have gotten worse."

"It's the world that's gotten worse, Edith. I'm just an observer."

"An observer with one of the finest minds I've ever encountered—and I hate to see you waste it. I don't know a practicing scholar in this country who has more insight into the history of religion and religious doctrine than you do."

The point was arguable, but Batty certainly knew a lot more than he probably should. *Too* much knowledge— and the curiosity that goes along with it—can sometimes get you in trouble.

He'd learned that the hard way.

So had Rebecca.

"But your mind can only take you so far," Edith continued, "and while there's room for a certain amount of cynicism when it comes to matters of faith, you don't always have to be so infuriatingly obnoxious about it."

Batty shrugged again. "The kids love me. Didn't you see the way they were cheering me—"

"Enough."

Batty closed his mouth. *Sour* Edith had been abruptly replaced by *Stern* Edith, and he knew better than to wander down that alley.

"As much as I hate to do this," she said, "I'm afraid I'm going to have to make this your last warning."

"Didn't you say that three or four warnings ago?"

"I'm deadly serious, Sebastian. Look at you, you can barely sit up straight. Are those bruises on your face?"

Batty said nothing. He vaguely remembered getting into a brawl last night. Or was that the night before? Fighting and fornicating were not exactly admirable pursuits in his line of work, but he'd done his share of both lately.

He caught Edith staring at the scars on his wrists. She shifted uncomfortably and averted her gaze. "I've been extremely patient with you, but that ends now. And if Arthur were here instead of me, he'd do exactly the same thing. So, please, for the sake of us all, sober up, get some help, and put your faith in God."

That last bit flipped a switch inside Batty's head. He thought of the night Rebecca died and no longer felt like being insolent or sarcastic or, as Edith had so delicately put it, infuriatingly obnoxious. He just stared at her, incredulous. "You want me to put my faith in God?"

"It was good enough for Arthur. It should be good enough for you."

Batty felt fury rising inside him, but he tamped it down and leaned toward her. "Do you ever smell them, Edith?"

She looked confused. "I beg your pardon?"

"Rebecca did. And so do I sometimes. That was both our blessing and our curse."

"What on earth are you talking about? What does Rebecca have to do with this?"

"Look around you, Edith. They're among us. They look just like you and me, but that smell, it radiates off their bodies like pig shit on a farmer's shoes."

"You must be a lot drunker than I thought."

"This has nothing to do with booze. The world isn't what you think it is. Contrary to what this school teaches the mindless zealots who walk its halls every day, God lost interest in us a long time ago. And that book you preach doesn't have all the answers. The sooner you accept that fact, the better off you'll be."

Edith's whole body went stiff then, and Batty knew

that he'd just kissed this job good-bye. Some people can't deal with the truth.

Not that Batty was a shining example of someone who could. This was the third teaching position he'd burned through in the last two years, so his record wasn't exactly stellar. But he was just trying to cope in the best way he knew how, and that didn't sit well with some people. Including him.

Edith said nothing for a very long moment, then closed her eyes, and Batty assumed she was sending up a prayer.

Good luck getting an answer.

When she looked at him again, she said in a careful, measured tone, "I want you to take some time off, Sebastian. Starting now. And I want you to get some professional counseling. If it's a matter of money, the college will pay for it."

A charitable offer, but no amount of therapy in the world would bring Rebecca back. "And if I don't?"

She sighed again. "Then may God have mercy on your pitiful soul."

6

MIAMI, FLORIDA

She couldn't remember what name to use.

Oh, she knew her *real* name. That one was easy. It was downright impossible to forget an albatross like Bernadette Imogene Callahan—as much as she might like to. But seeing as how she had passports issued to at least a dozen different identities, she sometimes felt as if she needed a Rolodex implanted in her brain just to keep track of . . .

. . . Wait now.

Stephanie.

Stephanie Hathaway.

Twenty-nine years old, newly divorced, using her alimony to travel the world. Had a layover in Dallas before heading into Miami, where she spent the weekend at the Viceroy. Thought South Beach was pretentious and overpriced, but shopped there anyway.

Was that the one?

She was pretty sure it was.

Standing at the airport ticketing kiosk, she tuned out a lobby full of anxious travelers, then hit the touch screen and began keying in the letters:

H-a-t-h-a-

She was up to *w* when she realized her hand was trembling.

Again.

Shit.

She flexed it several times, then held it out flat, studying her fingers as carefully as one might study a work of art, but with none of the appreciation or pleasure. The tremor was slight but unmistakable. Which meant that the first time she'd noticed it had not been an anomaly.

Damn.

She flexed the hand again, wanting desperately to hide it in a pocket or something. But hiding it away wouldn't change anything. The tremor wouldn't magically cease once the hand disappeared from view.

She could think of a hundred different reasons for the problem—the majority of them neurological—but in strict allegiance to Occam's razor, she figured the simplest explanation was the best one.

She'd barely had a wink of sleep in three days.

Three interminable days.

Not for lack of trying, mind you. But there it was.

And loss of sleep would also explain why she'd had so much trouble remembering which cover she was supposed to use. Not to mention the panic attack she'd had just before sunrise.

In short, she was falling apart.

"Excuse me, ma'am. Do you need some assistance?"

Startled, Callahan immediately dropped her hand to her side and turned to find a uniformed airline employee standing beside her. He was a short, stout young man who looked to be of Malaysian or Filipino ancestry, and had a pleasant, toothy smile—no hint of that tired, sourpuss expression she saw on the faces of so many airport front liners these days.

Which, of course, immediately gave him away.

Amateur.

Why did Section always use newbies as messengers? It made no sense. Here she was, trying like hell to be professional and the powers-that-be had sent in some lightweight to blow her cover.

Then again, maybe she was being too critical. And maybe there actually *were* airline employees who sported genuine smiles. Surely she'd seen a few in all her years of travel, hadn't she? No point in condemning an entire industry with one sweeping generalization.

But there was no doubt in her mind that, for better or worse, this young man was a colleague. And this surprised Callahan, because she'd had no indication that such a visit was forthcoming.

"Ma'am? Do you need some help?"

"I'm just punching in my name here. Trying to get a boarding pass."

The drill was a clever one. Probably a tad elaborate, but people in the intelligence field are prone to complicate things. You found the designated kiosk at the designated airline, punched in your cover name and received a boarding pass. Until that moment, you had no idea where you were going or what the particular assignment was.

Printed on the pass was a special 3-D bar code, which, when scanned into your government-issued smartphone, connected you to one of Section's private data servers that had enough firewalls and security traps to disappoint even the most aggressive hackers. The server held an encrypted mission dossier that could be downloaded at your leisure.

To the untrained eye, you were simply another tourist

queuing up for the long slog of airline travel. Even to a *trained* set of eyeballs you were unlikely to arouse any suspicion.

But apparently today's drill had been revised.

And that troubled Callahan. Even more than her tremors.

She didn't like revisions.

"I'm afraid this machine is out of order," the young man said, still smiling away. "I think kiosk number seven is free. Just touch the screen and type in your confirmation number."

By "confirmation number" he really meant her classified federal ID, a six-digit code that was given to every Section field agent the moment she or he came on board. It also meant that she'd be traveling under her real identity, as an official representative of the United States government.

Highly unusual. And not something she felt comfortable with. "Are you sure you aren't making a mis—"

"Move along, ma'am." The smile had abruptly disappeared. "I have to close this thing down."

Mission aborted, just like that.

Callahan furrowed her brow at him, then turned on her heels, scanning the lobby for kiosk number seven, which was located near a set of sliding glass doors that led to another section of the terminal. A beleaguered-looking woman with two small kids approached it, so Callahan sprang forward and quickly cut in front of her.

It was a rude, insensitive move, but she was in no mood to be polite.

The woman gave Callahan her deepest, most sincere scowl, then went away muttering, as her two kids tugged at her blouse, whining and crying for more Gummi bears.

Callahan had no idea where they'd be traveling to, but she felt great sympathy for the passengers on that plane.

Turning to the kiosk, she touched the screen, went through the menu selections until she found the appropriate entry box and hesitated only a moment before keying in her code. A split second later the screen showed her true name—Bernadette I. Callahan—and next to this was the time, flight number and destination. An all-night trip from MIA to GIG, then on to GRU.

Surprised, Callahan pressed the button to print her boarding pass. And despite the troubling nature of this entire enterprise, she could think of worse places to go.

She was headed to São Paulo, Brazil.

There wasn't much to the mission dossier.

A short overview of the assignment, a few police reports, some photos of a body, but nothing Callahan could really sink her teeth into.

What surprised her, however, was the number assigned to each of the downloaded files. They all ended in -078, which, for reasons Section had never fully explained to her, meant that this assignment was a balls-out, take-no-prisoners top-of-the-totem-pole priority.

Rumor had it that such assignments came directly from the White House.

Callahan had been given a -078 only once before in her career—a particularly sketchy op conceived by the previous administration. She'd been instructed to pose as a British millionaire's mistress, vacationing in the south of France, where she cozied up to a local businesswoman believed to be having an affair with a ranking member of the Senate Foreign Relations Committee.

No pun intended.

Callahan's objective was to gather embarrassing evidence against the senator, to help secure what would be the deciding vote on a highly controversial defense bill. In other words, pure politics of the most underhanded, self-serving kind. The kind Callahan despised, even if the idiot *was* cheating on his wife.

At least she hadn't had to kill anyone.

Killing always complicated things.

This current -078 was a puzzler, however. It was disconcerting enough that she was going in with very little cover, using her own name instead of an alias. She'd be representing herself as a State Department investigator, which, according to government payroll records, was technically true, although she had never once set foot inside the building on C Street or any of its branches.

But even more disconcerting was the nature of the incident she'd be sticking her nose into. According to the dossier, that incident was currently being referred to by Brazilian authorities as a *morte de minha desventura* or death by misadventure.

This could mean a dozen different things, of course, but the local *polícia* had decided that the victim's demise was either accidental or, more likely, a suicide.

So why on earth did Section give a damn about it?

Especially in São Paulo, of all places?

It made only slightly more sense when you considered who the victim was.

Gabriela Maria Abrino Zuada.

Normally, Callahan didn't know a pop star from a New Jersey car salesman. Her musical tastes leaned toward indie rock and euro-punk with a side of alternative jazz. And her interest in bubble-gum-smacking, coke-snorting, drunk-driving, party-loving, viral-video-making, IQ-challenged, Twitter-happy twentysomething pop icons had reached its peak somewhere south of the Britney Spears head shave.

But Gabriela Maria Abrino Zuada—or simply Gabriela to her fans—was something altogether different. At twenty-three years old, the Brazilian native had established herself as a worldwide phenomenon, the highest charting no-apologies Christian pop diva in the known universe. And even Callahan, who had long ago shed her Irish Catholic roots, knew who she was.

The announcement of Gabriela's death—which was wisely being delayed as long as humanly possible—would undoubtedly send a tsunami-size shock wave around the world, à la Michael Jackson. But as far as Callahan knew, nobody in the president's inner circle had sent a black ops emissary to check out Jackson's corpse.

So what exactly was going on here?

Callahan had no idea. And she hated like hell being kept in the dark.

She also had to wonder why her talents weren't being utilized more productively. Thanks to a tanking economy and a series of natural and not-so-natural disasters that had plagued the U.S. and the world of late, the international mood was about as sour as moldy rice. The world seemed to be going to hell in a handbasket and nobody knew quite what to do about it. People from all walks of life were scared and frustrated.

And, as always, the power brokers used that fear as a

tool. Hysterical politicians were shouting fire at every opportunity, and those who shouted the loudest seemed to be getting most of the votes.

Countries that were normally fairly docile threatened aggression against their nearest neighbors and those who wanted a slice of the ever-shrinking economic pie—which, of course, was *everyone*—were starting to make Armageddon-like noises.

Such noises were what prompted the fearful to flock to people like Gabriela. Rather than look for real solutions to their problems they simply wrapped themselves in the cloak of faith and abdicated all responsibility for their actions to false prophets and the Great Holy Whoever.

To each his own. None of that much mattered to Callahan.

All she cared about was the job.

But to her mind, she should be out in the field helping hunt down terrorists and the frighteningly high number of missing nuclear warheads that were floating around out there.

Instead, she was stuck on a plane headed to São Paulo, staring at a dossier on a dead pop star.

Which made no sense at all.

At the moment, however, she was too fried to try to figure it all out. She was only four hours into her flight and all she wanted was to forget about pop divas and politics and -078 file codes, and simply sleep for a while.

She had tried closing her eyes a few times at the beginning of the flight, had managed to doze once or twice, had even thought she'd made it all the way home for a moment there. But then a baby started crying back in the economy compartment, and Callahan had bolted awake as if she'd been slapped squarely across the face.

Before boarding the plane, she had taken a moment to Google sleep deprivation, and the news wasn't good. Not only did lack of sleep cause a myriad of health problems, including hypertension, heart disease and slower reaction times, *severe* deprivation could often lead to death.

Looking up from her smartphone, Callahan held out a hand again and checked for the tremor. Not only was it still there, it had gotten worse.

The guy in the seat next to hers was passed out, snoring slightly, a small bubble of spit in the corner of his mouth.

Callahan envied him.

Spit and all.

The crime-scene photos were pretty grisly, even on the smartphone's screen. The pop star looked like a crispy piece of bacon. She had been found in an empty storage room by her manager and bodyguards after the manager had smelled gasoline and heard her screaming.

Unfortunately, they'd found her too late.

It looked to Callahan like a case of self-immolation, and judging by the condition of the body, the victim had used a lot of gas to do the job.

But this bothered Callahan.

Self-immolation wasn't unheard of in Brazil, but it wasn't exactly commonplace either. Had Gabriela been an abused wife in Afghanistan, the scenario might have made more sense. Afghan burn hospitals were full of such victims.

But given Gabriela's profile, this particular method of suicide raised a big red flag.

An even bigger one, however, had nothing to do with the victim at all.

These photos could tell Callahan only half the story, and she'd have to take a look at the room and body herself before coming to any definitive conclusions—assuming she ever could.

But what she saw here was strange.

Very strange.

There seemed to be a complete lack of damage to the walls and floor surrounding the body. They were untouched by the flames. As if the victim had been burned somewhere else, then placed on the floor of this room.

Was this a murder?

Judging by the witness statements, that didn't make any sense either. And as strange as all this was, it still didn't tell Callahan why Section was interested in the case.

Her mandate was to "aid and assist the São Paulo Civil Police in conducting their investigation" and report her findings. An easy enough task on the face of it, but Callahan had a sinking feeling this assignment wouldn't be easy at all.

It was times like this that she regretted ever allowing herself to be recruited for the job. She should have stayed in graduate school and actually done something with this brain she'd been blessed with.

Or maybe she should have disappeared to some lighthouse somewhere and cut herself off from the world, blissfully ignorant of the growing turmoil around her. And every night, the moment her head touched the pillow, she would be whisked away to the Land of Nod and the pleasant dreams it promised.

So much for that idea.

7

HARRISON, LOUISIANA

Edith Stillwater's last few words had stuck with Batty for the rest of the afternoon and most of the night.

She was right. The absence of God notwithstanding, Batty *was* a pitiful soul. He was stranded in self-imposed purgatory here in this house. His only companions were the thick, earthy smell of the swamp and a humidity that wrapped itself around him like a warm wet blanket. No friends, no loved ones. Nothing but the Louisiana sky.

"It's hotter than the Devil's drawers," his mother used to say on nights like this.

She would sit on this very porch, fanning herself, her deck of blue Bikes spread out before her, her face scrunched up in concentration as she stared down at the array she'd laid out on the table. More often than not, there was a client sitting across from her, eyeing her anxiously, waiting for her to finish her reading, wondering if she'd be able to pull at least one small splinter of hope from those cards.

His mother tended to give it to them, even if she had to lie. She was a woman prone to sympathy, cared too much about other people, a trait she carried with her until the day she died.

She'd been gone now for a good fifteen years and this house was the only thing that Batty had left of her. A big old Southern monstrosity with columns and balconies and a fairly advanced case of swamp rot.

The place had been in his family for generations, and Batty was born here, in one of the bedrooms upstairs, his wizened old *mamère* playing midwife as his mother pushed him out into the world in what everyone in the family agreed was probably the most difficult delivery of the latter twentieth century.

Batty was born with an attitude, an eight-pound ten-ounce bundle of XY chromosomes, who, according to Gramma Jean, looked just like his daddy. He was never sure if this was supposed to be a compliment or an insult, or who it might be aimed at, but since Winston LaLaurie had spent most of his life in and out of jail, Batty had a feeling she wasn't trying to be kind.

Nowadays he was doing a pretty good job of living up to his heritage. Not the jail part, of course. Not yet, at least. But now that he was without a day job to go to—the one thing that had given him at least a semblance of legitimacy—he had officially become the most useless human being on the face of the planet.

A pitiful soul, indeed.

There's nothing worse than a man who can't hold on to a simple job. And nothing more disgusting than one who sits around feeling sorry for himself.

But then he had his reasons, didn't he?

He may have been born with an attitude, but he'd had it beat right out of him the night Rebecca died.

From the time Batty was three years old, he'd sit on the front porch while his mother read the cards for friends and neighbors and strangers who sometimes came down from New Orleans or as far away as Baton Rouge, rich and poor alike.

Everyone in Terrebonne Parish knew Patsy LaLaurie had The Vision and they all wanted to see what she saw. Batty had been proud to watch her work, knowing that half of what she did was designed only to make these people feel good. Not in a calculating way, not simply as a means to make money (although she never refused a donation), but because she didn't want a single one of them to walk away with fear in their hearts.

What good could it possibly do them?

"I can only *feel* what's coming," she'd once said to Batty. "I can't change it. So why make another human being suffer if they don't have to?"

Batty understood. Mostly because he could already feel what she felt. The thing his mother and grandmother called The Vision had been passed on to him. Nothing more, really, than a heightened sense of awareness. He felt things, smelled things, dreamed things and sometimes saw things that others couldn't. And he knew that there was enough darkness out there to scare the living daylights out of even the toughest old fart.

He remembered seeing Landry LeBlanc, a big, oafish bully of a man, cry like a baby when Mother broke from her usual routine and told him he had cancer. She did it, she later said to Batty, because she wanted the old fool to get his butt to the doctor in hopes he might at least slow down the inevitable, make his last days tolerable.

"Idiot spends most of his time winding his ass, scratching his watch and telling everybody it's daybreak when the sun's going down. But that don't mean he deserves to be in pain."

Batty missed his mother. Always would. And if that made him some kind of mama's boy—as the kids in school had so often reminded him—then so be it.

Setting his glass on the porch rail, he picked up the bottle of Tullamore he'd been nursing and poured himself another couple fingers of liquid. The irony of his preferred method of emotional medication was that he didn't really like booze. Not the taste of it, at least, which was something akin to kerosene mixed with rubbing alcohol.

But then he didn't drink for pleasure. And he had very serious doubts that there was anyone alive who actually did, no matter what they might claim. Alcohol—especially whiskey—was anesthesia, pure and simple. Designed only to kill the effects of the knife when it cut too deep.

And for Batty that knife was hitting bone right now.

"You take life too damn hard," his mother had always told him. Usually after he came home from school, covered in cuts and bruises. He'd never made it a secret that he had The Vision, too, and that made most of the kids afraid of him. He'd had to learn to use his fists to defend himself and had endured his share of verbal taunts.

That was where his nickname was born. The schoolyard. For the first few years of his life, most of the kids had called him Seb. But because Sebastian LaLaurie was the crazy kid with the crazy mom, a punk named Harley Wilks had started calling him Batty and it stuck.

He had resisted at first. Threatened to pummel anyone who repeated the name. But that only egged the other kids on, and over the years, he finally grew to accept it. Even thought of it as a badge of honor.

Yes, he *was* the crazy kid with the crazy mom.

So what are you gonna do about it?

But Batty really came to love the name when he met Rebecca. The way it rolled off her tongue with that sweet, subtle accent of hers. She was a Baton Rouge girl who showed up on the steps of Nassau Hall, ready to prove to these Princeton know-it-alls that even a late starter like her could kick some serious academic ass.

She stole Batty's heart the moment he met her. The moment she repeated his name back to him, those dark eyes smiling as she said it.

It didn't hurt that she'd had The Vision, too— although she'd been light-years ahead of Batty on that account. Light-years ahead of his *mother*, for that matter.

And he sometimes wondered if she'd known even back then the dark road she was destined to travel.

Batty sighed, knocked back his drink and set the glass on the rail, staring out at the warm Louisiana night, thinking he'd better get to bed before he turned into a blubbering old fool like Landry LeBlanc.

He didn't have cancer, but what he did have could be just as debilitating. And despite this current, rather sickening display of self-absorption, he wasn't about to go down easy.

He still had *some* fight left in him.

He just hoped it was enough.

Batty's bedroom was on the second floor.

Properly anesthetized, he stumbled to the bed and plopped onto his stomach, tucking his arms under the pillow as he laid his cheek against it.

He was about to pass out when he felt something digging into his left forearm. Something hard and pointy,
about the size of a peppercorn.

He fumbled for it, got it between his fingers, then
reached to the nightstand and turned on the light. It took
a moment for his eyes to adjust, and when they did he
saw that what he was holding was a diamond earring.

But this wasn't just any old piece of jewelry. It belonged
to the woman he'd met at Bayou Bill's last week. The one
who had walked into the bar looking as if she'd just stepped
out of a movie or a magazine. A redheaded, translucent-
skinned wonder who had sent a stuttering spike of electricity through just about every man in the room. And Batty
may well have heard angel trumpets the moment he saw
her.

He'd met his share of beautiful women over the
years—Rebecca foremost among them—but none of
them had prepared him for the pure sexuality that had
emanated from this one. She was the kind who instantly
made your groin stir and your gut ache, with a body so
taut and perfectly proportioned that it should have been
declared illegal in at least thirty of the fifty states.

Batty was by no means a letch, not even close. Was
not the type to sit around with the guys remarking about
women's physical attributes, pro or con. But this woman
managed to bring out the beast in him the moment she
walked into that bar. And he couldn't help thinking about
laying her across his bed, or on the living room couch, or
atop the dining room table—hell, he didn't care *where*, as
long as it was sometime very soon.

For the first time in as long as he could remember,
he'd actually been able to relegate his grief over Rebecca

to another part of his mind. The spell this redhead had cast was so strong that the animal came forth, begging him to take action.

And to Batty's surprise, he did, right here in this very house. The redhead had turned out to be more amazing than anything he could have imagined, a woman so free of inhibition, so willing to give him carte blanche to her limber little body, that he had almost felt guilty about making love to her.

Almost.

She was, he later realized, his anesthesia that night. An escape from the darkness that haunted him.

Unlike the whiskey, however, she didn't dull the senses. She heightened them. And she had returned his aggression in kind, doing things to him with her teeth and tongue and fingers that defied description. She was the most sexually adventurous creature he had ever encountered, and as he moved inside her, feeling her grip on him, her feverish flesh against his, he didn't want her to ever let go.

But then, when they were done, both of them slick with sweat, she surprised him even more. Had turned out to be so much more than just a willing body.

They had spent the rest of the night talking politics and religion and history—all the things that Batty had once felt passionate about, all the things that he and Rebecca would often argue about, right here in this very bed. The conversation took so many twists and turns that he could barely remember it with any specificity now. And, unlike his brain-dead students, the redhead had listened to him with an open mind.

And, it seemed, an open heart.

But it was what she *hadn't* done that got to him the most. When she saw the angry red scars on his wrists, the ones Edith couldn't help staring at, the ones he refused to hide, she didn't flinch, didn't ask about them, didn't judge him in any way. And later, she simply kissed them, very gently, one after the other, then climbed atop him and made love to him again.

As he looked up at her, he felt tears dampening his eyes. And for one brief, blissful moment, he thought he saw Rebecca there, smiling down at him the way she always had, her angelic face filled with a love that was meant only for him.

The next morning the redhead was gone.

No note. No good-byes.

He had been back to the bar several nights since, waiting for her, hoping to see her again, but she hadn't returned. And by the fourth night, Batty had wondered if he had dreamed it all. Had merely conjured up the fantasy in a drunken haze.

But, no.

This little diamond earring confirmed it.

She had been here. In this bed.

And the oddest thing about the whole experience, he realized, was that she had never told him her name.

8

SÃO PAULO, BRAZIL

Callahan hadn't been to Brazil in more than five years. Her last trip to São Paulo had been an overnight job, a quick and dirty snatch of a weapons manufacturer's laptop that hadn't given her time to fully appreciate the city's finer points. She had always hoped to come back here one day, but her gut told her that this trip wouldn't be much different from the last.

Except for the chaos.

It was apparent the moment she stepped off the plane that word of Gabriela Zuada's death had finally been unleashed. Television screens in the lobby flashed video of Gabriela's latest tour, along with a montage of interviews with her devastated fans. And every headline in the airport newsstands seemed to scream her name.

Callahan wasn't surprised. The death of a superstar is not the kind of information that can be easily controlled or contained, and there would undoubtedly be a dozen different harebrained theories surrounding this one, most of them postulated by self-aggrandizing cable TV pundits.

Callahan had learned long ago that what you saw on television news was little more than cheap soap opera theatrics, good old-fashioned storytelling designed to keep the viewers watching and the advertisers paying. Its relationship to the truth was often nonexistent and, depending on which network you chose, slanted to appeal to a specific demographic.

Callahan's approach was to always, without exception, treat such news as complete and utter bullshit and, when necessary, try to ferret out the truth for herself.

Assuming that was even possible.

But then her own job was all about deception, wasn't it? The veracity of the intelligence community wasn't exactly beyond reproach. And while she was often forced to compromise her beliefs, she was smart enough to know that the world was *built* on compromise, along with heavy doses of rationalization and deceit. Very little would ever get done without them.

Of course, looking at the sudden rise in unrest over the last several months had Callahan wondering if they were still working. While Section had always been an agency that played under the radar, priding itself in its ability to clean up the messes that politicians and the more visible intelligence agencies managed to create around the world, lately there was a sense within the community that there might well be too many fires to put out. Not that they all gathered around the watercooler and talked about it. But people *did* talk, and despite her relative isolation, Callahan knew that the concern they felt was quickly turning into panic—and that couldn't be good for anyone.

Despite this, the world kept turning, as it always had. But she had to wonder how much of it would be left in a few years.

The São Paulo airport was even busier than she remembered it, and navigating her way through the crowd took a seasoned agility that came only with years of traveling experience.

The customs lines were a bumper-to-bumper traffic jam. The heightened feeling of unrest around the globe was no doubt putting security personnel on full alert, looking for any possible contraband, and more people than ever were being pulled out of line and seeing their baggage X-rayed and carefully searched.

Not all of them appreciated the gesture and tempers were heated.

It was times like this that traveling under State Department cover came in handy. With a flash of her credentials and passport, Callahan was able to bypass the line and head straight for the lobby.

When she traveled by air—which was about 90 percent of the time—Callahan rarely carried more than a backpack and a small airplane-friendly overnight bag. All she needed were a few toiletries, some comfortable underwear, and half a dozen changes of clothes. Any additional wardrobe or luggage (or weapons, for that matter) were procured locally by Section and waiting for her in her hotel room, depending on the needs of the particular assignment at hand. The life Callahan led was often complicated, and traveling light was one of the best ways she knew to alleviate the stress of the job.

Not that this had been working lately. The panic attacks, the tremors, and the inability to sleep put the lie to that particular belief. And after years of back-to-back assignments, maybe what she needed was a vacation.

As she crossed the lobby toward the exit to the street, she noticed a young dark-haired girl sitting at a nearby bench, surrounded by luggage. The girl was sobbing uncontrollably, a newspaper clutched in her hands, Gabriela's face staring up at her from the front page.

This girl, she thought, was a live version of what was playing on the lobby television screens, her tears a palpable manifestation of a very real pain. By her reaction, you would think her sister had just died, yet it was unlikely she had known Gabriela beyond the carefully manufactured image that was projected on those screens.

For just a moment, their gazes met, and Callahan tried to show her a bit of sympathy, although she doubted it would matter. The poor thing was beyond consoling at this point.

But in that moment, Callahan was hurled backward to her own childhood, to a time shortly after her father killed himself. She had been very young when it happened, and she was devastated. Partly because he was everything to her, and partly because he'd left her behind with her stepmother, who was, quite possibly, the biggest stone-cold bitch on the face of the planet.

Leaving the girl to her tears—and her memories to the crowded lobby—Callahan carried her bag through the sliding glass doors and went outside, immediately struck by a stifling humidity that made her regret wearing a blazer. She went straight toward the curb, where she hoped to grab an air-conditioned cab.

The street was crowded with them, from small white Fiats to brightly colored VW vans, but before she could hail one, a teenage boy stepped into her path, said something unintelligible, then thrust a flyer into her free hand.

Callahan was about to tell him that unless he was handing her a portable swamp cooler, he could kindly fuck off, when he gave her a big toothy grin, then turned and headed toward his next victim.

Another messenger from Section?

No, she thought, not this time. He was a little too young to be a Section operative, and was more than likely just a kid trying to make a living.

Still, her gaze drifted to the flyer. It featured a photograph of a gaudily painted tour van rolling through what looked like a Brazilian shantytown. The text read, in English:

FAVELA TOURS
Experience true adventure! Explore the Wild
West of South America in São Paolo's *Favela
Paraisópolis*!

Callahan had heard of these tours before. They were usually taken by callous idiots who had a morbid fascination with how the poor and impoverished lived. The modern-day equivalent of a freak show. The very definition of the term *slumming*.

Shoving the flyer into her jacket pocket, she once again threw her hand in the air and flagged a cab.

It struck Callahan the moment she met him that Lieutenant Manuel Martinez didn't want her there.

This, in itself, wasn't an earth-shattering revelation. It doesn't matter what profession you practice. Anytime somebody new comes along, somebody foisted on you by management or, as in this case, the governor and the police superintendent, you tend to feel a certain amount of resistance to their presence.

But what surprised Callahan were Martinez's efforts to disguise this with the buttery charm of a Shopping Channel pitchman, a charm carefully accented by a disarming smile and a calculated twinkle in the eyes. The only thing that ruined the picture was a faint but unmistakable trace of fear behind that twinkle. Callahan had long ago learned to read people almost instantly, and her impression of the lieutenant was that he was a conflicted, frightened man.

What he was frightened of was anyone's guess.

"Agent Callahan," he said. "So wonderful to meet you. I'm so sorry we must become acquainted under such tragic circumstances."

He spoke in his native tongue, but Callahan had no trouble understanding him. She was proficient in nine languages and fluent in seven, including Portuguese. *Brazilian* Portuguese. Which was, undoubtedly, one of the reasons she'd been given this assignment in the first place. Martinez would have received word of this in the briefing packet Section had faxed him.

Callahan knew she had a choice here. She could play the charm card right back at him—something she was quite adept at—or she could simply play the cold, officious, no-nonsense State Department hard-ass who was here to get the job done.

Pulling her hand free, she went with option number two. "Why don't we forgo the formalities and get down to business?"

Martinez's smile froze. "Whatever you wish."

They were standing in the detectives' squad room of

the Special Investigations Department of the *Polícia Civil do Estado de São Paulo*. A couple of Martinez's investigators were slumped in chairs nearby, one of them running his gaze up and down her body without apology, as if she were nothing more than what the locals called a program girl, here to service the troops.

Had she not learned long ago to ignore such things, she might have been a bit perturbed by it. But this *was* Brazil, after all, in all its modern, complex, sexually liberated glory.

"These are Detectives Santos and Rivera," Martinez said. "They wish to express their gratitude that the superintendent has asked you to join our investigation."

"They do, do they?"

For a moment Callahan was tempted to tell them that they might want to consider adjusting that "gratitude" before she adjusted it for them.

But she was too tired to bother.

Instead, she opted for the high road. "Shall we take a look at the *victim's* body now?"

The word *body* was being kind.

Despite the crime-scene photos, Callahan was surprised by its condition, a charred mass of bones and wasted internal organs that were barely identifiable as human. What was left of Gabriela Maria Abrino Zuada lay in a heap on the medical examiner's table, giving off a sharp, putrid smell that invaded the nostrils without mercy, making Callahan's stomach do a sudden flip-flop the moment she walked into the crime lab.

She managed to hold back the airline peanuts long

enough for the nausea to pass, then turned to the medical examiner, a sober-looking guy named Pereira, who didn't seem at all bothered by the smell.

"So what can you tell me about this?" she asked.

"Other than the obvious? Very little."

"Run through it for me."

Pereira glanced at Martinez, who stood just inside the doorway. That trace of fear she'd seen earlier had gotten more pronounced and Pereira seemed to share it.

What the hell was going on here?

"The victim was female," Pereira said. "Twenty-three years old, identified through dental records as Senhorita Gabriela Zuada. The body was nearly incinerated by fire, and one of the witnesses said he smelled gasoline." He cleared his throat. "But this is where it becomes complicated."

"How?"

"There is no evidence of any gasoline."

"Then what kind of accelerant was used?"

"This is the complication. If the victim doused herself, as we originally suspected, she would have breathed in fumes, and some of the residue from those fumes would, in all probability, be in her lung tissue."

Callahan studied the mess on the table. "Good luck with that."

"I managed to scrape enough samples to examine, but I didn't find any trace of an accelerant at all."

It was Callahan's turn to frown. "That's a little hard to believe."

"Yes," Pereira said. "So I checked and rechecked. No chemical residue whatsoever."

"So then how did she catch fire?"

"It's quite obvious," Martinez said from the doorway. "If this wasn't suicide, it was an accident. Gabriela was a former meth addict who went back to her old ways and somehow managed to torch herself."

Callahan looked at him and could see that he didn't believe a word he'd just said. This was the public relations speech—a cover story—for something that couldn't be explained.

"That seems unlikely," she said. "Did you find any signs of drug abuse? A pipe? Matches? Anything?"

"We're working on that. Perhaps one of her friends removed the evidence to protect her reputation."

Pereira shook his head, apparently not willing to go along with the lie. "Without an accelerant, it wouldn't be possible to do this kind of damage merely by lighting a pipe, even if the substance in that pipe was highly volatile. So we have no real answer to your question. Unless . . ."

He hesitated.

"Unless what?" Callahan asked.

"As a man of science, my training tells me that there should be a rational explanation for the condition of this body, but in truth . . ."

He let the words trail again.

"What?"

"It almost appears that the combustion was . . . well . . ." He shifted uncomfortably, glancing at Martinez, as if he were too embarrassed—or too afraid—to continue.

"Go on," Callahan told him, her patience growing thin.

Pereira took a moment. Crossed himself. "That the combustion was spontaneous."

9

SHC. Spontaneous Human Combustion.

It seemed to Callahan that the so-called science surrounding this idea was sketchy at best and downright ridiculous for the most part. But she knew this wasn't the first unexplained death by fire to wind up on a coroner's slab.

Pereira went on to explain a documented phenomenon called "the wick effect," which more or less amounted to body fat turning the victim into a human candle, burning from the inside out.

A grisly thought if there ever was one.

Experiments on a pig were supposed to be proof that such a thing was possible—pigs and humans shared similar fat patterns—but Callahan had her doubts.

Judging by the videos she'd seen in the airport lobby, Gabriela Zuada didn't have more than a thimbleful of fat on her body, and as Martinez had said, there was no real evidence of drug paraphernalia in the room.

So unless the poor girl had somehow willed herself to catch fire, they were back to square one. And the way Callahan looked at it, there were four possibilities at work here:

1. Suicide
2. Accident
3. Murder
4. Act of God

Since Callahan didn't have a religious bone in her body, number four was immediately scratched off the list. Numbers one and two were still possibilities, but the preliminary forensic evidence didn't support either of them.

So what about number three?

Murder.

Callahan had briefly considered this on the plane, and maybe she should give the idea more attention. Was it possible that some crazed fan had managed to sneak backstage, snatch Gabriela away from her entourage and kill her by using some undetectable accelerant to light her on fire?

Based on the timeline mapped out in the dossier, this seemed even less likely than the other scenarios, but witness accounts are notoriously faulty and, at this point, all bets were off. Maybe the timeline was wrong. Maybe in the panic and confusion of finding their beloved Gabriela burned to a crisp, her friends had misjudged the sequence and duration of events.

It wouldn't be a first.

But the absence of any chemicals in Gabriela's lungs continued to niggle at Callahan. People just didn't burst into flames for no reason.

"Check the body again," she said to Pereira. "There's no way she wound up like this without some kind of help."

Pereira sighed. "I doubt I'll find anything."

"Keep trying," she told him, then turned to Martinez. "Shall we take a look at the crime scene now?"

Again that trace of fear flickered in the detective's eyes and Callahan wondered what he was holding back. She could see that he wasn't about to volunteer anything—

not yet, at least—so she decided to give him some room. Let this thing play out before she got aggressive about it.

She really did need to see the crime scene, however, and Martinez wasn't all that anxious to move—like a child who's reluctant to go to bed because he's afraid the boogeyman is hiding in the closet.

"Well? Shall we?"

"You're the boss," he said quietly, then turned and walked out the door.

A crowd had gathered outside the concert auditorium. Hundreds of Gabriela's fans stood shoulder to shoulder, some staring blankly, others openly weeping, still others carrying placards with her photograph, singing along with one of her songs that was piped through a portable loudspeaker.

It struck Callahan as both circus and wake, an outpouring of true affection for a lost star, tainted only by the attention seekers and rubberneckers who came here simply because it was the thing to do.

Wooden barriers had been placed along the entrance to the auditorium; armed state police officers watched the crowd carefully, waiting for any signs of unruliness. At their feet were dozens of bouquets and wreaths and crosses and candles and more photographs, a multicolored shrine to Santa Gabriela.

Callahan marveled at it all. Could not quite fathom how a simple girl who sang simple pop songs could garner such attention and adulation.

Martinez turned their squad car onto the main drive and waited for a guard to disperse a section of the crowd and wave them through. Callahan sat next to him, soaking it all in with a mix of dread and curiosity, knowing it wouldn't take a whole lot to get this crowd worked up.

Gabriela was dead and the details of her death were sparse and slow to surface. And the people here no doubt wanted answers. Sooner or later they'd start insisting they get some and Callahan didn't think they'd be too friendly about it. Despite the tears, that undercurrent of anger that plagued so much of the world these days was very much in evidence here.

Simmering. Waiting to explode.

The guard raised a megaphone, calling for several onlookers to step aside as Martinez gunned the engine and slowly drove toward a gate to the left of the entrance. Another guard unlatched it and waved the car through, giving Martinez a quick salute as they passed.

Martinez ignored him.

A moment later, they pulled up next to a loading dock as the gate closed behind them. A third guard came over and opened Callahan's door for her.

"Quite a crowd," she said to him as they climbed out. "They must have really loved her."

The guard nodded. "We all did. She was one of us."

Martinez turned sharply. "Speak for yourself," he said tersely. "She was in league with the Devil and paid the price for it."

Then, without another word, he moved toward the loading dock and gestured for Callahan to follow.

The room Gabriela had been found in wasn't much bigger than a walk-in closet. Twenty square feet at most and, as advertised, untouched by the fire—if, that is, you didn't count the burn mark in the middle of the linoleum floor.

It was hard to miss. Impossible, in fact. And the moment Callahan saw it, she thought she understood the reason for Martinez's mood.

The mark hadn't, however, been among the dossier photos. What was left of Gabriela's body had apparently been covering it. Yet it was the only real sign that anything unusual had taken place in the room, which was empty except for a few stacked boxes full of toilet paper, paper towels, seat covers and a mop and bucket tucked into a corner.

Callahan gestured. "Why wasn't this photographed?"

Martinez didn't seem to want to look directly at it. "I think that's obvious."

"It's potential evidence. All evidence needs to be photographed and catalogued. It wasn't even mentioned in the crime-scene summary."

"Our photographer was gone by the time the body was removed, and I saw no reason to call her back. There are certain . . . sensitivities involved."

"Sensitivities?"

"You saw the crowd outside. If something like this were to be released, there's no telling how they'd react. And if there are no photographs, there's no chance for a leak."

Callahan couldn't quite believe what she was hearing. "Did you actually work your way up through the ranks, or are you some kind of political appointee?"

Martinez's eyes went cold. "You're here to help us investigate, Agent Callahan, not impugn my integrity."

"Then *investigate*, for Christ's sake. Evidence is evidence, and you seem more concerned about public relations than solving a crime."

Martinez opened his mouth to speak, then closed it again. Then he said, "If you're trying to make me look foolish . . ."

"I just want to figure out what happened here. And this is a sign of possible foul play."

"Foul play?" he said. "I think it's much more than that."

Ignoring him, Callahan pulled out her smartphone, took several quick shots of the floor and added them to Gabriela's dossier. She stared soberly at the mark, which was quite small but looked as if it had been seared into the linoleum with a blow torch:

Callahan was no expert, but she knew this was an occult symbol. The kind you often found spray-painted on high school lockers by rebellious teenagers. If she remembered correctly, the *A* stood for "Anarchy."

But this was no high school prank. Far from it.

And the question was, who had put it here?

Gabriela?

Was she some kind of secret Devil worshipper who had burned the mark into the floor before setting herself on fire? And, if so, how exactly did she do it?

Considering the lack of tools, she'd have to be a magician to pull it off. And while Gabriela may have been a talented entertainer, it was doubtful she knew sleight of hand.

Which brought Callahan back to scenario number three.

Murder.

Despite the pop star sheen, Gabriela had managed to become a vaunted religious icon here in São Paulo and around the world. A phoenix who rose from the ashes, an inspiration to those who felt their lives were hopeless, especially amidst the turmoil they'd been witness to these last several months. So it was only natural that people flocked to the one thing that gave them any sense of calm.

Faith.

Was it possible that someone had done this to Gabriela in retaliation for her rising popularity and influence? Some wack job who somehow saw her as a threat to his existence? Who wanted to show the world that no one is immune to the final call, no matter how devout she may be?

Was this his signature? His mark? His *fuck you*?

A sudden uneasiness stirred inside Callahan, and she once again wondered why Section had sent her here.

What had they expected her to find?

This?

She could contact Section and ask, of course, but she doubted she'd be given an answer. She wasn't sure *they* even had one.

She turned to Martinez, who had wandered back out into the hallway, as if he were afraid to be in close proximity to the mark. He had lit a cigarette and was shakily lifting it to his lips to take a drag.

Callahan approached him. "So what do you make of all this?"

He exhaled noisily. "*Now* you want my opinion?"

"I wouldn't be asking if I didn't."

"I think I made my point of view clear when we first arrived."

Callahan frowned. "That thing you said about Gabriela being in league with the Devil?"

He nodded. Took another drag.

"You can't be serious."

"What other explanation is there? We've witnessed the impossible, Agent Callahan. And the impossible can only be explained by supernatural means."

"Neither of us has really witnessed anything, Detective, and I lean toward the school of thought that says there's always an explanation just waiting to be found. All we have to do is look for it."

"You don't believe in demons?"

"As much as I'd like to throw my hands in the air and blame this on some dark supernatural entity, I can assure you that if any demons are involved, they're all too human. I'm afraid I'll have to go with psychopath instead. So why don't we set the woo-woo stuff aside for a while and do some real police work?"

Martinez said nothing, and she knew she hadn't dissuaded him. But that was his problem, not hers.

"According to the inventory sheet, you found a cell phone in the room."

He nodded. "On the floor. Near the mop and bucket."

"I assume it was Gabriela's?"

"Yes."

"And I assume you went through the calls?"

Martinez looked for a moment as if he wanted to slap her, but held himself in check. "There was only one recent outgoing call, shortly before her death."

"To who?"

"Her manager. Alejandro Ruiz."

Callahan remembered the name from the dossier. "He's the one who smelled gasoline."

Martinez nodded. "That's what he told the responding officers, yes."

"I only saw his preliminary statement in the file. Did you ever follow up? Ask him about that phone call?"

"Why do I suddenly feel as if I'm on trial?"

"Look," Callahan said, "I know you don't like me much and I know you didn't ask for me to be here. But we have a mystery to solve and I intend to do my best to solve it—so just answer the question, all right?"

Callahan was acutely aware that she'd made an enemy for life. But in a contest of who has the bigger balls, it's best to assert yourself quickly and aggressively and without mercy, and she couldn't let this man's fear get in the way of her investigation.

"Well? Did you follow up or not?"

Martinez stared at her a moment. "Ruiz is in seclusion and I decided to leave him alone for now, out of respect. He and Gabriela were very close."

"All the more reason to question him," Callahan said. "Where do we find him?"

"He has a suite of private rooms in her penthouse."

Callahan raised an eyebrow. "I guess they *were* close."

10

When Callahan stepped through the doorway of Gabriela's penthouse, the first word that popped into her mind was *museum*.

She had half expected to find a sleek, postmodern, glass and chrome showroom, and there was certainly some of that. But what surprised her were the collection of artifacts Gabriela had amassed, a juxtaposition of her two worlds—music and religion.

There were enough guitars mounted on one large wall to fill a good-size Hard Rock Cafe, each one accompanied by an identifying placard: Gibson Les Paul, Paul Reed Smith Golden Eagle, pre-FMIC Stratocaster, Gibson SG, Martin D-28, Taylor 810ce. Callahan couldn't play these instruments, but she appreciated their beauty. The majority of them were signed by well-known rock stars, which meant this wall was worth a mint.

A Yamaha grand sat in a nearby corner atop a plush white carpet, and mounted above it was just the beginning of Gabriela's religious collection: a stark black-and-white etching of a winged Lucifer, cast out of heaven.

A Gustave Doré. And it looked like an original.

Framed copies of Gabriela's CD covers lined another wall, along with plaques commemorating their gold and platinum status. And just below this were two long glass cases holding more religious artifacts than Callahan had seen outside of the Alexandria National Museum.

Most of the statuary, artwork and jewelry inside these cases looked very old and quite valuable, and the sight of it all gave the young pop star a weight and depth that Callahan hadn't considered before. No one spent this kind of money, or surrounded herself with this kind of history, without a deep appreciation of both the artistry and message it conveyed. Maybe Gabriela had felt a kind of kinship with its creators—other artists sharing their love of God with the world.

There was something about this notion that saddened Callahan, and her suspicion that Gabriela had been murdered took even deeper root in her mind.

The timeline, she thought. There must be something wrong with the timeline.

Either that, or someone was lying.

Alejandro Ruiz?

The woman who had greeted them in the foyer—a middle-aged housekeeper named Rosa—stepped through a doorway behind them and said, "Mr. Ruiz will be with you in a moment. He's looking for his phone."

Martinez turned. "Thank you."

Rosa was about to leave when she hesitated and looked at Callahan. There was a trace of tears in her eyes. "Please go easy on him. He's taking this very hard. We all are."

Callahan wasn't quite sure why *she* had been singled out, but she nodded. "Were you at the concert hall when Gabriela died?"

Rosa shook her head. "I was at home. With my children."

"Do you know if Gabriela had any enemies? People who might want to do her harm?"

Rosa's eyes widened. "Why do you ask? Do you think someone—"

"I'm just trying to be thorough," Callahan said. "You were around her a lot, so I assume you know a lot about her private life. Does anyone come to mind?"

"No. No one. We all loved Gabriela. She was a good girl. Treated everyone like family."

"What about Alejandro? Did she treat him like family, too?"

The implication was clear and the question seemed to catch Rosa by surprise, but she managed not to stutter. "Yes. Of course. They were very fond of each other. Like brother and sister."

Uh-huh, Callahan thought. "While we're waiting, could you point me to her bedroom?"

Rosa looked conflicted, as if she were about to violate a trust. "Is that really necessary?"

"I'm afraid it is, yes."

Rosa glanced at Martinez, then said, reluctantly, "Just down that hall, first room on your right."

A bedroom tells you more about a person than any other room in the house.

This is where we feel most at ease. Where we keep the things that are most important to us, much of it within arm's reach. Where we have our most intimate moments.

Alone. With a lover. With our God.

The bedroom is where our secrets are held and revealed. Where we can be ourselves without fear of anyone watching or listening or judging. What's hidden within its walls is never meant to be seen by uninvited eyes, and Callahan felt a tiny twinge of guilt when she stepped into this one.

First impression: Gabriela was a reader. Voracious, from the looks of it. There was no television in the room and one wall supported several shelves of books. Fiction, nonfiction, hardback, paperback, some neatly vertical, while others were stacked horizontally on the edge of a shelf, as if waiting to be read: *The Heart of Catholicism, The Power of Miracles, Chastity and Spiritual Discipline.*

This last one suggested that Gabriela may not only have been trying to deepen her understanding of her faith, but was struggling to remain true to it.

There was an acoustic guitar tucked into a corner. A no-name brand, battered and scarred. A relic of her past, no doubt, and probably more valuable to her than any of the guitars in her living room.

On the neatly made bed was an open UPS box. Callahan checked the label and saw that it had come from the Garanti Auction House, Istanbul, Turkey. Probably another artifact. Pushing back the flaps, she reached inside and removed a small stone figurine of an angel fighting a dragon. She had no idea what it signified, but it was a beautiful piece and probably worth more than her yearly salary.

The opposite side of the room featured a window that

overlooked the city, a wash of skyscrapers disappearing into the horizon. To the left of it was a walk-in closet, two overstuffed suitcases sitting near the open doorway. The timeline had shown that Gabriela had arrived back in São Paulo the day of her death, and it looked as if she hadn't unpacked before heading off to the auditorium to prepare for her last show.

That the bags had been left untouched suggested to Callahan that the housekeeper's role here was limited to cleaning only. While Gabriela may have enjoyed some of the comforts of money, she was self-sufficient enough to deal with her own luggage, and for reasons Callahan couldn't quite explain, this made her like the girl.

Those untouched bags, however, also meant that Martinez and his team had once again proven their ineptitude. The suitcases should have been thoroughly searched for any possible evidence pointing to Gabriela's killer—assuming he existed. A letter, a notation, a diary, a photograph. Anything that might steer them in the right direction.

But nobody had bothered.

In fact, as Callahan looked around, it seemed as if the room itself had barely been touched. Was Martinez so convinced that Gabriela's death was some kind of otherworldly phenomenon that he'd decided to forgo any real police work?

Maybe Callahan should simply step away and let the man tell his ridiculous cover story about the poor girl's spiral into drug addiction.

Why should it matter to her?

But it *did* matter. There were too many unanswered

questions surrounding this case and she couldn't let them stand. Not without at least *trying* to figure them out.

Which was probably what Section was counting on.

Returning the figurine to its box, she moved around the bed, pulled the suitcases out of the closet doorway, and laid them flat on the carpet. Neither of them was locked, and when she opened the first one all she found was underwear. Tanks and socks and bras and enough frilly thongs and short-shorts to raise the eyebrows of even Gabriela's most progressive followers.

The second bag held pairs of neatly folded jeans and cutoffs, along with several printed T-shirts carrying messages like *Faith Inside* and *Pray It Like You Mean It* and *Property of God*.

One well-worn shirt carried a phrase that Callahan vaguely recognized:

> The mind is its own place, and in itself
> Can make a heav'n of hell, a hell of heav'n

True enough, but she'd be damned if she could remember where she'd heard it.

Continuing through the bag, she found more of the same, then did a quick check of all the pants pockets, hoping to come up with something interesting.

All she managed was a pack of spearmint gum and a few balls of lint.

Oh well, it had been worth a try.

As she closed the suitcases, her attention was drawn to the walk-in closet. She saw a tiny sliver of light in the darkness there, coming from the very back—like the light from beneath a door.

Was there another room back there?

Curious, she got to her feet, moved into the closet doorway and flicked on the light. The closet was paneled in bleached maple, with built-in shelves, drawers and shoe racks, but surprisingly few clothes hanging from the rods. Judging by the contents of the suitcases, Gabriela hadn't cared much about her offstage attire.

Callahan had expected to see a door along the back wall, but instead found more built-in shelves, divided into three columns.

So where had the light come from?

She certainly hadn't imagined it.

Flicking off the overhead, she crouched in the darkness for a different angle, and sure enough, a thin crack of light ran along the bottom of the center column, just about the width of a door.

A *hidden* door.

Getting to her feet again, Callahan crossed to the shelf, put her palms against it and pushed. She'd seen these types of doors before and wasn't surprised when it swung inward, a swath of sunlight spilling into the closet from the room beyond.

A small, private sanctuary. Not much bigger than your average bathroom.

The sunlight came from a solar tube high in the ceiling, and fell directly across an old wooden prie-dieu—or prayer desk—at the center of the room, which was essentially a narrow table with a padded kneeler in front.

A couple of half-melted altar candles flanked a small wooden cross atop the desk, and on the wall facing it was another symbol, this one far more elaborate than the one at the crime scene. It had been hand-painted in a deep cobalt blue, possibly by Gabriela herself:

Another occult sign?

Callahan had no idea what it meant, but seeing as this was a prayer room, there was obviously religious significance to the symbol, a notion bolstered by the lines of verse written directly below it in bold black letters:

> *Darkness ere Dayes mid-course, and Morning light*
> *More orient in yon Western Cloud that draws*
> *O're the blew Firmament a radiant white,*
> *And slow descends, with somthing heav'nly fraught.*
> *11:204–07*

A biblical verse?

Callahan didn't think so.

She was reminded of the quote on Gabriela's T-shirt and again had that vague sense that she knew it from somewhere. Not so much the words themselves, but the sound of the language. Its rhythm and tone.

Pulling out her phone, she took several shots of the room, including close-ups of the symbol and the lines of verse, and added them to Gabriela's dossier.

Section would undoubtedly want to see them, so she immediately uploaded the additions to the server and flagged them as a priority. Since she was obviously operating in need-to-know territory, she wondered if she'd get any kind of reaction.

With Section you could never tell.

Moving to the prayer desk, she studied the altar atop it. A thin leather strap hung from the cross, a small, circular medallion attached, about the size of a quarter.

Feeling a small stab of pain in her chest, Callahan took hold of the medallion and rubbed it between her fingers. Her father had given her a necklace very similar to this one for her fifth birthday. She'd worn it almost every day that year, until about three months after Dad died, when her stepmother had tossed it out, along with half of everything Callahan had owned.

This one was old, however, and probably a lot more valuable—monetarily, at least. Etched into its surface was the figure of a man carrying a child on his shoulders.

Saint Christopher. Patron of safe travel.

Turning it over, Callahan found another etching on the back—a beetle with the intials *CSP* engraved beneath it.

So who or what was CSP? Was this just another artifact Gabriela had procured, or was it more personal than that?

Making a mental note to check into the initials, Callahan released the medallion and shifted her gaze to a shelf beneath the top of the prayer desk.

There was a small stack of books there, their spines jumping out at her: *The Lesser Key of Solomon, Forbidden Rites, Angels, Incantations and Revelation* . . .

All of these seemed like unusual choices—especially in a prayer room—but it was the book at the very top of the stack that most caught Callahan's attention. A battered, well-thumbed paperback she remembered from one of her college literature classes. And all at once she knew where the lines of verse on the wall—and the quotation on Gabriela's T-shirt—had come from.

Paradise Lost.

Callahan's memory of the book was spotty. It was considered a classic and had something to do with God and Satan, but in college she had found it extremely difficult to read, its language so impenetrable that she'd been forced to seek out the CliffsNotes version just to make sense of it all.

Picking it up, she stared at the cover, which featured the same Gustave Doré etching that hung above the piano. She leafed through the pages and toward the end of the book she found that several of the numbered passages had been carefully highlighted, notes scribbled in its margins.

Shifting her gaze to the verse on the wall, she checked the citation—*11:204–07*—then quickly found the passage.

Sure enough, those same lines were highlighted in blue. And in the margin next to them, written in black ink, were two words:

Defende eam.

Callahan's Latin was a bit lacking, and the best translation she could come up with was . . . "protect her."

A curious little notation, but what did it mean? Who did Gabriela think needed protection? Was she concerned about someone she knew, or—

"That book was her obsession," a voice said.

Startled, Callahan turned to find a young man with bloodshot eyes standing in the doorway. He wore a robe, cinched at the waist.

Alejandro Ruiz.

"She took it everywhere we went," he said. "Every country, every city. Was always telling me what a work of genius it is. A gift from God, second only to the Bible." His eyes shifted, staring at nothing. "A lot of good it did her."

"I'm sorry for your loss, Mr. Ruiz." She offered a hand to shake. "I'm Agent Callahan."

Ruiz didn't seem to notice the offer. He was looking around the room, taking it in. "She didn't know I knew about this place. Thought she could hide it from me, but she didn't even bother to put on a lock on the door." He paused. "The knowledge always felt like a betrayal, yet here you stand, exposing her secrets."

Callahan ignored the jab. "Maybe she trusted you."

He smiled. "Gabriela had high hopes for humanity, and a lot of big plans, but her trust was reserved for the voices inside her head."

"Voices?"

"God. Angels. She was regular Joan of Arc."

"She told you this?"

He nodded. "Late one night, in a moment of weakness. But when I pressed her about it, she pulled away as if she realized she'd just revealed some sort of state secret." He paused. "Things were never the same between us after that."

"And this didn't worry you? Make you wonder if she had mental problems?"

Ruiz shook his head. "A lot of people hear voices when they pray, Agent Callahan. Especially people as blessed as Gabriela was. These last few months, she had a glow about her that's hard to describe. A sense of purpose."

"I can tell that you loved her very much."

"Ever since she was seventeen years old," he said. "Back when I had my own ministry. I still remember when she was busking on street corners, playing her music for spare change, struggling to overcome her addiction. I often thought she was in too deep to ever find the light. But she did."

Callahan thought of Martinez's cover story. "Do you think her addiction may have played a part in her death?"

"Not a chance. I saw how devastated she was when her friend Sofie died. She would never go back to that. Not after everything we'd accomplished."

"So what do you think happened to her?"

"I wish I knew. I just know she couldn't have done this to herself."

Callahan nodded. "In your statement to the police, you said you smelled gasoline, right before you and her bodyguards found her."

"Yes."

"And you're sure about that?"

"Yes."

"This was just before you heard Gabriela's screams, right?"

He closed his eyes. "Yes."

"How long had she been missing at that point?"

He thought about it a moment. Shrugged. "Three, maybe five minutes. Nothing more."

"And between the time you heard her screams and found her in the storage room?"

"No more than thirty seconds or so. And by that time she was already . . ." He stopped himself and stared at the floor, looking as if he were about to be sick.

"I'm sorry to keep pushing, Mr. Ruiz, but I want to be absolutely certain that you smelled gasoline."

He looked up sharply. "You think I'm lying?"

"I think you could be confused. How far away were you when you smelled it?"

"Pretty far. Gabriela was down a long hallway, around a corner. But there's no confusion."

Gas fumes are strong, Callahan thought, but would Ruiz have been able to smell them from that distance? And why hadn't any of the bodyguards corroborated his statement?

Could he have imagined it?

Ruiz slumped against the doorframe, and she could see that grief was weighing him down. "Can we be done with this, please?"

"Just a few more questions," she said, then gestured to the wall behind the prayer desk. "You say you've been in here before. Do you have any idea what that symbol represents?"

Ruiz glanced at it and shook his head. "I probably should, but I don't recognize it. I'm sure it meant something special to Gabriela. Her faith was deep."

"I think that's a pretty safe assumption," Callahan said, then showed him the highlighted passage in *Paradise Lost*. "You say she was obsessed with this book. What about this note in the margin—is this Gabriela's handwriting?"

"Yes."

"*Defende eam* means 'protect her.' Do you have any idea who she was talking about?"

Another shrug. "Could be anyone, I suppose. Gabriela dealt with a lot of people. Fans. Charity volunteers. Bible students."

"What about crew members?"

He nodded. "We're well staffed."

"Do you know if any of them practice the occult?"

He seemed affronted by the idea. "Of course not. Everyone on Gabriela's team has found the Way, including her bodyguards. Why would you ask such a thing?"

So he hadn't seen the mark on the floor.

And nobody had bothered to mention it to him.

"My job is to look at all of the possibilities," she told him. "Do you know anyone with the initials CSP?"

He thought about it and shook his head.

Callahan dropped the book to the prayer desk and gestured to the Saint Christopher medallion. "Any idea who gave her this?"

He looked at it. "It's probably just one of her trinkets from the auction house. Are we finished yet?"

"Just one more thing. What about your cell phone? Were you able to find it?"

He nodded and reached into his robe pocket, pulling out an iPhone. "I spend half my life on this thing, but I haven't touched it since Gabriela died."

"Then you haven't checked your voice mail?"

He waved a hand, dismissing the notion. "I'm sure there are dozens of messages. People calling with condolences. But I haven't had the energy."

"What about the one from Gabriela?"

His gaze snapped to Callahan's. "What are you talking about?"

"The outgoing calls on her cell phone show that she dialed your number just before she died. She may have left you a message."

His face went pale. "What?"

He looked down at the phone and, as Callahan watched, he immediately touched the screen, pulling up his voice mail application. He quickly scrolled through several dozen messages until he came to one marked *Gabriela*.

He stopped. Stared at it.

"Oh my God," he said quietly. "Oh my God."

11

Before Ruiz played the message, Callahan asked him to bring the phone into the living room. She wanted Martinez to listen in. It seemed like the right thing to do, considering this was allegedly his investigation.

Moving to the sofa and two chairs near the center of the room, they all sat. Then Ruiz placed the phone on the coffee table, touched the *speaker* icon and pressed *play*.

What they heard was a surprise to all of them.

It began with a loud clattering sound, as if the phone had hit the floor and rolled. Then Gabriela's voice echoed, her words unintelligible. She seemed to be babbling incoherently, but it was impossible to tell. She started to cry, her voice blurred by tears but rising in volume and intensity—

"No . . . Stay away from me!"

The plea had been directed at someone, yet there were no other voices in the room.

She began to cough now, violently, sobbing, struggling to breathe, begging to be left alone. This was abruptly followed by a commotion—feet shuffling, stumbling, crashing, Gabriela crying and coughing and gagging, continuing to beg.

Another crash was followed by a long silence, interrupted only by the sound of her rapid breathing, a cough or two.

She was close to the phone now, and after a moment she said something, then repeated it twice. But the words came out as little more than a croak, barely audible, her anguished whispers too soft to be understood.

Then, after another moment of silence, she began to scream.

Ruiz cut the message off midscream. He looked at Callahan with wounded eyes, then quickly averted his gaze, as if he couldn't quite handle the human connection. He'd be exposing too much.

"I can't believe I wasn't there for her when she called."

"Don't blame yourself. Phone service is always spotty in places like that. There was nothing you could have done anyway."

Ruiz just stared at the floor.

Callahan felt for him. Even for a detached outsider like her, that hadn't been easy to listen to.

She glanced at Martinez, who shifted uncomfortably in his chair, looking more rattled than usual, then got to his feet and gestured for her to join him over by the piano.

She followed him, bracing herself for whatever it was he had to say, knowing she probably wouldn't like it. She studied the Gustave Doré illustration as he spoke, keeping his voice low.

"There, you see? I was right. What we just heard wasn't natural. Not even close."

"Easy now, we've got sound and no picture, and

that's a pretty big leap. Someone had to be in that room with her."

"Nobody human—I can assure you of that. The only voice I heard was hers."

Callahan was reminded of what Ruiz had told her. About Gabriela hearing voices when she prayed. Could there have been more to it than that? Could she have had some kind of psychotic breakdown and done this to herself?

If so, that still didn't explain the *how*. And Martinez was right. On the surface, none of this seemed natural.

But his superstitious hysteria was starting to grate.

"Look," she said, "let's come back down to earth for a minute. What I heard on that phone was a woman who was obviously terrified. And despite how it may have sounded, I'm pretty sure she wasn't alone. I'm guessing the person in that room was someone she knew."

"Someone we *all* know," Martinez said.

Callahan struggled to avoid rolling her eyes and pressed on. "You don't achieve the kind of stardom or wield the kind of influence Gabriela had without making enemies. And with all the people she was surrounded by, there has to be someone who would want to—"

"De Souza," Ruiz told her.

They both looked over at him. He was on his feet now, moving toward them, his eyes more bloodshot than ever. "José de Souza's the one you want."

Callahan was surprised he'd overheard them. "Who's José de Souza?"

"The leader of the *Favela Paraisópolis* drug cartel."

"What's their connection?"

"In the old days, Gabriela did some courier work for

him, and she's spoken out against him many times since. She was pressuring the police to clean up the slums. Even talked about taking a trip there to encourage the children to honor God and stay away from drugs."

"And you didn't feel the need to mention this?"

"I told the officers at the scene. But at that point everyone seemed to think that Gabriela had committed suicide."

"We haven't completely ruled that out," Callahan said. "But at least we're getting somewhere. I take it Gabriela's interference in de Souza's life didn't sit well with him?"

"He threatened her more than once."

Callahan turned to Martinez. "Your men must have mentioned Mr. Ruiz's suspicions. Have you talked to this guy?"

She wasn't surprised when Martinez shook his head. "That's easier said than done. He rarely leaves the *favela*. And he's heavily protected."

She sighed. "I don't know how you manage to do it, Detective, but you continue to disappoint me."

"We can't just walk in there and demand his cooperation. It would take far more manpower than we can—"

"I don't care," Callahan said, "we need to interview him. He's the best lead we've got."

She could see by the look in his eyes that Martinez was still clinging to his fear. The man was useless.

Having something concrete to focus on gave her hope. But before she approached de Souza, she'd have to reinterview all the witnesses. Maybe one of them would remember seeing him at the concert that night. Maybe he'd been right there in the audience, waiting for Gabriela to go backstage.

Callahan thought about the sound of Gabriela's voice at the end of the recording, when she'd uttered those last few unintelligible words. It was barely a croak yet somehow purposeful, as if she were trying to send a message.

Was she giving them a name?

The man who had done this to her?

De Souza?

Callahan gestured toward the table. "Don't touch that phone," she said, then crossed the room to the foyer where she had left her backpack. Unzipping it, she pulled out her own smartphone and an audio cable, then moved to the sofa and sat.

Setting her phone next to Ruiz's, she connected one end of the cable to its input, and the other end to the iPhone's output jack. She had a forensic audio application installed that would allow her to clean up the recording and enhance the sound.

She called it up, then pressed *play* on the iPhone, transferring the message in real time. When it was done, she called up the audio wave—a graphic representation of the recording—and scrolled to a point near the end, where Gabriela's whispers were barely more than a few tiny spikes on a straight line.

Callahan isolated this section and normalized the sound, which enlarged the spikes and raised the volume by several decibels.

Then she clicked play, surprised by what she heard.

"*Defende eam*," Gabriela croaked. "*Defende eam . . .*"

The same two words she'd scribbled in the margin of *Paradise Lost.*

Protect her.

Callahan turned to Ruiz.

"There it is again," she said. " 'Protect her.' Are you sure you can't think of anyone Gabriela wanted to protect? Someone in danger? A child, maybe? One of her fans?"

Ruiz shook his head. "There's no way to know."

"She was obviously talking about herself," Martinez said. "She knew what was about to happen and was begging for God to protect her soul."

"Then wouldn't she have said protect *me*?" Callahan had had about enough of this idiot. She looked again at Ruiz. "You say Gabriela used to work for de Souza. Is it possible she may have been concerned about someone she knew from those days? A friend who's still caught up in that world?"

Ruiz shook his head. "Sofie was her only friend back then. And Sofie's long gone."

Maybe so, but if Gabriela had gone to all the trouble to say what she'd said—had even scribbled it in a book— then it obviously meant something to her.

Something important.

Callahan thought about the T-shirt and the verse on the wall and Ruiz's remark that Gabriela had been obsessed with *Paradise Lost*. There had been other notations in the book's margins. Other passages highlighted.

Could they mean something as well?

Getting to her feet, she headed toward the bedroom, Ruiz and Martinez following behind her, Martinez saying, "What? What is it now?"

Callahan ignored him and moved through the closet to Gabriela's prayer room. Grabbing the book, she leafed through it until she found the verse again, then continued turning the pages, finding more highlighted passages—each one as impenetrable as the last. Milton may have been a genius, but accessibility was not his strong suit.

Gabriela's notes seemed to be confined to the eleventh chapter—or Book XI. On some pages, only individual words had been highlighted and the notes scribbled in the margins did little to illuminate what might have been going on in the pop star's mind. Numbers and letters were written down and crossed out, then written down again, as if she were trying to puzzle something out. Break some kind of code.

But in *Paradise Lost*?

That didn't make a whole lot of sense. And Callahan again wondered if the girl had gone looney tunes.

"Look at this place," Martinez said, taking in the altar and symbol on the wall. He picked up the copy of *Forbidden Rites* from the prayer-desk shelf. "Look at what she was reading. I told you she was in league with the Devil."

Ruiz swiveled his head toward him, his face tight with anger. "Say that again and you'll be looking for a new job before the day is over."

The threat must have carried weight, because Martinez practically swallowed his tongue before shaking his head in disgust.

"I've had enough of this," he said to Callahan. "We all know what happened to Gabriela, and the more we follow this road, the more dangerous it gets." He turned, headed out the door. "I'll drop your bag at the hotel. You can find your own way there."

Then he was gone.

Fine, Callahan thought, no big loss. And Ruiz certainly didn't seem too broken up about it.

She gestured to *Paradise Lost.* "Do you have any idea *why* Gabriela was so obsessed with this thing?"

"No," he said. "And I have to admit, I've never read it. I tried a few times, but it was beyond me."

Except for a few religious scholars, a handful of uptight literary types—and maybe Gabriela herself—the same was probably true for most people.

Callahan thought about the facts surrounding this case. An improbable death, phantom gasoline smells, a victim who looked like barbecued roadkill, a satanic symbol burned into the floor of an otherwise untouched room, a secret prayer sanctuary, the strange, obsessive scribblings in the margins of an epic poem about the fall of Satan . . .

And, of course, the message in both the book and on Ruiz's cell phone.

Protect her.

Maybe Martinez was right, after all. There was enough weird going on around here to attract a bucketful of goth nerds, with a side order of religious fanatics. Something had been going on in Gabriela's life that was far beyond her role as a Christian pop star.

Something that had gotten her killed.

And call Callahan crazy, but she had a gut feeling that it somehow related to those two words, and the book she held in her hands.

Protect her.

But her knowledge of these things was far too limited for her to even begin to figure it out. What she needed was the help of an expert. Someone on call. A Milton junkie, religious historian and occult specialist all wrapped into one—assuming such an animal existed.

There was one sure way to find out.

Dropping the book to the prayer desk, she excused herself, then pushed past Ruiz and went back out to the living room.

She snatched up her phone, punched in the security code and was about to hit autodial when it buzzed in her hand. Checking the screen, she immediately put it to her ear. "I was just about to call you."

"We had a look at the data you uploaded," a voice said.

It was the same cold, disembodied voice she always heard when she dealt with Section. The agency wasn't big on formalities like names or ranks or identifying information in case you were unfortunate enough to one day find yourself compromised.

It simply gave orders. If you didn't follow them, you risked losing your job.

Or your life.

"I'm thinking I need a specialist," she said. "Somebody at the top of his game."

"We're a step ahead of you. Proceed as usual and we'll contact you when the arrangements have been made."

Then the line clicked.

12

HARRISON, LOUISIANA

It was nearing midnight when the trouble started.

Batty hadn't dragged himself out of bed until late in the afternoon, and had spent the first few hours of the new day fighting a raging hangover. By the time he had purged himself of the previous night's toxins, he was ready to start anew and didn't waste any time getting over to Bayou Bill's.

Bill's was busy as always and Batty was working on boilermaker number three (feeling generally sorry for himself that the redhead had once again failed to show), when the door blew open and a guy who may as well have had the word *tourist* stamped across his forehead stumbled in, looking lost and concerned and generally discombobulated.

He wasn't the source of the trouble, however. Just a curiosity that got Batty's attention right before the trouble began.

It was a hot night and the tourist was sweating like a man who wasn't used to the weather. But the moment he locked eyes with Batty, his entire demeanor changed, as if he'd found what he was looking for and was grateful to have it over and done with.

Batty half expected him to head straight to the booth. He was wondering what this was about and why he was about to be approached, when the guy surprised him by averting his gaze and taking a stool at the bar instead.

Batty watched old Bill put a bottle of beer in front of him and wondered if he'd been imagining things.

Wouldn't be the first time.

And a moment later, he was too distracted to care.

The trouble—when it finally came—came from the parking lot, just outside a window across from Batty's booth.

It was dark out there under the trees, but there was enough moon that he could see a handsome but worn-looking woman and her biker boyfriend in among the parked cars. They'd pulled up on a Harley shortly before the tourist wandered in, and started making out, looking like they were about to do the dirty right there on the hood of Ronny Cantrell's twenty-year-old Town Car.

Batty had been doing his best to ignore them ever since.

But some things were impossible to ignore. As he contemplated ordering another boilermaker, their voices began to rise—muffled behind the window, but loud enough to catch his attention. He looked over and saw that the make-out session had abruptly ceased and the biker now had hold of his girlfriend's wrist.

This was not, mind you, a little love squeeze. This was an all-out assault, fingers digging into the ulnar nerve, trying to elicit a reaction and not a favorable one. It was rough and mean and—window or no window—generally ill-advised in the presence of a gentleman like Batty. A gentleman who believed that you never laid a hand on a woman unless you intended to make her feel good.

Batty rose, feeling the booze sluice through him, but

he didn't let that slow him down. He called out a good-
night to Bill, who was too busy to notice, then went outside, staggering only slightly as he approached the biker
and his girlfriend.

The bearded bastard still had her by the wrist and
Batty could see from the look on her face that she wasn't
enjoying it one little bit.

"Excuse me," he said, moving in close. "I'd advise
you to let this poor lady go, and don't touch her again or
you'll be making an appointment with the dentist tomorrow, assuming you can still pick up a phone."

The biker looked at him, annoyed. Not a man who
liked to be interrupted when he was busy inflicting pain.

"Who the fuck are *you*?" He turned to the woman,
not bothering to release her wrist. "Is this guy a friend of
yours?"

She winced, trying to pull her hand away.

"No," she cried, the terror in her voice clearly reflected in her expression. "I don't know him."

The biker's eyes narrowed. "The hell you don't, you
little—"

That was when Batty swung, his fist connecting with
a solid crack. He had warned the man, but the man
hadn't listened, and Batty was a big believer in following
through on a threat.

The biker, however, was neither small nor flabby, and
despite nearly toppling to the ground with a bloody
mouth, he recovered from the punch much quicker than
anticipated.

The next thing Batty knew, the asshole was upright
and moving fast, and it was immediately obvious that he
hadn't yet had anything to drink—which, unfortunately,

gave him an advantage. In the flurry of punches that followed, Batty came up two for seven, only one of which connected in any substantial way.

It all ended with Batty faceup on the ground between two cars, staring into the eyes of the man who might very well have stomped him to death without even a twinge of guilt as the girlfriend shouted, "Kill the sonofabitch!"

So much for chivalry.

The biker wiped at his mouth, looked at the blood on the back of his hand, then rolled his tongue over his teeth, checking to see if there was any damage.

"You may be right about that dentist," he said thickly. "But they're gonna have to carry you outta here on a stretcher, you little mother—" He froze as the barrel of a gun touched the back of his head. Batty was surprised to see the sweating tourist standing directly behind him.

"Time to call it a night," the tourist said softly, looking considerably more confident than he had when he first walked into the bar.

The biker threw his hands up. "Easy, buddy. We just came here for a drink. He started it."

"And I'm finishing it. Grab your skank, get on your bike and get the hell out of here. Now."

There wasn't any room for negotiation in the tourist's tone, and apparently the biker wasn't as stupid as he looked. He glared at Batty, then grabbed hold of his girlfriend's arm, pulling her away, and a moment later, their bike was roaring down the street.

Batty got up on his elbows, squinting at the tourist, who tucked his gun away and crouched next to him, pulling him upright. "You okay, Professor?"

So it hadn't been his imagination. This guy knew who he was. "Still alive, more or less. Who the hell are you?"

"Just a friend."

"Well, I appreciate the help, friend, but I could've handled the sonofabitch just fine on my own."

"That's a debate we'll have to save for another time. We're running late."

Batty furrowed his brow at him. "Late for what?"

"You've got a plane to catch."

Then the guy quickly brought a hand up, and to Batty's surprise, something sharp and hot stung his neck.

He grabbed at his throat and fell back, but before he could say a word, the world tilted sideways and the tourist started to double and triple right there in front of his eyes as the moonlight suddenly grew very dim.

Then it disappeared altogether as Sebastian "Batty" LaLaurie fell down a deep, dark hole.

BOOK IV

Land of the Lost

Millions of spiritual Creatures walk the Earth
Unseen, both when we wake, and when we sleep

—*Paradise Lost*, 1667 ed., IV:677–78

13

LOS ANGELES, CALIFORNIA

He watched the girl get off the bus at the Greyhound station, her doe eyes taking in the world around her with obvious disappointment.

It was not, he imagined, what she had expected to find. The city wasn't as clean as it looked on network TV—cars choking the boulevard, trash clogging the gutters, the smog not as thick as it once was, but still smelling faintly of dirt and spit and sulfur.

There were no digitally enhanced blue skies here. And the only palm trees left were now victim to a slow-killing rot.

A homeless woman was huddled on the sidewalk near the bus station exit and the girl gave her wide berth, clutching her knapsack as she moved, looking as if she were afraid the old woman might spring to her feet and block her passage like a troll at the gates of Purgatory.

But the old woman remained still, only her eyes moving as the girl hurried past and made her way up Cahuenga toward Hollywood Boulevard, where surely things would look much better.

This was, after all, the land of dreams. Home to the stars.

But he knew that things would *not* look better. And as he followed the girl, staying a discreet distance behind her, he could see the change in the way she carried herself as her disappointment deepened. The footsteps slowed, the shoulders slumped, the head swiveled back and forth, hoping to find something—anything—that looked even remotely inviting.

The chicken hut on the corner? The check-cashing store? The urgent care clinic with iron bars on its front window? The tattoo parlor?

There was nothing. And he knew she was suddenly terrified, wondering if she'd made a mistake.

In this day and age she should have known better. But fifteen-year-old girls are not prone to critical thinking, especially when they want desperately to get away from home.

Some things just never change.

He had been watching her for many days now. Had followed her all the way from Lawton, Arizona. She'd gone missing from her home, but he'd found her at the bus depot there, counting the money she'd kept hidden in her dresser drawer, holding it close to her budding chest, eyes darting, hoping no one was paying much attention to her.

But he was.

And all the time he had watched her, from Arizona to California, he had been second-guessing himself, wondering if his instincts were wrong.

They'd certainly been wrong before. Many times, in fact.

There was the exchange student in eastern France. The painter in Hammersmith. The humanitarian in Macedonia. The missionary in northern Thailand . . .

He had searched the globe, year after year, and thought he'd heard her song. But what he'd really heard was his own wishful thinking. Nothing more. And he had begun to wonder if it was all a lie. A cruel deception, perpetrated by a father who no longer cared.

But this one was different.

This one gave him hope.

The kind of hope he had almost forgotten about. The kind of hope he'd felt in the long ago days, when he'd first made the decision to stop the killing, the debauchery, the self-serving narcissism that drove so many of his kind.

Maybe he was crazy, but it seemed that the circumstances were finally right for once. The fourth moon would soon be here, and he could hear the girl's soul calling out to him, so much stronger than any of the others.

And he knew that she was different. Special.

A gift from an absentee father.

His message to God.

After wandering up Hollywood Boulevard for several long blocks, her knapsack starting to weigh her down, the girl turned into a small coffeehouse on the corner of Gower, the kind of place that looked as if its prices might be right for her minuscule budget.

He waited as she bought a muffin and a cup of tea. She took a seat near the window, looking back the way she came with small-town eyes, full of trepidation and confusion, clouded faintly by tears. He knew it was really sinking in now, and before long the panic would start, and she'd be ripe for the taking by the first "kind soul" who came along.

She had been much safer back in Lawton. Despite her repugnant stepfather, the world around her had been smaller there, more easily controlled. But try to convince a teenager she's better off where she is and see how far that gets you. Especially when the aforementioned stepfather starts getting friendly and making comments about her changing body. Doing it while Mom is conveniently at work.

And Mom was always at work.

Stepping into the coffeehouse, he moved toward a table in back, careful not to make direct eye contact with her.

Too early for that. He didn't want to scare her away.

The girl gave him only a cursory glance as he entered—which was just fine with him. She kept her gaze on the street, sipping her tea, nervously nibbling her muffin, probably wondering if she had enough money to find a place to sleep tonight and still have any left over. There was a free shelter less than a block down Gower, but he doubted she knew about it. The only planning she'd done before getting on that bus was to buy a ticket.

And because he wasn't quite ready to make contact with her, he knew he'd have to find a way to guide her there.

Which, of course, was the difficult part.

One thing he had learned in all these years of "sobriety," as he called it, was that people had minds of their own, and getting them to do what he'd like them to do without resorting to treachery—and thereby breaking his code—took a lot of ingenuity. But he also found that if you presented them with the opportunity to make the right decision, they often did.

But as he well knew, it wasn't the decision itself that mattered. It was the intent behind it that counted.

Pulling the plug on a dying loved one because you want to inherit his estate is vastly different from pulling that plug because you want to end his suffering. You're either a murderer or a humanitarian, but you can't be both.

And the former will never get you that ticket to heaven, no matter how things may look to the world at large.

She was halfway through her muffin when a young man walked past the coffeehouse window. Twenty-five, slender but muscular, with raggedy brown hair and few days' worth of stubble on his chin. Hollywood pretty, like so many of them were out here—and a predator, no doubt about it.

He knew this before the guy had even disappeared from view.

A moment later, the pretty boy was back, now looking in the window at the girl, then breaking into a smile, moving around to the door.

As he pulled it open, he caught her gaze and said, "Carrie?"

The girl seemed confused and a little flustered. Then the guy was crossing to her table, giving her his best Jack Nicholson grin, but without the mischief or malevolent wit behind it.

"Carrie Whitman, right? You were in my Fundamentals of Scene class last year. We did that improv. The love scene, remember?"

The girl, looking slightly embarrassed, said, "I think you've got me mixed up with somebody else."

"No, no, no," he told her, then pulled out a chair and sat. "I'll never forget that kiss you gave me. And you're just as hot as you always were."

The girl started to redden. "Seriously, I'm not this Carrie girl, and I've never taken an acting class in my life."

The guy frowned. "You sure you aren't pulling my chain? Because I swear to God you two could be . . ." He paused, looking at her more closely now. "Yeah, yeah, I guess you're right. When I think about it, you're definitely a lot hotter than she ever was." He got to his feet, pushed the chair in. "Sorry for being such a douche."

Oh, he was good.

"Don't even worry about it," the girl said.

The guy flashed her another smile, then nodded to her and headed out the door. She was already on the hook, her head turning, following him with her gaze as he once again walked past the window.

Then he stopped, turned. Came back inside.

He was looking at her knapsack now. "Did you just get into town?"

The girl was an innocent, but she wasn't completely naive, and she hesitated before answering. "Yeah. Just a little while ago."

He held out a hand to shake. "I'm Zack."

She stared at it a moment, as if weighing a decision, then finally shook it. "Jenna."

"You looking for a place to stay tonight?"

"Uhh . . ." Another moment of hesitation. "Yeah, I guess I am."

"Me and a bunch of my friends are crashing at a place up in Burbank. There's plenty of room, you wanna join us. It isn't much, but it's way better than any of the shitty-ass hotels around here."

In the middle of all this, a woman wandered into the coffeehouse and ordered an Americano. Zack wasn't exactly speaking at a conversational level, so her attention was caught before she'd even closed her wallet.

Zack was still in the middle of his pitch, the girl starting to come around, weakening at the prospect of not having to sleep in an alley or a junkie dive, when the woman turned and said, "Bobby, get the fuck out of here before I call the police."

Her tone was flat, matter-of-fact, no-nonsense.

Zack wheeled around, annoyed by the interruption. But his demeanor changed the moment he realized who she was. Apparently, he and this woman had a history.

Jenna frowned at him. "I thought you said your name was Zack?"

"Middle name," he said, and of course he was lying. Everyone in Hollywood was trying to reinvent themselves. "And I don't like it when people call me Bobby." He shot a look at the woman now.

The woman didn't back down. "And I don't like when you prey on girls who are nearly a decade younger than you are. I mean it, Bobby, go now or I really will call the police."

She pulled out her cell phone to punctuate the threat. Zack looked as if he were about to get all hot and bothered, maybe go postal on her, but after a moment he merely glanced at the two women, muttered the word *bitch* and slinked out the door.

Jenna looked dismayed. "Who was that guy?"

"Nobody you want to get involved with, dear. He hangs around the shelter sometimes, harassing the girls, and I'm always having to chase him away."

"Shelter?"

"I run a homeless shelter down the street." She glanced at Jenna's knapsack. "We'll probably be full up tonight, but it'll be dark soon and if you need a place to stay, I'll be happy to put a sleeping bag on my office floor."

"Really?"

"Really. But you'll have to decide before my Americano comes, because there are a lot of other girls out there who could use that space."

A moment later the woman's order was ready, and Jenna hefted her knapsack and went with her out the door.

He considered following them but didn't think it was necessary. Jenna would be in capable hands tonight, and that was all that mattered. Zack the pretty boy was bound to be a complication—he had a feeling Jenna hadn't seen the last of him—but he could handle that in due course.

As the two women disappeared from view, he could still hear the siren song of Jenna's soul. Those high, sweet notes that told him he had finally found the one he'd been looking for for so many years.

What a shame she had to die.

14

SÃO PAULO, BRAZIL

"What you are about to experience, senhors and senhoritas, is the Wild West of Sampa."

Callahan had crowded into the back of the ancient tour van, finding herself pressed up against a fat American tourist and his wife.

Their driver and tour guide was a middle-aged Brazilian woman who wore a wireless headset that piped her voice over speakers mounted throughout the van. She gave her spiel only in a thickly accented English, so if you didn't speak or understand the language, you were shit out of luck.

"Keep your cameras ready," she said. "This is a sight you will want to remember."

Callahan had spent the previous afternoon and part of the morning reinterviewing witnesses—Gabriela Zuada's crew, her bandmates, her security team—leaning on them with questions about the pop star's potential enemies, especially those who might be involved in Satanic worship. But the only name that consistently came up was José de Souza. The drug lord Gabriela had once worked for.

Which only confirmed that, dangerous or not, the man needed to be questioned.

And Callahan would have to do the questioning.

So here she was, feeling the bump of the road beneath her as the van rolled along the highway at the edge of the city.

Off to their left were the beginnings of *Favela Para-isópolis,* a ramshackle shantytown, its multicolored, dilapidated metal-and-plywood shacks lining the highway, looking as if they might collapse at any moment.

The *favela* was located in the heart of the São Paulo suburb of Morumbi, one of the richest in Brazil. The contrast between unapologetic wealth and abject poverty was stark, visceral and depressing. Callahan wondered what it must be like to live in the shadow of such wealth, waking every morning and looking out at the glass-and-steel high-rises knowing they represented a world you would never be invited to enter.

She had to give Gabriela credit for managing to pull herself out of this rat hole. It couldn't have been an easy thing to do.

The van made a turn, pulling onto a narrow, debris-strewn street. There was a dumping ground off to the right, mounds of rubble and trash piled several feet high, blocking the view of the highway.

They rolled past it and stopped as a pack of teenagers on battered mopeds buzzed by, shouting obscenities and flashing what Americans would think of as the "A-okay" sign. In Brazil, however, it meant something quite different.

Ahead, the street was teeming with *favelados*—residents of the *favela*—young and old alike, some parked in rickety metal chairs, others looking down onto the street from second-story windows, still others standing in front of crude storefronts, hawking candy and bottled drinks to passersby.

Two boys who couldn't have been more than nine or ten stood near an open doorway, passing a joint between them in blatant disregard of authority. Assuming there *was* any around here.

Laundry hung from windowsills. Bundles of frayed electrical and telephone lines were strung between the buildings, crisscrossing the sky above the street like multicolored spiderwebs. The street itself was littered with old car tires, chunks of loose cement and overflowing garbage cans, one of which had been overturned by a mangy dog, hunting for food.

Overall, it looked to Callahan like a war zone, and probably was from time to time.

The driver rolled slowly forward through it all, weaving past the debris, giving the passengers a taste of what it meant to live in a country that was ill-equipped to handle its poverty.

"Each year, São Paulo's middle class becomes poorer and poorer," she said, "and the *favelas* grow in response. Many *favelas* have their own schools and day-care centers, but most of the children grow up in the streets, and must learn to be quick-witted and stealthy if they are to survive. Some people call this the Devil's playground."

God's dirty little secret, Callahan thought. The forgotten people, left to rot in their own waste, with little or no chance of ever moving beyond this hole they called home. They were born, grew up and died here—often violently—barely a blip on heaven's radar screen.

The van's driver would likely tell you that Barbosa Tours was helping these people by bringing visitors with cash to the slums. But the truth was, the tour companies who had come up with this hefty rationalization for their greed were nothing more than traffickers in human misery. These weren't tourists, but voyeurs. And Callahan didn't doubt that a large percentage of every dollar spent went into some fat cat's pocket.

The van turned a corner onto a slightly wider but no less desolate street, then pulled to the side and stopped next to an open storefront. Inside, the store's shelves were lined with cheap manufactured and home-crafted trinkets, along with a selection of local sweets like *beijinhos de coco*, *brigadeiros* and *olhos de sogra*.

The *favela*'s version of a tourist trap.

The driver set the brake and stood, calling for the passengers to exit the van, explaining that they'd be traveling on foot now. Callahan filed out along with the others, making sure to fall in behind the Long Island duo, knowing that this was her time to slip away.

Across the street, to the left, was a narrow alleyway. As her fellow passengers marched dutifully into the trinket shop, she circled behind the van and crossed to the alley without a backward glance.

She had carefully studied satellite images of the *favela* and had much of the layout committed to memory. Martinez and his crew had pinpointed what they believed to be de Souza's compound, and she knew she was headed in that general direction.

As she emerged on the other side of the alley, however, she was confronted by an almost impenetrable maze of tenement-lined streets. The earthbound view was much more intimidating than the satellite version and a wrong turn might impede her progress.

Pulling her smartphone out of her backpack, she called up her GPS app and studied the route she'd mapped out earlier that morning. She had hoped to navigate the less busy streets, to lessen the chances of being watched, but as she made her way through the maze, she knew now that this was a practical impossibility. The place was packed with *favelados*. She already felt eyes on her and was sure that it wouldn't be long before de Souza knew exactly what she was up to.

She turned a corner, moving into another alley, then stopped short.

A shirtless old man lay in the middle of it, flies buzzing around his head. He wasn't breathing, and Callahan couldn't tell if he was the victim of violence or had simply collapsed and died.

Whatever the case, she didn't like looking at him.

As she carefully stepped around him, something flickered at the periphery of her vision, and she whirled, catching only a glimpse of undefined movement, as if someone had just darted past the mouth of the alley.

Somebody following her?

The old man's attacker?

Callahan wasn't prone to paranoia, but this was the kind of place that nurtured it, and a sudden sense of unease washed over her. She knew how to handle herself in a fight, but she'd always taken the attitude that it was best to avoid one if at all possible.

Especially when she wasn't functioning at her optimum level. Lack of sleep had a way of dulling your senses, slowing your responses. She'd managed a couple hours last night, but it hadn't been enough to drive away the tremors.

If anything, they were getting worse.

Checking the GPS, she moved to the far end of the

alley and took a right. But the map couldn't tell her what she'd find here, and directly ahead of her was a barrier—a huge makeshift wall, cobbled together out of plywood and rope and corrugated sheeting.

A crude mural was spray-painted on the wall, featuring a stark landscape that was dominated by a large, rotting tree. The blackened fruit of the tree lay on the ground around it, amidst a litter of human bones.

Four words were spray-painted across the wall in English:

Welcome to Paradise City

Callahan's unease deepened as she stood there, staring at the mural. There was a gap in the middle of the tree, a hole in the wall, and she wondered if she should go through it or find another way in.

No point in wasting time.

Stepping forward, she angled her body sideways and squeezed through the gap, only to discover that the wall was much thicker than it looked. This was actually a kind of tunnel, formed by tightly packed piles of debris, and for a moment she found herself enveloped by near darkness.

She emerged on the other side to a narrow, pockmarked street crowded with yet more shacks made of cheap wood and corrugated aluminum.

To her surprise, however, the street was nearly empty. The only sign of life was a lone girl, about ten years old, who stood in a doorway several yards away, a cigarette burning in one hand, a sawed-off autoloader in the other.

The girl took a drag on the cigarette and looked at Callahan with hard, defiant eyes.

Come on, they said, *try and fuck with me*.

Callahan had no intention of taking her up on the invitation, but she knew this meant she was getting close to de Souza.

Moving to her left, she stepped into a narrow passageway between two shacks, hoping to pass through to the adjoining street. But the moment she entered, she slowed her pace.

Ahead and to the right was an open doorway, nothing but blackness beyond, and Callahan couldn't shake the feeling that someone—or some*thing*—was watching her from inside, waiting for her to get close.

There was no rational reason to believe this, but her scalp started tingling and her body instinctively shifted into survival mode. What she felt wasn't fear, exactly, but was certainly something akin to it. A gut-level awareness that all wasn't right here, and she should proceed with extreme caution.

Pulling her backpack off her shoulder, she unzipped a pocket and reached in, wrapping her fingers around a Glock 20. She'd found it and a backup waiting for her in her hotel room yesterday afternoon.

A gift from Section.

Keeping her hand on the grip, she continued forward, feeling the skin on the back of her neck prickle in anticipation with each new step, her heart thumping a few beats faster than normal.

Then a voice behind her said, "You're here because of us."

Callahan hitched a breath and whirled, dropping her backpack as she yanked the Glock free.

She froze the moment she saw who it was.

The little girl. The ten-year-old.

The girl stood about seven yards away, her cigarette gone, the autoloader held loosely at her side. Her gaze remained defiant, but there was something strange about her eyes now. A vague, amber luminosity to them that deepened Callahan's unease.

"You're part of Michael's army," she said. "He sent you here to spy on us."

She was speaking English, and Callahan had no idea what to make of this. In fact, now that she thought about it, the girl didn't even *look* like a *favelada*. She didn't look *Brazilian*, for that matter.

Why hadn't she noticed this before?

Callahan wasn't exactly comfortable pointing her Glock at a ten-year-old, but she had no intention of lowering it. Not with that shotgun in the kid's hand.

"Easy now. I don't mean you any harm."

"You *are* with Michael, aren't you?"

"I don't know anyone named Michael."

"He thinks he can save us. Bring us to God. But he's wrong. There's no saving us now."

The girl lifted the autoloader, and Callahan did what she knew she shouldn't—she hesitated, didn't engage, fully aware it could well mean the difference between walking away from this and landing facedown in the dirt.

But something about this little girl held her back.

She looked so . . . familiar.

Then the girl surprised her. Instead of pointing the weapon at Callahan, she pressed its two barrels against her own temple, her eyes softening now, the amber tint fading.

"There's no saving any of us," she said wistfully.

And as the realization of what she was about to do sank in, true fear thudded in Callahan's chest.

"No!" she shouted, and sprang forward—

—as the girl wrapped her finger around the trigger and pulled.

15

There was no gunshot.

No exploding ten-year-old head. No falling body. No blood.

Instead, Callahan blinked twice and opened her eyes, suddenly aware that the girl had completely vanished and that she herself was no longer standing between the two dilapidated shacks.

She sat on the floor of yet another alley. Her backpack was slung over her shoulder, her Glock safely tucked away inside, and she still held her phone in her hand, the GPS receiver showing that she was three streets away from where she'd stood only a split second ago.

What the *hell*?

Lifting her free hand, Callahan stared at it. It was shaking uncontrollably. Much more than a tremor now.

Had she fallen *asleep*, for Christ's sake?

Right in the middle of a mission?

Had that whole episode with the girl been a hallucination? Some kind of bizarre, somnambulistic nightmare?

What else could it be?

Leaning back against a dilapidated, graffiti-covered fence—a fence she had no idea how she'd wound up sitting in front of—Callahan closed her eyes again, trying to find her bearings, trying to will the tremors away. Get them under control.

It's okay, she told herself. Just a little glitch in the hardware. Nothing to worry about.

But who was she kidding?

This was no goddamn glitch. This was a sign of some very serious mental distress. Her problems with sleep deprivation had just gone from a solid five to a record-breaking one hundred fifty in about two seconds flat. And if she wasn't careful, if she didn't get some fucking shut-eye *soon*, she might well wind up on a slab at the morgue.

She could still see the little girl's face in her mind. Those defiant, amber-tinged eyes. And she was certain she'd seen the girl before.

But where?

There's no saving us now. There's no saving any of us.

Then it hit her.

Callahan could see herself sitting in her bedroom in her childhood home, years after her father had died, staring into the vanity mirror above her dresser, hating what she saw, hating her life, hating that Dad had shot himself and left her behind with the Wicked Witch of the West. Wanting more than anything to join him in heaven.

There's no saving us now.

The little girl in the alley was *her*. At ten years old.

As the realization of this wormed its way into her brain and lodged there, sucking away her self-confidence, Callahan tried to pull herself together.

This was no time to be having a panic attack or nervous breakdown or whatever the hell you wanted to call it. She needed to man up, right now, no excuses.

No. Fucking. Excuses.

Wishing there was a coffee hut nearby so she could order a double espresso with a shot of Red Bull—and knowing that was probably the *last* thing she needed—she did her best to center herself. She was, after all, sitting in the middle of a hell on earth, and as inconvenient as that might have been at the moment, she had a job to do.

She got to her feet. Took several deep cleansing breaths, telling herself to let it go, that this would pass, that everything would be just fine from here on out—and knowing full well that it wouldn't be. But that was okay. She'd gotten through a number of tough situations on a lie.

Like her entire life.

The trick now was to *pretend* everything was back to normal and keep plunging forward.

Purging the face in the mirror from her mind, she consulted her GPS again, then took another deep breath and continued on her way.

She just hoped she wouldn't wind up shirtless in a gutter somewhere with flies buzzing around her head.

De Souza's compound sat on the side of a hill, a large, squat windowless gray building that had about as much personality as a World War II bunker. Several teenage boys formed a loose barricade out front, each carrying an automatic firearm.

Several others stood on the rooftop, their weapons ready.

They seemed to be waiting for her.

As she approached, keeping her hands at her sides,

one of the older boys gave her the once-over and grinned, pleased by what he saw.

Another, younger boy, said, "This is not part of the tour, senhorita."

"I'm here to see José de Souza."

All the kids laughed, as if this were the most hilarious thing they'd ever heard. The older one had drawn closer now, still leering at her, and without even a hint of hesitation, he reached out and grabbed for her ass.

His hand was less than an inch away when Callahan caught hold of his wrist and twisted, pulling his arm behind his back as she quickly relieved him of his weapon and forced him to his knees.

Pointing the gun at his head, she said to the others, "De Souza. Tell him it's about Gabriela Zuada."

Calling José de Souza's home a rat trap was being generous.

It was a tad less filthy than the rest of Paradise City, but that wasn't saying much, and Callahan had to wonder why someone who was reportedly the highest-ranking drug lord in the area would be content to live in such squalor.

Despite a kind of dingy darkness to the place, there were some creature comforts in evidence. A sixty-inch plasma television played softly in a corner of the room, showing the never-ending news footage of Gabriela's ongoing wake. Another corner sported an enclosed toilet, its door hanging open, the room surprisingly free of offensive smells. And a doorway to the left revealed a king-size bed, a couple dozen half-melted candles of various sizes lining a shelf directly above it.

A naked woman, with flawless cocoa skin, lay fast asleep atop the mattress, her legs splayed out in front of her, leaving nothing to the imagination.

Spray-painted on the wall above the candles were yet more symbols—a pentagram, Lorraine cross, the now familiar *A* inside the circle, and others that Callahan wasn't as familiar with. They hadn't gotten there by accident, and only confirmed what she had already been told.

De Souza was a practicing Satanist.

But while the presence of these signs was certainly enough to raise her suspicions, it wasn't proof that he'd had anything to do with Gabriela's death.

Standing behind and to either side of Callahan were three of de Souza's teenage bodyguards, weapons in hand but pointed at the floor.

For now.

De Souza himself sat a few feet away from her, slumped in a battered armchair near the one and only window, which was really nothing more than a ragged rectangular hole in the wall that overlooked the *favela* and the jumble of high-rises beyond.

"I only agreed to see you out of curiosity," he said.

He was a lanky guy, much younger than she had expected, with dark, curly hair and a wispy black goatee on his angular face. He wore only bright red boxers, and several nasty knife scars were visible on his chest and abdomen.

"About what?" she asked.

"Why you would assume I know anything about Gabriela Zuada?"

Callahan saw no reason to beat around the bush. "There are people who think you may be responsible for her death."

His eyebrows raised. "Are you one of these people?"

Callahan shrugged. "Let's just say I have more questions than answers."

"I have a question myself. Why is the U.S. State Department so interested in something that happened on Brazilian soil?"

Callahan had brought her credentials with her, just in case, and de Souza's bodyguards had found them when they searched her backpack. They'd also found her Glock 20 and immediately taken possession of it.

She didn't yet know the answer to de Souza's question, so she fell back on a reliable lie. "We're here at the request of the governor of São Paulo. The United States is always happy to assist in cases of international importance."

"International importance?" De Souza shook his head in disgust, then gestured at the television. "I suppose with the world falling apart around us, it shouldn't surprise me that both of our governments are distracted by the death of a self-righteous demagogue. The Middle East and Central Asia are about to implode, Africa right behind them, yet all eyes are here on Brazil. What happened to our precious Gabriela?"

"You don't seem very upset by her death."

"Why would I be?"

"I'm told she worked for you at one time. As a courier."

De Souza shrugged. "A lot of people work for me. They live, they die. It's nothing unusual around here."

Callahan thought about the dead man in the alley and wondered if he'd worked for de Souza, too. "But Gabriela spoke out against you. Condemned you for selling drugs to children. Her boyfriend says you threatened her more than once."

"Ahh, yes, the demon de Souza. I make no secret of what I do or what I believe, and to some that means I should be feared and reviled. I've never understood why people are so quick to condemn those who don't buy into their feeble ideology. The truth is, the only threat I pose is philosophical. I'm nothing more than a man who fills a need, with no more power than any other human being. Including Gabriela."

"And you never considered *her* a threat?"

"To what? My luxurious lifestyle?"

Callahan glanced around her again. He did have a point, but she pushed anyway. "I'm told she was pressuring the police to clean up the *favela*."

De Souza shook his head. "A useless publicity stunt. The police know their place, just as I do. And they'll soon have a lot more to worry about than this little piece of hell."

"Meaning what?"

"Look around you, Agent Callahan." He waved a hand toward the hole in the wall. "It's obvious to anyone paying attention that the dragon is loose and systematically taking control of our planet."

"The dragon?"

"Satan. Lucifer. The King of Babylon. The God of This Age. We're surrounded by his influence—people dying in the streets, endless wars, the constant promise of terrorism and nuclear holocaust. The gates of hell are about to open and there's nothing we can do to stop it. I'd be a fool to align myself with anyone who might try."

De Souza smiled now, revealing that his left front

tooth had been carefully painted with shiny black enamel, an inverted white cross at its center. "I may be easily corrupted, senhorita, but that doesn't make me a fool any more than it means I killed Gabriela Zuada."

"So do you think Gabriela was murdered?"

He shrugged. "You'd know more about that than I would."

"Then if it wasn't you, can you think of anyone else who might want to harm her? Someone who practices the occult?"

De Souza straightened himself in his chair, then leaned toward her.

"Something's stirring in the air, Agent Callahan. Do you feel it?"

"What do you mean?"

"Dark forces at work. Stronger than ever. Dangerous, malevolent forces that may well be responsible for what happened to our sweet Gabriela." He paused. "I'd advise you to tread lightly, *querida*. Because you never know who's watching."

Callahan shivered slightly. Then, remembering that she was a skeptic who valued rational thinking over superstitious voodoo, she got hold of herself. The only dark forces at work here were man-made, and if Gabriela had been murdered, it was by human hands.

But not de Souza's. She was convinced of that now. He might be the obvious suspect, and he might not hesitate to kill a rival, but it was clear that he had considered Gabriela a harmless trifle and had neither the motive nor the desire to go after her.

In other words, Callahan was wasting her time.

"Thanks for the advice," she said.

De Souza studied her for a long moment, assessing her, but not in the same lewd way as the other men (and boys) she'd encountered in São Paulo. There was nothing lascivious in the look at all. And that only compounded her uneasiness.

He checked his watch. "You'd better return to your bus, senhorita. They're scheduled to leave soon. And once they're gone, I'm afraid I cannot guarantee your safety."

Then he smiled again, running the tip of his tongue along the edge of that shiny black-and-white tooth.

"*Vá com Deus*," he said.

Go with God.

16

When Batty awoke, he was blindfolded.

The blindfold was thick and had been pulled taut enough to keep any outside light from seeping in, and he had no idea whether it was day or night. The air around him felt humid, his clothes and skin slick with sweat, so he assumed he was still in Louisiana.

But where?

He couldn't move his arms and legs. He was sitting in a chair with his hands bound behind his back, his ankles strapped tight, and judging by the feel, whoever had done this to him had used those plastic zip-ties you always saw on the cop shows.

So what the hell was going on here?

He had been kidnapped, that much was clear. But if there was one thing Batty knew for certain, it was that he didn't have a thing of value to offer a kidnapper. No money. No rich relatives to pay ransom. In fact, the only human being on the planet who had really given a damn about whether he showed up for breakfast every morning was Rebecca.

And Rebecca was two years dead.

The last thing Batty remembered was the fight outside Bayou Bill's and the tourist poking a needle into his neck—followed by darkness. *Blissful* darkness, if you wanted the God's honest truth.

No nightmares. No troubling images. Nothing.

Until this.

Whatever *this* was.

He sat there quietly, telling himself not to panic. A mistake had obviously been made and that mistake would be corrected when his kidnappers realized he wasn't the man they wanted.

But then the tourist's words came back to him like a sledgehammer to the head—*You okay, Professor?*—and he knew he was wrong. Bayou Bill's wasn't exactly the type of place known to attract academics. You weren't likely to find anyone else from Trinity Baptist College knocking back a beer there—

—so this wasn't a mistake. Far from it. And the only explanation was that he had been targeted, just as he had suspected the moment he saw the tourist walk into the bar. The guy who had stopped a biker from stomping his brains to a pulp was not a Good Samaritan. He had come to Bill's specifically to kidnap Professor Sebastian LaLaurie.

The question was *why?*

Batty tried to separate his wrists to see if he could loosen the tie, but there was very little wiggle room. He shook his head back and forth several times, but the blindfold wouldn't give either.

"Hello?" he called out. "Is anyone here?"

Silence.

"If you're looking for money, you've been sadly misinformed."

No response.

Batty's heart was pounding and he suddenly realized he was starting to hyperventilate. Calming himself, he slowed his breathing and concentrated, trying to get a reading on the room, knowing he wouldn't get much without being able to feel it beneath his fingers.

Several moments passed before it came. Then, quite abruptly, a small part of the room's history skittered through his mind—vague but unmistakable feelings of fear and anger and pain—and he knew he wasn't the first person to occupy this chair.

And not all of its occupants had left here alive.

Callahan was suddenly very tired.

On the ride back to the Barbosa Tours building, she couldn't stop thinking about de Souza's warning and the dream or hallucination or neural breakdown she'd suffered in that alleyway.

She couldn't stop seeing the little girl—seeing *herself*—look up at her with those amber-tinted eyes.

There's no saving us now.

There's no saving any of us.

All Callahan wanted was to get back to the hotel and crawl into bed and hopefully sleep the afternoon away. Her mind and body were screaming for it.

Unfortunately, the moment she stepped off the bus and signaled for a cab, her cell phone rang.

Section.

"The asset has been procured," the disembodied voice said. "You'll find him at the safe house on Ribeiro de Lima."

"Was it really necessary to bring him here? This could have been handled over the—"

"NQN, Agent Callahan. The directive came from the top."

NQN.

No Questions Needed.

In other words, shut the hell up and do as you're told.

Callahan sighed. "Has he been briefed?"

"We're leaving that to you."

Of course.

Section was sometimes so callous and devoid of emotion it infuriated Callahan. It was too often all business, the powers-that-be failing to see the value in nurturing a relationship rather than simply pulling the trigger and worrying about the consequences later. That she was expected to do the debriefing only meant that they had run a basic smash and grab and it would be up to her to stabilize the asset and secure his cooperation.

Not surprising, but still an annoyance.

There were sixteen known elements to the United States intelligence community, including the CIA, the NSA and the FBI. Section was the seventeenth, a no-nonsense off-the-books ops unit that had been formed by the previous administration in direct response to the 9/11 attacks, and given more autonomy than all of the other elements combined.

Section's mission, however, was not restricted to hunting down terrorists. Its mandate included crisis management, facilitation and sometimes even instigation. And considering the coldhearted way it handled its assets, Callahan figured it was a miracle she'd been given a choice about joining, back when she was a potential recruit.

What would her recruiter have done if she'd said no?

But maybe her psychological profile had made it obvious that she'd jump at the opportunity. She was, after all, the perfect candidate. Single. No blood relatives. No emotional ties whatsoever. She doubted she would have been approached otherwise. Still, she was surprised Section didn't simply snatch her from campus, throw her into an iso tank and sweat her until she agreed to . . .

Callahan stopped herself.

Why was she dredging up all this nonsense? Shoving her thoughts aside, she signaled again and waited as a cab pulled up in front of her.

No point in wallowing in the weeds.

She had work to do.

Batty had been sitting there close to an hour, his arms and legs going numb, when he heard a sound: a door opening and closing somewhere above him. It was so faint that he wondered for a moment if he had imagined it, but then his gut told him that he was no longer alone here—wherever *here* was.

A moment later, he heard footsteps on stairs, then a door directly across from him flew open, letting in a waft of slightly cooler air.

"Jesus Christ," someone said.

Not the tourist, but a woman. And she didn't sound pleased.

"Who are you?" he asked. "What do you want from me?"

"Definitely not this."

Then he heard her footsteps and felt her moving

around behind him. He stiffened slightly as she grabbed hold of the blindfold and pulled it free.

Harsh fluorescent light assaulted his eyes and he squinted against it, catching glimpses of a small nondescript basement with a cement floor and walls and a workbench full of tools.

The woman came around in front of him now, and he did his best to focus on her. She wasn't as beautiful as Rebecca or the elusive redhead, but the package she presented had been put together quite well and he had no doubt she'd broken a few hearts in her time.

And balls.

She wasn't particularly large or muscular, but there was a definite solidity to her body and a fierceness of expression that led him to believe she could kick his ass without really trying.

Hopefully it wouldn't come to that.

"I want to apologize for the way you've been treated, Professor. The people I work for sometimes mistake brutality for efficiency."

"The people you work for?"

She pulled a wallet from her back pocket and flipped it open, showing him an ID card with what looked like an official seal. "Agent Bernadette Callahan. State Department."

Batty gaped at it. It looked real enough, but he had his doubts. What on earth would the U.S. government want with *him*?

"Since when does the State Department go around kidnapping people?"

"You'd be surprised," she told him.

Judging by the energy in this room, maybe he

wouldn't be. He glanced at the floor, saw a drain at the center, and wondered how much blood had been washed down it.

"This apology," he said, flexing his wrists behind him. "Does it include untying me?"

Agent Callahan didn't move. "That depends."

"On what?"

"On whether I can trust you not to do anything stupid."

"Too late for that," Batty said. "You'd need a score card to keep track."

"Which is why I hesitate. I've read your file. I know you sometimes like to swing first and ask questions later— and I'm assuming that's how you got all those bruises on your face."

"Guilty as charged."

"So, you see, if you were to try anything, I'm afraid I'd have to hurt you." She smiled. "I don't want to hurt you."

"But trussing me up like a hog is perfectly okay."

"That wasn't my call. If you give me your word you'll be nice, I'll let you loose and we can do this thing like two civilized human beings."

"We're off to a wonderful start," he said. "What exactly is this *thing*?"

"Do I have your word?"

He shrugged. "Do I have a choice?"

"I'll take that as a yes."

She crossed to the workbench and came back with a small pair of wire cutters. Crouching in front of him, she cut his legs loose, then moved around behind him again and cut through the plastic tie at his wrists.

Batty slipped them free, looking up at her as he rubbed them. "Now what?"

"Now we go upstairs and have a drink."

"I think I like that plan."

"A *non*alcoholic drink, Professor. I want you sober as a nun for this conversation."

"You must not know too many nuns."

17

S he gave him orange juice.

It came from a refrigerator in what looked like a neatly furnished studio apartment. The only thing unusual about the place was that it had no windows to speak of.

And, of course, the torture chamber downstairs.

Batty sat on a comfortable couch, staring at a door across the room, wondering if it was the way out of this place. He still had no idea why he'd been brought here, and he was considering not waiting to find out. If he timed it right, he could be out that door in seconds flat.

But where would it take him?

And what would Callahan do to him if he tried and failed?

"Where exactly are we?" he asked.

She took a seat in a chair across from him. "A safe house. We have them all over the world."

"So why am I not feeling particularly safe at the moment? I assume we're not in Louisiana?"

"A little bit south of there."

Batty frowned. The only thing directly south was the Gulf of Mexico, but he tried his best guess—which, of course, was ridiculous. "The Yucatán?"

"São Paulo, Brazil," she said.

Batty flinched involuntarily. This had gone from the surreal to the absolutely bizarre. "What the hell am I doing in Brazil, for God's sakes?"

"Again, not my call. I would've been happy to handle this long distance, but the people I work for seem to think you're needed here. And when they say jump, I usually say 'with or without a parachute?'"

Batty stared at her for a long moment. "Am I getting out of this alive?"

She smiled. "Relax, Professor. Nobody wants you dead. We just want your help."

"You have an interesting way of going about getting it. You never thought of maybe just . . . I don't know . . . *asking* me?"

"Would you have said yes?"

"That depends on what kind of help you need. And you'll have to forgive me, but I can't even imagine what that would be."

"We just want to pick your brain for a while."

Batty wasn't sure he liked the sound of that. Remembering he had a glass of orange juice in his hand, he lifted it to his lips and gulped it down. It was cool and sweet and half of it was gone before he came up for air, but he couldn't help wishing it had a shot of vodka in it.

Calming himself, he hoped she hadn't been lying about him getting out of here alive.

"Okay," he said. "Pick away."

"Why don't we start with a question? Have you ever heard of a Brazilian pop singer by the name of Gabriela Zuada?"

This was out of left field. "The Christian Barbie doll?"

"I'm not sure most people would characterize her quite that way."

Batty shrugged. "She's just another vapid young thing who preaches godliness to little girls, but really has no idea what she's talking about. I'm sure she steals most of her sermons straight from the scam artists on Sunday morning television."

"I take it you're not a believer?"

This was a loaded question and Batty didn't hesitate to jump onto his soapbox. Couldn't have stopped himself if he'd wanted to.

"I'm probably more of believer than all those TV morons combined. But that's got nothing to do with it. I'm just not big on hypocrites who claim to live by the word of God, only to cherry-pick Scripture to excuse their bigotry."

"You have pretty strong feelings about this."

"I have pretty strong feelings in general—but I think you already knew that. Why is the State Department keeping a file on me?"

"We keep files on all potential assets," she said. "And someone of your standing is very attractive to the people I work for. Leading academic. Biblical scholar. Expert on the occult . . ." She paused. "You had a pretty impressive profile before you started drinking."

"Does your file say *why* I started?"

She shook her head. "Not what I read. Is there something you want to tell me?"

Batty didn't respond, sorry he'd brought the subject up in the first place. But he'd gotten his answer, and that's all he cared about.

Callahan didn't push. Reaching into a pocket, she brought out a folded sheet of paper and handed it to him.

Batty unfolded it, saw a few lines of poetry.

> *Darkness ere Dayes mid-course, and Morning light*
> *More orient in yon Western Cloud that draws*
> *O're the blew Firmament a radiant white,*
> *And slow descends, with somthing heav'nly fraught.*

He didn't really have to read them. The words were as familiar to him as the Old Testament. Probably more so.

"*Paradise Lost,*" he said. "What about it?"

"That's what I'm hoping you can tell me. I'm told you're the leading authority on John Milton."

"Depends on who you ask. What does this have to do with the Christian Barbie doll?"

"You don't watch the news? Read the papers?"

"Not if I can help it."

Callahan nodded and gestured to the slip of paper. "What can you tell me about that passage?"

Batty glanced at it again. "Nothing particularly earth-shattering. You can Google this stuff and find out everything you need to know."

"I'm not a big fan of the Internet, Professor. Too much disinformation out there. I like the human element. Someone I can have a conversation with. Exchange ideas. Is there anything in that passage you find unusual?"

"In what way?"

"In a way that might explain why a murder victim would have it painted on her wall."

Batty looked at her. "What exactly are you getting me involved in?"

"Details to come. Just answer the question."

Batty reread the verse. "It's incomplete, for one thing. There's a whole lot comes before and after it. I'm guessing you know it's from Book Eleven, when the sun is eclipsed and Adam and Eve see a cloud descending from heaven."

Callahan nodded again. "I got that much from the CliffsNotes."

"But if you're looking for any kind of hidden meaning, I'm afraid you're out of luck. Taken as a whole, *Paradise Lost* is a work of genius, but a couple lines alone don't mean much beyond the simple fact that your victim may have had a thing for angels. Which, of course, leads me to believe you're talking about Gabriela Zuada, and that's my cue to say good-bye."

He set the glass and slip of paper on the coffee table in front of him and got to his feet.

Callahan didn't move. "Sit down, Professor. We aren't finished yet."

"As far as I'm concerned we are."

"Do you want me to take you downstairs and tie you up again?"

Batty looked at her. He may have been pretty good with a left hook, but he had no doubt that she could do exactly what she was threatening to do without breaking much of a sweat.

He sat back down. "You know, I'd probably be a lot more cooperative if you just told me what this is all about."

So she did.

She told him she was down here to help the local police investigate the death of Gabriela Zuada. That there were a lot of unanswered questions surrounding it, including possible signs of a Satanic ritual. Gabriela had apparently been obsessed with *Paradise Lost*, and she left behind a cryptic message that may or may not have been related to it.

Batty gestured to the slip of paper. "The lines of verse?"

"That's only part of what we found. The message I'm curious about was written in the margin of the book, which she repeated over the phone right before she died."

"And what was it?"

"*Defende eam.* Protect her."

"Protect who?"

"That's what I'm trying to find out. When a victim says something like that right before she's killed, you tend to think it might be important. Whoever she wanted to protect is potentially another victim, or a possible witness. So you can see why we'd want to locate this person."

"I'm afraid I can't help you much there."

"I know this is a shot in the dark, Professor, but you can't think of any way her message might relate to those lines of verse?"

Batty shook his head and sighed. "*Paradise Lost* revolves around Satan's fall from grace and the corruption of mankind, and despite your victim's obsession with it, I'd have a hard time equating any part of it to a murder or a Satanic ritual."

"Would you mind taking a look at the crime-scene photos?"

"If I refuse, will you let me go?"

"Not likely."

"I'm not sure how much good it'll do you."

"Just take a look and tell me if anything jumps out at you."

She brought out a cell phone, played with it for a moment, then handed it to Batty. "Just touch the arrow to flip through the photos."

Batty did as he was told and the screen came to life with a publicity shot of Gabriela Zuada. Before now, he'd only had a vague idea of what she looked like, but the moment he saw that face, his heart rate kicked up.

He'd seen her before. And not on TV.

This was the girl from his nightmare the other night. The one whose screams had awakened him. The one consumed by a wall of fire.

He sat there, unmoving, staring at her image, then reluctantly touched the screen again, advancing through the next several photos.

What he saw was a burned body. Burned beyond recognition. Then shots of a floor marred by dark scorches that roughly formed a circle with an A at its center.

Goose bumps rose on the back of Batty's neck.

He stared at the screen wordlessly, suddenly swept away to a place he didn't want to go. To a moment in time he had spent the last two years trying to obliterate.

Struggling to pull himself back, he said, "Where did they find this body?"

"In a backstage storage room at the local performing arts center."

"I need to go there. Right now."

Callahan frowned at him. "That's probably not a

good idea, Professor. I'm sure anything you have to con-tribute can be handled right—"

"You don't understand. I'm not asking, I'm telling you. It's imperative that I see that storeroom. You're in danger. Grave danger. And so is anyone else involved in this investigation."

"Danger? What are you talking about?"

Batty got to his feet again. She could try to stop him, but this time he had adrenaline on his side.

"This isn't a negotiation," he said. "Take me to the crime scene or stay the hell out of my way."

18

They took a cab to the performing arts center.

Callahan had tried to get LaLaurie to spill—to tell her what he'd seen in those photographs that *she* couldn't see—but he had refused to budge. On the ride over, he remained evasive, and the more time she spent with him, the more her irritation grew.

Danger. Grave danger.

What the hell was that supposed to mean? Did she have another Lieutenant Martinez on her hands?

As they were waved through the barricades, Callahan noted that the crowd outside had grown considerably, and she wondered how long it would be before it was too big to be controlled.

LaLaurie took it all in with a trace of wonder in his eyes. "A lot of fuss and bother for one little girl."

Callahan arched a brow. "Do you have any idea how famous Gabriela was?"

"Not a clue."

"There's the pope. Then there's Santa Gabriela. And in some circles even the pope has to play catch-up." She looked at him. "Are you ready to talk to me now?"

"About what?"

"About what you saw in those photographs."

"Not until I know for sure."

"Know *what* for sure?"

"I'll tell you when I know."

"And when will that be?"

"Soon," LaLaurie said. "Very soon."

Infuriating.

Less than five minutes later, they were climbing the loading dock steps. They entered the building, crossed through a small warehouse, then followed a hallway until they came to the storeroom where Gabriela's body had been found.

LaLaurie paused at the doorway, just short of the police tape. "You smell that?"

"What?" Callahan asked. "And if you say gasoline, I'll kick your butt."

"Sulfur," he said. "It's not strong, but it's there."

"You must have a better nose than I do." Callahan pulled the crime-scene tape aside and flicked on the light. "The reason I mentioned gasoline is because one of the witnesses insists he smelled it. But we haven't found any evidence of it."

"I'm not surprised. Who was this witness?"

"Her boyfriend."

LaLaurie nodded. "Like a husband having sympathy pains when his wife goes into labor."

"Say what?"

He didn't respond. He was staring at the scorch mark now, his jaw tightening at the sight of it. He seemed to go away for a moment, lost in a memory—and not a pleasant one at that. She was about to call him back, when he abruptly moved past her and put a palm against the wall, closing his eyes.

He stayed that way for what seemed an eternity, and

Callahan said, "Pardon the intrusion, Professor, but what the hell are you doing?"

"Trying to feel the energy in the room. Looking for signs."

What the hell? Was he some kind of psychic?

She didn't remember reading *that* in his file.

"Please tell me I misunderstood what you just said."

He moved to the scorch mark again and hunkered down next to it. He studied it a moment, then closed his eyes and slowly—almost reluctantly, it seemed—lowered his hand, pressing his palm against it.

The moment he made contact, his entire body went rigid. He clamped his jaw tight and began to shake, as if a current of electricity were shooting through him.

"Professor?"

She was sure he was about to go into a full-fledged grand mal seizure, when he suddenly jerked his hand away and opened his eyes. His face had gone pale and his breathing was labored.

She moved toward him. "Professor, are you okay?"

"I'm fine," he said, waving her off. Then he got to his feet, staggered slightly and steadied himself against a wall, struggling to catch his breath. "Just what I was afraid of. Take me to Gabriela's apartment."

"Maybe I should take you to a hospital instead. You look like you've been to hell and back."

"I told you, I'm fine. Take me to her apartment."

"Not until you explain to me what just happened."

"I'm not sure you're ready to hear it." His color was returning and his breathing was back to normal.

"What's that supposed to mean?" Callahan said. "Ready to hear what?"

"I'll explain it all when we get there."

"How about you explain it now and we can pretend we waited."

He looked at her. "Let's just say that what happened here isn't an isolated incident. That's why I warned you."

"You're gonna have to give me a hell of a lot more than that."

"At Gabriela's apartment. I promise I'll tell you everything."

Callahan gave the cabdriver the address for Gabriela's high-rise.

There was something about LaLaurie—his inflexible will, perhaps—that made it impossible to turn him down.

Or maybe it was the pain behind his eyes. She'd noticed it the moment she pulled that blindfold free, only to see it compounded by his little parlor act at the crime scene.

She had to wonder if it had something to do with the scars on his wrists, and was beginning to think that the file Section had given her had been heavily redacted.

He was damaged goods, no doubt about it, and she couldn't help thinking that whatever that damage was, it was somehow related to what he'd seen in that storeroom.

If LaLaurie was convinced Gabriela's death wasn't an isolated incident, then Callahan needed to know why. And as much as she wanted to smack him around until he finally broke down and told her, she decided to let him play this out.

It wasn't like she had anything better to do.

They were greeted at Gabriela's front door by Rosa, who frowned the moment she saw Callahan. "Mr. Ruiz is not available."

"We just want another look around," Callahan said.

Rosa shot a wary glance at LaLaurie; then she reluctantly let them in. Callahan ushered him into the living room, surprised by the way his face lit up at the sight Gabriela's collection.

"My God," he said, crossing to the cases full of artifacts, his gaze immediately drawn to something of interest. "Look at this. Do you know what this is?"

Callahan didn't really know what any of it was, but she was momentarily caught up in his enthusiasm and joined him at the glass. He gestured to a small greenish cross that looked as if it had been carved from stone, a crude figure of Jesus with outstretched arms adorning it.

"A bronze pendant," he said. "Seventh century, Roman Byzantine period. Soldiers used to wear these to battle. It must've cost her a small fortune."

"She had a big one, so I'm sure it wasn't a problem."

LaLaurie moved on to the next item as if he were the proverbial kid in the candy shop. "And this," he said, pointing at what looked like a tiny oval picture frame. "An antique silver reliquary with a Saint Leonard relic. This has to be over six hundred years old."

He went on this way for a few more minutes, pointing out each artifact and explaining what it was. Reliquaries, engravings, rare manuscripts, altar cards.

He certainly seemed to know his stuff.

As she listened, Callahan spotted a new item inside one of the cases: the stone figurine of an angel fighting a dragon. The one she'd taken from the box on Gabriela's bed yesterday. Rosa must have found it there and decided to put it on display.

She pointed it out to LaLaurie. "What about this? Any idea what it is? Besides the obvious, I mean."

LaLaurie nodded. "It looks about seventeenth century to me. It's from Revelation. Saint Michael fighting the dragon Satan in a war in heaven."

A sudden memory tumbled through Callahan's brain. *You're part of Michael's army.*

"Did you just say 'Michael'?"

"The patron saint of chivalry. Louis the Eleventh founded an order in his name. You've never heard of him?"

He sent you here to spy on us.

"I'm sure I must have, but I'm not big on religious icons."

"Well, the victim sure was. And maybe she wasn't such a Barbie doll after all." He gestured to the cases. "Nobody builds a collection like this unless they're very serious about their faith." He paused. "Or they're trying to protect themselves."

"Against what?"

He looked at Callahan. "Against exactly what happened to her."

He was about to turn away when Callahan grabbed his arm. "Professor, you've strung this out long enough. Do you have information pertinent to this investigation or don't you?"

"Where's her copy of *Paradise Lost*?"

Callahan sighed. "In a room off her bedroom."

Before she could say another word, he found the hallway and headed straight to Gabriela's bedroom without even the slightest hitch in his gait. Callahan followed, and by the time she stepped inside, he was already moving through the walk-in closet toward the hidden room in back.

When she caught up to him, she said, "How did you do that? How did you know where to go?"

"This room has an energy. I could feel its draw."

He stood just inside the doorway, taking in Gabriela's prayer room the same way he'd taken in the crime scene, and the look on his face wasn't easy to describe. Surprise. Awe. But also some uneasiness there.

He gestured to the painted blue symbol on the wall.

"You didn't tell me about this."

"You didn't give me a chance to. You know what it is?"

"It's a sigil."

"A what?"

"A sign, or a seal, with a very specific power and meaning. They're used in ceremonial magic. Even its color is significant."

"So what does it mean?"

LaLaurie found the copy of *Paradise Lost* where Callahan had left it atop the prayer desk. He leafed through it until he came to Gabriela's highlighted passages. He read for a moment, then looked up at Callahan.

"What it means," he said, "is that you were right about Gabriela having an obsession. First the figurine, then the painting, and now all these notations in Book Eleven. But the obsession wasn't limited to this book."

"Then what?"

"Not what. *Who*." He gestured to the wall. "That sigil represents the Archangel Michael. And blue is his color."

You're part of Michael's army. He sent you here to spy on us.

"And what about the notations in the book?"

"They're all in chapter eleven. Which is the part of the poem where Michael comes down from heaven to give Adam and Eve a message from God."

"Okay," Callahan said. "So we've established she had an obsession. What does that have to do with her death?"

"Pretty much everything."

"How so?"

He reached to the shelf beneath the prayer desk, pulled out the books that were stacked there and pointed to the first one. "*The Lesser Key of Solomon*. A seventeenth-century grimoire."

"Grim-what?"

"Grimoire. A textbook on magic." He showed her the next book. "*Forbidden Rites*. A manual on summoning spirits." And the next one. "*Angels, Incantations, and Revelation*. I think that's pretty self-explanatory." He looked at her. "Are you sensing a pattern yet?"

She thought about what Martinez had said. "You think she was practicing black magic?"

"Magic is just magic. It's the intent that makes it black or white, and there are varying shades in between."

"You almost sound as if you think it's real."

"Oh, it's very real."

Why did she know he'd say that? "I'm afraid you're looking at a bit of a skeptic, Professor, and I've already had my fill of superstitious nonsense for one case, so unless you have some concrete answers for me . . ."

"This is about as concrete as it gets. The way it looks to me is that Gabriela was trying to summon up an angel and it backfired on her."

Oh, brother. Should she even bother?

"Backfired?"

"She got the wrong angel," he said.

Callahan wanted to scream, but couldn't quite muster up the energy. She was just too tired to argue anymore.

The best thing to do, she decided, was to let this guy have his say, then put him on the next plane back to loonyville.

But she had to admit she was curious. "What do you mean by wrong angel? Aren't angels supposed to be good?"

"It's all about intent. Just like the magic."

She thought about Martinez's paranoia. "I always thought *demons* were the bad guys."

"They're the same thing," LaLaurie said. "The ancient Greeks thought of demons as benevolent spirits. Even Christians acknowledge they're nothing more than the so-called fallen angels. So what you'd call a demon is simply an angel who's made some bad choices."

"Why do I think my old catechism teacher would view this a little differently?"

"Most of what you hear in church was cobbled together by people who were long on faith but short on knowledge. And most religions are a jumble of ancient folklore, inconsistencies and convoluted logic."

"Yet here you stand, talking about angels and demons as if they're as common as wheat toast."

"Because this isn't about religion."

Callahan frowned. "I think you just lost me there."

"Religion is simply a by-product of people trying to explain the inexplicable. What I'm talking about here has nothing to do with any particular faith, and everything to do with reality. And angels are quite real. They just happen to occupy a different plane of existence than we do. Most of the time, at least." He paused. "The trouble starts when we try to invite them home for dinner."

"Okay," Callahan said. "For the sake of argument, let's pretend you aren't one sandwich short of a picnic."

"Thanks. I appreciate that."

"The bottom line is that you're saying Gabriela tried to summon up an angel and got more than she bargained for."

"Not just any angel."

"Then who?"

LaLaurie indicated the symbol on the wall. "I thought we already established that."

You're part of Michael's army.

"Saint Michael?"

He nodded. "But I have a feeling it wasn't Michael who answered her call."

"You said what happened to Gabriela wasn't an isolated incident. What did you mean by that?"

"Exactly what I said."

"And how do you know this?"

"Because I've seen it happen before."

LaLaurie was damaged, all right. Somewhere around the left temporal lobe.

Maybe that would explain why he was on indefinite leave from Trinity Baptist College.

Callahan had let this guy say what he had to say, and no words she uttered in response would express the depth of her disappointment. Or annoyance. Maybe *she* was the one who belonged in the loony bin for letting it get this far.

Time to wrap up this nonsense, put this guy on a plane back home and go to bed.

"Thank you for your insight, Professor. I just have one more question for you. One that might actually elicit a rational response."

"You don't want to hear the rest of it?"

"I'll leave that for you and your psychiatrist to sort out. But you do seem to have a lot of knowledge about Christian artifacts, so maybe you can tell me the significance of . . ."

She stopped herself as she looked at the wooden cross atop the prayer desk and noticed that the necklace was gone. "What the hell happened to it?"

LaLaurie was at a loss. "To what?"

"The Saint Christopher medal. It was hanging here yesterday."

The look on LaLaurie's face went from mild confusion to sudden surprise. "What kind of Saint Christopher medal?"

"What do you mean, what kind?"

"What did it look like? Did it have anything on the back?"

Callahan nodded. "Some initials and an etching of a beetle."

LaLaurie stiffened. "You're sure about that?"

"Why? Does that mean something?"

"It could change everything."

"How?"

"I need to see it. Right now."

"I just told you, somebody took it."

"And you don't have any idea who?"

As a matter of fact, she did. She doubted Alejandro had the emotional energy to do much of anything at this point, so that left the housekeeper. Rosa.

Turning, Callahan moved back through the bedroom and down the hall, LaLaurie at her heels. She called out Rosa's name, and a moment later, the woman appeared in the kitchen doorway, a quizzical look on her face.

Callahan said, "Gabriela had a Saint Christopher medal in her prayer room. Did you take it?"

"Yes, Senhorita. In preparation for the funeral."

"For the funeral?"

"Yes. She told me if anything ever happened to her, she wanted it buried with her."

"Did she say why?"

"I think it was very important to her. Very personal."

No kidding. Callahan told the housekeeper to bring it to them and Rosa disappeared down another hall, returning a few minutes later with the necklace in hand.

"You won't keep it, will you?"

"We just want to look at it for now," Callahan said. "But I can't make any promises at this point."

Rosa handed her the necklace and Callahan passed it on to LaLaurie.

He nearly froze in place as he took it, staring at it intently. Then he turned it in his fingers, looking at the etching on the back, his hands trembling, his face going through a dozen different changes before settling on complete and utter astonishment.

"CSP," he said quietly. "I was wrong about Gabriela. This is about much more than a summoning gone haywire."

"You know what those initials stand for?"

LaLaurie's face was pale again, but there was an odd excitement in his expression, as if he'd stumbled across a cache of hidden jewels.

"She was *Custodes Sacri*," he said softly. "That's the only explanation. No one else would have this. No one. Not even a collector. And that's why she was trying to summon Michael. She probably spoke to him on a regular basis."

"What the hell is *Custodes Sacri*?"

He turned the disk in his fingers again, gaping at it, then looked up at her.

"I think it's time for another drink," he said. "Something a lot stronger than orange juice."

19

"Have you ever heard of Archbishop Jacobus de Voragine? Or the Golden Legend?"

Callahan had decided to let this play out a little longer, mostly because LaLaurie had been so bowled over by the discovery of the medallion that she couldn't help getting caught up in his passion.

Maybe she'd been too quick to judge this guy. LaLaurie's belief in otherwordly phenomena didn't make him any different from half the world's population, so what could it hurt to practice a little patience, buy him a drink and see what else he had to say? There might be something amidst all the nuttiness that she could actually use.

She took him to her hotel bar. LaLaurie had ordered Tullamore Dew, and Callahan had settled for a glass of the house pinot.

"I've heard of the Golden Rule," she said. "Do unto others and all that?"

"This is different. The Golden Legend is a collection of stories compiled by the archbishop in the thirteenth century. Stories about the greater saints of the Catholic Church."

"Like Saint Michael."

He took a sip of his drink. "He was one of them, yeah.

But the one we're concerned with right now is Saint Christopher. Do you know his story?"

"I know he's the patron saint of travel, but that's about the extent of it."

"According to de Voragine, Christopher was a Canaanite warrior who wandered the countryside in search of a great king to serve. But when he finally found one, he quickly discovered that the king lived in fear of the Devil—which, to Christopher's mind, meant that Satan must be a greater king." He paused, took another sip. "So Christopher threw in with Satan, only to find that despite all of his power, the rebel angel was deathly afraid of someone called Christ."

"So let me guess," Callahan said. "He became a Christian."

"Right. And to serve Christ, he spent his days down at the river, helping people cross against a dangerous current."

Someone near their table laughed, and LaLaurie shot him a look, annoyed by the interruption. He waited a moment, then continued.

"Then one day, a boy walked up to Christopher and asked for his help to cross the river. So Christopher hoisted him up on his shoulders and gave him a ride. But despite his size, the boy was heavy. Christopher nearly lost his footing and barely managed to hang on. Once they were safely across, the boy kissed his forehead and thanked him. Then he said, 'I am the king you serve.'"

"Jesus?"

LaLaurie nodded. He had been holding Gabriela's Saint Christopher medal in his hands as he spoke. Now he held it out, pointing to the etching of the man carrying a child on his back.

"And that's why Christopher was named a saint."

"Okay," Callahan said. "But what does this have to do with Gabriela's death, or her being—what was it?"

"*Custodes Sacri Peregrinatoris*. Guardians of the Sacred Traveler."

Callahan balked. "Seriously?"

"I'm afraid so."

"Sounds like a crappy eighties' kid show."

"Far from it," LaLaurie said. "And by most accounts, they've never existed. You'd be hard-pressed to find anything about them in the usual literature. But there are one or two fringe accounts out there. You just have to know where to look."

"So who are these guardians?"

"A group of men and women who are said to have been chosen by the Archangel Michael to help those who want to make the journey from sinner to servant, just as Christopher did."

"Are they all Catholics?"

LaLaurie shook his head. "*Custodes Sacri* transcends religious ideology. They come from all walks of life. All cultures, all faiths. But each of the chosen has made the journey as well—Gabriela being a prime example. From drug addict to Christian superstar in a few short years."

He flipped the medallion over, pointing to the beetle etched into its back.

"This scarab symbolizes the promise of resurrection for all human beings. A symbol you won't find on any other Saint Christopher medal. In fact, if you ask most religious scholars, they'll tell you these don't even exist."

"So how do you know this isn't some kind of mock-up? A forgery?"

"The same way I knew how to find Gabriela's secret room. I can feel its energy."

Patience, Bernadette. Patience. She sipped her wine, half wishing she'd ordered a Tullamore herself. "So what do these chosen people get out of this?"

"The honor of serving God."

"That's it? No special seat in heaven?"

"That's not really the point," he said. He looked at the medallion in his hands. "Gabriela wouldn't have this unless she was one of the chosen. And it's only fitting that she had such an intense interest in *Paradise Lost*."

"Why?"

"Because John Milton himself was rumored to be a member of *Custodes Sacri*."

This was news to Callahan, but then her knowledge of Milton could barely fill a thimble. "Why Gabriela of all people?"

"Probably because she was so good at getting God's message out with her music. Just like Milton did through his poetry. But there are those who think that the guardians are much more than messengers."

"Meaning what?"

"That they're also protectors. Like Saint Christopher. Chosen to protect something or some*one* specific. That the sacred traveler is not just an idea, but a person or an object of some kind."

Callahan felt a sudden stutter of excitement. "*Defende eam . . .* Protect her."

"Exactly. It didn't make sense when you first told me, but now that we know what Gabriela was part of, it's obvious her last words were meant for her fellow guardians—or maybe even Saint Michael himself." He gestured to Callahan. "Do you have that copy of *Paradise Lost*?"

Callahan grabbed her backpack from under the table, pulled out the dog-eared book and handed it to LaLaurie. He flipped through the pages until he reached the eleventh chapter, then pointed to Gabriela's notations and highlighted passages.

"This isn't just random doodling," he said. "She was trying to crack a code."

"That's what I thought. But why?"

"I'm not sure, but I have a guess. Milton was known to be an admirer of Francis Bacon, and some historians think he may have subscribed to the Baconian theory."

"Which is?"

"Bacon often referred to himself as 'the secret poet' and there's a whole group of literary detectives out there who believe he was the true author of all of William Shakespeare's work. They claim Shakespeare was too uneducated to have written it himself."

"And what the hell does Shakespeare have to do with cracking a code?"

"The Baconians are convinced that if you carefully analyze his poetry, you'll find clear instances of cryptology— Bacon secretly signing his work so that the world would know who he really was. By extension, there are Milton followers who believe the poet may have done the same, in homage to Bacon. Only with a difference."

"Meaning?"

LaLaurie tapped the book with a finger. "In the opening stanzas Milton claims his words were divinely inspired. Most of us agree that what he wrote was a thinly disguised allegory, an indictment of the tyranny of his times. But some of those fringe accounts I told you about claim that the true meaning of *Paradise Lost* is hidden *within* its poetry. A secret message or prophecy from God that relates to who or whatever *Custodes Sacri* is trying to protect."

"So what *is* this prophecy?"

"That's the million-dollar question, isn't it? But I can tell you I've been through this book backwards and forward, and I haven't been able to find any kind of code at all. Neither has anyone else, as far as I know."

"So then it's bullshit."

LaLaurie shrugged. "I'm sure that's what the people who write for any of the Milton periodicals will tell you— assuming they've even heard the rumor in the first place. But Gabriela obviously didn't think so. And she was *Custodes Sacri*."

"But then wouldn't she already *know* the prophecy?"

"Another good question. Maybe the guardians' knowledge is limited only to what they *need* to know. And maybe she didn't like that. Curiosity can get you into all kinds of trouble."

Need to know. That was a concept Callahan was intimately familiar with.

She glanced at the scars on LaLaurie's wrists. "Why do I get the feeling you speak from experience?"

"Like I told you, I've seen this kind of thing before."

"Oh, I haven't forgotten. I've just been sitting here practicing my Zen."

"Does your mantra include the phrase 'Kill LaLaurie'?"

She smiled. "Maybe you really are psychic. But I'm

the one who blew you off when you tried to tell me about this at Gabriela's penthouse."

"Look, I don't blame you. You're a skeptic. I probably would be, too, if I were in your shoes. But I come from a long line of people who were acutely aware that there's a lot more going on out there than most of us want to acknowledge. And what I witnessed, firsthand, only confirms that."

She lifted her brows. "So do I have to keep chanting, or are you going to tell me about it?"

LaLaurie took a moment to gather himself, as if what he was about to say didn't come easily to him. He was dredging up a memory that he'd just as soon leave buried for a couple lifetimes.

He drained his glass and signaled to the bartender for another.

"What I saw was nearly identical to what happened to Gabriela. There was never any indication that *Custodes Sacri* was in the picture, but the body was in the exact same condition, and the exact same symbol was burned into the mattress beneath it."

Despite her doubts about good and bad angels and psychic energy and all other forms of supernatural hogwash, Callahan felt herself getting excited again.

Was this the breakthrough she'd been hoping for? Was it possible that whoever had killed Gabriela had killed before?

"Do you have any idea what that symbol signifies?"

"Hubris, vanity, arrogance—take your pick. Whoever left it has a very high opinion of himself."

"And you're sure the symbol on that mattress was the same?"

"I have eyes, Agent Callahan. I'm not mistaken."

Her heart was thumping. "When and where did you see it?"

"About two years ago," LaLaurie said. "In my own house." He paused, a somber look on his face. "On the night my wife, Rebecca, burned to death."

20

Batty had never told the story before. He had played it on his interior movie screen enough times to make him permanently nauseous, but he'd never said it out loud. Had never given voice to the horror.

"We were living in Ithaca at the time. My book on Milton had been published to good notices a couple years before, and I'd accepted an associate professorship at Cornell while I slogged through the next book."

"That's a long way from Trinity Baptist College."

No doubt about that, he thought. A lot had changed in the last two years.

"A return to Louisiana wasn't even on the radar then. We'd settled into a fairly routine life and Rebecca was feeling a little restless. She had her degrees in philosophy and religious studies but she wasn't working, and as ashamed as I am to admit it, I was too busy to pay much attention to her."

He often beat himself up for not realizing this at the time. Maybe if he hadn't neglected Rebecca, she'd still be alive today.

"Sounds like a pretty typical marriage to me," Callahan said. "How did you two meet?"

"In a dream."

It took a moment for the answer to compute, then her eyebrows went up. "And how exactly does that work?"

"Sometimes I dream things. See people."

"And your wife was one of those people?"

He nodded. "I was a graduate student at Princeton then. In the dream I saw Rebecca standing on the steps of Nassau Hall and was a little shocked when she turned and stared right back at me. Said my name. I found out later that she was psychic, too."

Callahan looked confused. "I don't follow."

"We were sharing the same dream."

Batty remembered that dream with great clarity, and the sudden stab of excitement he'd felt when he later saw Rebecca standing on those very steps and realized that she recognized him.

Dream sharing wasn't uncommon between sensitives, but it usually took a coordinated effort to make it work, and this one had been spontaneous and exhilarating. It didn't hurt that the girl he'd shared it with was breathtakingly beautiful.

Callahan said nothing, but Batty knew she was adding another item to her growing list of absurdities.

The waiter finally brought him his drink and he took a sip before continuing. "Anyway, back to Ithaca. Rebecca and I had settled in and she was feeling restless, but she'd always had this vast curiosity—another trait we shared—and she turned it toward the occult and angelology."

"Angelology? That's a new one."

"Not really. People have been studying angels for centuries."

"Is this where all your good angel/bad angel stuff comes from?"

Batty nodded. "There are as many theories about angelic spirits as there are tires in a junkyard, but Rebecca never did anything half-assed, and when she dove into it, what she discovered was that these so-called beings of light are really no different than their dark brethren."

"How so?"

"They're all fallen angels. Cast out of heaven by their creator."

"Even Gabriela's favorite?"

He nodded again. "Michael, Raphael, Uriel—all of them. At one time they were right down there in the fire alongside Beelzebub, Mammon and Moloch. The only difference is that Michael and the others decided to ignore Satan's call to arms and go their own way. Decided to honor their creator rather than fight against him. So a myth was born, promoting them to Archangels. The same myth that's sold to schoolkids every Sunday. But the truth is, they're not much different than us. Just struggling to do what's right."

Callahan took a healthy sip of her wine, then sighed. "I think my brain is about to implode."

"Imagine how I feel. Rebecca became more and more obsessed with this stuff and told me she'd started hearing voices in her head."

Callahan stiffened slightly. "That's exactly what Gabriela's boyfriend told me. But he claims a lot of people hear voices when they pray."

"A lot of sensitives hear them, too. So I didn't really give it much thought until she came to me one night and said she was afraid she might be in danger. She'd been experimenting with conjurations and was worried she may have summoned up a malevolent angel."

"Or maybe attracted some psychopath who *thought* he was one."

"You go ahead and hang on to that, if it makes you feel better. But I was there, and I'm here to tell you that this was no human stalker. There was a presence in our house. Something watching us."

He remembered waking up next to Rebecca and feeling that presence right there in the darkness of their bedroom, the faint smell of sulfur in the air. But oddly enough, the malevolence didn't seem to be directed at him. Only at Rebecca. And as he watched her sleep, he knew something had to be done.

"So we dove headfirst into the literature," he told Callahan, "looking for an incantation to rid the house of any dark spirits. But we were working with the original Latin text and we were both a little rusty at that point."

"So you got it wrong," she said.

He nodded. "*I* got it wrong, and Rebecca paid the price."

He was quiet a moment, mentally reliving that night. The dark angel plaguing Rebecca had become more aggressive in the last several hours, rendering her confused and nearly incoherent, begging for the thing to leave her alone.

He told Callahan this. Then he said, "I can't imagine it was much different for Gabriela."

Callahan didn't respond, but it was evident by her expression that he'd struck a chord.

"It must have been two in the morning by this time. I kept trying the incantation, even tried the standard

Catholic exorcism rights, but this thing had grabbed hold of her and wasn't about to let go until she gave in."

"Gave in?"

"That's how they operate. They can't make you do anything you don't want to. So they work on you from the inside—tempt you, seduce you, play mind games with you, throw hallucinations at you, scare the ever-loving crap out of you . . . It's like they're waterboarding your brain until you finally succumb. And the weaker you are, the faster you fall."

Batty had known that Rebecca was about to crack and had been desperate to stop it. What she was experiencing wasn't the same as a dream, but he tried to share it with her, to get inside her head, and when he finally did, he'd heard his *own* voice shouting at her, telling her how much he despised her—that he wanted her to die.

The room around him began to shake then, the windows rattling, the bed rolling, and before Batty could duck, a drawer shot out from the dresser, slamming into his head, knocking him cold.

"When I came to," he told Callahan, "the room was back to normal. Looked as if it had never been touched, except for her body on the bed, and that symbol burned into the mattress beneath her."

He closed his eyes, trying now to push the image from his mind, tortured by the knowledge that Rebecca's last moments had been filled with words of hatred, spoken in his voice. Had she known it was only a trick? He could only hope so.

He grabbed the glass in front of him and drained it. "I don't know why *I* was spared, but I was." He laughed softly. Mirthlessly. "If you can call this being spared."

"I assume there was an investigation?"

"Not much of one. I knew my story sounded crazy, so I called the police and told them I had just come home and found her like that, knowing full well that they'd consider me a murder suspect. But without a motive or even a workable theory about how she got that way, they never bothered charging me. They got a look at the books she was reading, then chalked it up to a freak accident and called it a day."

"Section had to know about this," Callahan murmured. "So why didn't they tell me?"

"Section?"

"Never mind," she said. "But you've gotta know I'm clinging to the lifeboat right now—one with the letters WTF stamped on the side."

"Like I said, I don't blame you. And you may think I'm certifiable, but I know what I saw. Put a goddamn straitjacket on me, lock me up in Chabert Memorial, and my story won't change."

He considered ordering another drink, but decided against it. For the first time in recent memory, he didn't want one. As if finally telling his story had somehow purged him of the need.

He watched Callahan drain her own glass and could see that she was struggling with all of this. Should she take that leap and believe him? Or simply fall back on what she knew, like the cops in Ithaca had?

But Batty wasn't done yet. "With Gabriela, we've got a whole new wrinkle in the fabric. She was *Custodes Sacri*, and if this angel came after her, he's bound to go after the other guardians, too, hoping to get whatever secret they hold. So they're all in danger."

"How many are there?"

"I'm not sure. I only know of one."

"Who?"

"An antiquities dealer named Koray Ozan. But until today, I thought his involvement was just a rumor."

"What changed your mind?"

"I get his quarterly catalogues and I recognized some of the pieces from his collection in Gabriela's apartment. I don't think that's a coincidence. As far as I'm concerned, it pretty much confirms he's *Custodes Sacri*. Which means he's a marked man."

"So where do we find this guy?"

"Istanbul."

Her eyes widened slightly and she nodded. "There was a box from the Garanti Auction House in Istanbul in Gabriela's bedroom yesterday. The figurine I asked you about was inside—Michael fighting the dragon."

"That figurine might have been a warning to her. That trouble was coming."

"These people don't have e-mail?"

Batty shrugged. "I'm not sure how they communicate. Or even if they do. The important thing is, we need to get a message to him before it's too—"

Callahan's cell phone cut him off. She reached for her backpack and fished it out, putting it to her ear. "Callahan."

She turned away from Batty and listened a moment, then murmured something into the mouthpiece before clicking off. When she turned to face him again, the color had drained from her cheeks.

"That was Section. I've been ordered to cut my losses here and pull up stakes immediately."

"Why?"

"They're sending me to Istanbul." She looked at him now as if she was finally starting to think that maybe, just maybe, there was some truth to everything Batty had told her. "Koray Ozan is dead."

BOOK V

The Sun Also Shines on the Wicked

So spake the false Arch-Angel, and infus'd
Bad influence into th' unwarie brest
Of his Associate

—*Paradise Lost*, 1667 ed., V:694–96

21

AMSTERDAM, THE NETHERLANDS

Dimitri Kovalenko did not like Amsterdam.

The city was always crowded, people pushing their way from here to there, always in a hurry, but never in *enough* of a hurry to suit Dimitri.

The worst of it was the Rosse Buurt. The red-light district. By day, the area was quite beautiful, with its cobbled streets and its centuries-old architecture. By night, however, those streets were so packed with human debris, looking for a private strip show or a cheap fuck, that Dimitri was quick to lose all patience with the place.

But Dimitri worked in the service industry. And sometimes that service required him to travel to cities he detested—which, when he thought about it, was probably any city but his own. He had been born and raised and still lived in Balta, a twenty-thousand-strong Russian Orthodox paradise in the Odesa province of southwestern Ukraine.

He had a wife and two children who missed him terribly when he went away on these business trips, which was far more often than he liked.

As he had packed for this latest excursion, Yalena had asked him, with some irritation in her voice, how much longer he would be doing this. Their son, Olek, was be-

ginning to act up both in school and at home, and Yalena
didn't feel she could handle him on her own anymore.

"He needs his father," she'd said. "He needs to know
you still love him."

The words had surprised Dimitri. How could Olek
not know that his father loved him? Was he not out here,
working hard to provide for him? Did the boy think he
enjoyed all of this travel?

"This is the last time," he'd told Yalena. "I will make
enough money on this trip to keep us fat and happy for
the rest of our lives."

"You've said that before, Dimitri. And every time you
do, it scares me, because I know what kind of people you
associate with."

Kovalenko had said nothing then. He did not speak
about business with her, but Yalena was not a stupid
woman. And she had seen enough of those associates to
justify her fear.

But he hadn't been lying to her. If things went well tonight, they would have more money than he'd ever thought
possible. And all of it would be theirs. Because the people he worked for did not know about this particular
transaction. They did not even know that he had left the
country.

Before coming to the Rosse Buurt, Dimitri had rented
a hotel room nearby and left the suitcase under the bed.
He was not foolish enough to bring it with him. He had
no idea if the German could be trusted, and until he saw
the money, until he was holding it in his hands, he would
not turn over the merchandise.

And should things go wrong and he wound up dead,
they would never know where to find that suitcase. An

outcome the German would, undoubtedly, consider unacceptable.

Dimitri made his way down Damstraat, weaving through the crowd of degenerates, keeping his gaze ahead, not wanting to look into the red-trimmed windows that lined the street. The half-naked women on display would be a temptation for him, and he had only succumbed to that temptation twice before. Although Yalena was a pedestrian lover, whose skills were limited, she was a good mother and a fine wife, and he had no desire to betray her again.

It didn't help that the meeting place was a brothel. He found it with little trouble, near the middle of the block, and took a flight of bright red stairs up to an equally bright red door.

He knocked. Waited. And a moment later it opened a crack and a tall, bored-looking brunette peeked out, a Black Devil cigarette dangling between her lips.

She blew smoke out of the side of her mouth and said something in Dutch that he didn't understand.

"I'm here to see Vogler," he said in Russian, gesturing for her to open up.

Nodding, the woman swung the door wide to reveal that she wore only a tiny pair of pink panties, and Dimitri couldn't keep himself from staring. She gestured him past her, and he stepped into a darkened room that could only be described as a bar or, more accurately, a social club. It was the same as any social club in Balta, men huddled at tables, nursing vodka or scotch. But in this place, each of those men had a half-naked woman hanging on to him.

Kovalenko forced himself to think of Yalena, which may or may not have been a wise thing to do. Slinging his backpack over his shoulder, he followed his hostess to another set of steps at the back of the room, where she gestured him upstairs.

"*Bedankt*," he said, the only Dutch word he knew, thinking he'd like very much to thank her more properly.

She blew smoke at him, as bored as ever, then turned and walked away.

Dimitri moved up the steps and found himself in a long hallway full of doors. These, he knew, were the courtesy rooms, and because none of them had been soundproofed, it was readily apparent what those courtesies were. He remembered a place very similar to this one, when he himself had occupied one of these rooms. To his amazement, he had discovered that the moans and groans around him had only heightened his pleasure.

But Dimitri drove such thoughts from his mind. He had business to attend to. At the end of the hall, there was yet another small set of steps leading to yet another door, and he made his way to it and knocked.

A moment later, the door was opened by a large, blond mercenary type wearing a shoulder harness, the grip of a nine millimeter protruding from its holster. Dimitri recognized him as one of the German's men.

The mercenary gave him the once-over, then gestured him inside. And the moment Dimitri crossed the threshold, a sense of unease washed over him and he wondered if he had been foolish in coming here.

Wouldn't it have been wiser to pick a more public meeting place?

The room was dimly lit, dominated by a large wooden desk. Behind that desk sat a dark silhouette that, for a brief moment, did not seem quite human to Dimitri. He felt his gut tighten at the sight of it and had the sudden urge to flee.

Then a lamp went on and he breathed a sigh of relief as Meinhard Vogler looked up at him and smiled. "Please, Mr. Kovalenko, have a seat."

Dimitri did as he was told, pulling his backpack into his lap. He had met Vogler only once before and could not help being intimidated by him.

A former member of East Germany's Office for National Security, Vogler had left service just months before the wall came down, only to reemerge several years later as the head of L4, a massive worldwide private security firm that had its fingerprints on nearly every military skirmish within recent memory.

Only a few years ago, L4 had been one of the big three private firms working for the U.S. government to help quell unrest in Central Asia. But bad publicity and a new president now limited their involvement to the periphery, and Dimitri—through his contacts in the Russian mafia—knew that they were looking for ways to recoup their losses. And because they no longer had any allegiance to a particular nation, they didn't seem to care how they accomplished this. Assuming they ever had.

It had occurred to Dimitri that what he was offering them might one day fall into the hands of someone quite dangerous (as if these people weren't dangerous enough), but he banished such thoughts to the part of his brain where the naked woman and the chorus of moans and groans now resided.

The less he thought about such things, the better off he'd be, and he had no desire to jeopardize this transaction with a sudden attack of conscience.

"So," Vogler said to him in Russian, "you've brought us the sample?"

It was only then that Dimitri realized that someone was standing in the shadows behind the German. A tall man in an impeccably pressed suit whose face was obscured by darkness.

A shudder ran through Dimitri. Why hadn't he noticed him before?

His surprise must have shown in his eyes, because Vogler smiled. "I must apologize. I neglected to inform you that there would be someone joining us tonight."

"Why do I think that wasn't a mistake?"

Vogler's smile faded. "Believe what you must. In any case, I'd like you to meet my associate, Mr. Radek. He'll be attending to the financial end of our arrangement."

The man in the shadows stepped forward then, and Dimitri's surprise deepened.

He had seen Radek before. Not in the flesh, but on CNN International, which he and Yalena watched with some regularity.

Raymond Radek was an American investment banker and former chairman of NASDAQ, who had only recently been cleared of all charges of investor fraud that had been leveled against him by the U.S. Department of Justice. A relatively young man, he was nevertheless a Wall Street icon who had risen to power quickly and, some said, ruthlessly. The U.S. Attorney's failure to bring him to trial—thanks to the recanting of testimony by several witnesses—had been a triumph for Radek. One that was trumpeted worldwide. And though his stature in the halls of finance had been diminished by these accusations and the severe downturn in the world economy of late, he was still a force to be reckoned with.

But nothing Dimitri had seen or heard had ever connected Radek with Vogler and L4, and his presence here seemed odd, to say the least. Dimitri wondered if he should be asking for more money.

Radek said nothing to him. Merely nodded.

Dimitri returned the nod and Vogler said, "Now that we all know one another, shall we take a look at that sample?"

Kovalenko stared at the two men, wondering again if he'd made a mistake in coming here.

But then it didn't much matter at this point, did it?

Unzipping a pocket of his backpack, he reached inside and handed a small metal cylinder across to Vogler, who then gestured to the blond mercenary and passed it off to him.

They all sat in silence as the mercenary went to a corner of the room and fiddled with the cylinder. He came back a few minutes later and nodded to Vogler.

Vogler looked across at Dimitri, and it could have been a trick of the light, but Dimitri was again struck by the notion that there was something not quite human about the man. Something in his eyes.

"I have to say I'm impressed, Mr. Kovalenko. How much of the merchandise did you bring with you tonight?"

"Fifty pounds. Just as promised."

Vogler's eyebrows raised. "A man of your word. Even more impressive."

He gestured to Radek and the businessman bent

down, hefting a small suitcase onto the desk. Laying it flat, he spun it in Dimitri's direction and opened it, showing him the two million euros in various denominations stacked neatly inside.

Dimitri felt something shake loose in his brain, as if a flood of opiates had suddenly been released and were slowly spreading throughout his body.

What an extraordinary sight.

And just as he was thinking what he and Yalena could do with so much money, Radek closed the suitcase, hiding the bills from view.

"I assume you have something for us?" Vogler said.

Dimitri nodded, then reached into his pocket and brought out his room key. "Hotel Hemel," he said, then tossed it to Vogler.

Vogler, in turn, handed it to the blond mercenary and the large man exited the room.

The hotel was less than a five-minute walk from the Rosse Buurt, and they didn't have to wait long before the phone on Vogler's desk rang.

Vogler picked it up, said something in German, then listened. A moment later, he hung up and smiled at Kovalenko.

"I continue to be impressed, Dimitri. I can't imagine a more promising start to our new relationship."

"Start? I only agreed to the one transaction."

Vogler gestured to the suitcase atop his desk. "I think once you've seen what's inside, you'll reconsider."

Dimitri frowned. "I've already seen what's inside."

"I don't think so," Vogler said. "Look again."

Kovalenko hesitated. What kind of nonsense was this? Leaning forward, he grabbed hold of the suitcase lid and lifted it. And to his astonishment there was nothing inside but a small framed photograph.

How could this be?

Were his eyes playing tricks on him?

It was then that he realized the photograph was one that normally occupied a spot on his night table beside his bed: Yalena, Olek, and his sixteen-year-old daughter, Kateryna, smiling happily for the camera.

Looking up sharply, Dimitri found both Vogler and Radek staring at him now, and their gazes were not close to being friendly.

"You have a beautiful family, Mr. Kovalenko. And I know many people who would pay dearly for such beauty. Your wife looks as if she might be a bit conservative in the bedroom, but I'm certain she could be properly trained."

Anger shooting through him, Dimitri jumped to his feet. But the moment he did, Radek's hands were on his shoulders, pushing him back into the chair. "Sit down, Dimitri."

How the man had managed to get behind him was a mystery, but there was power in those hands, and Dimitri did not doubt for a moment that Radek could snap his collarbone with very little effort.

"We have friends all over the world," Vogler said. "Men who will put the contraband you provide to very good use. All we ask is that you continue to work with us, and you'll soon have riches beyond anything you've ever imagined."

Dimitri was trembling all over. He knew what these men were capable of and he was certain they would follow through on their threat. He looked at the photograph and felt tears threatening to flood his eyes.

"Well?" Vogler asked. "Can we count on you to co-operate?"

"Yes," he said softly. "Yes, of course."

Vogler smiled again. "Excellent. I think it only fitting that we seal our agreement with a kiss."

And the moment Vogler said this, Dimitri realized that the hands on his shoulders were no longer Radek's. Radek, to his surprise, was again standing behind the desk next to Vogler.

The hands that remained moved up to Dimitri's chin and tilted his head back; then the tall, bored brunette in the pink panties leaned down and rolled her tongue into his mouth, her breath smelling faintly of tobacco.

"This is Klara," Vogler told him. "She has agreed to entertain you tonight."

Dimitri didn't know how or when she had entered the room, but he felt powerless, unable to resist her.

And as she took hold of his hand and led him to the door, he went along willingly, all thoughts of Yalena and his promises to her vacating his mind.

"We look forward to working with you," Vogler said.

But Dimitri barely heard him.

When Kovalenko and the girl were gone, the one who called himself Radek shook a Black Devil cigarette from the pack atop the desk and lit it, exhaling a plume of smoke.

"Nasty little thing," he murmured.

The one who called himself Vogler leaned back in his chair. "The Russian or the cigarette?"

Radek smiled and shook his head.

"Our secret interloper," he said, then turned his attention to a darkened corner of the room. "I know you're there. You may as well show yourself."

The darkness shifted, and as expected, the intruder emerged from the shadows looking radiant as always, her nearly translucent skin glowing in the lamplight. She looked even more beautiful than she had in Istanbul the other night. Had Radek not known what lay beneath the surface, he may have found her attractive.

She mirrored his smile. "Gentlemen. I thought I'd stop in and see how you're progressing."

"Perfectly fine without you," he told her. "As always."

"What's wrong, my darling? Are you upset with me? You two left that tea shop in such a hurry, I had to wonder if I somehow hurt your feelings."

Vogler scoffed. "Don't flatter yourself. We weren't interested in watching you seduce your little plaything."

She shook her head in amusement and sank into the chair in front of his desk.

"But isn't that what it's all about?" she asked. "Isn't that what you've done with this Russian and so many others?" She leaned forward and shook out a Black Devil for herself. "Taking a new skin and dressing up like a wannabe soldier doesn't change that fact. It all comes down to getting these insects to do exactly what we want them to do."

"A means to an end," Vogler said with a wave of the hand. "I'm afraid neither of us takes the pleasure from it that you seem to."

She lit the cigarette. "It's true. I do take pleasure in it.

Great pleasure. Turning them is half the fun. Then all we have to do is crank out a tune and watch the little monkeys dance."

"But the dance itself is all that matters," Radek told her. "Getting them to do what we need them to do. And our methods should always be simple and direct. There's no point in calling attention to ourselves. Something you obviously haven't yet learned."

"Meaning what?"

"The girl in Brazil. You put on quite a show there."

She shrugged. "I wanted information; she gave it to me."

"And you went about it in the most spectacular way imaginable, when what you should have done was approach her through the boyfriend. Worked through him to get that information."

"You two act as if we have all the time in the world," she said. "The fourth moon is only days away and there won't be another lunar tetrad for decades. I did what had to be done."

"And what has it gotten you? While we're busy making real progress, you're wasting your time chasing a myth."

She sighed. "Must we have this argument again?"

"If I think it's one worth having, yes."

"This is my party, remember? You both agreed to let me run with it."

"Not if it means seeing us fail," Radek told her. "You know me better than that."

"Indeed I do, Radek." She rose from her chair and moved around the desk toward him, stopping only inches away. "And you're starting to sound as if you consider me some kind of threat. Let's get it out in the open. I'm done sneaking around, pretending we're something we aren't." She took a drag off the cigarette, blew smoke in his face. "Am I a threat to you, my darling Mammon? Are you scared of little old Belial?"

Vogler spoke sharply, "Not here, not now. We can't know who's listening."

Belial turned to him, "And what of it, *Moloch*? Are you afraid the vermin will hear your real name? Do you think they look into your beady little eyes and don't realize what you truly are—even if in their coward hearts they can't admit the truth to themselves? Don't make me call our brother out west to back me up. You know how he feels."

Vogler didn't flinch. "Don't think for a moment you can intimidate me, Belial. And Beel doesn't scare me, either. Not anymore. Not since he became distracted trying to reach these creatures by manipulating their so-called *culture*. When all is said and done, we'll have our chance to settle our differences, and I don't think you'll be too happy with—"

A sharp knock cut him off.

"*Komm' rein*," he barked.

The door flew open and Vogler's assistant—Heinrich—stepped inside, hefting the black nylon suitcase he had retrieved from Dimitri Kovalenko's hotel room. Setting it next to the one on the desk, he unzipped it and threw it open.

They all stared at its contents: five lead cylinders containing fifty pounds of highly enriched U-235 weapons-grade uranium.

The one who called himself Radek eyed it appreciatively. "You see, my dear, *this* is how it's done. This is the kind of dance that can be useful to us. No myths, no fantasies. Just good old-fashioned human ingenuity—with *us* pulling the strings."

He looked at Belial, a self-satisfied grin spreading across his face.

"Welcome to the end of the world."

22

LOS ANGELES, CALIFORNIA

He spent his days watching the girl. Jenna.

He'd found a spot across from the shelter, a stretch of curb between two parked cars that he'd staked a claim on. To anyone observing, he was just another homeless waste-of-space waiting for the shelter to serve its evening meal.

In a way, that was true. He *was* homeless. He'd been thrown out of the only home he'd ever known a long, long time ago and had found himself feeling unsettled and lost, searching for a reason for his father's betrayal.

But his father had never been big on explanations.

Only consequences.

The shelter was a small, squat building in the center of the block that looked as if it had once been a store of some kind. Record shop. Used books. Auto parts. Pizza stand. Pawn shop.

Maybe all of the above.

It didn't matter. It was now doing double duty as a bunkhouse and a soup kitchen, with enough room for about ten beds—cots and blankets, really—that were folded up each afternoon to make space for a dozen or more tables and chairs.

He watched Jenna through the front window. Saw her with the woman from the coffee shop, who had apparently asked her and several of the other girls to help out in exchange for guaranteed bed space. They worked with her in the kitchen and carried trays full of food to a long, narrow table in the back of the room, then stacked paper plates and cups and plastic sporks and knives on one end.

At six in the evening, the doors opened and anyone who was hungry was invited inside for a meal.

Deserting his curb, he shuffled across the street and fell in line. He could hear Jenna's song, louder and more vibrant than ever, and any thoughts that he may have been wrong about her immediately vacated his mind.

She stood with three other girls behind the counter, scooping baked beans with a large serving spoon. She eyed him warily as he approached her and held out his plate, and he knew it must have been an effort not to look away. The skin he'd procured was young, but badly damaged by booze and cigarettes and drugs and couldn't have been easy to look at.

It served its function, but he knew it wouldn't last much longer.

"Thank you," he said softly, and offered her a smile, feeling the song of her soul wrap itself around him as he mentally counted the days until the fourth moon.

Everything would change for her then.

Everything.

And the world would never be the same.

He was sitting at a table, eating his dinner, when the pretty boy walked past the front window and glanced inside.

Zack the drudge.

The punk was merely trolling—just as he had been the

other night—but there was a noticeable hitch in his step as he caught sight of Jenna, then moved on.

He'd be back. No question about it. He'd wait for the woman who ran the place to disappear into her office, or go to the coffee shop for an Americano. Then he'd swoop in again and give Jenna another try. Pull out all the stops this time to put the lie to the woman's warnings and charm Jenna into coming home with him.

Could he hear her song, too?

No. Drudges weren't attuned to such things. But maybe someone had sent him here. He seemed just the type that Belial was drawn to, the kind of perfect specimen she took such pleasure in corrupting, so his presence here could well be her doing.

And that wasn't good.

Whatever the reason, Zack was an annoyance who needed to be stopped before he got his hands on Jenna again. Something that should have been done two nights ago, right outside that coffee shop.

Better late than never.

It took him a while to find the guy.

As darkness approached, he heard laughter and turned in to an alley off Western, just three blocks south of the shelter. He saw the pretty boy huddled near a cluster of trash cans with another young girl, lighting up a meth pipe. This girl was even younger than Jenna, maybe thirteen or so, with a premature hardness and enough open sores on her face to tell him she'd been on the streets for quite some time.

What a waste.

But he didn't hesitate. Walked right up to her, spun her away from Zack and the pipe and nudged her toward the mouth of the alley.

"Go home," he said. Wherever home was these days.

She didn't have to be told twice, and a moment later she was gone.

Apparently Zack didn't appreciate the intrusion. He paused midtoke and exhaled a plume of rancid smoke. "Who the *fuck* are you?"

"You don't know?"

"Am I supposed to, asshole? You just cost me a sweet fuckin' blow job."

"You really shouldn't have told me that."

He shot a hand forward, grabbing a fistful of Zack's shirt, then shoved him upward against the alley wall until his feet were dangling.

The pipe went flying and Zack struggled, kicking and waving his arms desperately, and you could tell by the look on his face, the sheer panic in his pretty-boy eyes, that he suddenly knew exactly what he was up against. "Holy shit, you're *him*, aren't you? The one they're always talking about."

"Who's your significant?"

Zack said nothing, struggling like an insect pinned to a bulletin board.

"Is it Belial? Did she send you here? Tell you to go after the girl at the shelter?"

Zack kept struggling. "I don't know what you're talking about. Let me go!"

He pressed harder, his knuckles digging into Zack's chest. "Answer the question, you little shit. *Is Belial your significant?*"

"Yes"—the punk huffed, wincing in pain now—"yes, yes."

"And the girl at the shelter?"

"Just another runaway. I found her on my own. I saw her the other night and decided to make a move."

"And Belial didn't send you?"

"No. She doesn't know anything about her."

"Good," he said, then released his grip.

Zack dropped to the alley floor with a grunt, grabbing at his chest, coughing and choking, trembling like a frightened dog. A puddle of urine spread out beneath his feet. "Please . . . ," he said. "Please let me go . . ."

"You know I can't do that."

Reaching under his jacket, he grabbed his knife. It was an old iron Roman folding knife he'd kept with him for many years, still in pristine condition. There was a time he would have carried a broadsword as well, but such things were a bit conspicuous these days.

As the knife came into view, Zack cried, "I can work for you! I'll do whatever you want. Belial doesn't need to know. I can be your spy!"

An interesting proposition, but the last thing he needed was a drudge of his own. Especially one who was so quick to betray his significant. He was about to dust the sonofabitch when he heard a shriek behind him and knew that he'd been careless—too quick to assess and dismiss.

The girl with the sores on her face was also a drudge.

And she'd brought reinforcements.

As her shriek reverberated against the alley walls, she shot forward and leapt onto his back, a switchblade snicking open in her hand. She brought it down hard, burying it in his neck, and he stumbled sideways, feeling the fierce white heat scorch through him.

Swinging around, he jerked an elbow back, smashing the girl's nose, knocking her to the ground. She shrieked again and he spun and kicked, giving it everything he had, nearly taking her head off at the shoulders. Her feral eyes suddenly went blank as her neck snapped back and she slammed against the wall—

—bursting into a cloud of black dust.

Then the others moved toward him, three more street kids—two boys and another girl. Much older and even more dangerous than the shrieker.

He tried not to make the same mistake with them. Tried not to humanize them, to think about how they'd once been innocent children. He tried to forget that they had parents who missed them, who waited by the phone or watched the door every night, hoping to see them walk through it. He kept reminding himself that they were no longer children but savage, empty vessels whose only purpose was to help their significant harvest more souls.

And kill anyone who tried to stop them.

As they circled around him, he yanked the switchblade from his neck, blood pumping from the wound, spurting across the alley wall, then running down the front of his jacket. With a knife in each hand now, he widened his stance and waited for their soulless gazes to connect—that silent signal that the attack was on.

Then it came and they all moved in unison, approaching him from three different directions. The girl and one of the boys had knives of their own and the second boy carried a length of two-by-four, three sharp nails protruding from one end.

The weapon came at him fast and hard, swung like baseball bat, but he deflected it with his right forearm, feeling the sting of one of the nails. Stepping forward, he arced his arm and scraped the Roman across the kid's chest, opening a deep, bloody gash. The kid's eyes went wide and he stumbled back, grabbing at the wound—but it was too late. The blow was fatal and the kid knew it.

A split second later he was dust.

One down, but the other two were still in motion, the girl coming up on his left side, thrusting her knife at him. It was a good six inches long and it sank deep, just under his rib cage, its heat radiating painfully through his body.

Without hesitating, he swung his left arm out, slashing her forehead with the switchblade, then brought a leg up and kicked, the sole of his boot slamming into her chest, knocking her to the ground. Then he turned his attention to her boyfriend, who came at him in a headlong charge.

The kid was making it too easy.

He simply sidestepped and swung the Roman, its blade slicing through the kid's neck with surprisingly little resistance. The kid's head tumbled to the ground and burst into a cloud of dust, followed shortly by his body.

But it wasn't over yet.

The girl was on her feet again, and despite the curtain of blood running down her face, she wasn't about to give up. He could see that she was ready to make another charge, and he didn't feel like wasting any more time on her.

Dropping the switchblade, he reached behind his back, freed his Glock 20 from his waistband, then swung his arm around and fired, putting two bullets in her chest.

She blew backward onto the asphalt, her mouth open-ing and closing like a grounded carp; then the inevitable happened and all that was left of her was a pile of black dust.

When he turned his attention again to Zack, he wasn't surprised to find that the punk had fled, leaving behind a smelly puddle of urine.

But there wasn't much he could do about it now.

He was hurt. Badly. And it wouldn't be long before this body gave out on him for good.

Clamping a hand to his bloody neck, he pulled the knife from his side, tossed it to the ground, then made his way toward the mouth of the alley, knowing he'd have to temporarily forgo his surveillance of Jenna.

Not something he wanted to do, but he had no choice.

It was time to find a new skin.

23

The one who called himself Jonathan Beel hadn't felt like doing the interview, but the moment he saw the reporter, he changed his mind.

She was quite fetching.

It was obvious that she had dressed up for the occasion, and he had no desire to disappoint her by politely feigning indifference to her appearance. He supposed he could uncross his legs and let her have an unvarnished view of her effect on him, but he decided that this might be pushing it. He didn't want to frighten her away.

Instead, he merely offered her his appreciative gaze, and she drank it up like a milk-starved kitten.

"So for the one or two readers out there who haven't yet seen the show," she said, "why don't you explain what *Saints and Sinners* is all about?"

They were seated in directors' chairs just to the right of the soundstage. He'd given her a tour of the new house they'd constructed, and she'd seemed suitably impressed by it. The truth was, this was first time Beel had seen it himself. He didn't normally spend much time on the set. He had an empire to oversee, and this was only a very small part of it.

"It's simple," he told her. "We put twenty people in a house and force them to live together. Ten of them lead what most of us would consider virtuous lives, and the other ten have run into a bit of trouble, so to speak. Saints versus sinners. After eight weeks of various challenges to their hearts and minds, whoever is left standing is awarded a million dollars."

"Well, it's obviously a winning formula."

Beel nodded. "Six weeks at number one. The network has already renewed us for another season, which is why we built this new set. We're casting now."

"Great news. But what do you say to those who claim that the show is fixed?"

"In what way?"

"The saints never seem to win any of the challenges. Only the sinners."

Beel laughed, waving off the accusation. "Isn't that the way the world usually works?"

The air outside the soundstage was chilly. As he walked the reporter to the parking lot, Beel pulled off his leather jacket and threw it over her shoulders. It was a shame to cover that smooth brown skin, but chivalry was a rarity in Hollywood and was sure to win him a few points.

He wanted to seduce her the old-fashioned way.

The interview had gone quite well. After she was done with her questions, the reporter had smiled and given him a look that said she was clearly interested. He knew that he could tempt her with a walk-on in one of his episodics (he was currently producing twelve shows for various networks), or maybe an on-air reporting audition for one of his cable news channels—but that would be cheating. Beel had no desire to use any tricks with this one. He considered her a challenge, and he had a feeling his efforts would not go unrewarded.

"Do you always wear your sunglasses at night?" she asked.

Her lips were full, but not altered by collagen or implants like so many of the women out here. He could imagine himself biting into the lower one, hearing her cry out in pain as he drew blood.

Then he'd move on to her nipples.

He had put on his sunglasses because he knew that his eyes gave him an unfair advantage with her. Inside the studio, she had so loved the feeling of his gaze as it washed over her that he had decided to give himself another handicap.

"Always," he said, in answer to her question, but didn't offer any further explanation.

"It just seems so . . . pretentious, I guess. And I like it better when I can see your eyes."

Of course she did.

Beel smiled. "If you could see my eyes right now, I'm afraid it might embarrass you."

Ten points for that one.

They reached the parking lot and she moved to the slot he had reserved for her, where a worn ten-year-old Miata waited. He had expected her to be driving something a little more upscale, but then he remembered that she was a newspaper reporter.

She definitely carried her poverty well.

Stopping at the driver's door, she opened her purse and dug around for her keys. When she found them, she turned, and Beel made sure to be standing close. Not close enough to make her uncomfortable, but enough to make his intentions clear.

She didn't shy away. In fact, she surprised him. "Do you feel like having a drink?"

"I'd love to."

"I have an apartment off Cahuenga, just over the hill. I might even have some vodka."

"Excellent. Lead the way."

She smiled now and leaned into him, brushing her fingers against his jeans. "And when we're finished with our nightcap, maybe I can do something about this little devil you've been trying to hide from me all night."

"Not so little," he said.

Her smile broadened, and she leaned up to kiss him. "I certainly hope you're telling me the—"

She stiffened suddenly and her whole body began to shake. Her eyes rolled back in their sockets until only the whites were showing.

Beel was momentarily startled, but then he sighed.

Shit.

He stepped back as the reporter continued to shimmy and shake in what, to the uninitiated, might look like some kind of medical emergency.

But Beel knew better.

Reaching into a pocket, he pulled out a pack of smokes and lit one up, waiting patiently for the moment to pass. Then, with the whites of her eyes still showing, the reporter stopped shaking and perched herself on the hood of her car.

"We've had an interesting development," she said.

Belial. Always one for the dramatic entrance.

"It had better be, my dear. I don't appreciate this interruption."

She stared at his jeans with her blank eyes. "That's obvious. You seem to be adjusting to this skin you've acquired. You look even better than you did in Istanbul."

He waved a hand at her. "Get to the point."

She nodded. Paused. "I have word from one of my drudges that someone we both know and love made a bit of a fuss today."

"Who?"

"My dear brother. And he took a few of my darlings in the process."

"Really," Beel said drily. "And I should care why?"

"Because the fuss was over a fifteen-year-old girl. He seemed very concerned about her." She paused. "Too concerned."

Beel took a drag off the cigarette. This *was* interesting. "Who is this girl?"

"All I have is a first name. And my drudge tells me she's quite a looker. Unfortunately, I haven't yet had a chance to get up close and personal myself. I've been a bit busy."

"This could be nothing. Your brother's interest in the creature could be purely predatory."

"Come on, Beelzebub"—she always used his given name—"you know him almost better than I do. He made up his mind about these things a long time ago, and I doubt he'll ever change it."

Beel shook his head. "He's no more a saint than the rest of us. This fable these moronic creatures have built around him is pathetic."

"True, but he's just arrogant enough to believe it, and I'm told he came out of nowhere today, so I can only assume he's been watching this girl. And that speaks volumes."

"We've been through this before," Beel said.

"But what if he's right this time? What if this girl really is the Telum?"

Beel wanted more than anything to believe it, but he wasn't so sure. Belial's brother had always played his cards very close to the vest, and there was no telling what he was up to. And as much as Beel would like it to, none of this meant that their former colleague had actually found what they'd all sought for so long. He could merely be trying to distract them, in anticipation of the coming moon.

Besides, identifying the Telum was only half the battle. They needed to find the key to releasing it, as well. And wasn't that the whole point of going after *Custodes Sacri*?

"Beelzebub?"

Beel shook himself from his reverie and looked at her. "Moloch and Mammon tell me you visited them in Amsterdam. That must have been pleasant."

She shrugged. "Mammon's the same as ever. He's predicting a massive collapse on Wall Street, and Moloch's still playing soldier, working tirelessly to get their weapons and drudges in place."

"But will it be enough?" Beel asked. "The eclipse is only days away."

"All the more reason to pursue this girl."

"And what about *Custodes Sacri*? If she really is the Telum, we need that key to seal the deal. Or *un*seal it, in this case."

"Unfortunately, I've hit a bit of a dead end. The one the Brazilian told me about has gone into hiding."

"Then *find* him," Beel barked. "You wanted the lead on this, so get me some fucking results."

She stiffened. "This isn't just about you, Beelzebub. We all have a stake in this race."

Beel knew she was right, and he didn't like letting his temper get away from him. But they had come so close so many times before, only to see their hard work undone by some foolish mistake or some petty dispute.

He thought about all the infighting, the backbiting, the conniving, the fractured alliances, the wars . . .

And where had any of it gotten them?

"Apologies, my dear. I've just been waiting so long for this, I sometimes wonder if we'll ever see it done."

"We will," she said. "I promise. But while I'm busy hunting down *Custodes Sacri*, I need you to keep an eye on my brother and the girl. I've already instructed Zack to make contact again and wait for our orders."

"I do so hope you're right about her."

Belial stepped toward him now, pressing herself up against him.

"Don't fret, Beelzebub. If all goes well, the Master will rise again, and bring the full wrath of Abyssus along with him." She kissed his cheek, lingering there for a moment. "*A posse ad esse.*"

Then she was gone.

BOOK VI

Traveling with
the Mr. and Mrs.

On they move
Indissolubly firm; nor obvious Hill
Nor streit'ning Vale, nor Wood, nor Stream
   devides
Thir perfect ranks

—*Paradise Lost*, 1667 ed., VI:68–71

24

ISTANBUL, TURKEY

Batty and Rebecca had come to Istanbul early in their marriage, when their interest in ancient history and biblical lore was in its prime. They had decided against the usual tours and had instead wandered the city on foot, soaking in its atmosphere—the sights, the sounds, the smells, the people.

Once hailed as the New Rome, Istanbul was a city of hills with a vast and varied narrative. Straddling both the European and Asian continents, it had been the center of the Roman, Latin and Byzantine Empires, and had seen the fall of Constantine Palaeologos during a fierce battle against the Ottomans.

A descendant of Constantine the Great—the first Christian Roman emperor—Palaeologos was said to have been rescued on the battlefield by an angel and was awaiting resurrection to this very day.

Batty wasn't holding his breath.

Like its culture, Istanbul was a mix of old and new, traditional and modern. Ancient mosques and synagogues and cathedrals adorned traffic-choked streets full of towering high-rises. Although its government was secular, the place breathed Old World spirituality, a feeling that was helped considerably by the call for prayer that blasted over loudspeakers at regular intervals throughout the day.

As he walked from the hotel toward Taksim Square, Batty remembered Rebecca's joy in immersing herself in the local culture. She had always embraced life with the unfettered enthusiasm of a child, and it was difficult to walk these streets without missing her.

Traveling with Callahan was a different story altogether.

"So here's the drill," she'd said to him as they boarded the plane in São Paulo. "We're Mr. and Mrs. Franklin Broussard from Baton Rouge, taking our first trip to the Middle East."

"Why the subterfuge?" he'd asked.

"There's so much tension in that area right now that we don't have much of a choice. My people tell me that not only can we expect zero cooperation from the Istanbul police, the government of Turkey doesn't want us there at all. Fortunately, the country's still cleared for tourists."

Batty knew Callahan didn't want him here. She was obviously someone who was used to working alone. But whoever was pulling her strings had insisted he go with her, and it wasn't hard to deduce that she was unhappy about it.

"Let's get one thing straight," she'd told him as they settled into their seats. "You're part of this assignment for one reason only, Professor—gathering and providing information. You have a unique insight into this stuff and as certifiable as you might be, we'd be stupid not to take advantage of that."

"Why do I hear a 'but' in there somewhere?"

"I sat in that bar and listened to your story, and I'm truly sorry about what happened to your wife, but I live by the credo that seeing is believing, and until I actually see something to convince me otherwise, I'm continuing this case on the assumption that what we're dealing with here is a very clever, very sophisticated and very troubled serial killer."

"And if you're wrong?"

"I'll be the first to admit it."

After arriving at their hotel, Batty had watched as Callahan used a program on her cell phone to forge credentials for the Istanbul police department. In the photo she wore a scarf and looked very much like an Istanbul native. But then Istanbul was a mix of Turks, Kurds, Jews, Georgians, and just about everything in between, so that probably wasn't saying much. The ID was written in Turkish, but he doubted it had her name on it.

"So who's this?" he had asked, looking over her shoulder.

"The new forensics tech at the Istanbul Crime Lab. I want to get a look at the remains."

"And what will I be doing while you're having all this fun?"

"I already told you. Gathering and providing information."

"Oh? What do you have in mind?"

"You're going sightseeing," she had said.

So here Batty was, crossing through Taksim Square on the way to the Garanti Auction House, where Koray Ozan's body had been found the previous evening. His task was to determine the exact location of the crime scene, and because Callahan was unable to secure blueprints of the building, she'd told him to check for entry points and potential security threats, then report back to her.

"What do you plan to do? Break in to the place?"

"I need access to that crime scene. And unless you've managed to get clearance from the local police, I don't see any other way."

"Seems pretty risky to me. The building's bound to be wired up tight."

"Let me worry about that part," she said. "Your job is to observe only. Don't get anxious and start sticking your nose in where it doesn't belong. You get yourself arrested, you're on your own."

The auction house was located a block north of the square and Batty didn't need a street address to find it. There were still several *polis* cars parked out front, uniformed officers milling about.

The building was large, rectangular and starkly modern, with a broad set of steps leading up to the entrance. Above the sliding glass doors was a huge red banner, written in both Turkish and English, announcing a special black-tie charity auction set for eight P.M. that night.

House officials had closed the place immediately after the discovery of Ozan's body, but the *Hürriyet Daily News* had reported that the auction would go on as scheduled. The exhibition room had been reopened this morning in order to display the pieces that were to be sold that night.

As Batty stood on the sidewalk out front, he felt a touch of trepidation, which wasn't surprising considering what had happened inside. Overcome by a sudden reluctance to enter the building, he glanced around and noticed a tea shop on the opposite side of the street.

He crossed to it, found a table outside, and a moment later a waitress came out to take his order. "Yes?"

She was a petite, attractive woman in her early twenties. Her name tag read AJDA.

"Black tea," he told her. "Extra sweet."

She forced a smile, nodded, went back inside.

It was only then that Batty sensed something odd about the woman. He wasn't sure what had stirred this feeling. There was no hint of sulfur in the air, although it could have been masked by her perfume or the smells of the city. Maybe it was that forced smile she'd given him or the strangely hollow quality to her eyes.

Or maybe he was just too paranoid for his own good.

As he waited for his order, he sat back in his chair and tried to relax, staring out at the auction house, knowing that his task was really nothing more than an exercise in redundancy. He didn't need to see the crime scene to know exactly what had happened here.

All he had to do was close his eyes.

It took Callahan all of fifteen minutes to find Ozan's remains.

The hardest part had been getting past the security checkpoint in the police department lobby, thanks to an overeager newbie who'd had to consult three different supervisors before letting her through.

In the end, the freshly minted ID and Callahan's flawless Turkish had done the trick, and she took an elevator up to the forensics wing, where the antiquities dealer's body was being stored for examination.

It frustrated Callahan that she had to go to these

lengths just to get a look at the victim. Section had a contact inside the department, but he'd developed a case of nerves and had told them his ability to assist them would be severely limited. So Callahan was on her own and flying blind.

But then flying blind seemed to be her standard operating procedure these days. Section had tasked her to find out if these two deaths were truly related, but she still had no idea *why*.

Was it possible they believed there was a paranormal component to all of this? Was it possible that out of all the experts they could have paired her with, they'd offered up LaLaurie precisely because of his backstory? And could this be why they'd insisted he accompany her to Istanbul?

These questions had been plaguing her ever since he'd told her about his wife. And Section's failure to fully disclose what they knew about him concerned her. She'd seen them do a lot of questionable things in her time, but forgoing a deep background check was not one of them, and it annoyed her to think that they didn't trust her.

She could only imagine what they'd do if they knew about her sleep irregularities and that episode back in Paradise City. They'd no doubt pull her from the field and eliminate her.

Section wasn't known for its sentimentality.

She didn't suppose their trust in her would be bolstered by her decision to send LaLaurie into the wild. But Callahan felt it was justified. Except for the two whiskeys he'd had in the hotel bar, he seemed to have gotten a handle on his drinking—had *twice* turned down the opportunity to indulge on the plane—and since Callahan didn't have the help of any local operatives, she figured she might as well put him to work. He wasn't a pro, but a little reconnaissance mission shouldn't get him into too much trouble, as long as he stuck to protocol.

The elevator dropped her off on the fourth floor. A sign on the wall indicated that the forensics wing was to her left down a bustling hallway, and she located the autopsy room without much effort.

It was small and busy, five exam tables laid out in a way that made the most economical use of the space allotted, while giving each of the lab techs room to move. Three of them were working right now, cutting into flesh, weighing organs, preparing slides for further examination as they dictated into microphones mounted above each of their tables.

Callahan found a rack of lab coats near the door and slipped one on, clipping her ID badge to the pocket. She went from table to table, nodding hello to the techs, carefully checking the bodies as she progressed. But none of them were Ozan.

There was a window to her right, a room full of lab equipment beyond it. She crossed to the door, stepped inside, and her gaze went immediately to a nearby counter, where the charred remains of a body lay atop a white towel.

Bingo.

Section had been right to be concerned. If these remains were any indication, the case *did* look as if it were related to the São Paulo death. The body was in almost exactly the same state as Gabriela Zuada's.

Callahan wouldn't know for sure until she got a look at the actual crime scene, but she doubted this was a coincidence.

There was a camera mounted on a stand next to the towel. One of the remains—a blackened femur—had been laid out on a rectangular platform, waiting to be photographed. Next to this was a computer terminal, showing a photo array, various parts of the body already catalogued and added to the police file.

Callahan reached into a pocket and brought out an SD memory card. Slipping it into a slot in the computer, she initiated a download and waited as the file's contents ticked off, photo by photo, document by document.

It was about halfway finished when a voice behind her said in Turkish, "Who are you? What are you doing in here?"

Callahan turned with a start and saw a mousy-looking guy in a lab coat glowering at her.

As Batty sipped his tea, he couldn't shake the feeling that something about the waitress wasn't quite right, and he knew he was starting to obsess.

Being sober definitely had its downside.

He had no doubt that hundreds, even thousands, of waitresses in this city would stir up the exact same feeling—along with cabdrivers, cops, doctors, construction workers, secretaries and everything in between. But that didn't make it any easier for him.

They were out there in force. Always had been. A battalion of compromised souls, willing to do whatever they were told in the name of their keeper. Yet despite his uneasiness, he knew that obsessing over it wouldn't do him a lick of good.

Knowing that this waitress was only a stone's throw

from the auction house, however, led him to believe that she might be involved in a little gathering and providing of her own. And if that was true, she could well be directly connected to whatever dark entity had attacked and killed Ozan. And Gabriela Zuada.

And Rebecca.

Finishing up his tea, he set the glass on its saucer, then rose and dropped a few coins on the table.

Enough stalling. Time to do what he came here for.

Crossing the street, he moved past the *polis* cars and milling cops and headed up the steps to the auction house entrance. The glass doors slid open as he approached, and the moment he stepped inside he felt it—

—The lingering residue of death.

There was a reception desk out front, a smartly dressed but somber-looking woman sitting behind it, undoubtedly still feeling the sting of their loss.

To her right was the exhibition room, the glass cases along its walls holding various antiques, artifacts and ancient statuary. Oil paintings hung above them in ornate frames—Baroque, Byzantine, High Renaissance. Heavenly landscapes full of winged cherubs stood in stark contrast to the more violent works, including one that depicted the beheading of Holofernes by the widow Judith.

The sight of her sword cutting into his neck made Batty shudder.

To his left was a set of open double doors, leading to the auction room itself, where several rows of chairs faced a podium and display table. Farther left was an elevator, a uniformed security guard standing next to it, and beyond him was a carpeted stairwell that led into the bowels of the building, another guard blocking passage to it.

Batty glanced at the directory on the wall between them. Also written in Turkish and English, it indicated that the building's offices and archives were located down those stairs.

According to Callahan's intelligence brief, this was where Ozan's body had been discovered, in a seldom-used archive room. But Batty didn't need a sign to tell him this. He could feel it rolling up toward him from that stairwell, a relentless, screaming brutality that was difficult to ignore.

He doubted there were any windows or other modes of entry down there, and if these guards stayed in place throughout the night, there was no way Callahan would ever get past them.

One of them was looking at him now. Batty smiled, nodded to him, then crossed to the exhibition room and pretended to browse, surreptitiously scanning the rest of the lobby.

Restrooms and pay phones directly across from the stairs. Fire extinguishers and pull alarms strategically placed along the walls. A tinted glass window next to a door marked GÜVENLIK—SECURITY.

He was contemplating the futility of his task when the elevator doors slid open and several men stepped out: plainclothes cops, along with three crime-scene technicians carrying their gear in plastic toolboxes.

They all looked weary, which meant that they had worked through the night and most of the day. And if the evidence they'd gathered was as sparse as it had been in São Paulo, they had a baffling mystery to solve.

Batty shook his head morosely.

They had no idea what they were dealing with here.

And he couldn't help but envy them.

"I asked you a question," Lab Coat said. "What are you doing in here?"

Callahan feigned irritation, returning her attention to what was left of Ozan's body. "What does it look like I'm doing?" she said in Turkish. "I'm cataloguing the victim's remains."

"I thought Leila was handling that?"

She fiddled with the camera. "Leila had an errand to run and asked me to cover for her."

"But I just saw her going into the washroom."

Callahan looked up sharply. "So are you the one who's been stalking her?"

He jerked his head back. "What?"

"She told me somebody from the lab has been harassing her. She's on her way to personnel right now."

He looked aghast. "And you think it's me?"

Callahan shrugged. "I wouldn't know. I just started here—where are Ozan's personal effects?"

He blinked at her, confused by the sudden change of subject.

"His personal effects," she said impatiently. "Where are they?"

"I . . . I'm not sure," Lab Coat sputtered. "Already in storage, I suppose. It's not my case."

"Then why are you wasting my time?"

His mouth dropped open as if he were about to say something more, but then he closed it again, shaking his head in dismay as he walked away.

Callahan let out a breath. She had a feeling he'd be back soon.

Turning to the computer, she saw that her download

was done and quickly removed the memory chip, dropping it into her pocket.

Less than a minute later, she was headed down the hallway toward the elevators.

Batty stood outside the auction house, watching the *polis* drive away. He'd seen enough of the place to know what Callahan was up against, and despite her confidence, he doubted she'd be able to get past those guards without a major bit of subterfuge.

Fortunately, he'd found one—although getting her to buy into it might be difficult.

As he watched the last of the patrol cars disappear around a corner, an icy wind blew through him. Glancing toward the teahouse, he saw a silhouette in the doorway.

The waitress. Ajda.

There was no doubt in his mind about her now.

She was a drudge.

Possibly even a sycophant.

And he knew that before he left Istanbul, he'd have to have a very serious talk with her.

25

"We've got a bit of a problem," Callahan said.

She was sitting in an armchair playing with her cell phone when Batty returned to their hotel room, and he was starting to wonder if the thing was superglued to her hand. She'd told him about the condition of Ozan's body, which hadn't surprised him in the least.

"What kind of problem?"

"According to the police reports, our new victim's been dead for a while. He went missing four days ago and nobody thought to take a peek into that archive room until a janitor happened by and smelled something sour."

"Four days," Batty said. "That means he was killed *before* Gabriela."

This revelation stirred something at the periphery of Batty's mind. A thought that slipped away as quickly as it came, leaving him grasping but unable to retrieve it. Something about Ozan, and . . .

. . . and what?

"It also means we're headed in exactly the wrong direction," Callahan said. "And God knows who our perp will go after next."

"I think that's pretty obvious. Another guardian."

"Yeah, well, I'm not so sure this whole *Custodes Sacri* thing holds up."

"Why?"

"I didn't get a look at Ozan's personal effects," Callahan said. "They'd been bagged and sent to storage and the clerk there wouldn't allow access without one of the investigators signing off on it. So all I have is an itemized list from the file, which isn't much. But it's enough."

"For what?"

She tossed the cell phone to him. No superglue in evidence. He looked at the screen and saw a bunch of Turkish writing. It was a list, all right, but not one he could decipher. "You're assuming I can read this?"

She was surprised. "You mean to tell me I've just discovered something you *don't* know?"

He tossed the phone back to her. "Translation, please."

"Five items," she said, and ticked them off on her fingers. "A watch, a pen, a wallet and two rings, one gold, one silver—little more than lumps of melted metal."

"And your point is?"

"Where's Ozan's supersecret decoder badge?"

"I beg your pardon?"

"His Saint Christopher medal. If he was one of these so-called guardians, wouldn't he have one, too?"

"Missing doesn't mean nonexistent," Batty said. "He could have kept it somewhere else, like Gabriela did."

"Or your whole theory could be hogwash."

"Then how the hell did I know about Ozan in the first place?"

"That's a good question. How *did* you know?"

The thought Batty had had a moment ago flickered through his mind again, but continued to elude him.

"How do I know any of it?" he said. "I'm a fanatic. I've had a massive interest in this stuff ever since I was a kid. But after Rebecca was taken, I became obsessed with it—just like she was. Spent every spare moment of my time in libraries and private vaults."

"And you believe everything you read?"

"Of course not. But I found a reference to *Custodes Sacri* and the Saint Christopher medal in a footnote of a book about secret societies, and that led me to explore further."

"That still doesn't explain how you knew about him."

"I tried to locate one of the medallions. I put out some feelers and was contacted by a collector in Jerusalem who claimed he'd seen one. That an antiquities dealer had shown it to him but refused to sell it."

"Ozan."

Batty nodded. "The collector knew about the guardians and told me he was convinced that Ozan was one of them."

"And you never contacted him?"

"He wouldn't return my calls. After a while I gave up. It was only a peripheral interest anyway. It didn't really have anything to do with what happened to Rebecca."

"Yet here we are."

"Yet here we are," Batty said. "And if you want proof I know what I'm talking about, what about the crime-scene photos? I can guarantee you'll find that same mark beneath Ozan's body."

Callahan nodded. "I'm not a strong believer in coincidence, so I don't doubt it. But the photos aren't in the file yet. And if the symbol is there, all it tells us is that we're dealing with the same killer. All the rest is speculation."

"You're wrong," Batty told her. "And I'll prove it to you once we get into that crime scene."

"We?"

"We're a team now, remember?"

Callahan seemed amused by this. "In the loosest sense of the word, maybe."

"Trust me, without my help you'll have a hard time getting down to where the body was found. You try going in there in the dead of night and even if you get past the alarms, there's still the security staff to contend with. And they don't look friendly."

"I'm not exactly a novice, you know."

"I don't doubt that. But why do this the hard way when there's an easier alternative?"

Callahan leveled her gaze at him. "All right," she said. "For the sake of argument, let's pretend I'm listening."

Batty took two tickets from his pocket and held them up. "Mr. and Mrs. Franklin Broussard are scheduled to attend an auction at eight o'clock sharp tonight, compliments of the Children's Relief Foundation."

He could see that she was intrigued by the idea.

"Not bad," she said. "That gets us through the door without a fuss, but then what?"

"A simple distraction," Batty told her. "The simplest kind of all. But if we're gonna do this thing right, we'll have to go shopping first."

She raised her eyebrows. "Why?"

"The auction's black tie. And I need a tux."

Despite poring over the antiquities catalogues whenever he could, Batty was more of an *admirer* of art than a collector, so he'd never been to a real live auction before. And the closest he'd ever come to wearing a tuxedo was back at Terrebonne High, when Angela McGee turned down his invitation to the senior prom, thus sparing him the humiliation of dressing like a blue velvet penguin.

Whoever had invented the tuxedo, he decided, had definitely been a sadist. Probably the same guy who invented the bra and the corset. The tux he'd rented this afternoon felt half a size too small, and the tie Mrs. Broussard had so kindly agreed to strangle her husband with was cutting into his neck like a dog taking to a particularly juicy bone.

Batty was convinced that Callahan was a bit of a sadist, too.

She was also quite a looker tonight. The black strapless gown she'd chosen hugged all the right places in just the right ways, and he wouldn't be a man if he didn't take notice. She sat next to him in the middle of the Garanti auction room, and he was fairly certain that she was not suffering the indignity of wearing either a corset *or* a bra.

Considering the size of the building, the auction room was small and intimate, no more than three hundred people of various persuasions crammed into it, sitting on stiff-backed chairs, dressed in their finest, including enough jewelry to cover half the U.S. deficit.

This was one healthy crowd.

Callahan had expressed doubts about Mr. Broussard blending in—but Batty thought he'd cleaned up pretty well. He'd even allowed her to apply a little CoverGirl to his bruises—the same stuff she was using to doctor the circles under her eyes—and if you didn't look too hard, you might consider him handsome.

"I have one hundred thousand lira," the auctioneer said into a microphone.

On the table next to him was a vase with a missing piece that was several centuries old. A relic, they'd been told, of the late Ottoman Empire.

"Do I have one-twenty?"

A man two rows ahead of Batty gave a subtle flick of the fingers and the auctioneer nodded.

"One hundred twenty thousand lira from the gentleman in forty-seven J. The bid now stands at one hundred twenty thousand. Do I hear—"

"One seventy-five," a voice called out.

Although Batty had witnessed some spirited bidding in the last half hour, the crowd seemed subdued. The night's festivities had begun in the lobby with a short, emotional memorial to Koray Ozan, who, according to the auctioneer, would have wanted them to carry on.

So carry on they did, their enthusiasm tempered by grief. Ozan had been a popular and well-loved figure in the city, a reformed smuggler and black marketeer who had turned his life around and donated millions to charity. This only convinced Batty that the collector he'd spoken to had been right. Missing medallion or not, Ozan had been a perfect candidate for *Custodes Sacri*.

"One hundred seventy-five thousand lira," the auctioneer said. "The bid is now one hundred seventy-five thousand. Do we have two hundred?"

Callahan touched Batty's knee and in her best Louisiana accent—which wasn't half bad—said, "Excuse me, darling, but I need to go visit the little girls' room."

This was their signal.

She rose and slipped past him, and he watched her glide up the aisle, lost for a moment in the graceful fluidity of movement. He was seeing her in a whole new light tonight. She stopped briefly to ask one of the auction house ushers for directions to the restroom. Then a finger was pointed, pleasantries exchanged, and Callahan pushed through the doors and turned right.

As the doors closed again, Batty returned his attention to the bidding war. It was up to two hundred twenty-five thousand now, and it seemed the value of the vase in question was about to double before everyone's eyes.

He waited. Knew what was coming.

He'd shown Callahan a sketch indicating that she had three easily accessible choices ahead of her, one of which was conveniently located near the restrooms, and not in the immediate view of any of the guards.

It was a simple but effective distraction. One of Batty's favorites from his days back at Jefferson Junior High.

Less than a minute later, the building's fire alarm started to ring.

After tripping the alarm, Callahan had hustled into the ladies' room.

Now she emerged, looking appropriately frightened and harried, as the guards mobilized around her and began herding people out of the building, urging them to "remain calm."

With their attention on the crowd, it was easy enough for her to slip away and move toward the stairwell, although working in an evening gown was not something she was fond of. She'd kicked off her Dolce & Gabbanas in the ladies' room, figuring she'd be much better off without the five-inch heels.

A moment later, LaLaurie was beside her, and as they moved wordlessly together down the steps, she had to admit his call for simplicity had been a smart one.

Or maybe not.

Halfway down, they were confronted by a security guard hurrying up the stairwell toward them. He gestured for them to turn around. "No way out down here. Please exit through the—"

Callahan knocked him back, then pulled a travel canister of hair spray from her purse and sprayed his face. He crumpled to the steps, out cold.

"What the hell is that?" LaLaurie asked.

"Something our lab cooked up. He'll be out for a while."

They continued down the steps until they reached a dimly lit room, cluttered with antique furniture, pieces of art, paintings, books, and other collectibles, some sitting on oblong tables, others peeking out from open wooden crates that were lined up along the walls. The tables were littered with rags and bottles of solvent and toothbrushes and polish, and Callahan realized that this was the staging area, where items were carefully cleaned and buffed and readied for auction.

She and LaLaurie moved through the darkness until they reached a brightly lit hallway, dotted with office doors. Each door had a pebbled glass window that was clearly labeled with the occupant's name, including one at the far end marked KORAY OZAN.

Beyond this was a narrow stone archway that led to another stairwell. A sign above it read ARSIV. The archive rooms.

Callahan signaled for LaLaurie to follow her, and they moved down the steps into darkness. When they reached the bottom, she fumbled for a light switch and flipped it on.

The light was dim but serviceable, revealing another hallway—or tunnel, really—this one made of old mottled stone. It had a low rounded ceiling with light fixtures strung along it and looked like something out of a horror movie. It occurred to Callahan that the auction house had probably been built here after an older structure had been torn down, leaving this part intact.

"Smugglers' tunnel," LaLaurie said.

"What?"

"If I'm not mistaken, that's what this was. Ozan was once a black marketeer, so I'm not surprised he was drawn to this place. I'll bet there was a lot of traffic down here once upon a time."

There were three wooden doors ahead. One to the right and two to the left—marked BIR, IKI and ÜÇ. But none of them showed any signs of a recent police presence. No crime-scene tape in evidence.

Callahan and LaLaurie worked their way along the curve of the tunnel and came to a juncture, where it branched off in two different directions. Callahan mentally flipped a coin and was about to go to her left, when LaLaurie took her by the forearm.

He gestured to the right fork. "This way."

"You're sure?"

"Trust me."

A moment later, they were standing in front of another wooden door, an *X* of yellow police tape across it. Callahan didn't bother wondering how LaLaurie had known where to go. It wasn't worth the headache.

She stripped the tape off and threw the door open. Finding a switch on the wall, she flicked it on and an exposed bulb came to life overhead.

The room was small and square and held nothing more than what auctioneers called "box lot" items. Inexpensive china, glassware, paperback books, old magazines, all stuffed into open cardboard boxes and stacked against a wall.

And burned into the center of the stone floor was the now-familiar anarchy symbol.

"What did I tell you?" LaLaurie said.

"Did I disagree?"

The symbol was one thing, but what she hadn't expected to see were the words scrawled in black marker across a cardboard box at the bottom of one of the stacks, written in Turkish with a weak, shaky hand.

"Jesus," she said softly. "Maybe you were right after all."

She crossed to the box, hitched up her dress, and crouched next to it, running her fingers over the words: *Onu koru*. A message left behind by a man who knew he was about to die.

"What does it say?" LaLaurie asked.

She looked up at him. "Protect her."

26

"So you believe me now? That he was *Custodes Sacri*?"

"Considering what he wrote here, it's certainly a possibility."

"No kidding. And what about the rest of it?"

"The woo-woo stuff?" Callahan shook her head. "Don't get ahead of yourself, Professor. I'm still leaning toward some nutcase who thinks he's some kind of dark avenging angel."

"What if I could change your mind? Make you see it my way?"

"Isn't that what you've been trying to do ever since we met?"

LaLaurie moved to the center of the room and squatted next to the symbol on the floor. "Give your hand."

"What? Why?"

"Just do it."

Callahan hesitated, not sure what he was up to, but finally reached out and took his hand. "Don't get any ideas. I saw the way you were looking at me tonight."

He ignored the remark. "When I was young," he said, "before I fully came into my own, my mother would do this so that I could see what she saw. To prepare me for what was to come."

"Meaning what?"

"Let me show you."

He looked at the symbol, then paused a moment as if to brace himself. Then, lowering his free hand, he pressed his palm against the floor and closed his eyes.

Callahan sighed. "This again? If I wanted to see the Amazing Kresk—"

She flinched as heat radiated up through her arm and tunneled straight through to her brain—a simmering bolt of energy that came at her so fast and furiously she didn't have time to react.

Her nostrils filled with an almost overwhelming smell of sulfur, as the floor tilted sideways and she felt herself falling. She yelped and tried to reach out, but realized she had no hands, no body. She was merely a *presence* in free fall, tumbling into a deep, dark nowhere.

Then light assaulted her, blinding light, sweeping past her, *through* her, all around her, and she felt as if she were spinning out of control. In the middle of it all she saw Koray Ozan, blurry but unmistakable, tears streaming down his face as he begged some unseen entity for mercy.

Then she was *inside* Ozan's head, the hiss of a thousand voices skittering through her brain, speaking in a tongue she didn't understand, uttering what she sensed were hideous, vile things. All she knew for sure was that they were unwanted voices, invading Ozan's mind—*her* mind—like an army of angry locusts.

Then the room around her burst into flames and Ozan screamed.

Callahan cried out, too, ripping her hand away from LaLaurie's as she collapsed to the floor, the flames gone, the voices fading.

Shaking uncontrollably, she stared at LaLaurie in horror and confusion. "What the hell did you just do to me, you sonofabitch?"

But LaLaurie didn't answer. *Couldn't* answer. He had collapsed himself, looking as if all the blood had drained from his body, his eyes closed, his face deathly pale.

Was he alive?

Somewhere in the distance, beyond the stone walls of the tunnels and the muffled braying of the fire alarm—

—was the sound of approaching sirens.

We need to get out of here, Callahan thought. Right *now*.

Once the fire department got here and realized there was no fire readily apparent, they'd start searching the building, looking for whatever had tripped the alarm. And when they found that guard on the stairs . . .

Still trying to shake off the effects of LaLaurie's mind meld—or whatever the hell it was—Callahan checked to make sure he still had a pulse and shook him awake.

"Come on, Professor, we're about to have company."

He moaned and opened his eyes, barely able to speak. "Stronger than I expected . . . Did you see it? Did you see Ozan?"

"At this point it doesn't much matter *what* I saw. We need to get moving."

She helped him to his feet, threw an arm around him, and urged him through the doorway. LaLaurie could barely walk and had to lean into her for balance.

Working her way through the tunnel, she found the

steps to the next floor, but with LaLaurie in his current condition, getting to the top would be problematic. Callahan had always taken pride in her athletic ability, but LaLaurie weighed a ton. And from the feel of his body, much of that weight was pure muscle. No way they'd get up these stairs on her strength alone.

As if reading her mind—which might not have been all that much of a stretch—LaLaurie muttered something, then shifted around, gathering his strength and started up the steps.

They moved at the pace of a newborn snail, Callahan trying to figure out what the hell had happened back there. Ozan's tortured face filled her mind's eye and she shut it quickly, not wanting to relive his horror.

When they reached the top of the stairs, the alarm stopped and she heard muffled shouts above them.

The fire department was here.

Steering LaLaurie to the right, she crashed through a doorway into the nearest office, then sat him in a chair and closed and locked the door behind them.

The room was dark, except for the incandescent light that filtered in through the pebbled glass. She could see the outlines of a cluttered desk, an old CRT computer monitor sitting atop it.

A search of the building would likely start upstairs, but it wouldn't take them long to get down this way and the sight of the guard on the stairs would stir up a whole different kind of trouble.

LaLaurie looked at her. "This is Ozan's office, isn't it?"

"I think so, yeah."

He gestured to the computer on the desk. "Can you hack into that thing?"

"*Now?* Why?"

"I want to see his records. He sent that figurine of Michael to Gabriela, so he may have sent something to the other guardians, too. Maybe we can figure out who they all are."

"We don't really have time to be playing around with this."

"We'll never get a better chance."

Callahan didn't know how much good it would do them if they were sitting in a Turkish prison cell, but she took a seat behind the desk and tapped the keyboard, bringing the screen to life. To her relief, Ozan's computer wasn't password protected. No hacking necessary. She called up the file system, quickly clicked through the menus, and found Ozan's client database.

"No time for a thorough search," she said. "I'll just download the whole damn thing."

Taking a memory chip from her handbag, she stuck it into the computer, hit a key, and seconds later, the database was on disc. As she ejected the chip, she heard a shout down the hall.

They'd discovered the guard.

"You ever been to jail?" she said. "It isn't fun. Especially here."

LaLaurie got to his feet. "We need to hide."

"Maybe if we turn sideways, they won't notice us."

He gestured to a closet against the left wall. A narrow, rectangular wooden wardrobe. "In there," he said.

"Both of us? There's barely room enough for—"

"We don't have a choice." He crossed to it and threw it open. There were a couple thick coats inside, but at least it wasn't stuffed full.

Callahan heard running footsteps in the hall, urgent voices.

She eyed LaLaurie with reluctance, then switched off the computer monitor and joined him at the closet. It took them a moment to squeeze in, chest to chest, a smashing of body parts that turned two medium frames into one large one. But they managed to make it work and get the door closed.

Then a two-way radio squawked and someone jiggled the office doorknob, barking a command in Turkish. "Open it."

A key chain rattled, a lock was turned and the door flew open.

Callahan sucked in a deep breath as a flashlight beam swept through the office, passing the crack in the closet door like a lighthouse beacon, once again reminding her of LaLaurie's mind meld.

A switch was flipped and the overhead light went on.

Through the crack, Callahan saw three uniforms in the doorway. One fire, two security. One of the security men stepped inside and crossed to Ozan's desk, checking behind and under it.

With sudden horror, Callahan spotted something—

—Her purse. She'd left it next to the computer monitor.

How fucking careless could she be?

Her heart started thumping. So hard she was convinced it would burst a hole straight through LaLaurie's chest. And just as she was sure the guard was about to find the thing—it was right there in plain *view*, for God's sakes—someone in the hallway shouted, "Hakki! Come quick!"

The guard in the doorway turned. "What is it?"

"Someone's been in the archive room where Director Ozan was found. They took away the tape."

Hakki gestured to the other guard. "Come on."

The guard by the desk nodded and crossed the room, then shut off the light and closed and locked the door behind him.

Callahan let out a shaky breath. "That was pleasant."

"I thought your chest was gonna explode. Do you always get so worked up, or is it this little bear hug we've got going?"

"Just for the record, Professor, I know twenty different ways to kill a man with one hand. You want to try me?"

"I think I'll pass."

"Smart move."

She was about to push the wardrobe open, when LaLaurie held her back. "Wait a minute."

"Look, buster, you've already copped your feel, so if—"

"No," he said, "I'm getting something in here. A feeling. We aren't the only ones who've been in this wardrobe in the last few days."

"What are the odds? It *is* a closet, after all."

LaLaurie threw the doors open and gestured for her to get out. Callahan didn't hesitate. As she squeezed past him, however, he immediately turned, shoved the coats aside and began to inspect the wardrobe's back wall, running his hand along it.

"What are you doing?" she asked.

"Ozan was once a smuggler, remember? And old habits die hard. What do you bet he had more than one way into the tunnels, in case he had to disappear in a hurry?"

She gestured. "And you think this is it?"

"There's a definite energy here." His hand stopped moving. "And it looks like Gabriela wasn't the only one who had a thing for hidden doors."

Callahan heard a faint *snick*; then LaLaurie shifted slightly and pulled, sliding the entire back panel of the wardrobe to one side, revealing another set of steps.

"Well, I'll be damned," Callahan said.

The steps led to a part of the tunnel that had been sealed off from the rest of the archives—smaller and narrower, curving sharply to the left. After waiting for Callahan to retrieve her purse, Batty took the lead, moving along the curve until he came to an arched doorway that opened onto a brightly lit, cavelike chamber with a vaulted ceiling.

He stopped in his tracks, taken aback by what he saw. "This sure as hell isn't Narnia."

"Another book lover," Callahan murmured, but her words were inadequate, giving short shrift to what lay before them.

It was a small library, with ten or more rows of bookshelves, each filled with exquisitely bound books. And if Batty was correct, not one of them was less than two hundred years old.

Ozan was not merely a book lover, but a bibliophile—in the grandest, most traditional sense of the word.

Batty stepped forward cautiously, as if his mere presence here might do damage to these treasures. The sight of this room electrified him, and he was suddenly alive, the most alive he'd felt since he'd lost Rebecca. More alive than that night with the mysterious redhead.

And that was saying something.

Crossing to the nearest shelf, he moved down the first row of books, gently running his fingers along the spines, feeling their age, their gravity. He began removing and examining them, one after another.

Demonomanie des Sorciers by Jean Bodin. *A Compleat History of Magick, Sorcery and Witchcraft* by Richard Boulton. *Basilica Chymica* by Oswald Croll. *Disquisitionum magicarum* by Martino Delrio. *Manuale Exorcismorum* by Maximilianus ab Eynatten.

First editions all. Each one pristine. Priceless.

And this was only a small sampling of Ozan's collection. Batty had never seen so many volumes on the paranormal and the occult gathered in one place.

"Check this out," Callahan said.

He turned and found her standing next to a cluttered worktable at the center of the room. On one corner of the table sat a small stone figurine of a winged Saint Michael, his sword held high.

"I'm sensing a shared obsession," she said, then gestured to the mess on the table. "Looks like he was trying to decipher code. Just like Gabriela."

Batty joined her there and she pointed to a spiral notebook with several lines of verse written on it in English, some of the words and letters crossed out, others circled—

—all of them from the eleventh chapter of *Paradise Lost.*

Sitting open next to the notebook was another pristine first edition, nearly five centuries old.

Batty picked it up. "*Steganographia*," he said, carefully leafing through it. Its pages held lists of spirit names, tables full of numbers, zodiac signs, planetary symbols. "He must have been using this as his guide."

"What is it?"

"A three-volume treatise on conjuring up spirits to send secret messages."

"Come again?"

"It was written by a fifteenth-century abbot named Johannes Trithemius. Kind of a how-to book on communicating with your colleagues through the use of angelic messengers. But when his friends found out what he was working on, it caused such a commotion he decided not to publish it. He even destroyed the parts he thought were particularly incendiary."

"What kind of commotion?"

"He was accused of dealing in the black arts and consorting with demons."

"There seems to be a lot of that going around."

"But here's the thing," Batty told her. "It's not really a book of magic at all. The stuff about spirits is all coded writing, and Trithemius clearly says in the preface that it's just an exercise in cryptology and steganography. But nobody believed him, and his reputation as an occultist was sealed."

"And it looks like someone published it anyway."

"Nearly a hundred years after he died," Batty said. He closed the book and returned it to the table. "The first two volumes were deciphered almost immediately, pretty much proving that the incantations were exactly what Trithemius had said they were—harmless encryption exercises. But the key for the third volume wasn't cracked until the seventeenth century by a guy named Heidel, and he hid his solution in his own coded message. So it effectively wasn't deciphered until about a decade ago."

Callahan gestured to the notepad. "And you think Ozan was using the same encryption keys to hunt for secret messages in these verses?"

"That's the way it looks."

"But why? What does he know that you don't?"

Batty shrugged. "Milton was a controversial figure in his day, who got into a lot of trouble for speaking his mind. Maybe Ozan was working on the assumption that he used Trithemius's encryption methods to conceal his later work—although you'd think, if anything, the material in *Polygraphiae* is a better choice."

"*Polygraphiae?*"

"Another one of Trithemius's books. His true masterpiece on cryptology."

Callahan sighed. "My head's starting to hurt."

"Welcome to my world. Whatever the case, Ozan or Gabriela strike me as naive amateurs more than anything else, yet they both seemed convinced that there's something in Milton's poetry that the rest of us haven't . . ."

Batty paused, his gaze now drawn to the stone figurine of Saint Michael at the corner of the table. He studied it a moment, suddenly aware that there was something off about it.

It was a familiar-looking piece, one he recognized from the Garanti catalogue, but the depth and pattern of the chisel marks didn't look right, and he'd bet his last dollar that it wasn't an original. In fact, it wasn't even that great of a reproduction.

"What's wrong?" Callahan asked.

"Probably nothing. It just seems odd to me that someone with Ozan's taste would have such an obvious fake on his worktable. Especially in a room like this. And especially of Saint Michael."

Callahan shrugged. "Maybe he liked it."

Batty reached over, picked it up. "That's like finding a jazz purist who likes Kenny G. Besides, there's something about this thing . . ."

"Let me guess. You feel an energy."

Batty looked at her. "Mock me all you want, Mrs. Broussard, but unless I'm mistaken, you were feeling it pretty strong back in that archive room."

But she was wrong—this was more instinct than energy. Flipping the figurine over, he examined the base, which was rounded and about the same circumference as a soda can. Grabbing hold of it, he pressed and twisted until he felt it give; then the lower half of the base swung to one side, revealing a narrow, hidden compartment.

There was a key inside. Hollow shank. Antique.

He looked at Callahan. "You were saying?"

"Luck. Nothing more."

There was some truth to that, but Batty would never admit it. He removed the key, set the figurine back onto the tabletop and scanned the room, staring at the bookshelves. "It's obvious Ozan was hiding something. What do you bet some of these books aren't real?"

"I think that's a pretty safe assumption."

Batty moved into the first row again and began running his hands along the books, this time looking for a faux book panel. Following his lead, Callahan went to another row, the two moving from shelf to shelf until, a few minutes later, Callahan called out to him.

"Professor, over here."

He found her at a bookshelf against the far wall. She had already put the faux book panel aside—a phony fourteen-volume collection on neopaganism and witchcraft—to reveal a locked wooden compartment.

Batty tried the key in the lock—a perfect fit.

He turned it, felt the mechanism give, then pulled the compartment door open to reveal a large rectangular wall safe, complete with LED readout and electronic keypad.

"Shit," he muttered.

"Relax," Callahan said. "Despite appearances, these things are cake to get into."

Pulling her purse from her arm, she rooted around inside until she found a small nylon tool case, then unzipped it and removed a miniature screwdriver. Moving up to the safe, she unscrewed a rectangular nameplate just below the keypad and set it aside.

Behind it was a lock cylinder. "This is the bypass lock," she said. "In case you forget your key code."

Returning the screwdriver to its case, she reached into her purse again and brought out a ring of what looked like keys, but were less defined.

She held one up. "Jigger key," she told him. "They're old school, but they work."

"You're like a Boy Scout," he said. "Only a lot better looking."

She arched a brow at him. "Careful, Professor. I wasn't kidding about killing a man with one hand."

"I've already come to the conclusion you're *never* kidding."

"Glad we have an understanding."

She inserted the key into the lock and jiggled it, but nothing happened. Choosing another key, she tried again—and again got nothing. The third and fourth keys wouldn't fit and the fifth one was a bust as well.

One last key.

She slipped it into the lock, gave it a jiggle, and Batty could tell by the look on her face that she'd done it. Not quite a smile, but a very faint smirk. As she turned the key, the electronic mechanism *thunked* and the LED readout flashed O-P-E-N.

"Impressive," he said.

"Not really," she told him, pulling the safe door open. "But let's hope it was worth it."

There was only one item inside: a moldering old leather-bound manuscript.

Batty gingerly removed it, staring in surprise at the thin leather strap wrapped around it, a familiar-looking Saint Christopher medallion glinting in the light.

Callahan was staring at it, too. *"Custodes Sacri.* I guess there's no question now."

Batty said nothing, his attention drawn to the manuscript itself and the initials J. M. discreetly etched into the bottom right corner of the cover. Feeling his heart kick up, he quickly removed the strap and flipped the manuscript open to reveal gray, aging pages—*handwritten* pages, in a faded violet scrawl.

"Holy Christ," he muttered. "This can't be right. The only known copy is a transcription. A printer's draft. And only thirty-three pages survived."

"Thirty-three pages of what?"

Her question was just a buzz in Batty's head. "This looks like the entire manuscript, for God's sakes, just as he dictated it. Where the hell did Ozan find this? It has to be another fake."

"*What* does?" Callahan asked. "What is it?"

Batty's eyes were transfixed on its carefully bound pages. If it *was* a fake, it was exquisitely rendered.

His hands trembled as he turned back to the first page and stared at its title. Then he looked up at Callahan, feeling an unbridled giddiness overtake him, as if he were an archaeologist who had just stumbled upon the lost city of the Incas.

"For the last time, Professor, what the hell *is* that?"

Batty tried to control the tremor in his voice. "It's John Milton's original draft of *Paradise Lost.*"

27

Spotting a leather book bag amidst the clutter on the worktable, Batty quickly moved to it and snatched it up. He dumped its contents onto the table—sunglasses, car keys and an iPad—then slid the Milton manuscript inside.

"What are you doing?" Callahan asked.

"Not leaving this here, that's for sure."

Ozan had apparently been planning to work from the original, and Batty wanted to examine it more closely. If it was genuine, maybe he'd find something that hadn't made it to the printing press. A line of verse or a stanza that might help him figure out what Ozan and Gabriela had been looking for.

He gathered up the notepad and the copy of *Steganographia* and shoved them into the bag, then reconsidered the iPad and added it to the mix. There might be something useful on it.

"We need to get back to the hotel so I can sit down with this stuff."

"I don't know if you noticed, Professor, but there are a few people out there looking for us right now. How do you propose we do that?"

"This is a smugglers' tunnel, remember? What do you bet there's another way out?"

Callahan seemed to like that idea. "Not bad, Mr. Broussard. You just earned yourself some brownie points."

"Why, thank you, dear. Does that mean I'll be sleeping in a nice warm bed tonight instead of the sofa?"

She smiled. "You pick the hospital, I'll be happy to put you there."

As they geared up to go, Callahan was thinking *she* was the one who needed a hospital bed.

Putting aside LaLaurie's mind meld—the effects of which were still lingering—she was completely, utterly and irrevocably exhausted. She'd managed a few hours' sleep on the plane. Enough to recharge the batteries a bit. But the day's events were weighing on her now and her body kept screaming for her to just lie down already. And the thought of getting out of this place, back to the comfort of their hotel room, was uppermost in her mind.

She waited as LaLaurie slung the book bag over his shoulder, then followed him out of Ozan's library into what turned out to be a labyrinth of interconnecting tunnels, designed, she supposed, to discourage any interlopers who managed to discover the place. They turned left, then right, went down steps through archways, then turned right, left, right again . . . And after several minutes of this Callahan had to admit that she was completely lost.

Which annoyed her no end. She could field strip and reassemble a SIG Sauer P226 with her eyes closed, but couldn't navigate a network of smugglers' tunnels?

Pathetic.

The good professor, on the other hand, seemed to know exactly where he was going. And after their little trip to Ozan-land, Callahan had pretty much given up on trying to talk herself out of what she now knew in her bones to be true. She might be reluctant to admit it to LaLaurie, but he didn't need to convince her of anything anymore.

What happened to Ozan was not even close to what anyone would classify as normal. And judging by Gabriela's phone message, she'd gone through the exact same thing. Which meant that the Satan-worshipping wack-job theory that Callahan had been clinging to for so long had gone straight out the window.

Bottom line, she owed LaLaurie—and Lieutenant Martinez, for that matter—a profound apology.

Whatever they were dealing with here, it had the ability to get inside your head and drive you bat-fucking insane.

And the idea of that chilled Callahan to the marrow.

Batty felt sure it would be just a few more turns, another set of steps, and they'd emerge somewhere on the streets of Istanbul.

He couldn't wait to get back to the hotel to give this manuscript a closer look. He could almost feel it vibrating inside the book bag, as if it were alive. Which lent some credence to Milton's claim that the words on its pages were divinely inspired.

But as he turned a corner, he suddenly stopped.

Callahan said, "What the hell are you—"

He held up a hand, silencing her.

Ahead, one of the light fixtures was broken, plunging the far end of the tunnel in darkness, and he sensed that someone was waiting there, in the shadows.

He could feel the heat. The hunger.

Keeping his voice low, he said to Callahan, "Don't move."

She squinted toward the darkness, whispered, "You *see* something up there?"

"The waitress from the tea shop across the street."

Callahan paused, as if waiting for a punch line. Then she said, "You're kidding me, right?"

"I wish I were. She waited on me when I stopped there this afternoon."

"What—you forgot to leave a tip?"

"Actually, I gave her a pretty generous one, but I don't think that matters much right now. If I'm right about her, and I'm pretty sure I am, she could rip us both apart in about thirty seconds flat."

Callahan considered this a moment. "Normally, I'd ask you to explain a statement like that, but I think I'm gonna take your word for it. What do you suggest we do?"

"Stay very still," Batty told her. "Believe it or not, she needs an invitation to attack. A sign of aggression."

"Ooookay . . . This is probably a stupid question, but how the hell do you know all this?"

"I thought we already established that. I read a lot of books."

She looked at him. "You ever considered fiction?"

"Never go near it," he said.

The shadows stirred ahead and Batty had a feeling their movement through the tunnels alone had probably been aggressive enough to pose a threat. Or maybe he'd already managed that back at the tea shop.

Whatever the case, it was already too late.

The shadows shifted and Ajda stepped forward into the light—not a drudge, as he had hoped, but a full-fledged, shape-shifting, throat-ripping sycophant.

And that was far, far worse than any drudge could ever aspire to be.

Worse still, she had shifted already, looking more animal than human. Freddy Krueger's long-lost daughter with a loving spoonful of junkyard rat thrown in, complete with bared teeth, sharpened nails and phosphorescent green eyes. Feral didn't even come close to describing this thing.

Batty felt Callahan sway beside him, and he knew that any doubts she'd had about otherworldly phenomena had just been swallowed whole by the Goddess of *Chew-on-This-Motherfucker*.

She was tough—probably one of the toughest people he'd ever met, man *or* woman—but there was nothing in her playbook that could have prepared her for something like this.

"I think I'm about to be sick," she gasped.

And as the beast let out a long, low growl, Batty said, "I've only got one word of advice for you."

"Which is?"

"Run."

Callahan didn't need to be told twice.

Without a word, she wheeled around and took off through the tunnel like a triathlete at the starting gun.

Running barefoot on stone with your purse tucked under one arm and your dress hitched up around your waist probably wasn't the most graceful way to make an escape, but she figured she'd save the performance evaluation for later and concentrate on staying alive.

LaLaurie was right beside her, breathing hard, and she could hear that thing—whatever the fuck it was— only feet behind them, skittering across the tunnel floor like something from a Kafkaesque nightmare, hissing as it ran.

The tunnel curved ahead, and Callahan leaned forward, picking up speed. But as she moved into the curve, the hissing got louder and more sustained. She heard a flurry of movement behind her. Then the thing screeched and LaLaurie grunted and went down hard.

Stopping in her tracks, Callahan spun around and saw him thrashing on the ground, the thing pinning him down like a cat with a hamster, its lips drawn back, exposing sharp, spiky teeth. Then it went directly for his throat.

Sweet holy Jesus.

LaLaurie grunted again, trying to block it, only to get a forearm full of teeth for his trouble. To his credit, he didn't scream, but Callahan knew she couldn't stand here and watch this fucking thing rip him to shreds. Yanking the hair spray canister from her purse, she leapt forward, spraying what was left of the stuff directly in the thing's face.

It screeched and fell back, but it didn't go down. Not even close. In fact, the assault only seemed to piss it off even more and now it was looking at Callahan, growling and hissing at her, getting ready to pounce.

But she didn't give it the chance. She knew she could

hurt it, so the trick was to strike fast and keep it off balance.

Hitching up her gown again, she turned sideways and kicked, nailing it in the side of the head, wishing she still had her heels on, could maybe drive a five-inch spike right into one of those baleful green eyes. The thing screeched a second time and went flying, slamming into the tunnel wall. Maybe it had the advantage of nails and teeth and agility, but despite its immunity to her magic hair spray, it didn't seem any stronger than your average everyday tea slinger.

And that made Callahan feel very confident, indeed.

Stepping forward now, she promptly got to work.

Batty clamped his arm, trying to stem the bleeding as he scrambled out of the way and watched Callahan in motion, a blur of kicks and spins and punches, and it was obvious she knew exactly what she was doing. It was, he thought, quite an amazing thing to see, and he knew that somewhere deep inside that rodent brain, little Ajda was wondering who the hell this crazy bitch was.

Callahan was relentless. Didn't pause, didn't slow down, didn't even seem to take a breath as she continued her assault, driving the beast down, every attempt at an attack countered by a solid, bone-jangling blow.

Then the beast was lying on the floor, hunkered up in the fetal position, bleeding, whimpering softly, as Callahan stood over it with her fists clenched, trying to catch her breath.

"Holy shit," she muttered, staring down at the thing as if seeing it for the first time.

But Batty knew what was happening. Still clutching his arm, feeling blood pool up in the sleeve of his tuxedo jacket, he climbed to his feet and stood next to Callahan, watching as the thing on the floor shifted again, morphing from beast to human before their eyes.

Then Ajda looked up at them, her face battered, her mouth twisted in fear and pain, tears streaming down her cheeks.

"Please," she begged. "Please kill me."

Batty crouched beside her. "Nobody's killing anyone. Who's your significant?"

". . . Please . . ."

He leaned in close. "Who turned you? Who's your significant?"

"I just want to die," she moaned. "I just want to . . ."

The sharp smell of sulfur filled Batty's nostrils, and he knew what was coming. The girl moaned and he grabbed her by the chin, forcing her to look at him.

"*Who's your fucking significant?*"

But it was too late. Jumping to his feet, he grabbed Callahan by the shoulders and pulled her away as Ajda began to spasm uncontrollably, crying out in agony.

Callahan's eyes went wide. "What the hell is wrong with her?"

"Just stay back. There's nothing we can do."

The spasms were so bad now, it looked as if Ajda might come apart. Instead, a dagger appeared in her hand, and she reached high in the air before plunging it into her breast. She sighed, and then burst into flames, releasing a long, high, animal wail as her entire body was consumed by fire. Then she imploded into a ball of black dust that disintegrated before their eyes, leaving nothing behind.

No flesh. No bones. No sign that Ajda had ever been there at all. Not even a scorch mark.

"Jesus," Callahan muttered.

Batty turned to her. "I guess that pretty much clears up any doubts you may have had."

28

"What are we doing here?" Callahan said. "Don't you think you should get that arm checked out?"

She looked a bit shell-shocked, but seemed to have recovered from their adventure in the tunnels. Maybe beating the crap out of a raging sycophant had been therapeutic—although Batty didn't think a lifetime of therapy would get the image of Ajda out of his head.

He had taken his jacket off and wrapped his forearm with it. The wounds were throbbing, but it didn't seem to be bleeding much now.

They stood in an alley adjacent to the tea shop, where Batty had found a door he assumed led to the kitchen. Across the street, a fire truck and several *polis* cars were parked in front of the auction house, the crowd of attendees still standing out front in their formal wear. He and Callahan had emerged from the tunnels in another alley, three blocks away, but Batty had insisted they double back.

He rattled the doorknob. "Can you pick this lock?"

"Look," Callahan said. "Do me a favor."

"What?"

"When I ask you a direct question, can you show me the courtesy of giving me a direct answer?"

He gestured to the door. "What about *my* question?"

"I'll make you a deal," she said. "You answer mine, I'll answer yours. See how that works? As it is, you're about a half dozen behind, and I'd really appreciate it if you'd get straight to the point for once."

Maybe she *hadn't* recovered, after all. She seemed a little touchier than usual.

"All right," he said, "fair enough. You want to know why we're here?" She nodded, and he gestured toward the auction house. "Like I told you, that thing you beat the hell out of back there—and I mean that literally, not figuratively—was a waitress at this shop. And when she waited on me this afternoon, I knew there was something off about her."

"Gee, you think?"

"She was what they call a sycophant," Batty said. "A human who's been turned."

"Turned by what?"

"What else? An angel. A dark one. They get inside your head, play with your emotions, your desires, your fears, but rather than dust you like Gabriela and Ozan and Rebecca, they turn you into one of their slaves."

"I think I need to sit down."

"You asked," Batty said with a shrug.

Callahan sighed. "So what else do I need to know?"

"Interaction with angels is tricky. They exist in a different realm than we do. And in order to work in our world, they need surrogates. Those surrogates come in three forms: skins, sycophants and drudges."

"Which are?"

"A skin is a physical host. People who have given the angels permission to use their bodies in exchange for a reward of some kind. It doesn't matter what that reward is, because it's rarely granted. It's just a trick they use to get what they want, and when they're done with the body, it's discarded and the soul that occupied it is obliterated."

"Be careful what you wish for."

"Exactly," Batty said. "Drudges and sycophants, on the other hand, are basically lackeys. A drudge is exactly what it sounds like. A menial laborer who doesn't have much brain power and does a lot of the heavy lifting. Think riots at ball games or soldiers run amuck or mindless news anchors, doing whatever their significant tells them to do."

"Significant?"

"The angel who turned them. You want me to keep going?"

"By all means. What's another nightmare or two?"

"Then you've got your sycophants," he said. "Like Ajda. When they're turned, their significant infuses them with a little piece of the otherworld, turning them into what you saw in that tunnel. Kind of a super-lackey who's been given some independence. But they don't tend to reveal themselves like that unless they're threatened somehow."

"So we were a threat because we're running around in Ozan's basement?"

"Maybe," Batty said. "But Ajda targeted *me* in that tunnel, so I have a feeling I'm the one she was worried about. I think it started when I sat down and ordered that cup of tea."

"But why?"

"That's what we're here to find out. So can you pick this lock or not?"

Without hesitating, Callahan brought up her foot and

kicked the door open, splintering wood, shattering the lock. "How's that?"

Batty gaped at her, then shot a glance toward the auction house, hoping she hadn't attracted any undue attention. "Not exactly what I had in mind."

"It worked, didn't it?"

She waved him past her and Batty stepped into the teahouse kitchen, which wasn't much more than a stove and a couple of countertops. They moved together through a doorway into the main parlor, which was dotted with chairs and small rectangular tables.

He felt the energy immediately. Knew that his instincts had been right.

"This is where the turning began," he said, then moved to the center of the room. Crouching down, he put his hand to the floor and closed his eyes. It took very little to call up the vision. A dark wind rose, began swirling around him, and he saw two figures on the floor, in this very spot—

—Two women, half naked, writhing in ecstasy, and one of them was clearly Ajda.

Then Batty found himself inside Ajda's mind, which was a swirl of confusion. She felt both exhilarated and afraid, but most of all free. This was something she had never experienced before and it was wonderful. She wanted more. As much as she could get.

But the face of the woman who was doing this to her—the dark angel's face—eluded Batty. Was nothing more than a blur. He knew from experience that his vision was limited to the amount of energy he could draw from the room, and even though it was strong, he wasn't sure there was enough here to bring that face into focus.

But he had to try.

Narrowing his concentration, he zeroed in on the other woman. Ajda's significant. His own energy, his *physical* energy, started to drain away, and he knew he wouldn't be able to sustain this for long or he'd wind up in that hospital bed Callahan had threatened him with.

But he didn't give up. Concentrated even harder.

The lens he was peering through began to turn and shift, the dark angel's face slowly taking shape, coming into focus. And when it finally did, it was like a knee to the balls. Batty felt the wind go out of him as bile began to rise in his throat.

It was the redhead.

The woman from Bayou Bill's.

The woman who had shared his bed and his body and had rarely left his mind since the night they spent together.

She stared up at him, smiling, and all at once it came to him. That elusive thought he'd tried to grab hold of when he'd told Callahan about Ozan's involvement with *Custodes Sacri*. He remembered lying in bed with the redhead, the two of them talking through the night—about politics and history and spirituality and God knows what else. But the one thing he now remembered more clearly than ever, was that he'd told her about Ozan. About the necklace, and his phone conversation with the collector.

About *Custodes Sacri*.

Which meant only one thing.

He had started this. *He* was the reason Ozan was dead. *He* was the reason Gabriela had followed. This bitch, this dark fucking angel, had destroyed them without mercy—

—just as she had surely destroyed Rebecca.

Looking into that smiling face, he wanted to reach out and rip her head off, send her straight back to hell. He cursed himself for letting her deceive him. Letting her seduce him. And he cursed her for coming into their house in Ithaca and taking the only woman he'd ever loved away from him.

Tearing himself from the vision, Batty collapsed to the floor, so drained of strength he could barely move.

He looked up at Callahan.

"Get me out of here," he croaked. "Get me the fuck out of here."

29

SÃO PAULO, BRAZIL

Belial was in bed with José de Souza's girlfriend when she heard it.

She'd been enjoying the sensation of the girl's tongue—what was her name again?—as it rolled across her belly and up toward her breasts. De Souza himself was sitting in a nearby chair, watching them with great interest, showing that blackened tooth of his that he seemed so proud of.

Belial closed her eyes, concentrating on the feel of the warm wet tongue against her flesh. She hadn't yet made up her mind about turning these two, although de Souza and his band of midgets would be quite an asset on the night of the fourth moon. But de Souza didn't strike her as someone who *needed* to be turned. Not immediately, at least. He was self-motivated. A homeschooled convert.

A fan.

And having someone like him on your side without having to sacrifice his intellect—which the turning always managed to blunt—was a very tempting proposition indeed.

But then she knew all about such temptations, didn't she?

Belial had returned to São Paulo after one of her contacts with the local police had told her that a woman from

Manessa was snooping around the crime scene, prying into the singer's death.

While this hadn't concerned her much, she *was* curious. So she had come back to São Paulo and discovered that the woman in question had now moved on to Esau. And this she found *doubly* curious, since she'd recently taken a trip there herself.

Was this woman's interest in the singer, and now, obviously, the antiquities dealer, purely professional? A connecting of the dots?

Or was she *Custodes Sacri*?

While retracing the woman's steps here in the city, Belial had found herself in the *Favela Paraisópolis*, with all of its glorious depravity (which was ironic considering what this place had once been), only to be introduced to its self-appointed king, a smart but overeager little rodent with a provocative, cocoa-skinned girlfriend.

The night had gotten predictable after that.

This wasn't necessarily a bad thing, but it *was* a distraction when the clock was ticking and she had work to do. Beelzebub's anger for her failure to locate the remaining members of her wayward brother's army was not misplaced, but it wasn't as if she'd abandoned the project. Her children were always out there working for her. Staying alert.

And what was the harm in a few stolen moments with a golden-tongued goddess? Surely Belial was allowed *some* pleasure . . .

But then, out of the blue, just as the girl was placing her lips on a hardened nipple and drawing it into her mouth—

—Belial heard it. The sound she so hated. The unmistakable scream of a soul turning to dust.

A soul that belonged to *her*.

She stiffened suddenly and shoved the goddess aside, pulling herself to the edge of the bed.

"Is something wrong?" de Souza asked, looking fearful. "Did she hurt you?"

The room was dark except for a few candles burning on the shelf above them, and Belial was glad for that, because she didn't want these humans to see her face. Unlike her brother, who wasn't afraid to show his torment (should the occasion arise), Belial preferred to keep her pain private.

And the loss of a soul was always painful.

For her, at least.

Especially since this wasn't the first one she'd lost today. Her brother had seen to that.

"It's nothing," she said to de Souza. "I'm bored, is all. It's time for me to go."

At moments like this the other clan leaders—Beelzebub, Mammon and Moloch—seemed to take as much pride in their ability to remain stoic as de Souza took in his enameled tooth. But for Belial, a loss was a loss. Each soul gone was a missing piece, a hole in the fabric she had spent so many centuries weaving.

These were not mere possessions to her. They were her children.

And to lose one always saddened her.

As she pulled her clothes on, de Souza leaned forward in his chair, an intense, concerned look on his face. "Are you sure you won't stay? We have so much to talk about."

The thought was absurd. "Like what, for instance?"

"The coming days, for one. We need to know how to prepare."

Belial looked at him and almost laughed. It was amusing how naive these self-absorbed converts could be. Did he really think he could prepare for what was to come?

Even *she* wasn't sure what to expect.

"Watch the moon," she said flatly. "Then do what comes naturally."

The second jolt came less than hour later. Belial had pinpointed her loss to Ajda, the young waitress she had met in Esau, and she knew this wasn't a coincidence. The woman she'd been told about was involved somehow. She was sure of it.

Ajda must have sensed something wrong about this woman and had foolishly taken matters into her own hands. And now that Ajda was gone, the hole in the fabric seemed larger than ever.

She'd been one of Belial's favorites.

So Belial had decided to stop wasting time and go to Esau immediately. Not to confront, but to observe. If a strategy wasn't working, you changed it, and confrontation had so far produced very little. And even if this woman did not turn out to be a member of *Custodes Sacri*, she could still prove useful.

But as she was preparing to leave, Belial felt a sudden jolt of pain in her chest. Someone pulling at her, trying to suck her out of her skin and into the swirling darkness of the otherworld.

When she realized who it was, she didn't resist. Let herself go.

How could she not?

She had invested a lot of time and energy into this

man. He was a laggard and a drunk, yes, but from the first moment she saw him—long before he'd taken that path—she had found herself inexplicably drawn to him.

His wit. His intellect. The complexity of thought. The ability to see what others couldn't.

She remembered what Moloch had said to her that night in the tea shop. "It's quite obvious you have a soft spot for this pathetic creature."

Moloch was a self-important dunderhead, but what he'd said was true. She did have a soft spot. And her decision not to turn the laggard had less to do with strategy—as in de Souza's case—and everything to do with . . .

Dare she say it?

Her feelings.

Just as she had no control over the sadness that overcame her whenever she lost a soul, she couldn't help how she felt about this man. A frame of mind that was both troubling and dangerous. She knew she should have turned him immediately, but she hadn't been able to bring herself to even try. Couldn't bear the thought of losing the qualities that made him who he was.

And after their glorious night together—a moment she had delayed for two long years—she had worked very hard to forget about him. Had distracted herself with the flesh of others in hopes that her thoughts of that night would soon fade away.

She had not returned to his home. Had not returned to his bed. And had almost convinced herself that he was no longer important to her.

Yet here he was now, pulling at her. Floating before her in the ether. Summoning up the lingering remains of that night in the tea shop with Ajda.

And this part puzzled her.

Was he there right now? In the tea shop?

Had *he* gone to Esau?

Before she could weigh the gravity of this turn of events, she saw him crouched near the floor, his face coming into sharp focus, and she could see that he wasn't happy. Far from it.

There was hate in those eyes. Fury.

And she knew with sudden certainty that—true to his intellect—he was now fully aware of who she really was and what she had done to that useless bag of bones, that supercilious whore he had called a wife.

And for the first time in as long as she could remember—

—Belial was heartbroken.

30

ISTANBUL, TURKEY

After the fifth shot of whiskey, Batty still wasn't properly anesthetized, but he was getting there. He'd brought the bottle to their hotel room and planned to finish it off before the night was over.

He was slumped on a couch near a window that overlooked the city, his forearm bandaged, the Milton manuscript lying on the cushion next to him. But he hadn't cracked it open yet. His excitement over it had waned. Died, actually. He was too busy getting drunk.

And thinking about the redhead.

He cursed himself for not recognizing what she was the moment he'd taken her into his bed. But then the smell of the swamp had been high that night, hadn't it? And the temptation strong.

But that was no excuse. No matter what desperate rationalization he might come up with, the end result was always the same.

He had slept with the creature who had killed his wife.

He'd had intimate relations with the dark angel—the fucking *demon*, all right?—who came into his home, burrowed her way into Rebecca's mind and drove the woman he loved to destruction—all the while using *his* voice to spew her venom.

His voice.

Yet despite knowing this, and despite his utter contempt for the creature, Batty's yearning for her—that animal instinct—had not gone away. Seeing her on that floor with Ajda had stirred a desire in him he could barely suppress.

And that made him sick to his stomach.

Hence, the bottle of whiskey.

"You ready to talk about it yet?"

Callahan sat in her armchair, Ozan's iPad in her lap, the copy of *Steganographia* and Ozan's notes on the table next to her. With Batty about as useful as a flashlight without batteries, she'd taken possession of it all and had spent the last couple hours working away, scribbling notes, checking references, consulting the Internet, texting messages . . . He had no idea what she was up to, but she was certainly keeping busy.

He, on the other hand, was merely passing time between shots.

He remembered that Ajda had targeted him specifically in that tunnel. Was it possible she had smelled the redhead on him? Was that why he was a threat? Had she attacked out of jealousy, of all things?

"Earth to LaLaurie."

He blinked. "There's nothing to talk about."

"Just answer one question. All this stuff you've been spouting about angels and drudges and sycophants—it didn't come from just books, did it?"

He looked at her. Realized he had involuntarily started rubbing the scar on his left wrist, as if he'd known what she was about to ask.

"No," he said.

She set her phone and the iPad aside, giving him her

full attention now. "Look. You don't have to tell me about this if you don't want to. I haven't exactly been the most receptive human being on the planet." She gestured to the bottle. "But it looks to me like you're on the train to oblivion, and by all rights, I should be in the seat right next to you. Call me selfish, but I'd rather that didn't happen."

"Does it really matter?"

"It does to me," she said. "I watched my father nearly drink himself to death right before he put a bullet in his head. And I'd just as soon not see that happen again."

Batty didn't often do this without permission, but she'd opened a small window and he took a moment to peek inside her mind. There was a lot of childhood anguish in there, and he knew she usually kept that window sealed tight.

"I'm not going to burden you with any details," he told her. "We'll save that for another day. Let's just say that most of what I know about this subject came my way because of two things: my curse and my stupidity."

"I'm gonna need a little more than that."

"The curse I was born with," he said. "This thing my mother called The Vision . . ." He raised his hands now, showing her his wrists. "And my stupidity."

"I assume you did that after your wife was killed?"

"After what I'd seen in our bedroom I thought I knew exactly where she was headed, and I was foolish enough to think I could go after her. And when I cut my wrists, I was swept away to a place I wouldn't wish on anyone."

Truth be told, his memory of that journey had faded over the last two years, becoming little more than a vague horror in a corner of his mind, like the murky remnants of a nightmare. But he'd come away from the place with its culture and its history imprinted on his brain, like data etched onto a microchip.

And knowledge like that wasn't easy to forget.

"I know I shouldn't be surprised by this," Callahan said, "but are you saying hell actually exists?"

"Hell, Lazaa, Tartarus, Kalichi—every religion has a name for it, and believe me, you don't want to go there if you can help it. I only had a small taste of it, and that was more than enough. And I'm pretty sure I brought a little piece of it back with me."

He could see that despite all she'd seen tonight, she was having trouble accepting this idea. But he had to give her credit for not dismissing it out of hand.

She was making progress.

"What do you mean, 'a piece of it'?"

"I don't know if you've noticed," he told her, "but I don't always have the sunniest of dispositions."

Callahan said nothing.

"I think part of the reason for that is what I've seen, but it's also something inside me, as if a living piece of the place attached itself to my soul before I was revived. Like a parasite. For all I know, I'm only one kiss away from being a drudge myself."

Which was why, he supposed, he still felt that attraction to the redhead.

"That's ridiculous," Callahan said.

"We went way past ridiculous a long time ago. And you can throw in absurd, ludicrous and laughable as well. Unfortunately, none of this is very funny."

"So what's your solution? Sit here and wallow in your misery? Or do you want to do something productive?"

"The two aren't mutually exclusive, are they?"

"Come on, Professor, I need you to sober up. You're not any good to me like this. What do you say we call down to room service and order a pot of that really disgusting coffee these Turks love so much?"

"You make it sound so inviting."

"It's better than no invitation at all, isn't it?"

He thought about it and sighed. "All right. I give."

"Good," she said. "I have something I want to show you."

The coffee was so thick and strong that Batty nearly gagged the moment it touched his tongue. He wasn't close to being sober yet, but he knew he needed to snap out of this and pay attention to what Callahan was saying.

"I went through Ozan's client list," she told him. "He had over six hundred active accounts, and the auction house is doing brisk business. In the last two months alone, they've shipped seven hundred and twenty-seven packages, all over the world."

"So the database is a bust. What about the iPad?"

"That's what I want to show you." She picked up Ozan's iPad from the table and touched the *home* button, bringing the screen to life. "His e-mail app is connected to two different mailboxes. Work and personal, both attached to the same server, run by an Internet provider here in Istanbul." She touched the screen and called up the browser. "But when I started exploring, I found a Web page in his cache. An anonymous mail service, running in the cloud."

"The cloud?"

"Out there on the Internet. Like Google apps or Sky-tap, where everything is centralized."

"So what does that mean?"

"In itself, not much. But when I found it, I had to ask myself, why would Ozan need a separate Webmail account, especially an anonymous one? Was he subscribing to porn sites and trying to cover his tracks? That doesn't seem likely."

Batty suddenly understood. "He was corresponding with the other guardians."

Callahan nodded. "Not often, but when I hacked into his account, I found four separate recipients, all of whom were sent messages by Ozan the day before he died. He'd already dumped them into his trash folder, but he hadn't bothered to empty it—a mistake amateurs always make. They assume that once a message is deleted, it's deleted."

"So who were the recipients?"

Callahan huffed. "I wish it were that easy. But they're all anonymous Web accounts, too."

"So it's a dead end."

"Not really. I managed to hack into the accounts, run an IP trace and found they'd last been accessed from four different Internet cafés. São Paulo, D.C., London and Chiang Mai, Thailand."

"We already know the recipient in São Paulo."

Another nod. "But Gabriela hadn't accessed the account since before she went on her last tour, so she never got the message."

"What *is* the message?"

"That's where I ran into a little snag. It's nothing but spam. 'Viagra at Internet Prices,' blah, blah, blah. The kind of stuff most people delete, which, of course, is the point. It's actually pretty ingenious."

She touched the iPad's screen, then handed it to Batty, and sure enough, the message she'd retrieved was a long, solid paragraph of a poorly written advertising come-on. Get one of these in your inbox and you immediately hit the kill button. But he knew there was more to it than that.

"It isn't spam," he said. "It's a hidden message."

"Right. I started thinking about what you told me in Ozan's library. About Trithemius—and *this* little puppy . . ." She patted the copy of *Steganographia* on the table beside her. "But if you look at the stuff on Ozan's notepad, you can clearly see that he was about as good at steganography as he was at e-mail security. So he took the easy route and used a shortcut to code his messages."

Batty glanced at the screen full of spam. "What kind of shortcut?"

"I checked his browser cache again and found a Web site that allows you to enter a phrase into a text box, then encodes it to look like this. I figure the guardians on the other end are using the same Web site to decipher it."

"So much for ancient tradition. I assume you decoded it, too?"

She nodded and touched the screen again, showing him the result:

Someone watching. Stay alert.

Batty studied the message grimly. "He obviously wasn't being paranoid. He was a sensitive, so he knew what was coming. Must've felt it."

"And, unfortunately, Gabriela was so wrapped up in her tour she never bothered to read the warning."

"I'm not sure how much difference it would've made. What about the D.C. and London accounts?"

"Both read and deleted," Callahan said. She touched the screen again. "But that wasn't the only spam Ozan sent. I found another exchange in his trash file—with the recipient from Thailand, dated a couple weeks earlier. I decoded it, but it's still pretty cryptic."

She showed him the results. First Ozan's message:

Tell me about C Gigas, 7 pages.

Followed by the Thailand recipient's reply:

Don't make the same mistake the poet made.
You may lose more than your eyes.

Batty felt his heart accelerate.

"I tried Googling this C. Gigas guy," Callahan said, "but all I got was a page on Pacific oysters. And I don't think Ozan and his buddy were discussing seafood."

"Or a person. They're talking about the Codex Gigas."

"Which is?"

"Another book."

"What—are these people obsessed?"

"Apparently so," Batty said. "But what surprises me is that it's Ozan asking the question. He has one of the most extensive collections on the occult I've ever seen, so it seems to me he'd already know all about the Gigas."

"That makes at least two of you. You mind filling me in?"

"It's also called the Devil's Bible," Batty told her. "It was written in the thirteenth century, supposedly in one night. With the help of Satan."

"Wonderful."

"It's about the size of a small packing trunk, and at one time it was considered one of the wonders of the world. This thing has survived fire and the Thirty Years' War. And right now it's housed in a library in Sweden." He looked at the e-mail again. "But like I said, Ozan would already know all that. His interest was in the seven missing pages."

"The what?"

"There are seven pages missing from the Gigas. Nobody knows how or when they disappeared, but there's been all kinds of speculation about what's on them, from a message from Satan to the secrets of God and the universe. And that's probably what Ozan was after." He tapped the iPad screen. "But it's the *response* that has me puzzled."

"Why?"

"Because it mentions the poet. 'Don't make the same mistake the poet made. You may lose more than your eyes.' I think we both know who he's talking about."

"John Milton."

"Exactly. He went blind nearly a decade before he wrote *Paradise Lost*. But this reply is couched as a *warning* to Ozan—don't make the same mistake—as if Milton did something to *cause* his blindness."

"So let me get this straight," Callahan said. "On one hand we have these seven missing pages, on the other hand we have two guardians searching for secret messages, and smack in the middle of it all we've got a blind fucking poet."

"There's obviously a connection there. We just need to figure out what it is."

Callahan got to her feet, stretched. "Well, maybe we'll get lucky when we talk to the monk."

Batty looked at her. "Monk?"

"I cross-referenced those e-mails with Ozan's client database," she said. "I got about a hundred different hits for D.C. and London, but only one for Chiang Mai. Three months ago he sent a package to a Christian monastery there. To a monk called Brother Philip. I've already chartered a flight."

"Then maybe he *will* have the answer. I guess it makes sense when you think about it."

"Why?" Callahan asked.

"The Devil's Bible was written by a Benedictine monk."

BOOK VII

The Fourth Moon of the Lunar Tetrad

Then in the East her turn she shines,
Revolvd on Heav'ns great Axle

—*Paradise Lost*, 1667 ed., VII:380–81

31

LOS ANGELES, CALIFORNIA

Finding a new skin was always a problem for him.

Had he been like his sister, Belial, he'd simply tempt, seduce and lie his way into getting what he wanted. But over the years he had formed a personal code. One he did his best to follow.

No subterfuge, no games.

He would get what he needed simply by asking.

So his choices were limited. There weren't too many humans out there who would willingly give up their bodies without the promise of some kind of reward. Which was why he found himself in Central City East, a section of downtown Los Angeles known as "the Nickel" or skid row, just blocks from the Angels Flight—a hillside rail tram that had only recently reopened for business.

The body he occupied—the body he was now forced to replace—had been found right here, a young man in his midtwenties who had been a heroin addict since he was seventeen years old and had no qualms about leaving this world behind.

The young man's speech had been slurred by drink and drugs, but he was cognizant enough to know what was being asked of him. Rewards no longer mattered. He had simply wanted a change, and was more than willing to take his chances in the afterlife.

"What's it like out there?" he had asked.

"Like nothing you've ever known."

"Will I see God?"

"I can't give you any promises, but I *can* tell you that what you'll see is a world *created* by God. What you make of it will be up to you—and it won't be without its dangers."

"I'm willing to take my chances."

"Are you? I don't want to do this unless you're absolutely sure."

"I'm sure," the young man had said. "There's just one thing I want to know before we start."

"Ask."

"Your name. I need to know your name."

He remembered resting his palm on top of the young man's head and thinking that, despite appearances, this was a good soul who would do well in the otherworld. Telling him his name was the least he could do.

"Michael," he'd said softly. "They call me Michael."

But that was then and this was now.

After the fight in the alley and the severe loss of blood, the young man's body was no longer useful to him. So Michael had patched up his wounds, gotten some much-needed rest, then used what little strength he had left to make his way back to skid row.

He hadn't felt good about leaving Jenna behind. His instinct was to stay with her, keep watching her—especially with Zack still on the loose. He hadn't intended to lose an entire day and much of the night, but what choice did he have? She seemed to be in good hands at the shelter, and with any luck he'd be back listening to her song before morning.

He began roaming the streets, feeling the life draining out of him with every step he took. He could, of course, abandon this body where it stood, but traveling through this world without a host was difficult and would only complicate his task. And he found it much easier to communicate with these beings when he looked and sounded like them.

As always, skid row was crawling with the wasted and the disenfranchised. Old and young, male and female, each one of them victim to human prejudices and often to their own mental or emotional weaknesses. They carried a sense of hopelessness so deeply rooted in their psyches that they saw no other remedy than to give up and give in. They drank and drugged themselves into oblivion, waiting and hoping for that final release.

Was he wrong to exploit that wish?

Maybe.

Maybe it made him no better than his brethren.

But his intent was pure. That much he knew for certain. He was here to *help* humankind, not hurt them. A cause he had dedicated himself to long ago.

He was a good hour into his search when he found a candidate. Older than he would have liked—late fifties or possibly early sixties—but there was a natural muscularity to his frame that couldn't be disguised by the oversize shirt and the ill-fitting jeans.

The man lay sleeping under the marquee of an abandoned movie theater, huddled close to the boarded-up ticket booth, his hair long and gray, the equally gray stubble on his chin making the transition to full-grown beard.

He looked physically healthy and didn't seem to be suffering the ravages of booze or drugs, so Michael had to assume he was mentally ill.

Which was both a blessing and a curse.

A blessing because his body wouldn't give out so quickly, yet a curse because it was difficult to explain to someone suffering from mental illness why you want him to make the ultimate sacrifice.

A dilemma that Michael would just as soon avoid.

So he continued on, moving past the old man and dismissing him from his mind.

Half a block up, however, he felt a stab of pain in his side and realized that his stitches had torn loose and he was bleeding again.

He didn't have much time.

Staggering to a bus stop, he sank onto the bench and checked the wound, doing what he could to stop the flow of blood. The moon hung low in the night sky, nearly close enough to touch, and as he sat there, holding his side, he thought about what was coming in just a few short days:

The last phase of the lunar tetrad.

The fourth in a quartet of full eclipses, unbroken in sequence, over the span of a single year. The last of four moons sliding through the umbra, turning a deep shade of copper.

A blood moon.

There were those who believed that consecutive eclipses were a signal from God. A sign that his son would soon return to the earth, that the dead would be resurrected and final judgment passed.

But there were others who knew better. Those—like

Michael—who had been here from the beginning and had witnessed the creation of man and the world he inhabited.

Those who wanted possession of that world.

The dark rebels who had once been Michael's friends.

The rebels had always thought of themselves as the heroes of the story. The bringers of light, the purveyors of truth, the bold few who had dared rise up against a tyrant to make their world a better place.

But history is written by the victors, and when the War in Caeli came to an end, those who had dared defy their father were beaten down and broken, labeled traitors, exiled to the belly of Abyssus.

To the world at large, they were seen as infernal spirits. Dark angels.

Daemones.

To their minds, however, the only thing that separated them from the so-called angels of God was their allegiance to individual freedom. They did not believe that their father, the creator of all things living, was infallible. Nor did they believe that he was fair or just or kind. And when he took it upon himself to create a colony of slaves, giving the poor hapless creatures the *illusion* of freedom, the rebels felt it only proper that they show him just how fallible he was.

These mindless beasts—these Homo sapiens, as they would later come to be known—were weak willed and violent, superstitious and easily corrupted, susceptible to the ever-changing and often conflicting mythologies their creator had conjured up in order to mollify and manipulate them.

The rebels decided to exploit these weaknesses. What better way to expose their father's arrogance than to lure his precious slaves into the endless fire? To tempt them into joining the New Rebellion?

Perhaps if he had treated these creatures with more dignity, this would not have been possible. But he had made a mistake in telling them that they were free to choose, only to punish them if they defied his will.

The contradiction did not go unnoticed.

While history would continue to be written by his followers, painting the rebels as evil and self-serving—using fear as a common motivator—the rebels worked quietly and with purpose, forging their own kingdom amidst the fires of Abyssus and doing all they could to undermine his authority.

Lucifer, a formidable warrior who was once God's most perfect angel, had demonstrated a capacity for ruthlessness beyond all others. He rose among the ranks to become the leader of the rebels, urging them to return to Caeli to fight again. To conquer their father's kingdom and take back the dignity he had stripped from them.

But on the night of the fourth moon, at the end of the first lunar tetrad, news of this rebellion reached their father's ears and he lashed out preemptively, showing the rebel king no mercy.

Too cruel to simply kill Lucifer, he instead banished him to the City of the Seventh Gate, locking him in a cell of fire to forever contemplate the consequences of his deeds.

And this was where Lucifer resided to this day. Forever in agony.

Although they considered their cause a noble one, the

remaining rebels disbanded, fearing their father's retribution. They began fighting among themselves, dividing into clans, each clan led by the strongest of them.

Belial. Moloch. Mammon. Beelzebub.

Michael.

And as time wore on, as century after century flew past—their spirits dampened and their memories blotted by war and greed and heartbreak—they forgot why they had come together in the first place. They themselves became tainted by their ever-growing thirst for power and the desire to control the playground their father had created.

But these earth creatures, these humans, turned out to be more resilient than they had expected, and that playground could not so easily be dominated.

Beelzebub, first brother to Lucifer, called for a meeting of the clans in Pandemonium, the one city in all of Abyssus that had not been marked by partisan politics—a neutral ground, built by the great Mulciber, where the leaders had no fear of a surprise attack.

And in that meeting, an alliance was formed. An agreement made.

A blood pact.

It was said that their father and his angels in Caeli had long ago turned their backs on the world he had created and had found other amusements to occupy their time.

No longer fearing his retribution, the clans would now work together for a common goal. If they could not return to Caeli, they'd create a heaven of their own. Their love for Lucifer had not waned, and because his fate had been cast under the bloodred light of the fourth moon of the tetrad, they would use the power of that moon to bring about the Final Conquest. They would open the seven gates of hell, release King Lucifer from his eternal bonds, and rule over their new paradise, forever enslaving these feeble humans as symbols of their father's indifference.

Only Michael objected to this plan.

Perhaps, he told them, there was another way to achieve their goal. Perhaps if they honored their father, stayed true to the original intent of his creation, they could work together with the creatures of earth and live in harmony.

Michael, however, was ridiculed by the others. Even his sister, Belial, called him naive, a fool to believe that honoring their father would bring them anything but more heartbreak.

But Michael could not be deterred. As the others continued to corrupt mankind, harvesting souls, which together with the power of the moon would open the seven gates and bring forth their beloved king, he worked quietly and with purpose, undermining them at every turn, urging peace among the humans, using the mythologies his father created to help persuade them to remain good and pure, untainted by the rebels' corruption.

And with each new lunar tetrad, he managed to beat back the forces of the alliance and prevent them from achieving their goal.

But it wasn't easy, and Michael's resolve began to weaken. In desperation, he called out to his father, insisting he listen, demanding that he pay attention to the world he had abandoned and bring it back to the light.

Then one night, when he was all but convinced that his call had gone unheard, his father came to him, amused by his demand.

"Look at this world you covet," he said. "The people who inhabit it are as corrupt and self-serving as Lucifer and his creed. Why should I care what happens to them? Why do *you* care?"

"Because I remember what it was to live in the light of your grace. And I want these people to know that feeling. Here on earth."

"They had their chance."

"But don't they deserve a second one?"

His father considered this. Then he said, "I'll do better than that, my son. Look to the skies, and with each new lunar tetrad these creatures you so believe in will be granted another chance. During that time, you must listen for the song, the song of the Telum."

"Telum?"

"A miraculous weapon so powerful that it will either give these creatures the peace you seek for them, or destroy them forever. And on the night of the fourth moon, whoever takes control of that weapon will control the fate of the world." He paused then, staring grimly at Michael. "But be warned, my son, I won't make it easy for you. That song will not be easily heard, and your enemies will know about this weapon as well."

"But . . . why?"

"Because they are my children, too."

Thirteen lunar tetrads had come and gone in the last several centuries, yet nothing had changed. Michael had failed time and again to hear the true song of the Telum, and with each new blood moon, the rebels drew closer to their goal.

But it would be different this time.

It had to be.

Because the rebels were closer than ever now, and he sensed that this was his very last chance.

A shout interrupted Michael's thoughts. A burst of laughter.

Keeping his hand clutched to his side, he turned and looked back toward the movie theater. Three men had stumbled out of a nearby bar and were eyeing the old man, working their way toward him.

All three were the size of college football players. Military haircuts.

Michael considered for a moment that they might be drudges, but he didn't think so. The vibe they gave off was all too human—even from this distance.

"Well, well," one of them said as they came to a stop in front of the box office. "Check out Gandalf. He ain't lookin' so good."

"Isn't that your pops?" another one said, and he and the third one doubled over in drunken laughter.

Unamused, the first one moved up to the old man and nudged him with his toe. "Hey, dirtbag, what do you think you're doing sleeping in my spot? I got this suite reserved."

The others laughed again.

Awake now, the old man flinched and cradled his head, muttering incoherently as he curled into a tight fetal ball.

The first guy nudged him again. "Get that dick outta your mouth and speak up, buddy."

A renewed wave of laughter overtook the other two,

but the first one still didn't join in. He was an angry drunk, and the hate and disgust in his eyes was difficult to ignore.

But the old man was trying. Kept muttering to himself.

Michael got to his feet then, feeling the sudden need to reassure him. He didn't normally do this—it was against his code—but there were always exceptions.

Always.

It's all right, he said, burrowing his way into the old man's brain. *I won't let them hurt you.*

But the old man didn't seem to hear him, his mind rapid-firing—

—Count to ten and they'll go away. Count to ten and they'll go away. Count to ten and they'll go away. One two three. One two three four. One two three four five. Count to ten and they'll go away—

But they didn't go away. The angry one crouched in front of him now, poking a finger into his shoulder. "You hear me, you stupid shit?"

—One two three. One two three four. One two three four five—

"Come on, Jimmy," the third one said. "This guy's a wack job. Let's get out of here."

But Jimmy shook his head. "Fuck that. I didn't spend six months in the desert so this asshole could collect welfare and wallow in his shit all day and night." He poked the old man again. "Where were you when I was chasing towel heads, you ungrateful prick? Sucking off Uncle Sam's tit?"

—Count to ten and they'll go away. Count to ten and they'll—

"Come on, Jimmy, give it a rest. He isn't bothering anyone."

"You might want to listen to your friend," Michael said.

He was standing less than three feet away from Jimmy now. Just off to his right side. The jump had been difficult in his condition, but he'd made it anyway.

Jimmy wheeled around and stood up. "Where the fuck did *you* come from?"

"That's a longer story than we have time for. But I'll tell you where you're going."

"And where's that?"

"Away," Michael said. "Right now. Whether or not it's voluntary is entirely up to you."

Interfering directly in human affairs was well beyond his boundaries, but he couldn't help himself. The old man had enough troubles and Michael couldn't stand there and watch this idiot treat him this way.

Jimmy did a slow burn, looking him up and down. "What are you—king of the bums or something?"

"Something like that."

Jimmy glanced at his two friends. "You believe this asshole?" He gestured. "Look at him, he's bleeding all over the goddamn sidewalk."

That much was true. The stitches had all ruptured now and the gash in Michael's side was widening. "You will be, too, if you don't walk away."

Jimmy stared at him. "You got balls of steel, buddy, I'll give you—"

Michael delivered the punch hard and fast, bloodying Jimmy's nose and knocking him on his ass. Then he turned to the other two, who had sense enough to back away.

"This isn't your fight," he said. "Pick your friend up and get him out of here. I really don't want to have to—"

The blow came from behind, delivered directly into the wound in Michael's side. It made a sick, sucking sound on impact, as pain radiated up through his central nervous system, nearly paralyzing him on the spot.

He grabbed at the wound and fell to one knee, knowing that Jimmy had once and for all rendered this body useless to him. He suddenly felt no connection to it, had no real control. And before he knew it, the three gorillas were standing over him, showering him with punches and kicks, Jimmy's the most vicious of all.

Then Michael was on the ground, staring into the frightened eyes of the old man—

—*Count to ten and they'll go away. Count to ten and they'll go away*—

But Michael knew they *wouldn't* go away. When they were done with him, Jimmy would again turn his drunken fury on someone who wanted nothing more than to be left alone.

So Michael did what had to be done. Once again violating his code, he burrowed his way into the old man's brain.

Let me in and I'll free you, he said. *Let me in and all of this will go away forever.*

—*One two three four five. One two three four five*—

Let me in and they can't hurt you. No will ever hurt you again. It's the only way. You know it's the only way.

He had no idea if the old man was listening, and as

the blows continued to rain down on him, Michael felt darkness closing in.

When the bum stopped moving, Jimmy spat on him and said, "Guess your balls ain't so big after all, are they, asshole?"

Cuddy crouched over the guy, feeling for a pulse. "Jesus, Jimmy. He's dead. We fuckin' killed him."

Jimmy shrugged. "Self-defense. Besides, he was already halfway there. We just gave him a nudge."

"You think the cops are gonna believe that?"

Jimmy saw a bulge in the guy's back and bent down, pushing his jacket aside. There was a Glock 20 in his waistband. "You see? Fucker was packing. And I don't see any reason to get the cops involved."

Cuddy's eyes were wild. "We're just gonna *leave* him here?" He turned to the old bum by the box office, who was still cradling his head. "What about this asshole? He saw the whole thing."

"Forget him," Weasel said, starting to back away from them. "He won't say nothin'. He's a wack job, remember? He won't do shit."

Jimmy pulled the Glock from the bum's waistband and stood up. "Maybe not. But I'm not willing to give him that chance."

"What're you gonna do," Weasel said, "*shoot* the guy?"

"I ain't gonna take his temperature."

Cuddy shook his head and let loose a nervous laugh. "Jesus, Jimmy, that's some cold-ass shit."

"Think about it. I shoot this asshole, put the gun in

the other one's hand and we got a bum fight gone wrong. Case closed."

Checking the magazine in the Glock, he snapped it back into place and stepped over to the box office, staring down at the old man.

What a waste of fucking space.

Jimmy pointed the Glock at him. "Better say a prayer, dirtbag, if you believe in that kind of thing."

"Oh, I believe," the old man said. And to Jimmy's utter surprise, he pulled his hands away from his head and looked up at him with unnerving clarity. "And so will you before I'm finished."

Then he shot a hand out, grabbing Jimmy by the ankle, pulling his feet out from under him. Jimmy brought the Glock up, but before he could fire, the old man had hold of his wrist. He felt the bones breaking and dropped the gun as he cried out in pain, begging for the old man to let him go.

He heard footsteps on the asphalt behind him, but they were headed in the wrong direction and he knew that Cuddy and Weasel were running away.

Now the old man was standing over him, a foot pressed against Jimmy's chest, an odd, amber tint to his eyes.

"You should've walked away when you had the chance."

Michael left the guy there by the box office. Not dead, but probably wishing he was. And once the police found him, good old Jimmy would have a lot of explaining to do about the badly beaten corpse that lay only feet away from him.

What was it he'd said?

A bum fight gone wrong?

Moving down the street, Michael flexed his hands and rolled his shoulders. The punishment he'd doled out had been a good warm-up, but it would take him a while to break in this new body.

He'd have to do it on the run, however.

It was time to get back to Jenna.

32

The rumblings of disaster began on the Internet.

Beel sat at his desk surfing the news sites. Maybe Moloch and Mammon were right: Maybe the cumulative efforts of the last several hundred years were about to pay off.

For weeks, the blogosphere and the social networks had been abuzz with the news of the release of a classified document. One that allegedly offered proof that Hezbollah militants had not only gotten their hands on a cache of nuclear weapons, but intended to deploy them against Egypt.

The debate raged over whether or not this document was real, but the damage had been done and the governments of Egypt, Syria, Iran and Lebanon were all on high alert, with Israel scrambling to cover itself as well. All parties concerned were spouting tough, heated rhetoric, which generally sent chills down the spines of anyone who was paying attention.

Less than a week later, North Korea renewed its threats of aggression against the South and attempts at diplomacy by the U.S. secretary of state were deemed an unmitigated disaster. War between the two nations was considered unavoidable.

Add to the mix the downward spiral of the world

economy, the riots during the recent G20 summit, violent skirmishes in third world countries, the rise in black market weaponry—including rumors of enriched uranium being smuggled out of Russia—and the general consensus was that the world was about to see a shit storm the likes of which it had never before experienced.

Rather than attempt to find real solutions to these problems, politicians took to the cable airwaves and blamed one another for their failings. Partisan mudslinging had reached a new high. Religious leaders told their followers to begin preparing for the Rapture as the rest of the world sat glued to their TV sets, wondering if they'd be alive for the next episode of *Saints and Sinners.*

Who would be kicked out of the house? Andrew or Tasha?

Beel smiled appreciatively every time his pet project entered the national conversation. To allow themselves to be distracted at such a critical time by television—well, in Beel's opinion, they'd get what they deserved.

Perhaps the tipping point was close, and his brothers' little experiment in Amsterdam would push it over. Or maybe Belial was right about the girl, and the elusive Telum had been found. The ultimate weapon. Beel allowed himself a moment to consider how sweet it would feel to free her.

The hard truth was that nobody really knew what was coming, including—and especially—the world's heads of state. And what chance did humanity really have with the four of them pulling the strings?

And if this girl really *is* the Telum, Beel mused, these pathetic little creatures won't know what hit them on the night of the blood moon.

BOOK VIII

Turbulence on the Road to Enlightenment

Of these the vigilance
I dread, and to elude, thus wrapt in mist
Of midnight vapor glide obscure, and prie
In every Bush and Brake, where hap may finde
The Serpent sleeping, in whose mazie foulds
To hide me, and the dark intent I bring.

—*Paradise Lost*, 1667 ed., VIII:157–62

33

ISTANBUL, TURKEY

Batty and Callahan caught a chartered plane at a small airstrip just west of Istanbul.

But as they crossed the tarmac, Batty felt an energy nearby. A darkness deeper than the darkness around them, as if someone were waiting in the shadows, watching them.

He remembered Ajda in that tunnel and wondered if this feeling was just the lingering residue of her attack. That seemed to happen to him sometimes. He had a hard time shaking this stuff off. But as they climbed the steps to the door of the plane, he stopped a moment and glanced around.

"What is it?" Callahan said, mimicking him, concern in her eyes.

He shook his head. "Nothing to worry about."

He just hoped he was right.

Batty didn't like small planes. Every one he'd ever flown in seemed to have a love affair with turbulence, and this one was no exception. But at least the seats were comfortable. If you had to spend hours bouncing around the sky in a tiny metal tube, it didn't hurt to do it in a chair the size of a Barcalounger.

As usual, Callahan—who sat across the aisle from him—kept her nose buried in her cell phone. She seemed subdued, but he knew her mind was probably racing, just as his had been when he'd first been forced to come to grips with the realities of the world. It was a credit to her tenacity that she was able to hold it together so well.

Callahan was what his mother had called "a woman with no backup." In other words, no reverse. Always moving forward, like a shark. And after seeing what she'd done to Ajda, he didn't envy anyone who got in her way.

He hoped this trip wasn't in vain. Even though Ozan and the monk had been somewhat careful about their e-mails, Batty knew that if Callahan could figure it out, others could as well.

And that meant Brother Philip was in danger.

Of course, they couldn't be absolutely sure that Philip was a guardian. Their information on him was almost nonexistent. It seemed to Batty that a monk wouldn't fit the typical Christopherian profile of spiritual redemption, but there was no telling where Brother Philip had come from. Callahan had requested a background check from her office in Washington, but had yet to hear back from them.

This whole government thing bothered Batty.

Back at the hotel, he had thought about D.C. and the e-mail Ozan had sent to an Internet café there. Knowing this was Callahan's stomping ground, it had raised a question in his mind.

"How did you get involved in this case in the first place?"

"Same way I always do," she'd told him. "They give me an assignment and I catch a plane. This one had a higher priority level than usual, but I'm not supposed to ask questions, just do my job."

"You ever stop to wonder why they sent you to investigate the death of a pop star?"

"Of course I have."

"And what's your conclusion?"

"That they know more than I do. But then they always do."

"Maybe somebody put a bug in their ear."

"Like who?"

Batty shrugged. "Somebody who knows enough to recognize a red flag when he sees one. Maybe somebody who got an e-mail message that said 'Stay alert.' They hear about Gabriela, happen to be close enough to your people to wield some influence, and the next thing you know, you're on a plane."

Callahan looked as if she was weighing a decision, then said, "I'm breaching protocol when I tell you this, but I think the order may have come directly from the White House."

"You think maybe our president is a guardian?"

Callahan laughed. "I highly doubt it, but he's been accused of worse. Maybe somebody in his administration is. And if that's true, then why bother with me? Why not warn the others directly?"

"Maybe he feels compromised. Thinks he's being watched and doesn't want to raise any alarms."

"None of which tells us what's at the root of all of this. Why Milton, of all people? Why *Paradise Lost* and the search for hidden messages? Why all the questions about missing pages and giant books? I can't stand being blindfolded."

"Maybe this Brother Philip will know."

"Assuming we can find him," Callahan said.

They had left it at that, taking a taxi to a remote airport in the dead of night so that some pilot for hire could lock them into a tiny metal tube and bounce them all over the cloudless sky.

But in the end, it wasn't the turbulence that terrified Batty.

It was the nosedive.

Callahan was exhausted. She'd spent the last few hours running the night's insanity through her head, visions of sycophants and human combustibles parading before her mind's eye, convincing her that her entire life had been a fraud.

It wasn't *her* fault that she hadn't known these things existed, had thought that they were merely fantasies created to thrill and entertain in movies and books and around the campfire. But maybe if she'd had an open mind, had not been so closed off to that world, had accepted at least the *possibility* that it existed, she wouldn't be paying for it now.

She thought about that moment in the alley in Paradise City. Seeing her ten-year-old self put a shotgun to her head. Had that merely been a product of her fractured past, or had something more sinister been at work? That whole place was knee-deep in the spooky.

She was, she suddenly realized, verging on another panic attack, and it took everything she had to tamp it down. Her hands were trembling worse than ever and she knew that if she didn't get some decent sleep, very soon, they'd have to carry her off this plane on a stretcher.

But, like always, sleep refused to come.

Unwilling to sit here and let her mind keep recycling the same events until they drove her completely nuts, she pulled Ozan's notepad out of her bag and started going through the verses he'd copied, concentrating on the crossed-out letters and words, trying to see if she could find what Ozan had been looking for.

She'd read up a little on Trithemius's code schemes and one of the codes featured in *Steganographia* was called the Ave Maria cipher, in which you looked for every other letter in every other word. But it was clear that Ozan had already covered that ground and had come up with zip.

And no matter how she rearranged these words, she got nothing. Absolutely nothing. If there were any hidden messages here, they were beyond her feeble mind. Still, she spent the good part of an hour running through the possibilities before she finally gave up in utter frustration.

And she still couldn't sleep.

Pulling Ozan's iPad into her lap, she thought about checking for more e-mails, but the labs at Section had already been alerted and were busy scouring Ozan's server, so she didn't see any real point. Instead, she navigated to the *New York Times* Web site and stared morosely at the home page:

STATE DEPARTMENT WARNS OF NUCLEAR
PROLIFERATION

The story warned that U.S. intelligence agencies had encountered evidence of the recent distribution of weapons-grade uranium throughout the Middle East and Africa. Some were concerned that several nuclear warheads had already been built and could well be circulating on the black market, and the impending threat of doom hung heavy over everyone in D.C.

The attorney general insisted that there was no need for alarm. He was working night and day and, with the president's help, was busy putting together an international coalition to study and address these concerns. Most experts, however, agreed that this was too little, too late. The fuse was already burning and might not be all that easy to put out.

Maybe it wasn't dark angels they had to worry about, Callahan thought.

Why the hell was she headed to Thailand?

Dumping the iPad in disgust, she settled back in her chair and closed her eyes. Maybe if she could just let herself go, didn't try so hard, her creeping anxiety would subside and sleep would find her.

When she was very young, and her father was still alive, he would perch himself on the edge of her bed at night and sing her a song. She could always smell the booze on his breath, but she loved him and he was there and that was all that counted. She remembered his voice, low and sweet, as he stroked her forehead with his fingertips.

Then, to her surprise, there it was—his voice—right now. There inside her head:

Sleep, Bernadette. Sleep.

The sound was as real as if he'd whispered in her ear. But she knew that was impossible. He'd been dead for most of her life.

Sleep, my angel. Sleep. I'm here with you. I always will be. So let yourself go and sleep.

Yes, she thought. Sleep.

Maybe she could manage it after all.

The moment she thought this, all of her cares began to melt away, like magic. Sleep was now a real possibility, an all-*consuming* possibility, and the temptation was too great to resist. Her anxiety would no longer be an issue. The tremors would stop. The world along with them. Everything would be better if she just let it take her.

Sleep, my darling.

And before Callahan knew it, sweet, blissful darkness wrapped itself around her . . . and swept her away.

Three minutes before the nosedive, Batty pulled the Milton manuscript from his book bag, finally ready to look at it.

It was a work of beauty. The worn leather cover. The time-aged pages. The fading ink. The flawless blank verse. Over ten thousand words. Words that had meant so much to him for so many years. Words that Milton claimed had come from God himself.

So was it possible that there was something in this draft that would open the door for them?

Batty supposed he should feel guilty for stealing it from a dead man, but he didn't. If it wasn't a fake—and he instinctively believed it wasn't—then it deserved to be in a museum somewhere, to be shared with the world, not locked up in a private library.

The most commonly seen version of *Paradise Lost*, the one taught in schools and found in the bookstores, was twelve chapters long. The twelve-chapter version had first been published the year Milton died, but that wasn't his original intent. The first incarnation of the poem, published several years earlier, had contained only *ten* chapters. But at the request of his publisher, Milton had divided chapters seven and ten and added short summaries to all twelve for the more poetry-challenged readers in the crowd.

The version Batty now held in his hands, dictated to Milton's daughter, held the original ten chapters, and several of its pages showed additions and corrections, and marks in the margins.

Maybe this was where the secret lay.

But in leafing through it, his mind nearly frozen with awe, Batty frowned as he came to the end of the last chapter—Book X. Something looked off here. A subtle but unmistakable anomaly in the binding. And on closer inspection, he saw what may well have been *torn* edges, as if several pages had been removed.

Could he be mistaken?

He didn't think so.

So was this *Ozan's* doing?

When he read through it, however, there seemed to be nothing amiss. The verses flowed just as they should, from Michael's revelation of the future to Adam and Eve's departure from Paradise.

Then the missing pages. If he wasn't imagining things.

So what had been removed?

He was pondering the significance of this when the jet suddenly bucked, a violent jolt of turbulence that dropped them several feet, leaving Batty's stomach behind in the process. He quickly set the manuscript onto the table beside him and tightened his seat belt.

Outside his window, a storm was brewing, threatening to make the previous bit of turbulence seem like child's play.

He glanced over at Callahan, but she was asleep. Lucky her. Then the plane buckled again and Batty grabbed his armrests, wishing to hell he had a parachute strapped to his back, because this wasn't looking good.

Suddenly aware of the smell of sulfur, he glanced again at Callahan, surprised to find her fully awake now and looking right back at him. Her gaze was unsettling in its directness.

"What's the matter, Sebastian? You afraid of a little turbulence?"

Her eyes didn't flinch, and that gaze was mesmerizing.

"You shouldn't be afraid, darling. I won't let anything happen to you. I'd *never* let anything happen to you. You mean too much to me."

Darling?

What the hell was going on with her? Batty tried to look away, but he couldn't. His eyeballs seemed frozen. His head wouldn't move.

Callahan unbuckled her seat belt now. "It hurt me to see you so angry, Sebastian. To see that hate in your eyes. You don't really hate me, do you? I only did what had to be done."

And all at once Batty realized that this wasn't Callahan at all.

This was the redhead.

She got to her feet and crossed the aisle toward him. "After all, it wasn't my fault, was it? *Rebecca* was the one who invited me into your home. *Rebecca* was the one who called. All I did was answer. So if you have to blame someone, don't blame me. Blame her."

Smiling now, she stood over him and began unbuttoning her shirt. "Besides, she could never give you a night like I did. She would never surrender herself, let you use her body the way I let you use mine."

The jet bucked wildly, but she barely seemed to notice, sidestepping only slightly as she dropped her shirt to the floor. "It's yours for the taking, my darling. Touch me anywhere you want."

Batty's mind was racing. He again tried to look away but he couldn't. Her gaze was too hard to resist. And now she was moving forward, straddling him, reaching her hands back to unhook her bra.

"Tell me you want me, Sebastian. I'm yours for the taking."

The engines began to scream, and the jet tilted into a dive, but suddenly Batty didn't care. He just wanted to lose himself in Callahan's gaze, to feel her flesh in his hands . . .

"Show me how much you want me, my darling. Feel me. *Taste* me. Put your lips on me. Let me feel your tongue."

A rush of pleasure washed through Batty's body and he still couldn't look away. And then, to his utter surprise, he saw Rebecca's face, smiling down at him, speaking in that subtle Louisiana drawl, "Show me how much you want me, Batty."

Then she leaned toward him, her tongue creasing his lips as she brushed her hand against his crotch, her fingers finding him, kneading him.

He couldn't believe it was her. Two long years without her, and now here she was, alive and vibrant, working her fingers until he grew hard against them.

Then the jet bucked again, knocking them sideways, and Rebecca reached out to steady herself. Her hand touched the Milton manuscript and she hissed, jerking it away.

Batty felt as if he'd been slapped in the face.

He blinked and looked at her, abruptly coming to his senses. And he was once again looking at Callahan's face.

But in that moment, he saw what truly lay behind her eyes:

The mind of a beast. A hideous, feral beast.

Thrusting his arms out, he shoved her away, knocking her backward into the aisle as the jet continued its rapid dive.

She hissed at him and pulled herself upright, starting to rise as—

—Batty flung his seat belt off and sprang from his seat, knocking her back down, sending her sprawling, shouting, "Callahan! Wake up!"

But she couldn't hear him, didn't respond, again getting to her feet, coming toward him with her teeth bared, her face curled up in a snarl. "You're fucking *mine*, you little insect."

Batty started to back away, glancing around him, trying to think what he could use to fight her off. But there was nothing.

Then his gaze shifted to the manuscript and he remembered how she had reacted when she'd touched it. It suddenly occurred to him that if it truly *was* the original manuscript, and it truly *was* the divine word of God . . .

Scooping it up off the table, he got it between both hands, and as Callahan advanced, he shoved it toward her, pressing it against her breasts. She howled as if it burned, her eyes filling with agony as she stumbled back.

And now she was *really* mad.

With a deep, animal growl, she surged forward again, coming at Batty at full speed. He threw his hands up, holding the book out, and she slammed into it, howling as it touched her flesh. They crashed into the aisle and Batty scrambled, getting on top of her, keeping the book pressed against her chest.

"Wake up!" he shouted.

She continued to howl and hiss and moan, writhing beneath him, the whites of her eyes turning red, as if the blood vessels were starting to burst. She hammered at him with her fists, landing several solid blows to his ribs—

—but Batty didn't let up. Kept the manuscript in place.

"Wake up, Callahan! *Wake the fuck up!*"

Then suddenly her eyes went blank and she stopped. Her arms fell to her sides and she was still.

Then the jet leveled off, steadying itself, the storm now behind them.

Batty pulled the manuscript from Callahan's breasts,

and stared down at her half-naked form, relieved, but barely able to catch his breath. .

Then Callahan blinked, the life coming back into her eyes.

And when she realized Batty was straddling her, she glanced down at her exposed body, then back up at him in horror and said, "What the *fuck*?"

34

CHIANG MAI, THAILAND

The place Brother Philip called home was the only Christian monastery in Chiang Mai.

Callahan hadn't spent a lot of time here and was frankly surprised that in a country that was overwhelmingly Buddhist, there were any Christian churches at all.

As usual, LaLaurie was all too happy to educate her.

"The Portuguese brought Christianity to Siam in the sixteenth century," he said.

They were riding through town in back of a *tuk tuk*, a three-wheeled motorized rickshaw. Their driver wore earbuds and seemed intent on killing someone as he blasted through the crowded streets.

"King Narai let the Roman Catholics in because he was curious about them and the world they'd come from. Unfortunately, that curiosity wasn't shared by everyone in government, and when Narai died, the Europeans were either killed or kicked out."

"Isn't that always the way?"

"Then around the late seventeen hundreds Taksin let some French missionaries come in, followed by the Baptists and the Presbyterians in the early part of the next century. They've never been more than a blip on the radar compared to the Buddhists, but they've made their mark."

As he spoke, there was a bit of a twinkle in LaLaurie's eyes, which annoyed Callahan no end. She knew what he was thinking whenever he looked at her now. She barely remembered anything that had happened on that plane, had just wanted to push past it and do her job. But she couldn't.

When she'd come to, with LaLaurie straddling her—vague images of their encounter dancing through the cobwebs in her brain—the thought that she hadn't been in complete control of her body had scared the crap out of her.

But that was something she could cope with. LaLaurie had assured her that even though she'd somehow given permission for that thing to use her, no permanent damage had been done. He'd managed to drive the invader away before it could get a lasting hold on her and suck out her soul.

Which was all well and good, she thought, but what bothered her most of all was one small, niggling detail—

—LaLaurie had seen her naked.

The feeling was irrational. Crazy. She knew that. She'd never been particularly modest. But the way LaLaurie kept looking at her now, she couldn't help but feel violated.

"There are a lot of expats and tourists in Thailand," he went on, "so you'll still find a number of churches, and several Christian hospitals in the country that—"

"Eyes up here," Callahan told him, touching her nose.

"What?"

"You're talking to *me*, Professor, not my bra."

LaLaurie gave her a slow smile. "Are you still stuck on that? Trust me, Callahan, I'm not fourteen anymore. Although I do have to admit—"

"Stop right there," she said. "If you value your life, just stop."

The monastery was not quite what Callahan had expected. It looked like any of the wood and terra-cotta structures you'd find in the neighborhoods of Chiang Mai, only on a larger scale, with multiple stories and a stone fence surrounding it.

When Callahan thought monastery, however, she imagined a massive compound with a church and housing for dozens of monks. But this place barely had room for a chapel and maybe twelve or so residences.

A bit of a letdown.

"Brother Philip is no longer here," the monk at the front door told them. He was a Frenchman, and Callahan knew that most of the monks were not Thai natives. "He left two days ago."

She had been expecting this. After that e-mail from Ozan, she wouldn't be surprised if *all* of the remaining guardians went into hiding.

"Is there any way we can contact him? He's had a death in the family and we're trying to locate him."

Not strictly a lie.

The monk gave them a quizzical look. "Family? I was not aware he had any family."

"His grandfather. He died suddenly and mentioned Brother Philip in his will. We know he won't be interested in the money, so we need him to sign a document to that effect."

"As I told you, he isn't here."

"Do you mind if we take a look at his sleeping quarters?"

"Why?"

"He may have left something behind that'll lead us to him," she said. "This really *is* important."

The monk stared at them for a long time, and Callahan wondered if he saw straight through her. But a life devoted to Christ did not necessarily make you clairvoyant.

"We have nothing to hide," he said and ushered them inside.

The good news: There were no scorch marks on the floor.

The bad news was that his room was not only small, it was also devoid of any personal belongings. Other than a chair and writing table, a neatly made twin bed, a sink and mirror and a mostly empty closet, there wasn't anything of use here. Nothing that might tell Callahan where Brother Philip had gone.

The only glimmer of hope was the wastebasket under the sink, which had some trash in it. Callahan had done her share of basket diving in the past, to varied success—itineraries, ticket stubs, scribbled phone numbers, boxes of hair dye. They all told a story if you took a moment to work it through.

But all she found in the wastebasket were a few used

tissues—mmmm, lovely—and a discarded wrapper for a bar of Parrot Soap.

"So much for that idea," she muttered as she turned to LaLaurie. "You want to do your thing?"

But LaLaurie was already at it, his palm pressed against the writing table, his eyes squeezed shut. He opened them and shook his head. "I'm not getting anything. This room is clear."

Callahan sighed, ready to call it a bust, when she glanced at the sink.

The usual toiletries were there, along with a cup and toothbrush. But what caught her eye was the soap.

It was a fresh bar, which wasn't surprising, considering the wrapper in the waste can. But what she found unusual was that one corner was flattened, worn down, as if it had been rubbed against something solid.

But what?

She was about to dismiss it when LaLaurie pointed and said, "What's that?"

There was only one window in the room, but the sunlight filtering in from outside shone directly across the mirror above the sink, which was what LaLaurie was pointing at. Callahan adjusted her angle, and that's when she saw it.

Soap marks on the glass.

Moving in close, she took a deep breath and huffed warm air across the surface of mirror. It took several tries, but when she was done, the message was clear, written in English:

PROTECT HER

She turned to LaLaurie. "We're too late. Brother Philip is angel food."

LaLaurie moved over to the mirror and pressed his hand against the glass, closing his eyes again.

"I'm still not feeling anything. I'm guessing he's alive." He looked at Callahan. "But there's only one reason to leave this message, and it's the same reason he ran."

"Which is?"

No smiles now, no drifting gaze. "He knows his time is short."

35

Batty liked helicopters even less than he liked small planes. But here he was, sitting in back of a black MH-6 Little Bird, trying to keep his stomach in check as the pilot worked the stick and soared above the slopes of the Loi Lar mountain range.

After leaving Brother Philip's living quarters, he and Callahan had questioned as many of the monks as they could find. But the rest of Philip's brethren were just as clueless about his whereabouts as the guy who had greeted them at the front door.

They had pretty much given up when the cleaning lady followed them outside and told them she'd spoken to Philip the morning he left.

"I come to work and he tell me not to clean his room." She was a middle-aged Thai woman who couldn't have been more than four foot five. She yanked at her collar with both hands. "He wear backpack, with food and supply. The one he always carry when he go to worship at the brothers' retreat."

"Retreat?" Callahan said.

She nodded. "They close it long time, but the brothers sometime go when they visit the hill tribe."

"Where? Where do we find it?"

The cleaning lady pointed past the fence toward the lush green peaks of a nearby mountain range.

"There," she said. "Close to God." Then she wished them *chok dee ka* and went inside.

Callahan immediately got on her cell phone and ordered up the helicopter. As they took another *tuk tuk* to the designated departure point, she opened an app and logged on to a satellite feed.

A moment later she showed Batty what looked like a large stone cross on the side of a mountain near the Doi Inthanon summit.

"Close to God," she said. "Let's find out how much good it did him."

The pilot was a scruffy-looking expat named McNab who did contract work for the U.S. government. He flew with a seasoned hand, but that didn't keep Batty from feeling the urge to lean out the fuselage door and heave the samurai pork burger he'd gobbled up on their way in from the airport.

He didn't know what samurais had to do with Thailand, but right now that sickly sweet teriyaki sauce was ripping up his insides like a freshly forged bushido blade.

McNab goosed the controls, then rose over a high ridge. Just beyond it lay a mountainside crowded with teak trees and mountain pine. A narrow dirt trail snaked down its long slope toward the sprawling lowlands, past the terraced rice fields and the rustic villages that the Kariang and Padaung hill tribes called home.

To the northeast lay Burma, which, along with Thailand and Laos, formed the Golden Triangle, once known for its thriving opium trade, but now home to a growing methamphetamine industry.

Banking right, McNab flew them around a large outcropping and found what they were looking for. High on a cliff and carved into the side of the mountain was a crumbling, moss-infested stone temple, fronted by a huge granite cross.

"Wow. That's quite a sight," McNab said into his headpiece.

Batty suspected the place was a couple centuries old, carefully built, stone by stone, by overzealous and severely misguided missionaries. The spread of Christianity had largely been a failure in Thailand, and the temple's remote location would have made it attractive only to the few converted hill tribes or the true believers.

Or to someone trying to hide.

Callahan was sitting up front with McNab. "You think you can put us down somewhere?"

McNab pointed to a small clearing to the right of the entrance. "No worries. There's more than enough room."

Less than a minute later they touched down and Batty and Callahan climbed out, ducking low as they passed under the rotors and crossed toward the temple.

Batty was happy to be back on solid ground. He slung his book bag over his shoulder and held it close. Now that he knew the manuscript's power, he didn't dare let it go.

The temple's massive teak doors were hanging open, nothing but darkness beyond them. Callahan moved up the crumbling steps to enter, but Batty held her back.

"Wait," he said. "I'm not getting a good feeling here."

"What's wrong?"

He stood very still, drinking in the temple's aura, absorbing its long history. There was a richness of spirit to this place—both good and evil—but nothing of immediate concern. The danger he'd felt was merely the remnants from some long past incident.

"False alarm," he said.

"You sure?"

He nodded. "We're safe. For now."

"Just remind me not to fall asleep," she muttered.

They continued up the steps until they reached the doorway, then paused at the threshold, peering cautiously inside.

The room beyond was cavernous, with stone pillars along either side and an enormous nave ceiling. The pillars had been painted with scenes from Scripture, full of cherubs and clouds and swooning maidens, but the colors were faded, the images worn away by time. The floor was made of intricately carved terra-cotta tile, but the years had been unkind and there were cracks in several places, with moss growing between them.

In fact, as Batty looked around, he thought it was something of a miracle that the place was standing at all. A sudden cough, and it might very well come tumbling down around them.

They stepped inside, moving toward an archway in back, neither of them saying a word. There were deep shadows beyond the pillars, but Batty wasn't getting any unusual vibes. Still, he half expected to find the remains of Brother Philip's toasted corpse somewhere.

As they stepped past the last pillar, Batty heard a faint *click* and something cold and hard touched the side of his neck.

"That's about far enough," a voice said.

So much for his sixth sense.

Batty and Callahan froze, and a husky guy with a shaved head, wearing a dark brown cassock, stepped from behind the pillar.

"Repeat after me," he said. "I accept Jesus Christ as my Lord and savior."

Callahan stared at him. "What?"

"Just say it or I'll pull the trigger right now. I accept Jesus Christ as my Lord and savior."

Batty and Callahan exchanged looks, but Batty knew what this was. He was giving them a test. If they could repeat the oath, they passed. If not, they were either dark angels, drudges or sycophants, and Brother Philip—assuming that's who this guy was—would blow Batty's head off.

Batty didn't have the heart to tell him this was probably a waste of time. He nodded to Callahan and they both repeated the oath. "I accept Jesus Christ as my Lord and savior."

Brother Philip seemed satisfied, but said, "Okay, step two. Before we get to introductions, if either or both of you have weapons, put them on the floor right now."

Batty had never seen Callahan carrying a weapon—hell, the way she could punch, she didn't need one—and he sure didn't carry any himself, so he just raised his hands, showing them empty and hoped this would be enough to make Brother Philip happy.

"Weapon free," Callahan told him.

"What about the guy flying the helicopter? Any chance he'll come in here and start blasting away?"

Batty and Callahan exchanged looks again.

"I think you're okay," she said.

Philip eyed them warily, a slight nervous tic in his jaw; then he finally relaxed and lowered the gun. "Okay, who are you and what are you doing here?"

36

"With all due respect," Callahan said, "you don't act much like a monk."

They were in an adjacent room now, sitting at a long table. Philip was camping out in here, his backpack and provisions piled in a corner. A kerosene lamp glowed beside him as he set out three paper cups and started pouring tea from a thermos.

He was full of nervous energy and it had taken them a few minutes to get him loosened up. "And what's a monk supposed to act like?"

Callahan shrugged. "I just expected you to be more . . . holy."

Philip nodded as if he understood. "I was pretty bowled over the first time I saw a priest smoking a cigarette and knocking back a shot of whiskey. We get these preconceived notions of what it means to be holy, and when somebody doesn't live up to the stereotype, we're surprised."

"You have to admit a monk with a gun is a little unusual," Batty said.

Philip finished pouring and pushed their cups across the table. "Hey, what can I tell you? I grew up in Jersey and I wasn't always with the monastery. And when your life is in danger, old habits die hard—you know what I mean? I haven't seen anything in the handbook says I've gotta be a hero."

Callahan frowned at him. "Are you *sure* you're Brother Philip?"

He glared at her. "What do you want, an ID? I'm afraid I left it in my other pants." He gestured to her cup. "You're not gonna drink your tea?"

Callahan eyed it suspiciously and didn't pick it up. "Why don't you tell us about the e-mail?"

"E-mail?"

"The one you sent in reply to Koray Ozan a couple weeks ago."

Philip had his own cup to his lips. He paused. "You know about that?"

"Ozan wasn't a genius when it came to computer security."

"Fair enough," he said, then took a quick sip. "What else do you know?"

"That you're *Custodes Sacri*," Batty told him. "And I'm guessing you're wearing the medallion right now."

Philip stared at him a long moment, as if trying decide whether he could trust him. Then he shrugged, reached into his collar and brought out the Saint Christopher medal hanging from a thick leather strap around his neck. "I'm starting to think this thing is costing me a lot more than it's worth."

"How long have you been with the order?"

"Long enough to know I shouldn't be talking to strangers about it."

"Let's get back to the e-mail," Callahan said. "Why was Ozan asking about the seven missing pages from the Devil's Bible?"

"Because he was a curious old fool. And curious fools wind up dead."

"Or blind," Batty said. "Like Milton?"

"Milton, Galileo and God knows who before them."

Batty was surprised. "Galileo?"

"That's how Milton got the bug. Galileo told him about the missing pages and he went looking for them. Or so the story goes. At this point, I'm not sure how much of it's true. These things tend to get distorted after a while."

"What's on those pages?" Callahan asked.

"A curse; I know that much. It's what drove both Galileo and Milton blind. But as far as I know, the pages from the Codex don't even exist anymore. When Milton realized how dangerous they were, he burned them."

"So how does this connect to *Paradise Lost*?" Batty asked. "What were Ozan and Gabriela Zuada trying so hard to find in Book Eleven?"

Philip looked from Batty to Callahan. "You two have been doing your homework. You'd better be careful, or you'll wind up just like Milton. Or Ozan. Although at this point it probably doesn't matter."

"Why?"

"Have you looked outside lately? What's happening in the world right now is enough to scare the Jesus right out of you. Everybody's favorite demons have been very busy—manipulating the stock market, flooding cities with drugs, whispering in the ears of those on the brink of waging war. And once the fourth moon comes, they'll finally be able to release all their slaves—a lot more than there ever were before—and that'll be the end of us."

"Fourth moon?" Callahan said.

"The fourth moon of the tetrad. It hits in two days."

She frowned. "What are you talking about?"

"An eclipse," Batty told her. "The fourth eclipse this year."

"Look," Brother Philip said, "do yourself a favor, go home and be with your loved ones, because the way it's looking, the bad guys have already won. And by this time next week, we'll either all be dead or so close to it, we'll wish we were."

"Are you talking the Apocalypse?" Callahan asked.

Philip snorted. "The Apocalypse is a fairy tale. But it pretty much amounts to the same thing. Only none of us will be seeing the Rapture anytime soon."

"And you're saying there's no way to stop it?"

"Not the way I see it. This train has no brakes. This is the modern age, with global communication, instant information, and opportunities to corrupt twenty-four/ seven on a worldwide basis. The pump has never been this well primed before. Unless Michael can pull off some kind of miracle, we're sunk. And if the bad guys get hold of the Telum before he does, that's a whole new level of—"

"Telum?" Batty said. "What's the Telum?"

Philip shook his head. "I've already told you too much."

"Then it won't hurt to tell us more. What *is* it? A weapon of some kind?"

Philip hesitated. Seemed torn. Then he said, "A wandering soul. A sacred traveler who's reborn every generation in human form."

"The one you're sworn to protect."

He nodded. "There was a time Michael thought *I*

might be the one, and Ozan before me, and the rest of the guardians. But he was wrong."

"Then who is it?"

"That's the million-dollar question, isn't it?"

"But if you don't know who it is," Callahan said, "how do you protect anyone?"

"By protecting the key. The key that frees her."

"And where is this key?"

Philip shook his head and gestured to their cups. "I'm done being friendly. I think it's time for you two to drink your tea and get out of here. Let me have my last hours in peace."

But Batty wouldn't let up. "Tell us about the key, Brother."

Philip drained the last of his cup and got to his feet. "Sorry, but that's all you'll get out of me. Right now, I'm just trying to protect myself." He lifted the gun from the table. "They can come after me, but I'm not going down without a fight. So if you two don't mind, I'd like to—"

Thunder rumbled outside and the temple floor began to shake. Violently. Batty and Callahan grabbed their chairs as Brother Philip stumbled back, his face going slack.

"She's here," he said.

Batty felt a sudden darkness spread through him. "Who's here?" But he could already feel her.

"Who do you think? Their enforcer. The angel of confusion."

Callahan furrowed her brow. "The angel of *what*?"

"You lead her right to me . . ."

Belial, Batty thought. The Demon of Lust. The Lord of Pride. One of the players in *Paradise Lost*. And Batty had a very strong feeling that she was currently inhabiting this earth as a drop-dead gorgeous, tongue-wagging, coma-inducing redhead.

Is *that* who he'd been dealing with?

Thunder rumbled again and the floor rolled beneath them. Pieces of the ceiling began to crumble and fall and Callahan shouted, "Let's get out of here. Go!"

But Brother Philip just stood there, frozen in place, as the temple crumbled around them. Callahan grabbed his arm, then yanked him around the table and through the doors as Batty snatched up his book bag and followed. The floor chattered and cracked, and he stumbled, nearly going down, but managed to stay upright and barreled out the door, dodging chunks of stone as he went.

And as they reached the main room, they stopped cold, staring wide-eyed at a woman standing in the open doorway, silhouetted against the malevolent sky.

She smiled. Stared directly at Batty.

"I have a little bone to pick with you."

The redhead. And despite himself, Batty felt a sudden tingling in his loins.

She was mesmerizing.

"That wasn't very nice what you did to me on that plane," she said. "After all we've been to each other, I'd think you'd show me a little more respect."

Visions of their night together filled his head, and he knew she was doing this to him. Feeding these images into his brain. He tried to resist, but her hold on him was strong, and he could feel himself giving in to her.

She gestured to his book bag. "You can start by giving me that manuscript. I think it might be just what I've been looking for."

The temple rocked again, parts of the wall crumbling, and Batty clutched the book bag to his side, mustering up every bit of his will. "Forget it," he said.

"Come on, now, Sebastian. I promise you'll enjoy the reward . . ."

Callahan turned to him now. "Who the hell *is* this chick?"

Belial shifted her gaze. "You don't recognize me, Bernadette? I'm the one who sang you to sleep today. I sang your daddy to sleep, too."

Her smiled widened.

As Batty watched, Callahan's expression shifted from confusion to realization then to outright fury.

Then she said, "*You have got to be fucking kidding me.*"

With a shriek of rage, she took a flying, headlong leap at Belial, but Belial seemed to have anticipated this. She sidestepped and swung an arm out, hitting Callahan with an invisible blow. It knocked her sideways, into a pillar, and she hit it with a grunt, dropping to the floor.

The dark clouds behind Belial rumbled and rolled. "The manuscript, Sebastian. Give me the manuscript."

"Why do you want it? What's in it?"

"A guarantee," she said. "But that's not your concern, is it? Just give it to me now, or I'll hurt your little—"

A gunshot rang out. Then another.

Batty jerked his head around and Brother Philip had his pistol raised, shakily aiming it at Belial. The bullets ricocheted around her and he adjusted his aim and fired again. The third bullet rocketed straight toward Belial and she shot a hand in the air, catching it in her palm.

"Quaint," she said, then suddenly whipped the hand out, flinging the bullet right back at Brother Philip. A dark red hole opened up between his eyes, and he slumped to his knees, the gun slipping from his fingers.

He croaked once, then fell forward onto his face.

Thunder rumbled and the floor shifted again, Batty struggling to maintain his balance as he looked in horror at Philip's body.

"Such a shame," Belial said. "I so wanted to have some fun with him." She looked at Batty. "Last chance, Sebastian. Give me the manuscript or—"

Callahan came out of nowhere. A flying tackle straight to Belial's gut. The redhead screeched as Callahan wrapped her arms around her, and the two tumbled through the doorway and down the steps, disappearing from view.

The floor shifted and swayed as more debris showered down around Batty. Staggering toward Brother Philip, he snatched up the gun and ran outside.

Callahan and Belial were at the bottom of the steps, Callahan straddling her now, reaching for her throat. But then, in the blink of an eye, Belial *vanished*, and Callahan tumbled forward. A split second later, Belial was behind her, delivering a kick to Callahan's ribs.

Callahan grunted and tumbled sideways. But to Batty's surprise, she was on her feet again in an instant, bringing her arms up in a combat stance. Batty had seen what she'd done to Ajda, but Belial wasn't any sycophant and wouldn't be so easily tamed. Still, the body she occupied was human—and built for seduction, not fighting—and she could feel pain just like anyone else.

He considered using the manuscript on her again, but she was so entrenched in this particular skin that he doubted it would have any effect on her. And he didn't want to risk her taking it away from him. She seemed to believe that there was something special about it, that it had some special power—a guarantee, she'd said—and he'd be damned if he put that power in her hands.

As she lunged for Callahan, he raised the pistol, aimed for her back, then squeezed off a shot. It hit home and Belial grunted, stumbling forward, blood pumping out from a hole just below her shoulder blade. Batty thought he'd feel joy in putting a bullet into the creature who had killed his wife, but it was a joyless act.

All he felt was contempt.

Belial whirled and glared at him, her eyes angrier than he'd ever seen them—a hot, luminescent yellow. Then the ground began to shake harder than ever, chunks of stone breaking away from the temple walls and shooting out like mortar fire, slamming into the earth around him. She swiped an arm in his direction and the impact to his chest was as sharp and painful as if she'd delivered the blow directly. The gun went flying as he tumbled back onto the temple steps, the wind knocked out of him.

Taking advantage of the moment, Callahan advanced on Belial and swung out, landing a solid punch to her throat. Belial made a gagging sound and staggered back, grabbing her neck—

—but Callahan kept moving forward. She shifted her body sideways and kicked out, the sole of her boot landing smack in the middle of Belial's gut.

Across the yard, the pilot—McNab—was climbing out of the helicopter, staring at them in utter disbelief.

Even from this distance, Batty could see the panic in his eyes, and he knew what was coming next. He tried to call out to McNab, but no words would come, he could barely breathe.

Then McNab scrambled back into the helicopter, and a moment later, the whine of its engines filled the air as the rotors started whirling.

He was about to leave them behind.

"Stop!" Batty shouted, finally able to breathe, but his voice was drowned out by the roar of the rotors and the rumbling of the sky.

Chunks of the temple showered down around them as Callahan continued her assault, fueled by anger, punching and kicking, knocking Belial back.

But Belial wasn't close to being down or out, and she suddenly vanished—

—only to reappear *behind* Callahan again.

Then *Belial* was advancing, waving her hand like a wand, each wave sending a jolt of energy in Callahan's direction, Callahan grunting and stumbling, trying to recover but finding it harder and harder with each new blow.

Batty spotted the gun where it had fallen and clambered across the steps, reaching for it, getting it in his grip. Pulling himself upright, he aimed again and squeezed the trigger—

—but the gun clicked. Empty.

Shit.

And now Callahan was on the ground, and he could see that she was weakening. She tried to strike out, but Belial knocked her back with another invisible blow. Then the redhead moved forward and stood over Callahan, blood pouring from the wound below her shoulder blade.

Raising her voice so that she could be heard over the roar of the rotors, she said, "Give me the manuscript, Sebastian, or I'll rip her head off and drink her fucking blood."

And Batty had no doubt she'd do it. No doubt at all.

But then something unexpected happened.

Batty heard a sound, a soft *plock* that registered just below the whine of the chopper blades. Belial's eyes went blank and she stumbled forward slightly, as if buffeted by a sudden wind.

Then she turned, and he could plainly see the hole in the back of her head, a small trickle of blood seeping from it, turning her copper-colored hair a darker shade of red. He hadn't seen an exit wound, so he could only assume the bullet was lodged in her brain—or what was left of it. The impact had surely mushroomed through her skull, destroying everything in its path.

Then another shot rang out, hitting her in the cheek, spinning her around, the side of her face turning into raw, bloody hamburger. A third shot quickly followed, putting a hole through the back of her neck, and she dropped to her knees, her eyes now filled with shock and rage and dismay.

It took Batty a moment to figure out where the gunfire was coming from. Swiveling his head, he looked toward the helicopter.

Across the yard, McNab lay on his belly, a sniper rifle in hand. He smiled, as if satisfied by a job well done, but Belial suddenly screeched and swept an arm through the air.

A chunk of the temple broke free, rocketed across the

yard like a small comet and slammed into the helicopter's gas tank.

As McNab jumped to his feet, the chopper exploded in a ball of fire behind him. He screamed as the flames enveloped him, instantly turning him into a roasted human marshmallow. Then he slammed to the ground and stopped moving.

The concussion lifted the helicopter several feet into the air; then it dropped back down, landing on its side, its rotors snapping as the flames quickly gutted it.

And as they burned away, Belial teetered a moment, turning to Batty, her eyes now full of sadness, a fountain of blood pouring from the hole in her neck and down the side of her face. Then she toppled onto her back, the blood spreading on the ground beneath her.

As he slowly regained his senses, Batty staggered to his feet, shell-shocked, not quite believing what he'd just witnessed. He stumbled to the bottom of the steps and stood over a broken Belial, once again wondering how he could ever have taken her into his bed.

After a moment, Callahan got up and stood next to him, her fists involuntarily clenched, as if she were waiting for the bitch to make another move.

Then Belial's mouth opened and blood bubbled up on her lips as she tried and failed to speak.

But Batty heard her voice inside his head.

This isn't over, my darling. We're connected, you and me. That was Rebecca's gift to us . . .

Then air escaped from between her lips as the life went out of her eyes and her body abruptly went still, abandoned by its occupant. It was, after all was said and done, just a human vessel, a skin, a means to an end that meant nothing more to her than a wrecked car or a torn dress. She had no use for it now and she was gone.

A moment later, the rumbling stopped.

The sky was clear.

The earth still.

Even if Batty's heartbeat wasn't.

37

"That old woman with the really long neck is staring at me," Callahan said.

They had been hiking for what seemed like hours, following the winding trail down the mountain past the rice fields and the tribal villages, both of them on edge, but exhausted after the debacle at the temple.

And that's exactly what it had been. A debacle.

What else could you call it?

Two good men were dead, the temple in ruins, a helicopter destroyed, and Batty and Callahan were lucky to have gotten out of there with their souls still intact.

One of the only blessings to come of it, Batty thought, was the dispatching of Belial—at least in her current human form. But he knew they hadn't seen the last of her.

This isn't over, my darling.

Belial might not return in the form of knock-'em-dead redhead, but she'd be back, stronger than ever. You could count on it. It would take a lot more than a couple of clueless mortals to destroy her, and all he could think to do was to keep moving forward in hopes they'd get lucky again the next time.

At least they'd come away from the debacle with a bit of knowledge. Thanks to Brother Philip, they now knew this went well beyond a few calculated attacks against the guardians. There was a plan in motion and it was an ugly one. A plan that would reach its conclusion during the coming eclipse.

The fourth moon.

Batty knew about lunar tetrads, knew they were rare, but he'd never considered that there was a power in them that would help Belial and her friends open the gates of hell. And he knew in his gut that this was exactly what they were planning. After years of trying, they had finally harnessed enough corrupted souls to overwhelm all the good in the world and deliver to them the paradise they sought.

The paradise they had lost.

But based on what Brother Philip had said, he could conclude only that Saint Michael had a plan of his own. A plan that involved the sacred traveler, whoever that might be.

A wandering soul. The Telum.

The word itself was Latin for *weapon*—which was why he had asked Philip about it—but how could a person be a weapon?

And what about the key the guardians were protecting? Was its secret somehow hidden in this manuscript he had tucked under his arm?

Was that why Gabriela and Ozan had worked so hard to decipher it?

Why Belial had wanted it?

"She's really giving me the evil eye," Callahan said. "Should I be worried?"

Pulling himself out of his thoughts, Batty looked off to their left where an old tribal woman with gold neck rings was watching them work their way down the trail.

"I doubt Belial would be able to find a new skin quite that fast. Besides, she'd do a lot more than stare."

"You can understand why I'm a little jumpy," Callahan said. "And I don't like the way she's looking at me."

"Relax. She's a Kayan villager. She doesn't mean you any harm. In fact, if you asked, she'd probably take you into her home and feed you."

"Just as long as she doesn't try feed *on* me," Callahan said. "I've had enough excitement for one day. And what's with the neck rings?"

Batty threw her a glance, surprised that in all of her travels, Callahan hadn't encountered such a sight before.

"The Kayan consider an elongated neck a sign of beauty," he told her. "The rings force the collarbone and ribs to compress and make the neck look longer than it really is."

"You truly are a font of information, aren't you? My own personal Internet." She looked at the Kayan woman again. "How can they do that to themselves?"

"Correct me if I'm wrong, but weren't you wearing five-inch heels when we went to that auction?"

Callahan conceded the point with a shrug. "Speaking of which, my feet are killing me. Along with every other part of my body. Let me check to see if I've got a signal now. Maybe we can get somebody to pick us up."

She stopped and pulled her cell phone out of a pocket, checking the screen and not happy with what she saw.

"Shit. You'd think if the missionaries can build a temple up here, someone could erect a cell tower."

Batty shook his head. "I sometimes wonder how the world survived before those things were invented."

"Why don't we ask the lady with the stretched neck?"

They were moving through a forest of pines when Batty thought about Milton and the seven missing pages from the Devil's Bible.

It was a foregone conclusion now that Milton was a guardian himself—an idea that might seem far-fetched to some, but to Batty's mind, only made sense. Milton was a deeply religious man and a passionate civil servant who often spoke out against the king. He had almost gotten himself killed for it, and had spent much of the latter days of his life in sightless seclusion, his reputation tarnished. And it wouldn't have been outside his nature to take on the responsibilities of *Custodes Sacri*, especially if it meant he'd spend those last days in the service of God.

But Brother Philip had said that the curse on those pages had driven Milton blind—just like Galileo before him. And that Milton had *destroyed* the pages when he realized how dangerous they were.

But could any of this be true?

Could both of these men have had possession of the pages at some point in their lives?

Philip had said that Galileo had given Milton "the bug," and Batty knew that the poet had visited the astronomer on his travels through Europe. Had an obsession been born during that visit? An obsession that had eventually been satisfied, only to drive Milton blind?

And why had Ozan wanted to know about the pages? Were they somehow mixed in with his attempts to decipher those verses from *Paradise Lost*? And did it all relate in some way to this mysterious Telum?

There was a connection here. There *had* to be.

But Batty had too little information to figure it all out.

So maybe he needed to start with Ozan's and Gabriela's obsession. In chapter eleven of *Paradise Lost*, the Archangel Michael takes Adam to the highest hill in Paradise and shows him a vision of the future. Adam witnesses the death and destruction of Noah's flood, the rise of the tyrant Nimrod and the Tower of Babel, the deterioration caused by old age, the ravages of war and disease—all of which could be prevented if man were to live a virtuous life.

But there were no secret messages to be found in that chapter. No codes to be deciphered. Batty himself had been through the book time and again and had never found anything.

But then he suddenly remembered something. A small bit of curiosity he had set aside when things started getting crazy on the plane. Before Belial had hijacked Callahan and the plane started its nosedive, he had been looking through the manuscript, marveling at the ink on the pages, the words crossed out, the inserted revisions.

But as he had flipped to the end of the book, he had noticed something odd. Something wrong with the binding.

Something *missing*.

Could it be that simple?

Batty stopped in his tracks, fumbling for the book bag. As he reached inside and grabbed the manuscript, Callahan realized that he was no longer walking beside her and turned to look.

"What is it? What's wrong?"

Batty found the stump of a fallen pine and sat, pulling the book into his lap. "I think I may have just figured it out."

She came over to him. "Figured what out?"

He quickly flipped through the manuscript until he reached the last chapter—what would have been chapters eleven and twelve in the revised version, but was actually chapter *ten* here. He checked the binding, saw the torn edges, as if several pages had been removed.

"Is it possible?"

"Is what possible? What's going on?"

He looked up at Callahan. "Ozan and Gabriela were trying to decipher the wrong chapter eleven."

"What do you mean, the wrong chapter eleven? What other chapter eleven is there?

"*Paradise Lost* was originally divided into ten chapters," he told her. "Until the publisher asked Milton to split two of those chapters to make it seem longer and look more appealing to the readers."

He showed her the manuscript. "This is the original ten chapters." He gestured to the torn binding. "But there are pages missing here. Torn out of the back of the book. But if you look at the verse, it's complete. It ends exactly where it's supposed to end."

A light came into Callahan's eyes. "He wrote another chapter. The real chapter eleven."

"The *right* chapter eleven," Batty said. "The one they should have been trying to decipher all along. And look how many pages are missing."

He handed her the book and she took a closer look at the binding, the torn edges, mentally counting them, moving her lips as she did. Then her eyes went wide.

"Seven," she said.

"The seven missing pages of the Devil's Bible. And this isn't a coincidence. That has to be what was there."

"But that doesn't make sense. Philip said Milton burned them, and look at these edges. This is the same paper he used in the rest of the manuscript. And you said the Codex's pages were huge, and written several centuries before."

Batty thought about this and shook his head. "I don't have an explanation, but I know I'm right. And this has something to do with the key Philip told us about. It's a prophecy of some kind, an instruction manual—who knows?"

"But you'd think if anyone would, it would be Ozan and Gabriela."

"Not necessarily," Batty said. "Like I told you before, they could be operating on blind faith. Remember that e-mail? And what Philip said about Ozan being a curious old fool?"

Callahan shook her head and handed the book back to him. "We could sit here and speculate from now until doomsday—which, if you believe Brother Philip, is not that far away. But there's no way we'll be able to figure all this out unless we get one of the remaining guardians to spill. And the chances of that look pretty slim right now."

"Maybe not," Batty said.

"Do you know something I don't?"

"The e-mail to D.C., remember? The guardian who probably started you on this whole quest in the first place. The guy in the president's administration."

"Hey, that was as much speculation as all this other stuff."

"I don't think so," Batty said. "And as soon as you can get reception on that cell phone of yours, I think you need you to call your people and set up a meeting."

"For what? You don't know Section. They're a closed shop."

"Say you want to discuss the Telum. If one of the guardians is behind this, he's sure to swallow the bait."

"And if he does?"

"I guess we'll just have to wait and see what happens."

They were nearing civilization when Callahan got a signal.

After dialing in her com-code, she waited a full ten minutes before the disembodied voice came on the line. "Yes?"

"We have a situation."

"What sort of situation?"

"I can't go into much detail over the phone."

"This line is secure, Agent Callahan. You know that."

She did indeed. Section spent a considerable amount of time and money making *sure* it was secure, but that didn't help her much right now.

"I need a face-to-face," she said. "And I'm bringing the asset with me."

"Impossible. Follow procedure and upload your report."

"We have to speak to whoever originated this assignment. Someone upstairs."

"That can't be done. Even asking is a breach of protocol."

"Then breach it," she said. "I guarantee he'll want to hear from me. It's about the Telum."

"The Telum?"

"I don't have time to explain. If you can't handle my request, pass me along to someone who can."

There was hesitation on the line.

"This is highest priority," she insisted. "It doesn't get any higher than this."

A long pause, then the voice said, "Wait for our call."

The line clicked and Callahan lowered the phone, looking over at LaLaurie, who was resting at the side of the trail. They made eye contact, his gaze hopeful, but she shook her head and gestured to the phone, indicating she was waiting for an answer.

She knew her handler was passing the message along, and a flurry of calls would follow, sending it up the chain of command until someone who carried enough weight could figure out what to do with it.

Fifteen minutes later, her phone rang and she put it to her ear.

"Your request has been denied," the voice said.

"What? Did you tell them—"

"Continue with the investigation, Agent Callahan, and report back to us."

Then the line clicked.

BOOK IX

The Evil That Men Do

Deep to the Roots of Hell the gather'd beach
They fasten'd, and the Mole immense wraught on
Over the foaming deep high Archt, a Bridge
Of length prodigious joyning to the Wall
Immoveable of this now fenceless world
Forfeit to Death

—*Paradise Lost*, 1667 ed., IX:299–304

38

LOS ANGELES, CALIFORNIA

Jenna wasn't at the shelter.

Michael had gone there to watch their morning ritual—the opening of the blinds, clearing away of cots, sweeping and mopping and setting up tables before heading into the kitchen to help prep food. And with the blood moon approaching, he had planned to make contact in a more meaningful way today, in hopes of getting Jenna to trust him.

Instead, what he saw was a fresh new face among the handful of regulars, and he knew this wasn't good. Space was limited here and this new girl could very well have taken Jenna's slot.

So where was she?

Had she even spent the night? Or had Zack tried again?

Something nasty fluttered in Michael's stomach.

A feeling of dread.

Even though it couldn't be helped, he cursed himself for leaving Jenna alone. His need for a new skin had not only compromised his ability to function in this broken world, but had also impaired his judgment—and Jenna (and the world) could well be paying the price.

She was an innocent. An unsullied soul. A simple girl who had run away—not to rebel, but to escape an intolerable situation—and she hadn't yet had time to adjust to her new surroundings. To understand the dangers she faced.

To know the power she held inside her.

And because of Michael's weakness, his carelessness, she was gone before he could tell her who and what she was.

He found the woman who ran the shelter on a smoke break in the alley out back. As he approached her, she took one look at him, saw a fit but aging man with gray hair, beard and fresh, new thrift-store clothes—including a well-seasoned army jacket—and immediately showed him her cell phone.

"I've got the police on speed dial," she said.

"I just want to ask you some questions."

"I don't have any money. And if you're looking for food, you can come back tonight. We open at six."

"Thanks, but I'm not interested in that."

She stiffened slightly. "Then what?"

"I saw you in the coffeehouse up the street a few nights ago. You were there with a young girl."

The woman's eyes narrowed. "And?"

"I know the girl's been staying here at the shelter, but I haven't seen her this morning. Did she spend the night last night?"

"Why are you so interested?"

"I think she may be the daughter of a friend of mine," Michael lied. "A woman in Arizona." He was making all kinds of compromises lately. "I would've approached her before now, but I had to be sure she was the right girl. Her mother's dying."

The woman's eyes widened slightly, but remained suspicious. She was used to being very protective of her girls.

"That's funny," she told him. "We had a nice long talk that night and she didn't mention anything about her mother being sick. All she talked about was her perv of a stepfather. That wouldn't be you, would it?"

"I told you, I'm a friend of her mother. And Jenna doesn't know she's sick. I don't think she would've run away if she had."

The woman stared at him, assessing his story—assessing *him*—then slowly shook her head. "Sorry. I wish I could believe you, but I don't."

"Then what can you tell me about the guy who was with her? The one who called himself Zack?"

The eyes narrowed again. "How do you know all this? I don't remember seeing you that night."

"I was there. Sitting in back."

"So . . . what? You're some kind of stalker?"

"I told you, I just want to do what's right. Get Jenna back home. Now tell me about Zack."

"I think you need to get lost."

"I don't want any trouble. Just tell me and I'm gone."

She sighed. "What's to tell? He's a creep. Uses those looks of his like a weapon. He was there. Then he was gone. I haven't seen him around since then and I don't expect to, if he knows what's good for him."

"Do you have any idea where he hangs out?"

"Not a clue," she said. Then she held up the phone again. "Now, do I have to make that call or what?"

Michael spent the day wandering around Hollywood, hoping to pick up even the smallest of vibrations, but the world around him was chaotic and he couldn't hear a thing.

He'd gone back to the coffeehouse, and the Greyhound station, walked along Hollywood Boulevard, the Sunset Strip and several streets in between, but Jenna was nowhere to be found.

He wondered if this new skin of his was making it difficult to hear her song. But that seemed unlikely, and its sudden absence made him doubt himself.

Had he been wrong about her all along?

Had he let his desire overtake his reason? His senses?

He was, after all, directly related to Belial, and she was the queen of such behavior.

But no. He didn't think he was wrong.

In fact, he *knew* he wasn't. Sooner or later he'd hear that song again, as bright and clear as ever.

At least he hoped he would.

Because time was running out.

It was late in the day when he finally got his wish.

The moment the sound wafted through him, he felt a relief so intense it made his legs tremble. An odd reaction, certainly, but he wrote it off to the continuing struggle to get mind and body to work in harmony.

Breaking in a new host was akin to a transplant patient adapting to a donated kidney.

Or maybe it was the other way around.

Whatever the case, Michael knew it would take time to fully adapt, and unexpected physical sensations were part of the territory.

But none of that really mattered.

He could hear Jenna's song—as clear as could be— and all he cared about right now was that she was safe.

Following the sound, he moved up Hollywood Boulevard and found himself standing across the street from the Rocket Bar & Grill, a modern take on an old fifties diner. She was right there in the front window, sitting at a booth with another young girl—one he recognized from the shelter—and they were laughing together like old friends.

As Jenna sucked down the last of her Coke, the other girl dug through her purse for a few dollar bills and laid them on the table. Michael had no idea how the girl had managed to get the money, but the hardness of her face suggested the worst, and he hoped he was wrong.

Before he could give it much thought, however, a battered blue Chevy Malibu pulled to a stop out front and honked its horn. Jenna's new friend looked out the window and smiled, waving to the car as they both got to their feet and went to the door.

Michael's gaze shifted to the driver, a young punk of about twenty. He was trying to decide whether the guy was a drudge, when the punk moved his head and the person sitting next to him came into view:

Zack.

The sight of him sent a chill through Michael. He wasn't sure how Zack had approached Jenna, but had a feeling he was using the other girl as a proxy. Someone to convince Jenna that, despite what the woman at the shelter had told her, Zack was actually a pretty good guy.

Michael didn't know if the friend herself was a drudge, but at this point it didn't make much difference. Contact had been made, and from the look on Jenna's face as she stepped out of the diner's front door, the ploy had worked. She was smiling as if she and Zack had known each other for decades.

Zack climbed out of the car then, throwing the rear door open as the girlfriend got in front and Zack gestured for Jenna to hop in back.

Michael knew he had to stop her.

Couldn't let her get into that car.

And at this point, there was only one way to do it.

"Jenna!" he called, waving a hand, his voice nearly drowned out by the traffic streaking by.

She didn't hear him.

"Jenna!" he called out again, and this time Zack looked up sharply, staring at him with quizzical eyes.

Michael needed to get over there. Now. But when he tried a jump, his body resisted. It wasn't yet ready for lateral travel.

He'd have to do this the old-fashioned way.

Reaching under his jacket, he jerked his Glock free and headed across the street. Zack saw him coming and despite the change in appearance seemed to know exactly who he was.

Grabbing hold of Jenna's hand, he hurried her into the car and climbed in after her, closing them inside.

"Jenna!" Michael shouted, as loud as he could.

And as she settled into her seat, she heard him and turned, looking out her window at him, her face churning up in confusion.

Who was this guy, and why had he just called her name?

Now Zack was pounding on the back of the driver's seat, shouting for his buddy to "Go! Go!"—

—as Michael picked up speed and raised the Glock, ready to blow out one of the tires.

Then, without warning, a horn blasted, long and loud, off to his right. Michael jerked his head around just in time to see a city bus bearing down on him, the driver frantically flashing his headlights.

Michael dove to the blacktop and rolled as the bus came to a groaning halt, just inches from where he'd stood. Then tires screeched, horns honking wildly, as another car smashed into the back of the bus, several more piling up behind it.

As Michael pulled himself upright and got to his feet, he saw the Malibu roaring down the boulevard.

And there was Jenna, craning her neck, staring out the back window at him with wide, frightened eyes.

39

LAS VEGAS, NEVADA

The first of the riots was in Sin City, of all places.

No one was quite sure how it started, but the Vegas Strip and the hotels downtown were unusually crowded, and that may have had something to do with it. People from all over the world had packed the casinos, hoping to win it big and cash in on the American dream—a dream that seemed even more remote than usual. So the anxiety level was high and tempers were frayed.

Rumor had it that it began with a simple altercation. Two tourists at odds over which slot machine belonged to whom—along with the three-million-dollar jackpot it was spewing. One of them claimed she'd been straddling two machines and had just turned away for a moment when the other came up and dropped the winning coins, thus robbing the straddler of the reward she surely had coming.

Their fight was brief, but vicious, ending with one woman dead, and the other practically foaming at the mouth, victim of a rage and frustration so virulent that it spread like a contaminant. And the next thing everyone knew, there were people fighting everywhere, taking it into the streets.

But, again, that was just a rumor. The truth is, anything could have set it off.

In an interview on the evening news, one man said it was all the fault of our godless society. That it was the goddamn atheists and the homos and them terrorist camel jockeys who had brought this down upon us, with their craven depravity and their hatred for their fellow man. As far as he was concerned, every last one of them should be publicly executed, used as examples for the rest of the heathens. Get Jesus or get bent.

Later that day he was shot dead by his wife, who claimed he'd been abusing her for twenty-five years.

It took a few hours for the mayhem to spread to other cities, but spread it did. Political protests, impromptu strikes, small skirmishes that seemed to escalate for no reason other than that people were either scared or fed up. Tired of living in a world that provided them no hope.

Or just plain tired of living.

It was as if humankind had finally given in to its baser instincts and started listening to that little cartoon devil on its shoulder, damn the consequences.

And as things got worse, the faithful sent up their prayers, asking for protection and guidance.

Unfortunately, no one seemed to be listening.

The three dark angels watched it all from the board-room of L4, which stood high above the Strip—one of the many branches they maintained around the world. The creation of a security company had been Moloch's idea—

—L4 or Lucifer's Four—

—which was about the extent of his creativity.

Moloch, the Lord of War—who was currently calling himself Vogler—stared at the street below, shaking his head in contempt. "Seed the crowd with few drudges and the lemmings follow. It's amazing how predictable these creatures are."

"Be thankful for that," Mammon said. "As you well know, it hasn't always been this easy."

In this world, Mammon—the Lord of Greed—used his human name Radek.

They all preferred to use human names when dealing with humans.

All but Belial, that is.

They'd often told her that the goal was to blend in, which could hardly be accomplished with names so familiar to so many, thanks in large part to the poet, who had stolen their story. But Belial possessed an immeasurable amount of arrogance. Had chosen to inhabit this earth as a *woman*, of all things, so that told you all you needed to know about her.

Jonathan Beel, or Beelzebub, Lord of the Flies, said, "Don't start celebrating quite yet. The moon is two days away, and while your efforts have been admirable, they're no guarantee of success."

"Always the naysayer, eh, Beelzebub?"

"Need I remind you of our record of failures? No matter what we throw at these creatures, no matter how we might tempt them, they always manage to survive."

"Not this time," Mammon said. "Moloch and I have planted these seeds all over the globe. What we're witnessing here is only the beginning."

"We shall see."

"The point—as I seem to have to keep reminding

you—is that this world has never been so corrupt, never been so full of weak-willed mortals who blame one another for their failures. I can't remember a time when I've seen so many so willing to exploit the pain of others or kill over petty differences, or claim to worship their so-called father as they wallow in their own hypocrisy. We've harnessed enough tainted souls to do exactly what we need to do."

"Nice speech," Beelzebub said. "But it doesn't change anything. Without the power of the Telum, we could well fall short."

Mammon laughed, his voice laced with derision. "A few moments ago you were braying about Belial's claim she may have found the sacred traveler. What happened to all that confidence?"

"The Telum is only half the battle, and you know it."

"You surprise me, Beelzebub. For someone who's so anxious to see the Master released from his cage, you seem awfully dependent on this fairy tale. Here Moloch and I give you concrete results, and Belial is still wasting her time with Michael's little fan club, looking for something that may not even exist."

"She found the girl, didn't she?"

"Her *brother* found the girl, and she's childish enough to think that actually means something. But Michael's irrelevancy on this planet has never been so clearly defined."

"I happen to agree with her," Beelzebub said.

Mammon shook his head in disgust. "Miraculous weapons, singing souls . . . you two are as gullible as those fools who think the one we put on the cross was some kind of—"

"Enough," Moloch said, moving toward them. "You two fight like schoolchildren. I thought we were past all of this nonsense."

"I simply don't like the idea of all of our hard work being discounted in favor of something that has yet to be proven," Mammon said.

"No one is discounting anything," Moloch told him. "But Beelzebub is right. Let's not be so arrogant as to believe that the game has already been won. Telum or no Telum, there's still a lot of work to be done."

"Hear, hear," Beelzebub said.

"So why don't we save the celebration for a night when we can all drink a toast with Lucifer?"

The other two nodded; then all three raised their hands.

"*A posse ad esse.*"

40

CHIANG MAI, THAILAND

Seven missing pages.

The key to the Telum. The sacred traveler.

In order to protect her, the guardians had to protect her secret—a secret that had been removed from the Codex Gigas centuries ago, only to fall into the hands of Galileo Galilei—if Brother Philip was to be believed.

The curse on those pages had driven Galileo blind. And Milton after him.

But if Milton had burned them for fear of what they might do, then how and why had they wound up in the manuscript for *Paradise Lost*?

And, for that matter, who or what exactly *was* the sacred traveler?

A wandering soul, Philip had said, but what was her purpose? It sounded as if Michael was the one in charge of finding her, but once he did, what did that mean?

Was she a weapon of some kind?

Too many questions, Batty thought. Too many unanswered fucking questions.

And with the fourth moon of the tetrad coming, what were the chances of answering those questions before it was too late? What were the chances of finding those pages—the key to whatever Michael was looking for—

before the gates of hell sprang open and all of humanity was destroyed?

It wasn't looking good.

It was looking even worse when they got back to the heart of Chiang Mai.

The streets were filled with angry protestors, police in riot gear trying to control the crowd with fire hoses and batons. But the police seemed overwhelmed, and it looked as if the crowd was winning.

"Jesus," Callahan said. "It's already started. Just like Philip warned us. It happened so fast."

"He said it would."

They found refuge in a bookstore, several blocks away from the action. The place was practically deserted, and the guy behind the register looked visibly nervous, as if he'd be all too happy to close up and get to the safety of his home.

The few customers who were in here didn't seem to be all that interested in the books surrounding them. They huddled together on the sofa and chairs at the center of the room, fugitives from the chaos.

Batty and Callahan found a grouping of chairs in back and as they settled in, Callahan reached for her cell phone. "I need to call Section again. Get them to listen to me."

"If they didn't listen before, I doubt they'll listen now. For whatever reason, they're letting us handle this on our own. But where do we take it from here? We're running out of guardians."

"London," Callahan said. "That's all we've got left."

"London was a pretty big place the last time I looked."

"We start with Ozan's e-mail. Go to the Internet café where it was downloaded, then work from there. Maybe we'll get lucky."

Batty didn't have much faith in locating whoever had received the e-mail, but they had to try. Still, he wondered if there was another way to ferret out the truth about all this. There had to be some way to . . .

Then it struck Batty.

The Vision. Maybe he could use The Vision.

One thing he'd learned over the years was that his vision worked best when there was a lingering darkness in the room. That it was strongest when he encountered death or pain or destruction of some kind. So it didn't immediately occur to him to try to use it on something good.

Something *divine*.

Reaching into the book bag, he took out the Milton manuscript. He'd already discovered on the plane that it truly *was* inspired by God, but he'd never thought to try to tap into its energy.

"What are you doing?" Callahan asked.

"Looking for the missing pages."

"What?"

Batty opened the book and quickly flipped to the last page. He stared at the imperfect binding, the faintly ragged edges where the seven pages had been removed. If they'd been torn out after Milton died, then the history here was centuries old, and it wouldn't be easy to grab hold of. He'd have to concentrate harder than he'd ever concentrated before, and there was no telling what it would do to him.

Bracing himself, he took a deep breath, then put his palm against those edges and closed his eyes.

But nothing happened.

He stopped. Centered himself. Tried again.

Concentrate, Batty. *Concentrate*.

He wasn't getting anything.

Desperate, he grabbed the Saint Christopher medal and hung it around his neck.

He turned back to the manuscript. And then he felt it. Heat radiating up his arm and into his brain. The medal had been the key. And instead of the usual dark tunnel, he was assaulted by an explosion of light, like fireworks inside his head. Then the light seemed to consume him, to suck him in—

—and he was gone.

When he opened his eyes he was standing. But as he realized this, he wasn't quite sure *where*. All he saw was a wash of colors, vibrant blues and greens and yellows so bright that they hurt to look at.

He squinted against them, willing them to come into focus, shielding his eyes with a cupped hand as they slowly adjusted to the light. And then he saw before him a place more beautiful than any he could ever have imagined.

Rolling hills. Blue, cloudless sky. Fields of yellow flowers so far and so wide they seemed to go on forever. And trees. Trees bearing flawless fruit—reminding him, oddly enough, of the bowl of plastic apples and pears on his mother's dining table.

This world vibrated against him, seeping into his skin, releasing some kind of drug into his system, a drug that produced a pleasure so intense that he wondered if he could remain standing.

"This is the world as it could have been," a voice behind him said.

Male. British. Refined.

Batty turned and saw a shimmering, ghostlike image walking toward him, moving with a graceful fluidity. And as the image came into focus, he saw that the man wore his hair long, in a style from another time, his suit and collar from another century.

His eyes clouded over by cataracts.

The man—who Batty now knew was the poet—turned to the tree beside him and plucked a bright red pomegranate. "But because of the frailty of mankind," he continued, "our world will soon be this."

He bit into the fruit and the moment he did, the tree beside him caught fire and began to melt. Batty turned and saw that *all* the trees were on fire, their fruit withering. Then the sky darkened, the flowers beneath it wilting and dying as the hills grew barren. And soon everything around him was the color of slate, as a dark, cold wind kicked up and blew through him, rattling his soul.

Within seconds he was caught in the center of a black tornado, a cacophony of sounds rising in his mind as the wind whirled around him, growing tighter and denser with each revolution. Batty opened his mouth to scream, but nothing came out, as the tornado gathered speed, the growing darkness threatening to swallow him whole . . .

Then abruptly it was gone.

He stood on a hilltop overlooking a small, crumbling villa, the poet beside him. Below, a young man exited the front door, moved quickly across the courtyard and mounted a horse.

"When he first told me about the Devil's Bible," the

poet said, "I thought poor Galileo has lost his senses. A dark, pernicious toxicant seemed to have spread throughout that place, making it impossible for me to breathe."

The young man rode his horse to the front gates, signaling for the guard to open it.

"The astronomer had wanted to use me as his eyes, now that his own were gone. He had thought I would understand, but I saw him only as a feeble old man whose wild imagination had taken possession of him."

A flash of light assaulted Batty's eyes, and when it cleared, they were standing in a study lined with bookshelves, the young man—slightly older now—sitting at a writing desk, hard at work with pen and paper.

"Shortly after his death, I made no mention of that meeting, unable to tell the world that one of our most cherished minds had grown feeble in his last years."

Again the light assaulted Batty. Then they were standing in a room lit by candlelight, several men—including the poet—sitting around a table, deep in conversation.

"But imagine my surprise, when shortly after the end of the Thirty Years' War, I got word that the Swedish army had plundered the treasures of Rudolf the Second, and had brought back with them the very book the astronomer had spoken of—the Codex Gigas. The Devil's Bible."

Now Batty had a bird's-eye view of a grand parlor surrounded by books, and at its center a large glass case containing an enormous tome. It lay open at a page that featured an elaborate multicolored portrait of a demon with horns, and the poet stood with another man, staring at it in awe.

"Within a year, I found myself in Stockholm, where

the book was on display at the Swedish Royal Library. The curator not only confirmed the tale of its creation, but that seven pages were indeed missing, just as the astronomer had told me."

Light flashed and they were once again standing over the field of yellow flowers, the poet's blank gaze fixed on Batty.

"I soon became obsessed with finding those pages, wanting to know what secret they held. The astronomer's estate had no knowledge of them, so I prepared to travel to Rome, to the private archive where he claimed to have viewed them. But before I left, I received correspondence that the collection they were part of had been sold to an antiquities dealer in London. They had been close to me all along."

The poet paused, reflecting for a moment, then said, "The antiquities dealer had since died, and the collections he had most recently obtained were languishing in a vault beneath his shop in London while his children quarreled over his estate."

The light once again flashed and now Batty found himself in a small cluttered vault, the room lit only by flickering lamplight. The poet sat a table, carefully removing several enormous sheets of parchment from an equally large portfolio. His hands were shaking, and Batty strained to see what was on those pages, but they wouldn't come into focus.

"I cannot explain to you what I felt at the moment I saw them. Joy, elation—yes—but also a power, a power so overwhelming that they seemed to draw me in, to wrap themselves around me in a loving embrace, and I knew I was in the power of God. These were *His* pages that He had once hidden in that enormous book forged by the Devil."

But now the poet began rubbing his eyes, moving the lamp closer.

"The astronomer had warned me that only those whose motives are pure can read the pages without fear of the curse, but I had foolishly ignored him, believing his blindness to have been caused by the constant use of his telescope. I was wrong, however, and within minutes my vision began to blur."

Batty saw the poet on the street now, the portfolio tucked under his arm as he stumbled toward a horse and carriage.

"But I had seen enough to know that what was on those pages was an ancient prophecy, the key to a miraculous duality of power, a power so rich that should it fall into the wrong hands, all of humankind could be in danger. That the gates of the bottomless pit—of the Abaddon itself—would be opened, spewing forth all the horrors of Pandemonium and beyond."

Suddenly Batty was looking down at a view of a city ravaged by war, cracks opening up in the earth between the buildings, spraying molten lava into the air.

Now the poet was back in his study, surrounded by flickering candles; his eyes clouded over, his hands extended, palms outward, as his lips moved in silent prayer.

"But what frightened me most of all was my sudden desire to invoke that power myself, under the grace of God, even though I knew that such an invocation would be impossible without its source. The sacred traveler. So I began searching for that source, and soon found myself consumed by the black arts, in hopes that I might hear the song of a wandering soul.

"The astronomer had told me of the coming eclipse, and I knew that if I could free that soul during the darkness of the fourth moon, I could deliver to the world a new paradise, and I alone would be the *ruler* of that paradise, the new creator.

"But in a moment of clarity I came to realize that what I was seeking was a product of my own false pride and my selfish desire to control my world. That what I was trying to do could only end in disaster. So in a moment of strength, I destroyed the pages."

The poet now stood before a fireplace, tossing the portfolio into the roaring fire. The light of the fire flared, and Batty and the poet were once again standing on the hillside, beneath a cloudless blue sky.

Batty finally found his voice. "But that wasn't the end of it."

The poet slowly shook his head. "Years later I had finally moved on, had learned to live with my blindness and had renewed my devotion to God and the gift he had given me. My poetry. I had long wanted to write an epic, but I thought, what if I could write one that not only celebrated God's grace—a prayer of contrition, you might say—but examined the corruption of man? A corruption I knew all too well.

"I asked God to assist me, but I never received an answer. I made claims of a divine muse, but the truth was that no such muse came to me until the very last chapter of my epic was long finished.

"Late one night, I was visited in my sleep. Despite my blindness, I could suddenly see, and before I knew it, I had several sheets of paper in front of me, my finger etching itself into them as if controlled by another being, and I knew in my heart that these were the very pages I had destroyed. They had taken on a life of their own, insisting to be seen.

"Then the angel Michael came to me and told me that I was to be the first guardian of the pages. That I had proven myself trustworthy when I had attempted to destroy them, and now I must hide them away so that they never fall into the wrong hands. Until the time came that they could be used to serve God.

"The original copy of my epic still lay on my writing table. A final transcription had already been prepared and sent to the publisher, and though I was blind, the manuscript still had sentimental value to me. So the following morning, I gathered up these new pages, added them to the bottom of the stack—my own personal Book Eleven, you might say—and asked my daughter to summon a bookbinder. I stood there with him in the room as he bound all the pages together. Then I locked it away in my personal vault.

"It stayed there for nearly ten years. And as Michael continued his long search for the sacred traveler, he asked others to join me in protecting her secret."

The poet lowered his head, as if exhausted by the story, and Batty said, "But the pages were removed after you died. Who removed them?"

"One of the new guardians, of course."

"And where were they taken?"

"To where I could continue to watch over them."

"I don't understand."

"Let me show you," the poet said, then waved a hand in front of Batty's face.

Suddenly the world went dark again and Batty found himself at the center of a swirling tornado, its walls closing in on him. Then, with startling abruptness, the whirlwind came to a stop and he was floating—floating above an open wooden coffin, looking down on the poet's body as those milky, sightless eyes stared up at him.

"They are with me," the poet rasped.

Then, with equal abruptness, Batty awoke. He was sitting in the chair in the all-night bookstore, his palm pressed against the binding of the manuscript as Callahan eyed him with grave concern. He slumped back, feeling as if every bit of energy had been sucked out of his body.

He was barely able to move his lips.

"You were right," he gasped. "We need to get to London. Now."

BOOK X

Orgy of Disorder

Why else this double object in our sight
Of flight pursu'd in th' Air and ore the ground
One way the self-same hour?

—*Paradise Lost*, 1667 ed., X:201–03

41

LOS ANGELES, CALIFORNIA

H e didn't find the house as easily as he would have liked.

Remembering what Zack had told Jenna that first night, that he and his friends were "crashing at a place up in Burbank," Michael had stolen a Buick convertible and hit the freeway.

Unfortunately, Burbank, a sprawling suburb in the San Fernando Valley, boasted a population of more than a hundred thousand, and traveling from one neighborhood to the next playing a potentially fruitless game of Where's Jenna? was a time-consuming process.

He supposed he could have used another means of travel—a means he and his brethren were accustomed to—but his first attempt since he'd acquired this skin had been an unqualified failure, and he knew that for the time being it was best to stick to the laws of this world for fear he might weaken himself unnecessarily.

His skills would return in time.

Finding the house was a thankless task, but Michael had not prevailed against Belial and her friends these last several centuries by giving up easily. His one advantage was that Jenna's song still hummed faintly in his chest, fading in and out like distant radio signal, and his only solution was to keep moving block to block, house to house, in hopes that he'd eventually find her again.

He worked slowly and methodically through the night—a game of hot and cold—backtracking when necessary. And by early the next morning he found a rundown house on the outskirts of the city and instinctively knew that it was the right place.

There was no sign of the battered Chevy Malibu in the driveway, however. And the house itself—an abandoned rental with an overgrown yard—looked empty.

They'd been here and gone.

Disheartened, Michael found the back door unlocked and went inside. The kitchen was a disaster that smelled of rancid milk. The living room was filthy and devoid of furniture. Crude graffiti were spray-painted on the walls. The stained carpet was littered with pizza boxes and burger bags, and there were several ratty blankets on the floor, along with enough discarded needles and drug paraphernalia to stock a small medical clinic.

The thought that Jenna had slept in such squalor (if she'd slept at all) deepened Michael's depression. He had a hard time believing that such an innocent girl could be so easily seduced by Zack's oily charm. But maybe that innocence had been a figment of his imagination. Maybe he'd been romanticizing the girl because of who she was and what she meant to him. Maybe she was no different from the countless other runaways who had found their way to this sadly corrupted town.

Her song had grown weaker than ever now, only its residue remaining, and he had no idea why the signal was dying.

But he couldn't give up. Not now. Not ever.

Taking a last look around, he was about to head outside when he heard a soft moan, coming from the down the hall.

Jenna?

Feeling his heart kick up, he crashed through the hallway, moving from bedroom to bedroom. In the corner of the master was an open bathroom door.

He stepped inside and froze.

There was a petite teenage girl lying faceup in the tub, her head canted, a string of vomit running down her chin, a syringe still stuck in her bruised, needle-marked arm.

Not Jenna, but her girlfriend from the café.

Michael quickly moved to her and sat her upright, slapping her face to wake her up. But she didn't respond. He felt for a pulse, but it was barely there and he knew it was too late. The girl would be dead before he could get help.

Something sour churned in his gut, and all he could think was that this could easily have been Jenna.

Placing his palm against her forehead, he blessed her and sent up a silent prayer. It was a formality more than anything else, but he hoped it meant something to someone out there and that this poor girl's soul would do well in the otherworld.

As her pulse finally came to a stop, he glanced down at her hand and noticed a mark on the back of it, just above the crook of her thumb.

A faded stamp of some kind.

Lifting the hand, he tilted it toward the light from the doorway and took a closer look:

An orange flame. The numbers 904 below it.

He recognized it: an underground dance club named 904, near La Brea and Wilshire, that had derived its name from the local police code for fire. It was rumored to be owned by a media mogul named Jonathan Beel.

Beel, of course, was just a skin. A shell. Occupied by Michael's old friend and nemesis—brother to Lucifer, and sometime lover of Belial.

Beelzebub.

Michael had never been to the club, had never had the desire to walk right into the lion's den. But he knew now that he had no choice.

He was certain he'd find Jenna there.

42

"What're you gonna do to her?" Zack asked.

Jonathan Beelzebub Beel flicked his gaze toward the annoying little insect, his voice weary with contempt. "Are you still here?"

"I'm just curious, is all."

"I'm beginning to think Belial didn't do a thorough enough job when she turned you. Or are all of her drudges so nettlesome?"

"What does that mean?"

"Never mind," Beelzebub said, and waved a hand at him dismissively. "Just sit the girl on the bed, then go wait in the hall."

Beelzebub had been living above the club for several months now. He had a house in Bel Air and a penthouse in Century City, but he preferred the atmosphere of 904. He particularly enjoyed the feel of the relentless beat that seeped up through the floor all day and night. It made him feel alive.

"I had to give her a little taste," Zack told him. "She didn't want to at first, but she finally—"

"Didn't I just tell you to go?"

"Okay, okay." The insect took the girl by the shoulders and led her to the bed. She was indeed high. A little too high. And Beelzebub wished he'd simply handled the matter himself.

But he was a busy man. He had been using his network of media outlets to help fan the flames of insurrection around the world (humans believed anything they saw on TV) and the task was often difficult and time-consuming. He had people to help him, of course, but he'd always been a hands-on kind of guy.

Now he wished he'd been a bit more hands-on with young Jenna.

Zack sat the girl down and she teetered slightly, but caught herself before she fell. Despite the drugs, she was a lovely little thing. Beelzebub had always been attracted to older women himself—like the reporter he'd met the other night—but this one was something special. She was at that point in her life where her face and body had not yet betrayed her, and the smooth tautness of her young flesh was quite captivating.

If it turned out that Belial had been wrong about her, he might consider putting her on the market.

As the insect headed for the door, Beelzebub said, "You did as I instructed, right? With the other girl?"

Zack nodded. "We left her in the bathtub."

"And the stamp?"

"Just like you told us."

"Excellent," Beelzebub said, then waved him away.

Michael found the battered blue Malibu parked in the lot behind the building.

The building itself was made of crumbling red brick, an old garment factory with boarded-up windows. The rear door looked like something out of a medieval torture chamber, and he assumed this was his old friend's decorative addition to the place. During the Middle Ages, Beelzebub had spent many years in the skin of a lieutenant at the Tower of London, the proud inventor of a racklike device that would compress a subject's body until blood ran out of his ears and nose.

The door was unlocked and Michael stepped inside. With the windows boarded up, the only light filtered in through the cracks and seams. The place was huge and musty and mostly vacant, except for the row of old sewing machines on one side of the room, covered with cobwebs, most of them still carrying giant spools of thread. Several bolts of faded fabric were stacked in a nearby corner.

On the other side of the room was a pile of old plumbing pipes, and at the far end was another door. Michael moved to it and pushed it open, and the moment he did, he heard the steady *thump thump thump* of a dance beat.

A set of steps led downward into darkness, black graffiti and shallow gouge marks covering the walls on either side—signs and symbols that were very familiar to Michael, including Beelzebub's sigil, buried beneath a string of profanity.

Somebody obviously knew him quite well.

Moving down the steps, he followed a dingy hallway to another door, where a drudge about the size of a Winnebago stood guard, staring at him as if he were an invader from Mars.

Michael tried to push past him, but the guy put a hand on his shoulder. "Who's your sig?"

"The man himself," Michael said.

The Winnebago gave him a snort. "Yeah, I'll bet."

But then he stepped aside anyway, letting Michael into another hallway with graffiti-scarred walls. As Michael moved toward the far end, he listened carefully for Jenna.

Her song was still weak, but he had no doubt that she was here somewhere.

Beelzebub crouched next to the girl. "How are you feeling, my angel?"

Jenna wobbled slightly, tried to focus on him. "Kinda weird . . . Who're you?"

"My name is Jonathan. I'm a friend of Zack's. He said you weren't feeling well and asked if he could bring you up here for a while."

She looked around the room. Blinked. ". . . I don't like it here. Where's Zack?"

"Dancing. Do you like to dance?"

She shrugged. "Yeah, I guess so . . ."

"Well, I'll tell you what. As soon as I get the phone call I'm waiting for, I'll have Zack take you downstairs so you can have some fun. Okay?"

". . . I still feel weird . . ."

"Don't worry. That'll wear off in a few minutes and you'll be fine. Would you like to lie down?"

"Yeah . . . ," she murmured. "I think I better."

She carefully pulled her legs onto the bed and lay on her side, closing her eyes. Beelzebub studied her, admiring her delicate features, the pale white throat. Too bad Belial wasn't here. She'd so enjoy this.

He reached over and smoothed her hair. "Zack tells me you've had some bad things happen to you, Jenna. Is that true?"

She stirred. ". . . What kinda things?"

"He says you ran away from home because of your stepfather."

She hesitated. "I don't want to talk about that."

"Does it give you pain, Jenna? Thinking about what he did to you?"

"Yes . . . Stop."

"What if I could make all that pain go away, my angel? Would you like me to help you take away the pain?"

She opened her eyes. There was a trace of tears in them. ". . . Who are you? Why are you asking me this stuff?"

"Because I want to help you, Jenna. There may come a time when you'll have to make a choice. And I want to help you make the right one. Will you let me do that?"

The phone rang before she could answer.

He reluctantly got to his feet, went to his desk, and hit the intercom. "Yes?"

"Guy just came in. Could be him."

"What did he look like?"

"Solid. Gray hair. Beard. Maybe sixty or so. But not somebody you'd wanna go one-on-one with."

The same description the insect had given him. Assuming the idiot knew what he was talking about.

"All right," Beelzebub said. "Call me back when it's done."

He clicked off, glanced at the girl, then went to the door to get Zack.

Michael pushed through a set of swinging doors into a room the size of a warehouse. The place was packed shoulder to shoulder with gyrating bodies, the music loud enough to break the sound barrier.

Strobe lights flashed red and yellow and white, in perfect time to the beat, and Michael didn't think he'd ever seen so many people jammed into one place. He saw dark leather and jeans and short skirts and fishnet stockings and half-naked women throwing their heads back in laughter as men—and other women—pressed up against them, bodies grinding, hands roaming.

He started circling the crowd, peering into it as he concentrated on Jenna's song. But it was too dark, and there were too many people out there. And if Jenna had been brought here by force, he doubted she'd be tearing up the dance floor.

So where would she be? A holding room of some kind? An office?

Michael scanned the periphery of the club, looking for stairs or an elevator. He looked back the way he came and saw a cluster of sofas and chairs, where exhausted dancers rested their feet and drank exotic beers. To the right of that were the swinging doors he'd just come in through.

And farther to the right was an elevator.

Michael moved. Headed straight for his target. A couple of dancers got in his way, but he didn't slow down, shoving them aside. He was still several yards away when a light above it flashed and the doors slid open.

And there inside were Zack and Jenna.

Zack had her by the hand, and when he pulled her out of the elevator, she stumbled slightly. Drugged. They looked for a moment as if they were about to step onto the dance floor; then Zack made an abrupt left turn and pushed through the swinging doors, dragging Jenna behind him.

They were headed outside. Fast.

Michael ran, barreling through the doors into the hallway. No sign of them. He picked up speed, slammed through the next door, and still didn't see them. He flew down that hallway and up the graffiti-covered stairwell, then burst through to the room with the sewing machines—

—and stopped.

Froze in his tracks.

Zack and Jenna stood in the middle of room, facing him, Zack wearing a wide, shit-eating grin on his face.

"What's your hurry, Mikey? You don't like to dance?"

There were four more drudges with him. Two on each flank. Three men, one woman. And one of them was the Winnebago. They spread out to block Michael's path.

"Yeah," the woman said. "Come dance with us."

She was covered with tattoos and piercings and looked as if she were completely willing to rip out your throat and feed it back to you without even the slightest hint of remorse. There was a swastika on the side of her neck, and her hair was black and spiky.

The other three didn't have as many tattoos or as much metal sticking out of their faces, but they had enough muscles between them to start a gladiator show.

He'd been set up. The stamp on that dead girl's hand had been deliberately put there to see how he'd react. And his presence here had proven to Beelzebub that Jenna was someone special. The someone they'd all been looking for.

Michael took his Roman from his waistband, kept his focus on Zack. "Step away from the girl."

"Sorry, asshole. Can't do it."

"I really think you should reconsider. Ashes to ashes and all that."

The tattooed chick edged sideways, moving to the pile of pipes to her left. "I sure hope you got a spare skin back home, 'cuz we're gonna have some fun with this one."

She snatched up some pipes and tossed them to the others. They hefted them in their hands and spread out, waiting for Michael to engage. Zack spun Jenna around and pushed her toward the sewing machines. "Sit down and watch, bitch."

Jenna stumbled and grabbed hold of one of the machines.

"You really don't want to do this," Michael said, stepping toward them now. "Just let me take the girl and we'll save the dustup for another day. I couldn't care less about a worthless bunch of drudges."

"Worthless?" Zack said. "You trying to hurt our feelings?"

"That would require you have a heart and a mind and a soul. And you're oh-for-three at—"

The Winnebago roared and came at Michael, swinging the pipe hard, aiming for his head. Michael ducked with plenty of room, but the Winnebago swung again, going for another head shot. The pipe *whooshed* past Michael and he jerked back, watching it brush past his chin, a little too close for comfort. Then he sidestepped and spun and sliced the Winnebago's gut with his Roman.

A split second later, the guy vaporized, dust scattering violently in the air, blowing directly into the faces of Zack and the others, as the pipe he'd held clattered on the floor.

But Michael didn't slow down. Not waiting for them to attack, he spun and swung, effortlessly knocking the pipe out of the tattooed chick's hands, then doubled back and brought up the Roman again, the edge of his blade slicing through the swastika on her neck. She burst into fine ashes, her piercings scattering across the floor like jacks on asphalt.

Deciding he didn't have time to waste on this nonsense, Michael ripped his Glock from his waistband and opened fire, taking out the two remaining muscle men with two quick shots.

Then he turned the gun on Zack.

Zack took one look at the bead rings, the nose hoop, the star plugs, the barbells, the ear studs, the nipple piercings and God knew what else on the floor in front of him and stumbled backward, dropping his weapon, throwing his hands up. "Okay, okay, okay, man! I give! I give!"

Michael stopped, lowered the gun. "What do you do when you see a roach on your kitchen floor, Zack?"

Zack looked confused. "What?"

"Just answer the question. What do you do when you see a roach?"

Zack kept backing away. "I don't know, man, I don't know—I-I step on it. What *you* do?"

Michael smiled. "Show it no mercy."

Then he brought the gun up again and fired, the bullet piercing Zack's chest, turning him to dust.

Good riddance to bad rubbish.

Michael crossed to the sewing machines, where Jenna stood frozen on the spot. Despite the drugs, there was a look of stunned disbelief on her face.

Had she really just seen all that?

"W-who *are* you?" she stuttered. "What just happened?"

"I'll explain later," he said, grabbing her by the wrist. "There's bound to be an army coming up those stairs any minute now and we need to get out of here."

She jerked her arm, trying to pull free. "You're a lunatic. I'm not going anywhere with you."

Michael held her firm and leaned his face toward hers. "Listen to me, Jenna. I didn't want it to happen like this, but if you stay here you're in danger. We have to go. Now."

He could see that the drugs were still confusing her, that she didn't know what to do, but she stopped resisting and he tightened his grip on her and pulled her toward the door. Without a backward glance, they ran to his Buick, jumped in.

"Put on your seat belt," he said, firing up the engine. Then he jerked the car into drive.

Two minutes later, they were blasting down Wilshire, weaving in and out of traffic, and the girl had come out of her stupor enough to realize how scared she was.

"What's going on?" she cried. "Who are you?"

"That's hard to explain."

"How do you know my name? Did my parents send you?"

"No. They don't know anything about this."

"Then what's going on? What happened to those people back there? They just . . . disintegrated."

"There are things in this world that are hard to understand, Jenna. And I can't give you an explanation that'll make a lot of sense to you. Not like this. So right now you'll just have to trust me."

"Trust you? I don't even *know* you. You're just some gross old man!"

She seemed more alert now, which might have had something to do with the speed of the car and the wind rushing through her hair.

"Pull over," she said. "Let me out of this thing."

"I can't do that, Jenna."

"Pull over! Or I swear to God I'll—"

Suddenly they heard shouts and the revving of engines as two cars pulled up on either side of them, packed with drudges from the dance club. One of the drudges scrambled out of the back passenger window and sprang onto the trunk of the Buick.

Jenna screamed, and another one leapt from the car on Michael's side, diving into the Buick's backseat. Pulling himself upright, he wrapped his hands around Michael's throat.

As Michael struggled to breathe, the first one went for Jenna.

Grabbing his Roman, Michael swung out, slicing him across the face, and a shower of dust blew back and away, disappearing into the sky.

Jenna screamed again.

Then the second one tightened his grip, and Michael's vision narrowed. It was a miracle he was even able to drive. Fumbling the Roman, he grasped for it and missed, and it tumbled into the backseat. He tried to grab hold of his Glock, but he fumbled it, too.

He grasped Jenna's arm. "My gun," he croaked. "Find my gun . . ."

Jenna's face was pale with panic. Her eyes wild.

"Do it!" Michael croaked. He hammered a fist at the drudge's head, but the guy didn't let up.

His vision was almost gone, the street in front of him a dark blur. He felt Jenna moving around beside him, but had no idea what she was up to. Then, just as he was about to black out, Jenna screamed again, a shot rang out—

—and the pressure on his neck disappeared, the drudge disintegrating behind him, sending a swirl of black dust into the air.

As Michael's eyes came back into focus, Jenna dropped the gun to the seat as if it were contaminated, and started to tremble, tears springing into her eyes.

Throwing his arm across her, he told her to hold on, then jerked the wheel, taking them into a hard right turn down a side street. The other cars faltered only slightly, then regained speed, once again pulling up alongside the Buick.

Then the driver on the left side jerked his wheel hard and slammed into the side of the Buick. The jolt hammered through Michael but he didn't slow down.

The car slammed into the Buick a second time with brutal force, the impact knocking Michael's hands off the wheel.

The Buick careened toward the sidewalk but was cut short by a row of parked cars. Metal screamed as they came to an abrupt, jarring stop, pitching Michael forward. His face hit the wheel, pain rocketing through him as blood burst from his nose and the world started spinning around him.

Suddenly there were drudges swarming all over the

Buick, and Jenna screamed as hands grabbed at her, ripping her seat belt free and pulling her out of the front seat.

Dazed, Michael lifted his head, his vision blurred, as another car pulled up alongside them.

A black limousine.

The rear passenger window rolled down and Beelzebub signaled to the drudges. "Bring her to me."

Jenna struggled as the drudges dragged her over to the limo. "Let go of me!"

As she got close to the window, however, Beelzebub reached out and took her hand. A gesture that calmed her a bit.

"It's all right, my angel. I won't let him hurt you."

"Who are you people? What do you want from me?"

"We have time enough to talk about that. But first we need to get you somewhere safe."

Michael tried to move, but his legs were pinned under the dash. "Leave her alone."

Beelzebub ignored him. "What do you say, Jenna? Would you like to come back home with me? You'll be safe there. Not a thing to fret about."

"Don't pay any attention to him," Michael told her. "You can't trust him."

Jenna looked confused. She glanced at Michael, then returned her gaze to Beelzebub. "He killed Zack. Just shot him point-blank. It was awful."

"I know, my angel. But don't you worry, God will punish him. Why don't you get in and I'll take you home?"

Jenna hesitated, then finally nodded. The door opened, the drudges released her, and she climbed inside, disappearing from view.

Then Beelzebub turned to Michael. "See how easy that was?"

"Don't think it's over," Michael told him.

"Oh, I certainly hope not."

And as Michael struggled to free himself, Beelzebub's window rolled up and the limousine pulled away.

43

LONDON, ENGLAND

St. Giles' Cripplegate was one of the few medieval churches in all of London. It sat on soil that was believed to have held holy structures as far back as a thousand years. In the middle of the Barbican, London's now-thriving cultural arts center, it was the only building left standing—although damaged considerably—when the area was destroyed by the blitz during World War II.

It had also managed to survive the Great Fire of 1666, and Batty didn't think these were insignificant facts.

The church was an imposing structure, constructed of Kentish ragstone in the fourteenth century in the name of the hermit Giles, the patron saint of cripples—although, ironically, the name Cripplegate had nothing at all to do with this. It featured a high bell tower, and the churchyard was bordered on one side by a surviving piece of the Roman wall, which had been erected several centuries earlier to protect the port town of Londinium from interlopers.

Stepping onto its grounds was like stepping through the looking glass into another time and place.

Batty and Callahan had arrived in London early, and were forced to wait until well past nightfall to approach the church grounds. The streets here seemed only slightly less crazy than those in Chiang Mai, and as the unruliness continued, the police did their best to keep it contained.

They had spent the day holed up in a cheap hotel nearby, Batty fidgeting like a teenager, unable to sleep or eat, just anxious to do what needed to be done. He tried to bide his time by reading sections of the Milton manuscript and *Steganographia*—both of which he carried in the book bag—but his mind kept wandering, remembering his vision.

Only those whose motives are pure can read the pages without fear of the curse, Milton had told him. But were Batty's motives pure?

Was anyone pure?

Part of what had fueled him, what had taken hold of him in São Paulo in the first place, was his desire to know who had ripped Rebecca out of his life. And when he found out, he had been filled with a rage and anger he hadn't felt since the day she died.

Yet when he'd put that bullet in Belial's back, when he'd seen what McNab had done with his sniper's bullets, Batty had felt nothing more than relief. Relief that Belial had been stopped—if only temporarily—from destroying more lives.

So did that make his motives pure?

No way to tell, unfortunately.

And now, deep into the night, he and Callahan made their way across the churchyard to the main entrance. It was locked, as expected, and if there was any kind of security guard, he was nowhere to be found, undoubtedly spooked by the pandemonium in the streets these last couple days.

Or maybe joining in.

Callahan checked for alarms and found none, then got through the lock with little effort. Fortunately, she didn't use her foot this time.

They carried flashlights to guide them. Batty had been here before, in his quest to know everything Milton, and noted that it hadn't really changed. Even in limited light, the church was impressive, sporting polished wooden pews and lined on either side with carved stone columns and archways.

To their right, beyond the archways, stood a bronze statue of John Milton.

Callahan put her flashlight beam on it. "This is a good sign."

"Here's an even better one," Batty said, then shone his light on a nearby wall that held a bust of Milton atop a plaque that read:

JOHN MILTON
Author of Paradise Lost
Born Decr 1608
Died Novr 1674

His father John Milton
died 1646
They were both interred in this church

"The question," Callahan said, "is where?"

"That part could be tricky."

She knitted her brow. "How so?"

"It's been a few centuries since he was buried," Batty

said. "And the place has been rebuilt and refurbished a few times since then, so finding the exact location could be problematic." He paused. "Then there's the issue of grave robbers."

"What issue?"

"It's said that during one of those rebuilds—about a hundred years after he died—Milton's coffin was broken into and he was stripped of his teeth and hair. The coffin was supposed to have been moved after that."

The more Batty thought about this, however, the more he had to wonder if it was just a cover story. What if it had been the guardians who had moved him, at Saint Michael's bidding? To protect the pages. The corpse with the missing hair and teeth may not have been Milton at all.

"So, in other words," Callahan said, "we have no idea where the hell we're going."

"Then might I suggest you turn around and leave," a voice told them.

They both froze as a figure stepped out from the shadows beyond one of the archways. He was tall and slender, in his midfifties, and had a shotgun resting on his forearm, casually pointing it in their direction. The security guard, no doubt. Although he wasn't wearing a uniform.

He was British, of course. "Picking locks, carrying torches . . . looks to me as if you two are up to no good."

"Easy," Callahan said, her eyes on the shotgun.

"I don't shoot, luv, unless someone provokes me. And you're not going to provoke me, are you?"

"Listen to me," Batty said. "I can't explain any of this without it sounding completely crazy, but we need to see John Milton's remains."

"I was getting that impression, the way you two were talking. The question is, why? I've seen some Milton crazies in my time, but not all that many of them have been anxious to get a look at a few rotting old bones."

"Like I said . . ." Batty spread his hands.

The guard pointed to Callahan. "You. Do you have some form of identification on you?"

"Why?"

"Because I'd like to know who I'm about to shoot, should it become necessary." He turned a palm up and waggled his fingers at her. "Let me see."

Callahan pulled her State Department ID out of her pocket and tossed it to him. He opened it, gave it a glance, then suddenly relaxed, tossing it back to her.

"It's good to meet you, Agent Callahan." Then he set the shotgun aside and held out a hand to shake. "My name is Grant. Jim Grant. I was told to expect you."

Batty and Callahan exchanged looks. Then Callahan said, "You're with Section?"

"I presume that's who you work for, but no, I answer to a higher authority." He reached into his collar and brought out a Saint Christopher medal. "I'm the caretaker here, but I'm also here to protect what needs to be protected."

Callahan looked confused. "But how could you know we were coming?"

"Quite simple. I received a telephone call."

"From who?"

"That's a question I don't have an answer to, I'm afraid. But whoever he is, he knows about *Custodes Sacri*, so I can only assume he's one of Michael's associates. Recruited the same as I was."

Batty turned to Callahan. "The D.C. connection, no doubt. He obviously prefers to remain anonymous."

"Whatever the case," Grant said, "we're wasting time." He turned and gestured with his fingers. "Follow me."

I t was a vault. A burial crypt located beneath the church down a long, narrow stairway, behind a locked metal door.

But the crypt itself obviously hadn't been touched since it was built centuries ago, and the sight of it sent a sustained shiver of revulsion through Callahan the moment they stepped inside. She'd seen plenty of death in her time, but places like this gave her the creeps.

It started with a narrow ossuary, or bone house. A stone wall to their left was lined with long wooden shelves—and on those shelves, sitting side by side, were several hundred skulls, yellowed by age. To their right were two large pallets carrying piles of neatly stacked bones.

"The plague," Grant said, without offering any further explanation. Not that Callahan needed one. She was surprised by his complete sense of calm. His demeanor seemed much more monklike than Brother Philip's ever had.

LaLaurie, on the other hand, seemed to be on edge the moment they stepped through the crypt doorway, and she had to wonder if being surrounded by all this death had an effect on him. Those enhanced senses of his had to be going into overdrive.

"This way," Grant said, motioning with his flashlight.

They stepped through an archway on their right and into the main chamber. It was the size of a small warehouse and Callahan was instantly reminded of the staging room in Istanbul. But instead of boxes full of antiques, this one held rows of coffins, some in the center made of ornately carved stone, while those lining the wall—in neat, horizontal rows—were shallow wooden caskets, warped and weathered by years of neglect.

There was a smell down here that was hard to miss. A mustiness. And beneath this, faint but unmistakable, the scent of rotting corpses. Callahan had no idea how fresh some of these bodies were—she didn't figure this place had hosted anyone new in quite some time—but the smell was there and she recognized it immediately.

Either that, or she had an amazing imagination.

Grant moved to a stone casket in the center of the room. "This is the one," he said. "John Milton."

LaLaurie nodded and crossed to it, pressing a hand against it, trying to suck up its energy. Callahan half expected the lid to crack open on him, letting loose a vampire or some other deadly creature.

But nothing happened, and LaLaurie opened his eyes, shook his head.

"You're wrong," he told Grant.

Grant's eyes widened slightly. The most emotion Callahan had seen in him so far. "How can that be? This is the one I've been guarding for the last fifteen years."

"Well, I hate to break it to you, Jim, but you've been guarding the wrong coffin."

LaLaurie looked down the row, and over the next several minutes, moved from coffin to coffin, pressing his hand against them, coming away from each one looking a little less whole, and she knew this process was taking its toll on him.

Grant was scratching his head. "I can't believe we got it wrong. All this time and we got it wrong."

"Maybe you didn't pick up the phone often enough," Callahan said.

By the time he'd finished touching every coffin in the room, LaLaurie looked a bit green under the gills. And he still hadn't found what they were looking for.

He turned to Grant. "I assume you have a pauper's vault?"

"Pauper's vault?" Grant said. "I hardly think Milton would be—"

"Maybe one of the previous guardians thought it was prudent to hide him where someone would be less likely to look."

Grant nodded and pointed his flashlight beam toward the back of the room. There was a wooden door there, and he motioned for them to follow. They moved with him and he pulled the door open to reveal another set of steps leading to a subbasement, Callahan again reminded of the auction house.

These steps, however, were old and rickety and creaked so loudly as they descended them that she was sure they were going to wake someone up.

When they got to the bottom they found a smaller, narrower room, with no caskets in the center. Instead the walls were lined with cubbyholes holding cheap wooden boxes, most of them falling apart, arm and leg and foot bones protruding through the cracks.

There was one that didn't belong here, however. An

actual casket stuffed into a dark corner, weathered by age, but clearly out of place.

LaLaurie glanced at Grant and Callahan, then moved to it and pressed his palm against the lid. He closed his eyes, but didn't keep them closed long.

"This is it," he said. "John Milton."

"You're sure?" Grant asked.

"No doubt whatsoever."

"So what are we waiting for?" Callahan said. She stuck her flashlight under her arm and reached for the lid, pushing it open, not at all surprised when they found yet another skull and a set of bones, these mostly intact. The clothing that had covered them was long gone.

It suddenly occurred to her that this is how we wind up.

All of us.

Some leave behind a legacy, as Milton had, a piece of themselves that will be remembered for centuries to come. But most of us die in obscurity. A pile of bones that lie forgotten in some grave, our lives no more important to the world at large than the quarter-inch column of ink that announces our departure from it.

One day we're here; then we're gone. And unless you get lucky, a couple hundred years later nobody knows who the hell you were.

She shone her flashlight inside. Some of the coffin lining was still intact, but no sign of any pages in sight.

"Check under the bones," LaLaurie said.

Callahan looked at him. "You first."

He frowned at her, then reached inside, shoving his hands beneath the body and patting the tattered lining there. She could tell by his expression that he wasn't having any luck.

Then she noticed something—on the right side of the casket where the lining was torn. She shone her light directly on it for a better look, and saw a tiny seam in the wood.

Another hidden door?

Reaching over, she tore the lining away to reveal a narrow oblong panel. Digging her nails into the seam, she pried the lid back and found a hollowed-out space behind it, a burlap bag stuffed inside.

She looked up at LaLaurie, saw the excitement on his face and gestured to the bag. "Be my guest."

With shaky hands, he took it out, untied a leather string at the top, then reached inside and pulled out a familiar-looking Saint Christopher medal. *Custodes Sacri.* He handed it to Callahan, then reached inside again and this time pulled out a roll of time-worn pages, bound by another leather string.

"Careful," Grant said. "Remember the curse."

Batty nodded. "You two might want to close your eyes."

"What about you?"

"I'll take my chances."

Grant didn't hesitate, but Callahan shook her head. "I'm good for now."

Shutting the casket lid, LaLaurie took the Milton manuscript out of the book bag and laid it atop the casket, opening it to the last chapter. Then, as Callahan trained her flashlight beam on it, he untied the string around the roll of pages.

"You'd better close them now," he said.

Callahan nodded, and keeping the flashlight steady, she closed her eyes and listened as he flattened the pages out next to the manuscript. She knew he was checking to see if they lined up.

But then he went still. "This doesn't make any sense."

"What? What's wrong?"

"The pages . . ."

"*What?* What about them?"

LaLaurie paused. Then he said, "They're completely blank."

44

"I don't fucking believe this," Callahan said.

Both she and Grant had their eyes open now and were staring at the pages in shock. And they were definitely blank.

Grant said, "This is what I've been guarding for fifteen years?"

Callahan turned to him. "No, you were guarding somebody else's casket, remember? And it looks like someone slipped in here and switched out the pages."

Grant looked resentful. "They'd have to get past me and a double-locked metal door to do it. And I can assure you, Agent Callahan, this didn't happen on my watch."

"So you're here twenty-four/seven?"

"Well, no, of course not, but—"

"They weren't switched out," Batty said. He had carefully lined up the pages next to the manuscript and the edges matched. He had no doubt in his mind that these were genuine.

"So what are you suggesting?" Grant said. "That this is some sort of cruel hoax? That our first guardian made the whole story up?"

Batty didn't respond. He was thinking back to his vision, to what the poet had told him.

I had several sheets of paper in front of me, my finger etching itself into them as if controlled by another being.

His *finger*, not a pen. Etching itself into the pages.

Then a thought occurred to Batty. "What have you been told about these?" he asked Grant.

"Certainly not that they're blank."

"You've spoken to the angel Michael, I assume?"

"He doesn't ring me up every day, but I wouldn't be here if he hadn't recruited me."

"And he said nothing about this?"

"It's my understanding he can't read the pages himself. None of the angels can. They need humans to translate. In fact, I'd say they seem to need us for quite a *few* things."

Batty nodded, his mind still clicking away. "Both Ozan and Gabriela were trying to decode Milton's verse in Book Eleven. Except they had the *wrong* Book Eleven. Were you told at any time that the pages were encrypted?"

"Yes," Grant said. "But I'm not sure *why*. It's just a story that's been handed down through the generations of guardians."

"Then maybe that's what we have here. Encrypted pages."

"What are you thinking?" Callahan asked. "Invisible ink?"

Batty shook his head. "Invisible ink wasn't invented until the nineteenth century, by a guy named Henry Wellcome."

"Is there a bottom to that well of information you draw from?"

"I hope not," Batty said. Then he reached for the

book bag and brought out the copy of *Steganographia*. "You remember what I said this book was really about?"

"Of course. Steganography, cryptology."

"That's what the experts discovered when they broke the code and I'm sure that's what Ozan was using it for. But the thing that frightened Trithemius's friends and convinced them he was an occultist is that on its surface it's a treatise on how to pass secret messages through spiritual entities."

"Right. But that was just a cover story. Trithemius said so himself."

"But what if he was lying to protect his reputation? What if he really *was* an occultist, and these really are recipes for communicating through spirits?"

"Wait a minute, wait a minute," she said. "Slow down a little."

"In my vision, Milton told me he was visited by another being in the middle of the night. That it forced him to etch these pages with his finger. He was blind, so he couldn't know that the pages were blank. But they were clearly a message from a spirit." He picked up the copy of *Steganographia*. "So what if we were to use one of Trithemius's incantations to decode that message?"

Callahan thought about this. "I think you might be onto something."

"I hope so."

He placed the book next to the blank pages and cracked it open. It had been a while since he'd studied the thing with any depth, and as he stared at the words, he wasn't sure which incantation to choose. Remembering what had happened to Rebecca, he didn't want to summon up the wrong spirit.

He read through them all carefully, then finally found one that seemed most appropriate. A simple, straightforward summoning.

"All right," he said, "Keep your fingers crossed."

Both Grant and Callahan stepped back slightly is if they were afraid they might get in his way. He quickly scanned the page in front of him, committed the incantation to memory, then touched the stack of blank pages and closed his eyes.

Then he said, "*O magne spiritus, si placet, mecum communica nuntium his in paginis. O magne spiritus, si placet, mecum communica nuntium his in paginis. O magne spiritus, si placet, mecum communica nuntium his in paginis.*"

For a moment nothing happened and Batty was afraid it hadn't worked. Then he felt heat in his hand and his fingers began to tremble. He half expected them to take a life of their own and begin writing across the page. Instead, the pages themselves began to glow, infused in a warm yellow light.

Grant and Callahan stepped back even farther, shielding their eyes, as the glow grew stronger; then a fountain of light rose toward the ceiling, illuminating the entire room, a shimmering image appearing at its center.

Batty didn't back up. Didn't move. Didn't shield his eyes.

His gaze was transfixed on that image, and a strange feeling welled up inside him. A feeling of warmth. Not *physical* warmth, but a sense of emotional fulfillment that enveloped him like a loving embrace.

The embrace of a mother and child.

A father and son.

A wife and her husband.

Then the image in the light began to take on form and substance and Batty's chest seized up, tears springing to his eyes. His mouth dropped open and he wanted to say something, wanted desperately to form words, but there were no adequate words for what he now saw.

The image smiled, and the warmth inside him doubled. Quadrupled. He was weak with it. Drunk with it. And not just his fingers were trembling, but his entire body.

"Hello, Batty," she said, in that subtle Louisiana drawl.

It was Rebecca.

"Becky," he croaked.

He hadn't called her that since she died. Not even in his mind. Couldn't bring himself to use the name she had introduced herself with, all those years ago on the steps of Nassau Hall.

But now she was here and it just seemed right. She was his Becky, and he wanted to spring forward and pull her into his arms. But he knew she was only an apparition, impossible to hold.

"How is this happening?" he said. "Where are you?"

"I'm here, Batty. With you."

"But I don't understand."

"Your time in the otherworld was too short. You may have learned many things, but there is so much more to know. It's a vast place, filled with wonder and miracles."

"All I saw was darkness. And I couldn't find any miracles. I couldn't find you."

"But you did," she said. "You didn't know it at the time, but you did."

His eyes widened. "I don't understand."

"You know that piece of the otherworld you thought you brought back with you? That was part of me. Part of my soul. I'm always with you, Batty. I always will be."

Tears welled up in Batty's eyes again. "But I thought . . . Belial . . ."

"Belial destroyed my human form, but one of the incantations you spoke before I succumbed managed to protect me from her, from taking my soul as her own." Becky paused. "But she knows I'm with you, Batty, and she knows my song. That's why you must always be vigilant."

Batty said nothing. He didn't know *what* to say. To know that Rebecca had been with him all this time, had seen what he'd done with Belial in his bed, had watched him drink himself into oblivion time after time, fighting in bars, embarrassing himself at the college. He suddenly felt ashamed.

"Don't fret, Batty. You're human, just as I once was. We make mistakes. We learn from them and we move on. We've been on our own for so long, left to face heartbreak that's almost impossible to bear. Left to deal with the darker angels—not only from the otherworld and beyond, but the darker angels inside us. That pull at our hearts and prod our psyches. It's a miracle that we've survived this long. But that's what it means to be human, Batty. That spirit of survival. The need to create and procreate and love and be loved." She paused again, smiling. "Yet despite your failings, here you are. And that's why he chose you. You've seen the darkness, but your soul— our soul—remains untainted."

"Who?" Batty said. "Who chose me?"

"Michael, of course. He came to me, shortly after you left the otherworld. Belial is his sister and he could feel you through her. He knew of the coming tetrad. The coming struggle. And he wanted me to bring you this message."

"Wait a minute," Batty said. "He *knew* I'd be here?"

"Nothing is certain, but many things can be predicted. And hoped for."

"But what does he want from me?"

"He wants you to free her. To free the sacred traveler. To release her from her human bonds and give mankind the chance it deserves. To let her be a message to God."

"But . . . how?"

"The pages will tell you," Rebecca said. "But you must not fail, Batty. If the dark angels manage to corrupt her soul before you have a chance to free her, all will be lost, the seven gates will open and Lucifer instead will be freed, to rule the earth forever."

Batty felt sick. How could he be responsible for something like that? He was barely responsible for himself. He couldn't even keep Rebecca from being taken from him.

"This has to be a mistake."

"Not a mistake," she said. "But it won't easy for you. You will be tested. But remember that I'll be with you. Always. If you feel your resolve faltering, just call to me and I'll listen."

Becky's image began to shimmer now, starting to blur.

"Wait," he said. "Don't go."

"It's time, my love. The message has been given. You

have difficult choices ahead of you. Just remember to heed the pages. They will tell you what you must do."

Her image continued to shimmer and blur, then finally faded away.

Then the glowing light was gone, the room once again dark except for the beams of their flashlights.

Batty took his flashlight from the casket lid and shone it down on the pages. They were no longer blank, but what he saw surprised him.

Not poetry, as he had expected. No final verses to *Paradise Lost*. But seven carefully rendered illustrations—much like the Gustave Doré etching in Gabriela's apartment—black-and-white drawings of a world gone mad, ravaged by pain, people struggling, fighting, killing. And in each new drawing a huge full moon hung high above them, each one farther along in the progression of a lunar eclipse.

But it was the seventh drawing that told the tale.

A story of two opposing outcomes.

On the right side of the page was a ravaged world, barren and lifeless, a dark-winged Satan hovering above it. On the left side was a lush, verdant paradise with rolling hills and fruit-bearing trees, a great warrior angel looking down upon it.

And at the center, kneeling beneath the moon in full eclipse, was a small figure, a dagger held in her right hand, aimed directly at her throat. Her left hand was held palm outward, as if in oath, toward a man wielding a sword.

Below them, a sacred incantation was written in bold black ink—*Quod apertum est, id aperiri non potest*.

What is opened cannot be closed.

But it was the figure of the man with the sword that told Batty what he was expected to do, reminding him of the painting he saw in Istanbul, of the widow Judith attacking Holofernes. Reminding him of Saint Christopher's selfless martyrdom.

The man with the sword was cutting off her head.

aLaurie stumbled slightly and fell back. Callahan and Grant quickly stepped forward, grabbing his arms, holding him upright.

"What's wrong?" she asked.

He looked at her. "You didn't see it?"

She hadn't seen much of anything. "A bright light, that's about it. I covered my eyes for a couple seconds. Then it went away. Next thing I know you're about to collapse."

He turned to Grant, but Grant just shook his head.

Callahan gestured to the pages. "They're still blank. What happened?"

"Blank?" LaLaurie said. "You don't see the drawings? The incantation?"

"All I see is a stack of really old paper."

LaLaurie pulled away from them now and turned again to Grant. "I need to speak to Michael. I can't do what he wants me to. Do you have a way to contact—"

He stopped suddenly, glancing around the crypt, then turned to the casket and quickly gathered up the manuscript and the pages. "We have to get out of here."

"Why?" Callahan said. "What's going—"

A rat skittered across the casket. Callahan jumped

back, and something squished underfoot, squealing in pain. She whipped the flashlight beam downward, shining it on the floor.

More rats, maybe four or five. And as she swept the light around the crypt, she saw that the walls were moving—still more rats crawling out of the darkness, their tiny feral eyes squinting back at her.

Callahan had never had a problem with rodents. One or two on their own was fine. But this many of the hideous little creatures was just too much to take.

They started swarming toward her. One tried to sneak up her pant leg and she yelped and kicked out, flinging it aside. LaLaurie and Grant were kicking, too, shaking them off their feet.

Callahan watched in horror as more rats skittered toward them. Then the walls of the crypt began to shake, and one of the wooden coffins cracked open. A bony arm fell out, and Callahan may have been imagining this, but the fucking thing looked *alive*.

Then more rats began to crawl up her legs, two, then three, now four . . .

Grant grabbed her arm and dragged her toward the stairs, pointing the way with his flashlight, LaLaurie trailing behind them.

The steps were teeming with rodents now. Moving together, the three started kicking and stepping, working their way upward, the rats squealing and peeping and hissing, clinging to their pants as they moved. Several more were crawling up the walls beside them.

Suddenly one leapt onto Callahan's head, trying to burrow into her hair. She smacked it with her flashlight, but it didn't shake loose. She hit it again, then again, the thing squalling louder with each blow, until it finally gave up and fell to the stairs.

Reaching the top, Grant and Callahan dove through the doorway into the main vault, LaLaurie stumbling in after them, slapping a rat from his book bag. They were about to start back toward the ossuary when a sea of the little bastards skittered toward them like a hideous black wave.

Grant spun, shining his flashlight toward the back of the vault. There was a door back there.

"Come on," he shouted. "Come on!"

They all moved together, kicking their way toward the door. Then Grant flung it open to reveal another set of steps that led toward yet another door above. Grant gestured Callahan ahead of him, and they took them two at a time.

She was almost to the top when, behind her, LaLaurie yelped and fell. Within seconds, the rats were swarming up and over him.

As he flailed, trying to fling them off, Grant turned and got him by the collar, yanking him toward the top of the stairs. As they drew closer, Callahan grabbed a sleeve and pulled, swinging her flashlight mercilessly, feeling tiny bones crunch beneath its weight.

When they got LaLaurie to the top, she threw the door open, feeling the sweet night air rush in. Then they pulled him out onto the church lawn.

Swatting the last of the rats away, Grant slammed the door shut, then helped Callahan pull LaLaurie to the center of the yard.

They collapsed next to him. There was blood on Callahan's flashlight and she tossed it aside in disgust.

"Thanks," LaLaurie huffed, trying to catch his breath.

Grant nodded. "Happy to oblige."

And as they all struggled to breathe, Callahan saw something dark and malevolent seep out from under the door they had just come from—a black vapor that hung in the air, as if taunting them. Then it shot across the yard and disappeared into the night sky.

"Was that who I think it was?" Callahan asked.

LaLaurie sucked in a breath and nodded.

"I get the feeling she doesn't like us much."

"That's not the worst of our problems," he said. "I think she was inside my head. Saw what I saw. And if that's true, she knows the incantation."

"Incantation?" Grant asked.

"The key to freeing the sacred traveler."

46

They didn't have to call Michael.

When they stumbled into Grant's lodgings, located at the edge of the church property, Grant flipped on a light and found a bearded man in his early sixties huddled in the center of the room, looking broken and abused, his face bloodied.

Callahan thought he was a homeless guy, but after a moment of hesitation, Grant seemed to know who he was and immediately grabbed him by the arms, helping him over to a twin bed tucked into the corner of the room.

He left a weapon on the floor behind him. A curved, antique knife of some kind, its blade covered with blood.

Callahan picked it up. "This guy means business. Who is he?"

"It's Michael," LaLaurie said. He was hanging back by the door, a somber expression on his face.

"As in *Saint* Michael?"

"That's the one," Grant told her.

She studied the guy. "No disrespect, but I was expecting somebody—I don't know—a little more . . . shiny."

"Shiny?"

"You know, all white, with wings and all that stuff?"

Grant gestured impatiently to another doorway. "Get me a wet cloth, will you? The loo is through there."

Callahan went into the bathroom, found a washcloth hanging from a rack, then quickly wet it and wrung it out. When she went back into the main room, the guy on the bed—Michael—was stirring.

She tossed Grant the washcloth and he pressed it to Michael's forehead, wiped some of the blood from his nose.

LaLaurie was still hanging by the front door, looking as if his cat had just died.

What was going on with him?

Before she could ask, Michael's eyes blinked open. He looked momentarily disoriented, but shook it off and turned to Grant.

"I found her," he said.

Grant's eyes widened. "The traveler?"

Michael nodded. "There's no mistake this time. It's her. I know it's her."

"Where is she?"

His eyes clouded. "I had her with me, but I lost her. Beelzebub and his drudges." He looked up at Callahan and LaLaurie. "It's good that you're both here. I hoped you would be."

"You *know* who we are?" Callahan asked. Thoughts of the D.C. connection popped into her mind and she had to wonder how many people were involved in this thing.

Reaching into the pocket of his jacket, Michael pulled out two leather straps and tossed one to Callahan, the other to LaLaurie.

Surprised, Callahan caught it, then stared at the Saint Christopher medal attached. "What's this for?"

"We've got a few vacancies," he said. "Consider yourselves deputized."

Callahan couldn't believe what he was suggesting, but before she could say anything, LaLaurie piped up.

"We've already collected enough of these," he said. "And I can't do this."

He tossed the medallion to the floor, then turned and walked out.

Batty was halfway across the yard when Michael materialized in front of him. He staggered slightly as if the task hadn't been easy.

Batty faltered, but didn't slow down. As he tried to move around the angel, Michael grabbed him by the arm. "The decision is yours, but hear me out."

Batty stopped. Waited.

"You know I can't ask you to do something you're not willing to do."

"That's right," Batty said.

"But I think you also know the importance of this. Especially now that Belial and the others have the sacred incantation."

"You know about that?"

Michael nodded. "Grant told me. But I expected it. I knew she had a hold on you. And the father said this wouldn't be easy."

"Tell me I'm misinterpreting that drawing. The man with the sword isn't me."

"I wish I could, Sebastian, but if we could simply snap our fingers and release the sacred traveler without any effort, what would be the point? This is about choices. And the intent *behind* those choices, and proving to the father that humans are still capable of making the right ones. And this is a choice not made through malice, but out of love. A love for humankind."

"You sound like a fucking serial killer."

"Don't cheapen this. You know what this means. *Rebecca* knows. She wouldn't have agreed to carry that message if she didn't."

Batty thought about her shimmering image.

The warmth of her embrace.

If you feel your resolve faltering, just call to me and I'll listen.

"The choice is yours, Sebastian, but we still have time. You don't have to make a decision right now."

"But isn't this all academic anyway? They already have the traveler and the incantation. How can we stop them?"

"I'm afraid I've never been known to give in too easily."

Michael brought out his knife and sliced it through the air as if he were slicing through a thin membrane. A hole in the atmosphere opened up and beyond it was a darkness that Batty recognized.

The otherworld.

A place he barely remembered yet hoped he'd never have to see again.

Then Michael took him by the wrist, turned his palm upward, and placed the Saint Christopher medal there. "You and your friend have come this far. What do you say we finish the journey together?"

Batty looked down at the medallion. "What do you have in mind?"

"We go after her," Michael said.

BOOK XI

The Road to Paradise

Death is the golden key that opens
the palace of eternity.

—John Milton

47

THE OTHERWORLD

They traveled by foot down a long, winding trail through the Forest of Never—the angel, the scholar and the spy.

They were, from all appearances, a ragtag crew, the angel brandishing a gun and knife, the spy carrying a shotgun she'd borrowed in the overworld. The scholar had nothing but his fists to rely on, and his wits, but the angel vowed to protect him should anything go wrong.

And many things could go wrong here.

The otherworld was a vast and frightening place, and no one who had visited could claim to know it all. Even the angel himself—who had a home here—had seen only a part of it.

They traveled in silence, each harboring their own thoughts, their own fears. The forest around them was quiet. Too quiet. And the angel knew that its inhabitants were well aware that their home had been invaded by strangers. They would wait and watch, and evaluate . . . and should they feel threatened, they would not hesitate to defend.

The trail seemed to wind on endlessly, and had the scholar not been lost in thought, weighing the decision that lay before him, he might not have been able to continue. Though his memories of the place were vague, the forest stirred up intense feelings of dread and heartbreak, blunted only by his determination to see this thing through and make the right choice.

As they moved through the trees, a mist began to descend, and the spy thought that it might be a living entity, with thoughts and feelings of its own. It clung to them as they walked, seeping into their skin and clothes, seeming to speak to them in low, ominous whispers, and the spy remembered what the scholar had told her about bringing a piece of this world back with him.

It was a thought that did not comfort her.

After traveling through the mist for several hours, they found themselves at the edge of the forest overlooking a yawning canyon, its jagged hills blackened by fire. They stood in a row, looking down at the deep crevices in the canyon floor, waiting for the angel to speak.

After a moment, he pointed toward the largest and deepest crevice of them all.

"There," he said. "The path to Pandemonium."

The spy looked doubtful. "All I see is a giant hole."

"It's the only way in."

"How do we get down there?" the scholar asked.

The angel turned. "What I'm about to ask you to do will go against your better nature. You'll have to shed your earthly prejudices and follow my lead."

"I think I shed my earthly prejudices when the mist started talking to me back there," the spy said, "so what do you have in mind?"

The angel tucked his weapons in his waistband, then moved to the very edge of the cliff and turned his back to the canyon.

"You must let yourself go," he said. Then he did, allowing his weight to carry him backward over the edge of the mountain, his jacket billowing as he fell. The other two watched in disbelief as he plummeted toward the canyon floor—

—then the mist billowed out from his clothes and his skin, slowing his descent until he was merely floating.

A moment later he touched the ground unharmed.

He signaled for the others to follow, but they both hesitated, unable to grasp what they had just seen.

Then the spy shook her head, said, "Ahh, hell . . ." and moved quickly to the edge before she could change her mind, clutching the shotgun to her chest as she spun around and let herself go.

The scholar watched for a moment, then moved to the edge and followed her down.

They landed without incident, the last of the mist rising from their skin, whispering softly as it evaporated. They were surrounded now by jagged mountains and razor-sharp rocks. A misstep, a fall, and a piece of the earth here would slice through your flesh and bone as if it were nothing more than soft butter.

The large chasm was still a mile away, and they traveled a well-worn path toward it, stepping carefully around the rocks, ever mindful of the unseen creatures who watched them from the shadows.

The spy heard a low growl and turned her attention to her right, where a pair of green luminescent eyes carefully followed her.

"Keep facing front," the angel said. "Make no move to provoke it."

The spy snapped her head back around, trying very hard to keep her legs from trembling.

This was, the two humans thought, the longest mile they had ever traveled. As they finally neared the edge of the chasm, however, they felt no relief. They saw a long dark pathway leading toward the glowing light, a pathway that held no promise. No hope.

Several black scorpions skittered up the path toward them, and the angel held up a hand and said, "They will only sting you if you show them fear. But if one becomes aggressive, merely rub a finger along its back and it'll immediately calm down."

"You have *got* to be kidding me," the spy said, her voice laced with disgust.

"All creatures, dark and light, want to be loved."

A moment later, the angel again took the lead and they made their way down the path. The scorpions skittered up close, but did not attack, instead turning and following like excited children, as the three continued forward.

They soon passed through the mouth of the chasm, entering a narrow cave with a low ceiling. They all ducked to keep from bumping their heads, and saw roaches and spiders clinging to the rocks, the roaches rubbing their wings together as if ready for flight, their feathery whispers faintly reverberating against the walls.

The spy and the scholar exchanged brief, uneasy glances as they followed the angel into a shadowy tunnel. The angel withdrew his knife, spoke a brief incantation, and the knife began to glow, illuminating their path. Several multi-legged insects that the humans didn't recognize scattered away in fright, disappearing down a dark hole in the tunnel floor.

The three stepped around the hole and continued on,

moving along a curve until the tunnel opened out onto another cave. The angel came to a stop and pointed his glowing knife toward a stone archway on the opposite side.

"The entrance to Pandemonium."

"At the risk of sounding like a complete idiot," the spy said, "what exactly *is* Pandemonium?"

"A city built by the great Mulciber in honor of Satan. We call it the City of Lost Souls."

They heard a sound and something moved in the shadows of the archway. Then a thing that looked like it should be a wolf or a dog stepped forward and began growling at them.

All three heads.

"A trinine," the angel said. "It won't harm you unless you upset its master."

"Its master?"

As if in answer, a figure slithered out from the shadows behind the three-headed dog. It had the body of a serpent below, and that of an old woman above, her breasts sagging, her hair stringy and gray, her face etched with lines, her teeth crooked and yellow.

"Well?" she said. "Are you going stand there staring, or come inside?"

The two humans exchanged glances again, then followed the angel as he crossed to the old woman.

"What's the fee today?"

"Same as always," she said. "Nothing more than a kiss."

The thought of this turned the humans' stomachs, but they were soon distracted by movement in the shadows on the opposite side of the archway. The shadows shifted and something dark and menacing moved forward, a shape with no real definition.

Whatever it was, it was watching them carefully.

"Go back to sleep, boy," the old woman said. "They'll pay their fee." Then she looked at the three visitors. "Won't you?"

"With pleasure," the angel told her, then stepped close to her and leaned down, kissing her on the lips. The woman snaked her arms around him and held him there for a moment, then finally released him.

"Be on with you, then. Next."

The two humans once again exchanged glances, neither of them anxious to move forward.

"Come on, come on," the old woman said, "or I'll sic my son on you."

The trinine growled and the shadows on the far side of the archway shifted again. Not one to waste time, the scholar leaned down, giving the old woman a kiss. Again she snaked her arms around him, holding him there, and when she released him, he stumbled back, his eyes wide and slightly embarrassed, as if he'd enjoyed the moment but didn't want to admit it.

Then it was the spy's turn, and she clearly did not want to do this. Steeling herself, she tucked the shotgun under her arm, then sidled up to the old woman, crouched down and hesitated, not sure she could go through with it.

"Oh, for Lucifer's sake," the old woman said, then grabbed the spy and yanked her close, planting her lips on her. A slick tongue slithered down the spy's throat and a burst of pleasure flowed through her. Then she, too, stumbled back in a daze and struggled to stay on her feet.

"All right, boy," the old woman said. "Open the gate."

A moment later they heard a faint creak as the gate was opened, and the humans took the path toward the City of Lost Souls.

Pandemonium.

48

The place was at once familiar, yet like nothing Callahan had ever seen before. They seemed to be in a canyon of some kind, with dark, cavernous walls, but with no sky to speak of.

No moon. No stars.

Yet something was stirring up there. Something oppressive. Hostile. A malevolent turbulence—as if some dark specter was watching over them.

A long row of burning torches lined the narrow road, and the walls on either side looked like huge, blackened beehives fashioned out of dark stone.

Homes, Callahan thought, but left it at that.

She didn't want to consider what might be living inside. And she hoped she'd never have to find out.

Up ahead was what looked to be the center of the "city"—if you could really call it that—a cluster of ancient stone structures with pillars and archways surrounding an open square.

But a normal city would be bustling with activity, and this one wasn't. In fact, it was deserted. A ghost town. No one milling about. No lights in the windows. No sounds. No nothing.

And Callahan wondered why.

"Where is everyone?"

"Asleep," Michael said quietly. "And be thankful for it. In a few hours this place will be crawling with creatures you'd best not see. Otherwise you might not get back to the overworld with your sanity intact."

Too late, Callahan wanted to say, but she remained silent.

She'd been to cities all over the world, traveled to some of the most dangerous places imaginable, but as they moved toward the empty square, she'd never been so unnerved before. Never felt a *weight* like this. An uneasiness so deep that it seemed to drag her down.

The threat here was not so much *ex*ternal as it was *in*ternal. And she suddenly realized that what she felt was despair. The despair of a thousand lost souls all gathered in a single place, buzzing inside her like bees in a hive.

If her father had felt only a fraction of this before putting that gun to his head, then she understood why he'd done it.

No one could live with this feeling for long.

She glanced at LaLaurie and knew he felt the same. He'd already had his taste of hell, and she was pretty sure it had been more than enough.

They came to a stop; then Michael ushered them under the shadows of an archway.

"Wait here," he whispered. "And keep your voices low. You really don't want to wake anyone up."

Callahan frowned. "I thought you said this was neutral ground?"

"For angels," he told her. "Everyone else is fair game. That's why they call it Pandemonium."

He was gone for an eternity.

After leaving them behind, Michael had crossed to another archway and disappeared beneath it, swallowed up by a curtain of darkness. When several minutes had passed and he hadn't returned, Callahan started feeling restless.

"What the hell is taking him so long?"

"Give him time," LaLaurie told her. "He obviously knows what he's doing."

Until now, LaLaurie had been uncharacteristically quiet. Callahan wasn't sure what was bugging him—other than the obvious—but he hadn't been the same since they'd escaped Belial's most recent assault.

She knew he had seen something on those pages that she wasn't privy to, but she figured it couldn't be any more horrific than what they'd experienced so far.

Deciding to risk getting her head bitten off, she said, "What's going on, Professor? You've barely uttered a sound since we left the church."

LaLaurie looked at her with pain in his eyes. Then he said, "They want me to kill her."

Callahan wasn't sure what he meant by this. "Kill who?"

"Who do you think?" he asked. "The sacred traveler."

"What are you talking about? Who put that crazy idea in your head?"

"The pages."

Callahan frowned, knowing by his look that what he'd seen must have been extremely disturbing. "So are you ready to tell me about them now?"

"I just did," LaLaurie said, raising his voice.

The sound echoed and something fluttered nearby.

Something coming awake. They both froze. Waited. Then it settled down and was quiet again.

LaLaurie kept his voice low.

"According to the pages," he said, "releasing the traveler has two possible outcomes. In scenario one, if the traveler stabs herself at the pleasure of the dark angels, Satan will be released and the gates of hell—the Abaddon—will flood open."

"And scenario two?" Callahan asked.

"If she's released by someone with an untainted soul, she'll become a warrior angel, drive the demons back to hell and create a paradise on earth. At least that's the way I interpreted it."

Callahan shifted uncomfortably. "I think I'd prefer option two."

"You don't get it," LaLaurie told her. "We're talking about a young girl here. In either case, she dies. And in that particular scenario, *I'm* the one who has to kill her."

Callahan said nothing for a moment. Then she asked, "So what do you plan to do?"

"That depends on you."

"What do you mean?"

"I'm thinking of going with option three."

"Which is?"

"We take the girl and *nobody* kills her. We hide her away until the eclipse has come and gone and she lives to see another day."

"I know your intentions are good, Professor, but wouldn't that work to the dark angels' advantage? If we believe what Philip told us, they're planning on opening those floodgates with or without the sacred traveler."

LaLaurie shook his head. "They can try, and I'm sure

they will. But they've tried before and didn't make it. The human spirit is too strong. And I'm betting they won't be able to do it this time, either. Not without the girl."

"And you're willing to take that risk?"

LaLaurie looked into her eyes, and she could see that there was no doubt in his mind about this. "If creating some kind of utopia on earth requires me to take the life of another living, breathing human being, I'm sorry, but you can count me out. Self-defense is one thing, but this is flat-out murder." He paused. "We're talking about the future of humankind, right? And the way I see it there are only three actual human beings directly involved in this little drama right now. The two of us and her."

There was some sense to what he was saying. "But what about Michael?"

"What about him? I don't think he'll stop us."

"Are you sure? He has a lot invested here. Centuries of looking for the traveler. What makes you think he'd just throw his hands up and walk away?"

"He wouldn't be bothering with any of this if he didn't respect humanity and the concept of free will. He already told me it was up to me to decide, and I think he'll respect that decision, whatever the consequences." He paused. "So are you with me?"

"Look, Professor, I understand what you're saying, and I appreciate the sentiment behind it, but I'm not sure *I'm* willing to risk the alternative."

"What's the oath of *Custodes Sacri*?"

"I think you know."

"Protect her. That's what it's been all along, right? What better way to protect her than by protecting the human being she's become?"

"You haven't even met this girl," Callahan said.

"And that makes a difference? I'm sure in your profession killing someone is no big deal, but—"

"That's not fair."

"Isn't it?"

He was right. Callahan had been asked to kill before and she hadn't hesitated. It wasn't common, but it was part of the job. And she honestly had no trouble targeting a bad guy.

But this was different. This was an innocent girl they were talking about. She wasn't a drudge or sycophant, who had given her soul away. And she hadn't asked to be who or what she was.

The line had to be drawn somewhere, didn't it?

"All right," Callahan said. "I'm with you."

And as they stood there contemplating their decision, Michael emerged from the darkness and approached them. To Callahan's surprise, he'd added an additional weapon to his arsenal—

A battered gold broadsword hung at his side.

"It took a few threats and some arm-twisting," he said, "but I'm told she was taken to Lucifer's old palace. They're keeping her there until the ceremony."

"And how far away is this place?" LaLaurie asked.

"Too far to walk, but there's another way."

"And what's that?"

"We'll be cutting through Purgatory."

Purgatory was a seldom-used place these days.

Once considered necessary for the purification of the soul, it was no longer relevant. With God's abandonment of earth and its outer dimensions, no souls went to heaven anymore, so no such purification was considered necessary.

Rebecca had told Batty that the otherworld was a vast and often wonderful place. He had yet to see the wonderful part, but was relieved to know that she was somewhere safe. And after seeing her in that crypt, he missed her more than ever before.

There was an odd, troll-like being at the entrance to Purgatory who demanded payment before letting them through. Michael dropped some equally odd-looking coins into his palm (they reminded Batty of puzzle pieces), and the troll let them pass.

Purgatory itself didn't look much different from what they'd already seen of the otherworld—if you didn't count the oppressiveness of Pandemonium.

Wide valleys. Dark, craggy mountains. They might as well have been stranded on the moon.

As they traveled along the road, Batty's gaze fell to the broadsword at Michael's side. He knew exactly what its purpose was, but Michael had yet to say a word about it. And the sight of it only made his resolve grow stronger.

After less than an hour of traveling along a winding road, Michael stopped, pulled his knife from his waistband, and tore a long gap in the atmosphere.

Then he made the knife glow and they stepped into yet another cave and followed him through a maze of interconnecting tunnels until they were outside again, facing yet another bleak landscape.

Several yards in the distance, silhouetted against a darkening sky, was an old castle, with high towers and crumbling ragstone walls. It looked as if it hadn't been occupied for centuries—

—except for a single glowing window, high on a wall.

"No one's been near this place since Lucifer was banished," Michael said, then gestured to the window. "I guess they thought it was safe to bring her here." He smiled. "Let's prove them wrong."

49

They waited until the sky was almost completely dark. This gave them the advantage of cover, but it also made it more difficult to see and maneuver.

The castle was fronted by a small forest, and Batty knew that, like the Forest of Never, there were creatures here, watching them, waiting for them to make a wrong move.

"Same as before," Michael said. "They won't attack unless provoked. And they couldn't care less what's going on in that castle."

The three had split up, he and Michael taking one flank, while Callahan took the other. As they moved cautiously through the trees, Batty kept his eyes on that glowing window, knowing how terrified that poor girl must be.

Protect her.

That's what he intended to do.

As they got closer to the castle, Batty saw several ways in. Although castles are generally built for defense, this one was so old and decrepit that there were large gaps in several places along the front and side walls.

But it wasn't unprotected. There were two men sitting guard on a low wall out front, smoking cigarettes—

which to Batty's mind, seemed a bit incongruous, considering where they were.

"Drudges," Michael whispered. "He must've brought them with him."

"And who's *he*?"

"Beelzebub."

Batty knew the name well. Straight from the pages of *Paradise Lost*. Second in command to Satan. Articulate. Well-mannered. Deadly.

He looked at the two drudges, who, from all appearances, were just the opposite. "What do you want to do?"

"I hope your friend is ready," Michael said.

"Why?"

"I have a confession to make."

"Which is?"

"I've never been very good at this stealth shit."

Then Michael jumped to his feet, ripped the gun and knife from his waistband, and shot through the trees like an angel possessed, his long gray hair blowing out behind him as he headed straight for the two drudges.

The term *all hell broke loose* never seemed more appropriate.

Callahan couldn't believe how quickly things went south. One minute she was sidling up to a gap in the castle wall, the next minute Michael was flying across the yard like maniac on steroids, firing his Glock at the two drudges out front.

He was obviously a guy who liked to get straight to the point.

Unfortunately, he must have forgotten there were a few mortals around. This bold move of his had alerted somebody inside the castle and suddenly the whole yard was flooded with drudges, Michael taking them down one after the other, enough dust in the air to create a sandstorm.

All of this would've been fine if some of those drudges hadn't spotted Callahan trying to sneak inside through that gap.

Someone screeched, sending out an alarm, and the next thing Callahan knew, she was confronted by two snarling sycophants. And with all due respect to Ajda, the tea shop waitress, these things were motherfucking *monsters* compared to her.

Fortunately, she had the shotgun, which was a pump-action autoloader, and she started firing away, blowing the fuckers to the seventh level of hell.

Then she was inside the castle and running for a set of stairs, until her path was blocked by an army of drudges, some of whom had knives, others with guns.

She opened fire again, blasting a couple of them to smithereens. But then the knives started flying and the guns were barking and Callahan dove behind a stone pillar.

A split second later, Michael popped into view like a TV genie and started firing and reloading, firing and reloading, moving with blinding speed, taking them down like shooting gallery targets, working with a fluidity and grace—and most of all, *accuracy*—that Callahan could only envy.

She spotted LaLaurie on the stairs behind Michael.

He'd come in through a gap in the wall and was taking the steps two at a time toward the hallway at the top. A couple of drudges scrambled down toward him and it looked as if he were in real trouble, until he ripped the book bag off his shoulder, yanked the Milton manuscript out and pressed it against the first drudge's face.

The drudge screamed and toppled over the stairs, landing hard on the stone floor before bursting into a cloud of black dust. Then the second one came at LaLaurie, but he seemed to have a bit more of a brain, and he grabbed for the book, screaming as it burned his hands. Still, he managed to rip it out of LaLaurie's grip and fling it aside.

Then he went in for the kill, baring his teeth, which was kind of funny considering he wasn't a sycophant. Maybe he was working on a promotion. He went at LaLaurie's throat like a coyote after a cat, but LaLaurie didn't falter. He sidestepped and delivered a left jab straight to the drudge's face and down it went.

But the wannabe was the least of the professor's worries. At the top of the stairs was the real thing—another sycophant—and if those two below had been monstrous motherfuckers, this one was Godzilla, and he was blasting down those stairs like a greased monkey shot out of a cannon—

—his mouth opened wide enough to swallow LaLaurie whole.

Batty saw the thing bearing down on him, thinking, this is it, it's over now, when he heard a shout behind him and Michael was at the bottom of the steps. Michael ripped the broadsword from its scabbard and flung it toward Batty.

To Batty's surprise, he caught it with little effort. Then the thing was on top of him, but he swung out hard, slicing into its torso, and with a screech, it burst open, blowing a thick, oily black dust right into his face.

The stuff burned and Batty coughed and wiped frantically at his eyes. When he could see again, he bounded up the stairs, finally reaching the top.

There was a dark hallway ahead, flickering lamplight coming from an open doorway, and standing there, wide-eyed, was a girl of about fifteen or so, wearing a brown ceremonial robe. She looked as if she'd been expecting someone else, her gaze dropping to the sword in Batty's hand.

And he could see that she was about to bolt.

"Wait!" he called. "Stop! I'm a friend of Michael's!"

But she didn't stop. She took off like a startled kitten, tore down the hall and skidded around the corner, disappearing from view. Batty called out again, was about to go after her, when he heard her yelp in terror.

Then a guy with long hair and sunglasses came back around the corner, one hand over the girl's mouth, a dagger in the other. Batty didn't need an illustrated guide book to know who he was.

Beelzebub.

The girl was squirming, trying to get away, her screams muffled against his palm, but his grip was strong. He smiled at Batty and said, "*Quod apertum est, id aperiri non potest.*"

What is opened cannot be closed.

The sacred incantation.

Batty felt something thud in his stomach as Beelzebub sliced the dagger through the air, opening a hole in the atmosphere.

Then they were gone.

50

Batty turned to Michael. "Tell me you know where he's taking her."

"I have a guess. I only hope I'm right."

"What's your guess?"

"To Eden."

"*Eden?*" Callahan said as she came up the stairs behind them. "As in the *Garden of*?"

"Yes. Or at least what *used* to be Eden, before the corruption began. He's taking her to the spot where the tree of knowledge once stood. It's his way of thumbing his nose at the father. It doesn't hurt that they'll have a perfect view of the fourth blood moon."

"Can you get us there?" Batty asked.

"Are you ready to do what needs to be done?"

Batty looked at the sword in his hand, then glanced at Callahan. She was covered with dust, looking as if she'd rolled around inside a vacuum cleaner bag.

Then he said to Michael, "Just get me there and you'll find out."

"I can't get us to the exact spot, but I can get close. But be warned, a lot has changed since we left. The unrest will have escalated and the eclipse is about to begin. We need to work fast to make this happen."

"Then maybe we should stop talking and get moving," Batty said.

Michael nodded and sliced open a hole.

Michael wasn't kidding when he said things had changed.

Callahan could barely believe her eyes. When they squeezed through the hole he'd made, what she saw was a city under siege, a battleground that lay beneath a turbulent night sky, the thunder of guns pounding her eardrums.

"Moloch and Mammon have done their work well," Michael said. "It won't take much to tip the scale."

Callahan was stunned. "This isn't tipped?"

The city was in chaos, a riot gone viral, men and women with weapons darting through burning rubble, pausing to fire on one another, some in police uniforms, others in street clothes. But Callahan got the feeling it was every man for himself—although she couldn't be sure who was human here and who wasn't.

What surprised her most of all, however, was that they stood in a city she knew. A city she had just visited.

They were in *São Paulo, Brazil*.

"What the hell are we doing *here*?" LaLaurie said to Michael. "I thought we were going to Eden."

Machine-gun chatter forced them to duck. They all dropped down, taking cover behind a row of parked cars. This was insanity.

"We are," Michael said. Then he jumped up and darted to an abandoned Chevy in the middle of the street, its engine still running. He climbed in, spun the wheel and hit the accelerator, backing toward them. "Get in."

Callahan glanced at LaLaurie and he looked just as confused as she was. Then she ran to the passenger side and jumped in, LaLaurie following close behind. When they were both inside, Michael punched the accelerator and they took off down the street.

Callahan checked the sky and saw a huge moon, a centimeter of shadow washing across it.

"It's starting," she said. "The eclipse is starting."

They brought the girl up the stairs to the rooftop.

Belial couldn't quite believe how beautiful she looked, all dressed up in that ceremonial robe. She had been drugged, but still she resisted, showing a lot of spirit.

Belial wished she'd could have taken some time alone with the girl. It would have been her last chance to understand what it meant to be a woman.

The two drudges had her by the arms. They stopped in the doorway, Jenna struggling between them, and waited for Belial to give her approval.

Moving in close, she smiled and ran a finger under Jenna's chin.

"So beautiful," she said.

The girl jerked her head away, tears filling her eyes, her speech slurred by the drugs. "Why are you doing this? What you want from me?"

"Michael didn't tell you?"

"Leave me alone," she cried. "I wanna go home. I want my mother."

"Your mother?" Belial said. "Now why would you

want to go home to that vile creature? Isn't she the one who betrayed you, brought that man into your happy home? Or is that story all a lie?"

"Please . . . ," she begged. "Please, let me go . . ."

"That's exactly what we're about to do, my darling. By freeing you, we free the world."

Stepping back, she nodded to the two drudges and they carried Jenna past her toward the center of the rooftop, which was crowded with otherworld dignitaries.

Before they got her there, however, the earth rumbled, shaking the building, and everyone cheered as they looked up at the moon.

It hung low in the night sky like a giant blind eye, a shadow slowly creeping across it.

The new beginning was near.

"**D**id you feel that?" Batty asked.

They were blasting down an eerily vacant highway, and this was the first time he'd ever felt an earthquake while riding in a car.

"It's starting," Michael said. "The opening of the Abaddon. And unless we get to that girl soon, all seven levels of hell will be released on earth and Lucifer will be free."

They looked at each other, the thought of this a lingering foul odor.

Then Batty glanced at the shadow on the moon. "It seems to be moving faster than usual."

"You can't think of this as a natural event anymore. The speed of the eclipse will accelerate with each new soul corrupted."

"How long before we're in full eclipse?" Callahan asked.

"Minutes, rather than hours."

The earth rumbled again and the rooftop swayed.

More cheers went up as lights blew out in the distance. Then buildings started to topple, a spray of yellow-orange lava erupting into the air.

The two drudges pushed Jenna to the ground, and Beelzebub—who stood nearby, looking quite handsome in his own ceremonial robe—signaled to Belial that it was time to begin.

She nodded, then moved over and knelt before the girl, still smiling as she grabbed hold of the robe Jenna was wearing.

"I think we can dispense with this."

She pulled the robe up over the girl's head and Jenna, naked underneath, flung her arms around herself and started crying again.

Belial leaned forward and kissed her tears, murmuring against her cheek. "Don't fret, my darling. This will soon be over."

Then she looked directly into Jenna's eyes.

Probing them.

Going in deep.

The orange light of the lava was reflected in her tears and after a moment Jenna started to relax, letting her arms drop to her sides, not so concerned anymore about modesty.

"That's right, my darling. Let us see you, in all your

glory. Present yourself to the Lord Satan and ask him to bring you home."

Then, as if in answer, the earth rumbled again.

This one was a doozy. The earth shifted and everything around them started to sway. Suddenly the road cracked, a fissure opening up in front of them.

Michael slammed the brakes and spun the wheel, the Chevy's tires burning up blacktop as they came to a screeching halt—

—just as a gusher of lava shot into the air.

They all jumped out and scrambled back, barely avoiding molten patches of the stuff that landed at their feet.

Heat radiated off it, and they fell back even farther as the earth rumbled again.

Batty looked up at the moon and saw that the eclipse had hit the halfway mark. They didn't have a minute to spare.

"Enough of this bullshit," he said to Michael. "Where are we going? Where is she? Where did they take her?"

Michael moved over to him, got very close, staring him directly in the eyes.

"Are you ready to do what has to be done?"

Batty couldn't look away from him.

And he couldn't lie, either.

"No," he said. "I can't do what you want. I can't kill an innocent human being."

"Then what do you plan to do? How do you plan to stop this?"

"They won't succeed without her. I know they can't. This can be fixed. We've done it before."

"Look what's happening around you, Sebastian. This is just the beginning of it. What you're about to witness is hell come to earth. Is that what you want?"

Batty's head was spinning. What he wanted was to scream.

The world was falling apart around them, but he had to believe. He had to have faith. And he couldn't bring himself to say what the angel wanted to hear.

"Just tell me where they took her."

Michael studied him, searching his eyes, then backed away and pointed. "There," he said. "They took her in there."

Batty looked across the street. Michael was pointing toward a cluster of ramshackle shacks. A shantytown made of plywood and aluminum siding.

One of the shacks had a word spray-painted across it in Day-Glo green:

Paraisópolis.

"Holy shit," Callahan muttered. She was standing beside him now, gaping at the shantytown. "You've gotta be kidding me? The *favela*? *This* is Eden?"

"What does it say?" Batty asked.

She looked at him. "Paradise City."

51

Batty hadn't expected this.

For centuries, biblical scholars had been arguing over the location of Eden. Some believed it could be found in the heart of Iraq, while others said they had uncovered evidence of it in the industrial city of Tabriz, Iran. Still others claimed Turkey or Egypt or India.

There were those who pointed to Mount Olivet, in Jerusalem, where Jesus wept, was crucified and rose from the dead. Where he had ascended to heaven.

Batty himself had always thought of Eden as a frame of mind. An ideal. A symbol that didn't really exist. It didn't matter where it was located, but what it represented.

The dawn of sentience.

But if Michael were to be believed—and Batty saw no reason *not* to believe him—then the ground on which this shantytown stood had once been Paradise.

And apparently still was.

Paraisópolis.

Paradise City.

The earth rumbled again, and somewhere in the distance behind him Batty heard cries of pain. He realized that he was still gripping the sword, had carried it with him from the car, and as he thought about what Michael had said, he found himself starting to have second thoughts.

What if he was wrong about this?

What if it couldn't be fixed without sacrificing that poor girl?

Yes, she was an innocent, but hadn't innocents died before in the name of freedom?

And wasn't this about the ultimate freedom? The freedom of thought?

John Milton had fought strenuously, had risked his life in the name of free expression, had burned those pages because he feared they'd fall into the wrong hands and humankind would be stripped of that freedom forever.

And now that they *had* fallen into the wrong hands— because of *Batty* when it came down it—wasn't it his duty to set things right? Not merely slow their progress by snatching the girl away from them, but to create the heaven on earth that so many desired?

Yet it kept coming back to the girl.

That single, breathing, walking, talking, *living* human being.

And as he and Callahan and Michael crossed the street toward Paradise City, he had absolutely no idea what choice he would ultimately make.

Beelzebub watched as the others gathered around Belial and the girl. Make no mistake about it, Belial was a master at what she did, and he could see young Jenna succumbing to her power, giving in to her will.

It was thing of beauty. A true gift. And as he looked

up at the darkening moon he was happy he had trusted Belial's instincts. Was happy that Michael had betrayed the traveler with his impulsiveness. Had it not been for him, they never would have known that she was one.

That was something he'd have to live with for a long, long time, as he sat in his cell in the seventh city.

Beelzebub thought it only fitting that they had brought the girl here to this rooftop. The place where the tree had once grown. It was, he thought, a final, symbolic *fuck-you* to their fraudulent, self-aggrandizing father and his precious creation.

All along the skyline, he saw more eruptions, the earth giving way to a seething abyss. The gates breaking open.

And he knew it was like this all around the world. Soon his brother would rise from the fires of Abyssus, once and for all, and take possession of his true dominion.

Lord of the Earth.

King of the New Creation.

Father to all who embraced his sovereignty.

And Beelzebub was fairly certain they would not be given a choice in the matter. This was one of God's mistakes that his brother would not repeat.

What a shame, he thought, that he didn't have a piece of fruit with which to tempt the girl. That idea, however, seemed a bit simplistic now. Human beings had become such complex animals over the years, and while they could certainly be predictable, they couldn't always be relied upon to succumb to such easy temptation.

Better to let Belial do what she did best.

To persuade the girl to take her life in the name of Satan.

The moon was in three-quarters eclipse now.

Batty, Callahan and Michael moved together through the *favela*, Michael taking the lead. They wound through its streets, surprised to find it curiously empty, but then many of the people here had probably fled during the chaos, and those who were left had undoubtedly gathered near where the ceremony was to be held.

Except for the dead. As the three guardians moved from street to alleyway and back to the street again, there were bodies everywhere. Some with weapons at their side. Others shot down without mercy.

Michael snatched up a couple of guns along the way and tossed them to Batty and Callahan.

"Through here," he said, then cut to the right, moving up a narrow cement pathway. The shacks on either side were in ruins, thick black smoke billowing from within them, spewing its noxious fumes into the air.

They were turning the corner when the earth began to shake again and before them a row of shacks shuddered and collapsed, sinking into a fissure in the ground.

Fire shot up in front of them and they pulled back, quickly changing direction.

But then something moved from inside the fissure.

"Look out!" Batty shouted.

And out of the fire and smoke came a platoon of creatures, the likes of which Batty had never before seen, their skin charred, their teeth bared as their feral eyes took the three guardians in with a hunger that sent chills up his spine.

One of them dove for Callahan, but she ducked away as Michael jerked his knife from his waistband and cut the thing in two. It howled and burst into flames, tumbling to the ground, as three of its friends advanced on Callahan.

She brought her shotgun up, shot one in the chest, then kicked, whirled, and kicked again, knocking the other two aside as Michael quickly finished them off with a couple bullets of his own.

But still more came at them, and Batty brought his own gun up, blasting them back into the hole.

Then it was over. For now, at least.

But as they gathered themselves and continued on, Batty knew there would be more to come.

It was time for the ceremony, and it looked as if Belial had the girl primed and ready. She came over to Beelzebub now.

"She's all yours," Belial said. "When she sees that dagger, she'll think it's candy."

Beelzebub smiled and kissed her full on the lips. And they were very nice lips indeed. "I really do like this new skin."

"The girlfriend of the local drug lord. He used to own this place."

"Used to?"

She smiled. "He's one of ours now. Are we ready to begin?"

Beelzebub checked the moon. "Just waiting on Moloch and Mammon. Where are those fools?"

A voice behind him said, "I'd watch that tongue, if I were you."

They turned to find Moloch and Mammon walking toward them across the rooftop.

"I have to congratulate you two," Mammon said. "You were right after all." There was a sneer in his voice that led Beelzebub to question his sincerity. "But before we begin, we have a little surprise."

"Surprise?"

Now Moloch stepped forward and pointed toward the far horizon.

"Watch," he said.

Within milliseconds of speaking the word, a mushroom cloud rose in the distance, followed by a thunderous *boom*.

The shock wave rolled out across the landscape, toppling everything in its path.

"**D**own!" LaLaurie shouted. "Get down!"

Callahan dove to the ground, feeling the earth rumble beneath her as the shock wave leveled the buildings behind them, stopping just short of the *favela*.

"Oh, Jesus. Oh, Jesus," she moaned, buffeted by a hot, harsh wind.

She kept her face buried in her arms, not wanting to see the destruction behind her, not wanting to move.

But when she finally forced herself to look up, she found nothing but a fine dust swirling around her, and she was unable to see more than three feet in front of her. Then the dust began to clear, blowing back the way it came, to reveal that half of São Paulo had been reduced to nothing but ash.

"Oh my God," Callahan moaned, tears filling her eyes.

This couldn't be happening.

It just couldn't be.

But just as she thought she'd seen the worst of it, the ground began to shudder again, and a fiery chasm splintered and forked, two enormous cracks cutting to the left and right, spewing flames. And from within those flames came the bodies of the dead, crawling over the cracks like ants from a mound, silhouetted by the massive bloodred ring of the eclipsing moon, only a sliver of which still shone in its glory. The animated bodies of the dead seemed to take their power from it, spreading out toward Callahan and the others, their eyes filled with malice.

"Oh my God," she said again, and scrambled to her feet.

This wasn't going to end well.

52

The dark angels and their drudges cheered and applauded. They had never before seen anything so glorious.

As the dust cleared, Beelzebub looked up and saw that the eclipse was nearly full. The moon glowed a brilliant bloodred in the sky.

"Let us begin," he said, and those in robes formed a circle around the girl as he approached and stood over her. "Are you ready to give your soul to Lucifer?"

The girl looked up at him, her eyes glazed.

"Lucifer . . . ," she muttered.

Beelzebub smiled, slipping the dagger from his pocket as he turned to the others and spoke the sacred incantation. "*Quod apertum est, id aperiri non potest.*"

What is opened cannot be closed.

"*Quod apertum est, id aperiri non potest,*" the others repeated in unison, then began walking in a circle around the girl and Beelzebub, chanting the words over and over.

Beelzebub knelt down. "It's all right, my angel. Nothing to be afraid of. Soon all your pain will be gone. You want that, don't you?"

"Yes," she said softly.

"You want me to take away your pain?"

"Yes . . ."

He held out the dagger. "All you have to do is give yourself to Lucifer. Are you ready to do that?"

"Yes," she said a third time, then took the dagger into her hand.

Batty watched in astonishment as the cracks in the ground started to multiply, chunks of the earth breaking away, tumbling into the ever-widening pit, a wall of molten lava shooting up from within.

The dead things were still crawling toward them and Michael fired his Glock with one hand and arced his knife with the other, severing arms and torsos and heads.

Batty and Callahan opened fire alongside him, putting bullets between their eyes, knocking them back into the abyss.

Batty felt a prickling on the back of his neck and turned to where one of the shacks had collapsed behind him. A short distance away, he saw a cement bunker on the side of the hill, and there, standing on its rooftop were a dozen or more people in brown robes, moving in a tight circle.

He was instantly reminded of the drawing on the seventh page.

Firing off one last shot and nailing another dead thing in the chest, he shouted to the others and took off toward the bunker.

"*Quod apertum est, id aperiri non potest,*" the crowd chanted as the girl knelt there, staring at the dagger in her hand. "*Quod apertum est, id aperiri non potest.*"

"It's all right," Beelzebub said. "It'll only hurt for a moment. One small prick of the flesh and all is yours."

The girl swayed slightly, still staring at the dagger. Then she raised it into the air and Beelzebub smiled.

"Yes, yes . . . Give yourself to Lucifer."

He could see that she was his. That she was about to do it.

"*Quod apertum est, id aperiri non potest.*"

He glanced at Belial, who had broken from the circle and was watching with quiet rapture in her eyes.

The moon was in full eclipse now, everything aligned and perfect, and he knew that all he had worked for, century after century, would finally be his. His beloved brother would soon be free and the world would be theirs to rule together.

The girl raised the dagger higher, then higher, aiming it toward her throat.

Batty was only feet from the bunker when he saw the girl raising the dagger.

No, he thought, no . . .

He had to stop her.

Shoving his gun into his waistband, he dropped the broadsword and picked up speed. Hurdling over a low cement barrier, he jumped onto a platform, then leapt toward the bunker, grabbing onto the lip of the rooftop.

His legs swung free and he struggled to pull himself up and over the ledge, but he couldn't get enough momentum and the strength in his fingers was waning fast.

One of the drudges on the rooftop spotted him and snarled, heading in his direction. But just as the drudge was about to reach him, a shot rang out and a bloody red hole opened up in its forehead.

It blew back hard, bursting into a cloud of black dust.

Batty closed his eyes as the dust blew across his face. He heard shrieks and cries of alarm from the rooftop and he knew that others would soon be coming. His fingers were starting to give out, and as he struggled to hold on, his gun shook loose and clattered to the ground below.

Shit.

Just as he was sure he was about to follow it, he felt a burst of energy behind him, a rush of hot air that sent him hurdling up and over the lip of the rooftop, and he knew that it was Michael's doing, delivering an invisible blow.

He rolled and jumped to his feet—

—and there, just five yards away, was the sacred traveler, her eyes glazed, staring at the dagger in her hand.

Beelzebub was vaguely aware of a disturbance around him, but paid it no attention. The little witch wasn't doing what had to be done.

He glanced at the moon.

"Go on, my angel. The time is now."

But the girl still didn't move. Kept staring at the blade.

"You want to give yourself to Lucifer, don't you?"

"Lucifer . . . ," she murmured.

"One small prick and the world is yours."

"Mine . . . ," she said.

Then, just as he was about to give up hope, she tightened her grip and raised the dagger even higher, ready to plunge it home.

"That's it, my angel, that's it! Time to take away your pain."

Then all at once, something shifted in her eyes. She suddenly focused on Beelzebub, then screamed and brought the dagger down—

—plunging it straight into his throat.

Beelzebub's eyes went wide as he grabbed his neck and teetered back, blood pouring between his fingers. Getting to her feet, Jenna kicked him hard, knocking him backward. "Go to hell, you sonofabitch!"

Belial shot forward, grabbing for the girl, as angels all around them started shouting, several of them reaching for Beelzebub as he tumbled to the ground.

Batty barreled forward as a crowd of drudges and dark angels descended upon him. He spun and swung, connecting with every blow, but there were too many of them and he knew he wouldn't last.

He did his best to drive them back, looking desperately toward the girl, relieved to see that she was on her feet now, standing over a figure writhing on the ground, the dagger in her hand, and murder in her eyes.

A dark-skinned Brazilian woman was reaching for her, and as Batty was about to move in, someone hit him from behind, knocking him sideways.

Wheeling around, he punched out blindly, sending another drudge sprawling.

Then gunfire rang out, and he saw Callahan moving toward him, blowing away drudges left and right, clouds of black dust bursting like fireworks in the air around her.

But when he turned to face the girl, the Brazilian woman had her by the arm, struggling to wrestle the dagger from her. The woman glanced up at Batty, and as their eyes made contact, something warm and wet rolled over in his stomach.

He knew instinctively who she was.

Belial.

It was Belial. Already comfortable in a new skin.

She shook the dagger free and it fell to the rooftop, and now Beelzebub was being helped to his feet, his eyes filled with fury.

Batty tried again to move toward them, but his path was blocked by a rampaging drudge. More shots rang out and as the drudge disintegrated, Batty charged, heading straight for Belial and Beelzebub.

Callahan saw LaLaurie making his charge and was about to join him, when someone tackled her from the side, knocking her to the ground.

Her gun spun away as one of the robed idiots landed on top of her and smiled, revealing a blackened front tooth.

It was de Souza. José de Souza.

"I told you this was coming," he hissed, then suddenly his face began to distort, his eyes narrowing, his teeth growing sharp and nasty.

He was a sycophant.

Opening his mouth, he went for her throat, but Callahan ducked away and brought a fist up into his stomach. He howled and rolled off her and she scrambled desperately for her gun, snatching it up in her fingers as she turned to face de Souza. But before she could get a good grip on it—

—he swiped a hand at her, knocking it away. Then he lunged, moving in for the kill.

But Callahan reared back, brought her foot up and kicked out with everything she had. The heel of her boot smashed against his teeth, nearly pulverizing them, the blackened one ripping free at the root and splatting on the rooftop.

De Souza howled and fell back, grabbing at his mouth—

—as Callahan found her gun, pointed it at him and pulled the trigger.

A split second later, the sonofabitch was dust.

As Batty made his charge, Beelzebub wheeled around, waving a hand at him.

Knowing what was coming, Batty dove, flattening on the rooftop as a deadly wave of energy rocketed past him, nearly creasing the top of his skull. Then he jumped to his feet again, and a voice behind him shouted—

"Sebastian!"

Batty turned, saw Michael near the edge of the rooftop, broadsword in hand. Repeating the gesture he made at Lucifer's palace, Michael thrust his hand out, releasing the sword.

It flipped end over end and Batty caught it midair, then turned without hesitating and lunged toward Beelzebub, whose attention had returned to the girl.

"Look out," Belial cried, and Beelzebub wheeled around, again waving a hand at him.

Batty thrust the sword upward, blocking the blow, feeling it vibrate in his hands, the force of the energy nearly knocking the weapon from them. But he held on tight and lunged again, swinging out hard.

As the edge of the blade sliced straight for Beelzebub's stomach, the dark angel's eyes widened—

—and he suddenly vanished.

A split second later, he was behind Batty, but before he could make a move, *Michael* was there, slicing at Beelzebub with his knife. The blade scraped across the dark angel's back and he stumbled forward as Michael advanced on him.

Returning his attention to Belial, Batty saw that she had scooped up the dagger and was backing away, the girl struggling in her grip.

"I'm really starting to think you have a thing for me, Sebastian."

"Let her go, you bitch."

"How can you call me that after all we've meant to each other?"

Batty felt her trying to get inside his head, trying to use her power against him. But he refused to let her in. He thought of Rebecca and how she was part of him now, and he knew she'd never let Belial get close to him again.

"Let her go," he said, raising the sword.

Belial ignored him and grabbed the struggling girl's hand. Prying it open, she forced the dagger into it and pushed the girl to her knees.

For a moment, everything around Batty seemed to shift into slow motion—

—Belial holding firm, hand clamped over the girl's, once again raising the dagger high.

—Michael and Beelzebub locked in hand-to-hand combat, a fluid ballet of blows.

—Callahan charging through the sea of drudges and dark angels like a rampaging warlord, fists flying, gun ablaze.

—The moon still in full eclipse, its fiery crimson surface alive with power.

—And the dust, always the dust, bursting in the air.

It all seemed so surreal to Batty. Dreamlike. Not of this world. And he wished he could open his eyes and find himself two years in the past, back in his bed in Ithaca, Rebecca—sweet Becky—sleeping quietly beside him.

But the dream was broken by another shout, Michael standing only feet away. "The moon, Sebastian! The moon! It's not too late—do what has to be done!"

Batty glanced again at the blood moon, then looked at the girl, still kneeling in front of Belial, struggling in the bitch's grip, the dagger poised above her throat, utter fear in her eyes.

But as their gazes connected he saw something else there. Something *more* than fear, coming from the very depths of her soul. She seemed to understand—to *know*—what was being asked of him.

"Do it, Sebastian! Now!"

Tightening his grip on the sword, Batty moved toward them, but something within him still resisted.

She was a human being.

Flesh and blood.

Who was he to decide who should live and die? Who was he to decide the fate of the world?

He wasn't a god. Not even close. There were times he barely felt like a man.

"Do it!" Michael shouted, sensing his hesitation.

Batty looked again at that hovering dagger, at the fury in Belial's eyes. He felt her trying again to push her way into his brain, but again he resisted. He was no longer drawn to her. Could deflect anything she threw at him.

Strengthening his resolve, he raised the sword, knowing that the decision he'd made could change the world forever. Then he closed his eyes, letting his vision guide him, swinging the sword home, feeling it cut into flesh, slicing through bone.

And when he opened them again, he saw Belial's pretty Brazilian head tumble across the rooftop and roll over the side.

53

As Belial's headless corpse flopped to the ground behind her, the girl staggered forward and burst into tears.

Batty dropped the sword and grabbed for her, pulling her into his arms. And as she sobbed against his chest, he felt Rebecca smiling inside him.

But it wasn't over yet.

All around them, the battle still raged, Callahan fighting off the last of the drudges as Michael and Beelzebub continued trading blows. Then the moon began to darken, turning a deeper shade of red, as the ground beneath them trembled and rolled.

Batty wondered if this was it.

Had he made a mistake in keeping her alive?

Were the gates of the Abaddon about to open, once and for all?

But then the girl began to tremble violently in his arms and to Batty's surprise, she pushed away from him. Stepping several feet back, she looked up at him without even a hint of fear or confusion in her eyes.

Something had changed about her.

There was a maturity in her gaze. An awareness. She was no longer the young girl he'd seen trapped in Belial's grip.

Then her body began to shimmy and shake, her naked flesh falling away, as if she were shedding a cocoon, and a bigger, bolder, more radiant being rose from within, her wings unfurling, opening, spanning fifty feet or more.

She was, quite possibly, the most beautiful creature Sebastian LaLaurie had ever seen. And as she levitated several feet above the ground, she smiled at him.

"You made the right decision, Sebastian. God sent me to watch over you. Over all of you. I am your second chance."

"But I don't understand," Batty croaked. "I was supposed to kill you."

The angel shook her head. "No, Sebastian. It was the *third* choice that mattered. The *hidden* choice. The one not shown in the prophecy that demonstrated your humanity to God and told him there was still hope for humankind. The one that came from reason and emotion, with no promises attached to it. It was the *right* choice, Sebastian. The only choice."

Free will, Batty thought. That's what it ultimately came down to. And what so many people thought of as weakness—the ability to empathize, to *care*, the thing that seemed so absent in the world of late—was really man's strength. His lifeblood.

The angel flicked a wrist and the sword at Batty's feet suddenly leapt through the air and landed in her hand.

Then she was moving, gliding, sweeping the blade in wide arc, a wave of energy rolling out across the rooftop, drudges disintegrating in its wake, dark angels dropping their skins where they stood, their vaporous life-forms fleeing in terror.

With a roar of rage, Beelzebub broke from Michael's

grasp and flung an arm out, firing his own ball of energy straight toward the warrior angel's chest. But she deflected it with the blade, hurling it right back at him, the impact slamming him to the ground.

He landed in a heap at the edge of the rooftop, his body twisted, broken beyond repair. Looking up at her in stunned disbelief, his eyes went blank—

—and he was gone.

And as the last of the demons abandoned their skins and fled into the darkness, the angel waved her sword once more. Thunder rumbled, and all throughout the city, the fiery crevices of hell sputtered and died, sealing up before Batty's eyes.

Then the angel looked at him and touched her heart.

"Go with God, Sebastian . . ."

And before Batty could say a word, she let her wings carry her into the sky, taking her upward toward the heavens. As she disappeared from view, a ray of golden light broke through the darkness above and swept across the landscape, restoring everything in its path.

It looked to Batty as if someone were running the film in reverse, buildings rising from the rubble to their former glory as the city was restored.

And all around him, the *favela* began to shift and change—battered aluminum shacks turning into houses; trees and grass sprouting and growing, flowers blooming, as the moon faded away and the sky turned a brilliant, cloudless blue.

Batty looked at Callahan and Michael, all of them standing there, frozen in place, covered in fine black dust, their weapons limp in their hands, their mouths agape—

—as they stared in awe at the world around them.

t was almost as if it had never happened.

As if the clock had been turned back a few hours, leaving the city to blithely go about its business. Traffic in the streets, schoolchildren on buses, drive-time radio stations playing the latest hits from São Paulo and around the globe.

But it had also *changed* somehow.

They all felt it as they stood there in the center of the city. They couldn't know for certain, of course, but it seemed as if a giant pressure valve had been opened, releasing all the tension from the world.

Replacing it with hope.

They had walked here from the *favela*, dazed and exhausted, the three of them looking as if they'd emerged from a coal mine. And as they paused to take it all in, Michael said, "You do realize this isn't the end of it."

Callahan gestured to their newly restored surroundings. "Looks pretty definitive to me."

"Don't let any of this fool you," Michael said. "It's a second chance, nothing more. A shot at redemption, not a return to Paradise. There are no guarantees for humankind. There are no guarantees for *any* of us."

Batty nodded, a familiar line of poetry coming to mind. "Long is the way, and hard, that out of hell leads up to light."

Callahan looked at him. "Milton?"

"*Paradise Lost*. Seems appropriate, don't you think?" He turned to Michael. "This isn't the last we've seen of Belial, is it?"

"If I know my sister, she and Beelzebub are already licking their wounds and planning their next move." He paused. "But that's not the worst of it."

"What do you mean?"

"This isn't the same world our father created. We've entered a new age now. And the enemies of humankind aren't limited to a handful of disgruntled angels. There are forces out there—human and otherwise—waiting, watching, looking for weaknesses to exploit. And if this second chance is to mean anything, we'll have to remain vigilant, always alert."

"We?" Callahan said.

"*Custodes Sacri*'s job is far from done."

"So what are you suggesting?"

Michael turned to face them now. "You've proven yourselves today. There aren't many who could do what you've done. Yet you prevailed. *We* prevailed."

Batty instinctively touched the medallion hanging from his neck. He'd forgotten he'd put it on.

"I think it's time we transform ourselves," Michael said. "Broaden the view, so to speak. Become the eyes and ears of humankind and do what we can to help God's new angel watch over the world."

What he said made sense to Batty, and for the first time since Rebecca died, he almost felt whole again.

"But that's an enormous undertaking," Callahan said. "And there aren't enough of us to go around."

"Yet look what we've managed to do. Three solitary

beings who came together to make something happen. Never underestimate the power of determination."

"Or desperation," Batty said.

They all laughed, but there was very little humor in it.

"We aren't alone in this," Michael told them. "There are others out there who remain unseen—human and angel alike."

Batty thought of the anonymous D.C. connection and glanced at Callahan, wondering if she was sharing his thought.

"We can build a *network* of guardians," Michael continued, "and work together to keep *all* of our travelers safe."

They looked at one another, nodding in agreement. Then Michael offered them his hand, palm up, and said, "*Defende eos.*"

Protect them.

Batty and Callahan exchanged another glance, then clasped his outstretched hand and said it again. In unison.

And as they watched Michael slice a hole in the atmosphere to lead them back home, Callahan turned to Batty.

"What do you think, Professor? A drink to celebrate?"

"Only if it's orange juice," he said.

She grinned. "It may take me a while to sort all this out, but there's one thing I know for sure."

"What's that?"

"I'll be sleeping like a baby tonight."

ACKNOWLEDGMENTS

This book could not have been written without the creative guidance of Brian Tart and Peter Harris, and without the editorial genius of Ben Sevier, who kicked my ass when it needed to be kicked and helped me write the best book I possibly could. Thank you to all of them.

I'd also like to thank Brett Battles, Toni McGee Causey, and my son, Matthew, for listening patiently and giving me some amazing suggestions that solidified and deepened the story, and Lee Child, who graciously answered a call for help and got me the information I needed.

As always, thank you to Scott Miller of Trident Media Group, who has worked tirelessly on my behalf—the world's greatest agent at the world's greatest agency.

And finally, to Leila and Lani, my wife and daughter, who put up with my nonsense and make my life complete.

ABOUT THE AUTHOR

Robert Browne is an award-winning screenwriter with a keen interest in angels, demons, and the cultural and spiritual history of the afterlife. In writing *The Paradise Prophecy*, Browne was inspired by the works of John Milton, particularly *Paradise Lost*, along with the many obscure and in some cases long-suppressed documents that make up the dark narrative history of the original War in Heaven. He lives on the West Coast.

THE LAST TEMPLAR

Raymond Khoury

In present day Manhattan, four masked horsemen dressed as Templar Knights emerge from Central Park and ride up the steps of the Metropolitan Museum of Art during the blacktie opening of a Treasures of the Vatican exhibit. Attending the gala, archaeologist Tess Chaykin watches in silent terror as the leader of the horsemen hones in on a strange geared device. He utters a few cryptic Latin words as he takes hold of it with reverence before leading the horsemen out and disappearing into the night.

In the aftermath, an FBI investigation is led by anti-terrorist specialist Sean Reilly. Soon, he and Tess are drawn into the dark, hidden history of the crusading Knights, plunging them into a deadly game of cat and mouse with ruthless killers as they race across three continents to recover the lost secret of the Templars.

From the *New York Times* bestselling author

Paul Christopher

VALLEY OF THE TEMPLARS

Retired Army Ranger John Holliday and his friend Eddie travel to Cuba in search of Eddie's mysteriously vanished brother—and find themselves desperately trying to stop a shocking plot devised by a secret Templar cabal that has been growing for five hundred years. As the conspiracy tightens the corrupt and dying Castro regime in an iron grip, Holliday must find Eddie's brother before it's too late—and the secret horror of what lies in the Valley of Death is revealed.

**Available wherever books are sold or at
penguin.com**